PRAISE FOR

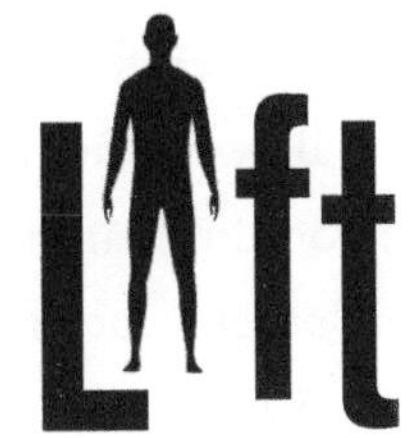

"An outstanding achievement . . . Ray Anderson's extraordinary grasp of mathematics, music, and human behavior are all on display here . . . His world-building is impressive, and yet the all-too-human players in this tale don't become lost in it. The natural reactions among many of the characters as the stakes go up coalesce into conflict or cooperation, and the doomsday clock keeps ticking toward what may be its final chime."

**—Vincent H. O'Neil, author of *Glory Main*, book one of The Sim War series**

"So much science fiction rests on the caveat at the core of Mary Shelley's progenitor novel Frankenstein: 'Watch what you wish for.' For over two hundred years this cautionary theme has infused the genre with the warning not to tamper with nature, human or otherwise.

*Lift* is a mind-bending and brilliantly engaging twist on that theme, suggesting that human nature be altered to set it free from the so-called 'Curse of Cane'—murder and war.

Set in the year 2489, the world is at the threshold of World War IV and inching toward extinction. Because it is believed that violence is 'embedded in our psyche,' mathematicians decide that the only way to eliminate the self-sabotaging evil is to devise an optimal language that eliminates miscommunications and misunderstandings among people of diverse cultures.

An ingenious concept, *Lift* clearly and meticulously demonstrates how mathematics, linguistics, and music theory coalesce to save the species. Thus, humans can join the galactic community of other species which have long conquered their violent nature.

Brilliantly researched and well-crafted, the novel's title refers to a scientific breakthrough that allows for a finite number of historical individuals to be resurrected or 'lifted' into the present. Euclid, Bach, Marie Currie, Jonas Salk and other great thinkers help fabricate a language that obviates 'the virus of evil.'

The title *Lift* also refers to the literal upward movement to the stars as well as an apotheosis of the human race based on humanity evolving out of its own bestial nature. This is a must-read piece of speculative fiction that accomplishes what the best of the genre does well—educate, entertain, and inspire [a] new way of thinking."

**–Gary Braver, bestselling and award-winning author of *Rumor of Evil***

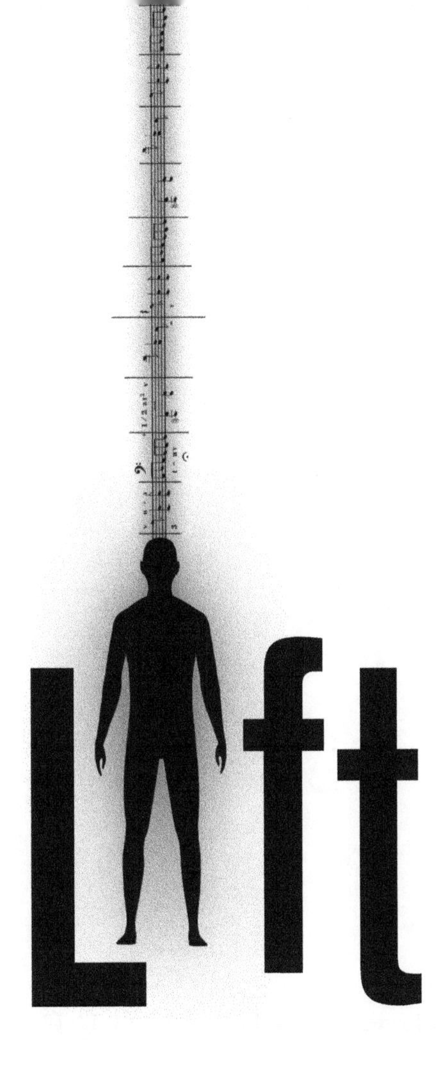
Lift

## ALSO BY RAY ANDERSON

*The Trail*

*Sierra*

*The Divide*

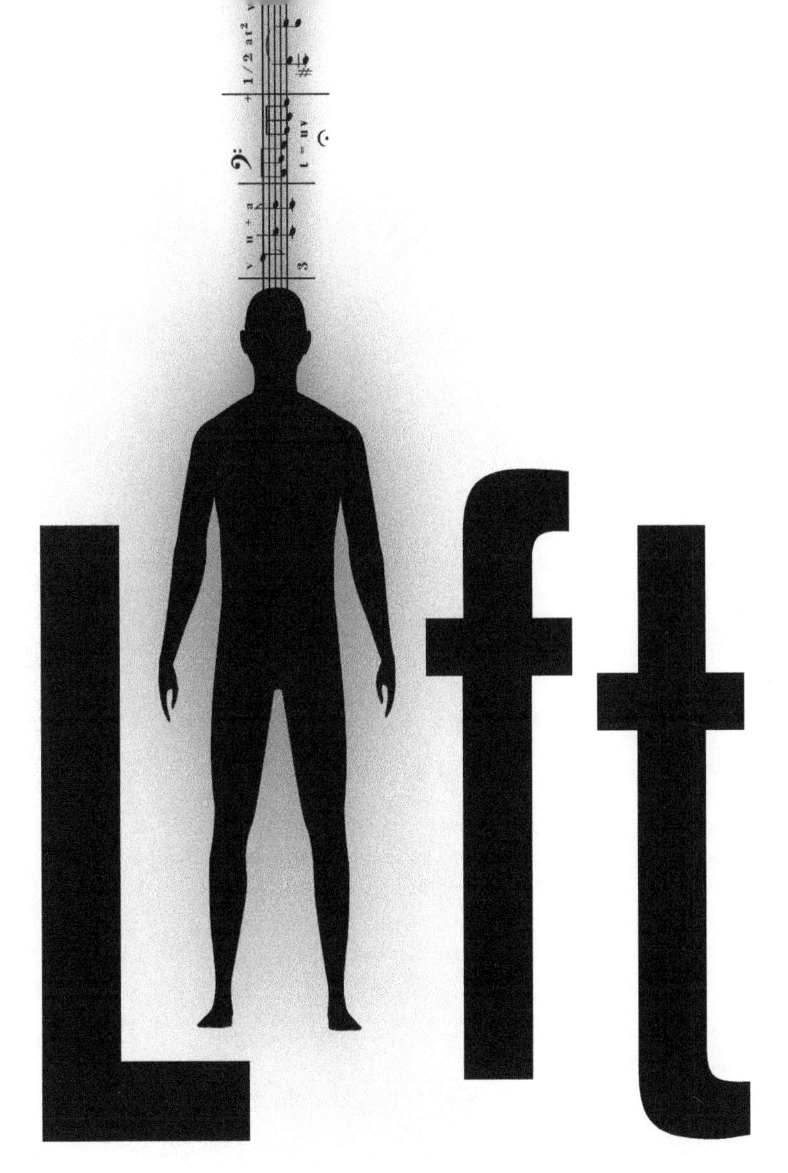

# Lift

## THE RISE OF MATHE-LINGUA-MUSICA

---

RAY ANDERSON

Keylight Books
an imprint of Turner Publishing Company
Nashville, Tennessee
www.turnerpublishing.com

*Lift: The Rise of Mathe-Lingua-Musica*



Cover design by Archie Ferguson
Book design by William Ruoto
Author photo by Donnat C. Mitchell

Library of Congress Cataloging-in-Publication Data

Names: Anderson, Ray, 1942- author.
Title: Lift : the rise of M-L-M / Ray Anderson.
Description: Nashville, Tennessee : Turner Publishing Company, 2024.
Identifiers: LCCN 2022050680 (print) | LCCN 2022050681 (ebook) | ISBN 9781684429660 (hardcover) | ISBN 9781684429677 (paperback) | ISBN 9781684429684 (epub)
Subjects: LCGFT: Science fiction. | Novels.
Classification: LCC PS3601.N54475 L54 2024 (print) | LCC PS3601.N54475 (ebook) | DDC 813/.6—dc23/eng/20230714
LC record available at https://lccn.loc.gov/2022050680
LC ebook record available at https://lccn.loc.gov/2022050681

Printed in Canada

To—

All Mathematicians, Linguists, Musicians,
and admirers thereof.

# PRINCIPAL CHARACTERS

**World Council of Mathematicians:**

**Juanita Colleen Popov**—*Chairperson*, expert in number theory and primes. Internationally acclaimed harpist.

**Yoganda Sein Anand**—Specialist in game theory. Psycholinguist, fluent in nineteen languages.

**Sean Pablo Boucher**—Expert in fractal and chaos theory. Eidetic memory.

**Wang Chen De Costa**—Leading mathematician in computer simulations. International Bridge champion.

**Sven Olaf Gunderson**—Specialist in quantum theory. Leading topologist and discoverer of the Minus Three Dimension.

**Joiacham Aaron Heinz Reed**—Expert in probability and metamathematics. Author of *Dragoon* fantasy series. Born on First Moon Colony.

**Katherine Sorche Tuan**—Specialist in bio-mathematics and nano-technology. Former Random-Fisher, 3-d, world chess champion.

**World ARMY:**

**General Roy Braun**—*Chief*, Graduate Powell Military Academy

**General Janice Osteen**—Graduate Powell Military Academy, 7th-degree black belt, karate

**Students:**

**Charles Wang De Costa**—Student, mathematics academy, 16-year-old son of Wang Chen De Costa

**Andrica Saint-Saens**—Charles's girlfriend, student, mathematics academy

**Conrad**—Charles's rival, student, mathematics academy

**Other Characters:**

**Veced Lobashevsky**—Russian peasant, puzzle solver, Liftee

**Pauperito**—Italian servant, discovered by Leonardo da Vinci, Liftee

**Helena Kosovsky**—Pupil of Ludwig Wittgenstein, Liftee

**Magnuson**—Mathematician, discovered and enabled Lobashevsky, Liftee

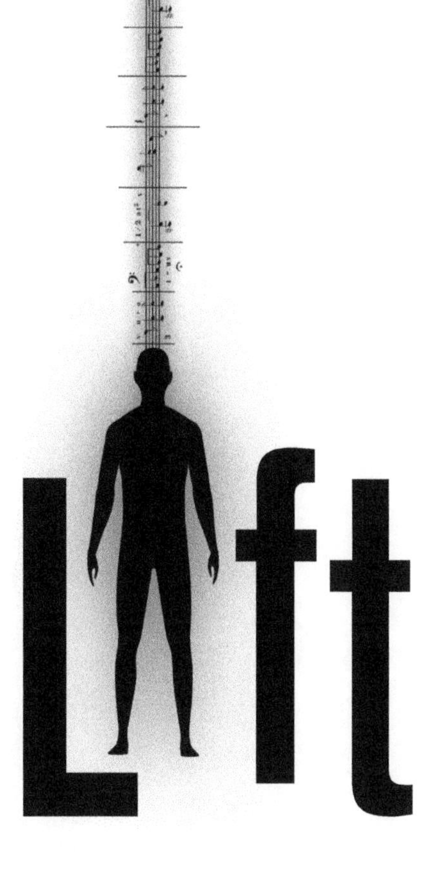
L ft

# PROLOGUE

THE WORLD COUNCIL OF MATHEMATICIANS (WCM) HAS BEEN Earth's supreme governing body since the discovery of historical time travel in 2411. Present-day humankind cannot go forward in time; they can only go backward. But a recent breakthrough in quantum-entanglement physics allows any deceased human to be Lifted into the modern world. The deceased can be Lifted forward in time, but only in the continuum of their past to the present. No person can be Lifted or sent beyond now.

Humanity had discovered that mathematics provided innumerable scaffolds in the universe. As the finest minds climbed and penetrated new mathematical pathways, it became ever more obvious that deeper understanding in all fields of mathematics would improve world leadership, science, and government. And it proved to be true. Weather forecasts became reliable to the point that the accuracy of prediction for any square-mile location on the planet was 99 percent for up to a month and six days out. Cancer was next. Genetic research infused with the newest quantum calculations revealed the particular inchoate chromosomes and organelles of a person that would be infected. Data pages in the billions were accumulated in what became known as "Cloud Plus," and specific fixes were found for all cancer victims of all nations. A year later, mathematics linked Alzheimer's disease to tobacco and secondhand smoke. The discoveries, cures, and wins continued as mathematics explored, discovered, and prevailed.

Despite these advances, humanity was sick, due to an untreatable "virus"—the human propensity to covet, take, and kill. Humankind's dependency on violence and war is more pronounced than ever. It is the worst of times.

In an effort to correct for violent futures, attempts were made to improve the past, but humanity did not perceive the deeper repercussions that would make the future worse. For example, when a young struggling artist named Adolf Schicklgruber was waiting for official acceptance as an art student in Vienna, and the WCM found the key person who would grant that wish, it was viewed as a tremendous gift for humanity. Yet, after the deed was done and this artist was on his way to acclaim, new histories were simulated and rolled to the present, only to learn that the Soviet Union had conquered Europe, killed even more people, and performed additional atrocities and pogroms. Just when the miscalculation was understood and attempts made to re-correct, an unseen and previously unaccounted-for asteroid slammed into Earth, killing millions.

It wasn't a coincidence. We knew. There was no other plausible explanation that could account for the asteroid that seemingly came from nowhere. It was punishment for tinkering with history and a warning to never try to change it again.

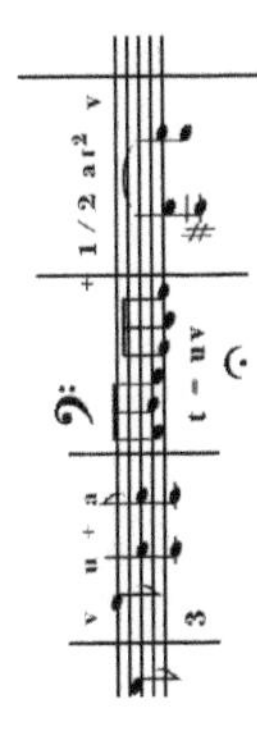

# I

Our world, so worn and weary,
Needs music, pure and strong,
To hush the jangle and discords
Of sorrow, pain, and wrong.

—Frances E. W. Harper, "Songs for the People"

# 1

## 21 October 2489
## Indonesia

"SO, HOW DO WE PACK IN THE MUSIC?" CHARLES ASKED.

The master organist stared at him. For a gifted mathematician, he thought, this young man is a disaster. "Aside from mathematics, Charles, what else do they teach sixteen-year-olds at academy?"

"Mostly all math, from age ten." Charles thought to add: "depending on how exceptional we may be."

Johann Sebastian Bach blinked and blew his nose into his hand. Charles rolled his chair back sharply. They were ensconced in a five-square-meter soundproof room, busy at their keyboards. Charles's face reddened as Bach wiped his smeared hand underneath the desk where they were seated. "Terrible," Bach said. "You pay close attention to me and what I do here." He tapped on the keyboard and entered the standard musical scale in letters. "We have a lot of time to make up, and your teachers should be whipped."

When Bach found the corresponding musical scales in Mathe-Lingua-Musica, he transposed the latest mathematics. "What do we do about sharps, flats, and naturals?" Charles asked.

"Thank God you asked. Perhaps there is a flicker of hope in you yet."

.................................

TWO DAYS LATER, BACH AND CHARLES PRESENTED THEIR NEWEST update to the World Council of Mathematicians. The seven WCM members sat around an oval table, while Charles and Bach sat beside each other among them. To Charles's surprise and Bach's frustration, the five men and two women, the finest mathematical minds on the planet, scratched their heads and were lost.

"What do you mean by atonals?" one of the men said.

"Imbeciles. Give me asses and they would understand better," Bach said. "What is wrong with you, Sir?"

"Restrain yourself, Mr. Bach, or you will be sent back to your era-time by the end of the day," Juanita Popov, Chair of the Council, said. Bach stuck his pinkie into his ear and wiggled his I-Trans, which looked like a miniature hearing aid tucked in his ear.

Charles whispered to Bach, "Go back and begin with our premise." Bach blew his nose into both hands. Charles knew what Bach might do next and offered the master his handkerchief. Bach looked puzzled as he accepted the wrinkled cloth.

"Right," Bach said. "I ask the Council, what is considered to be the universal truth in our universe?"

"Mathematics." All answered as one.

"Correct. Two plus two equals four; three squared equals nine; et cetera. At least in *our* universe." With a snort, he paused. "And what is considered to be the universal language in our universe?"

Juanita Popov, for the first time, smiled at Master Bach. "One universal language is music. The other is mathematics."

"Ah. I would add that music is our only universal language." The great composer-organist angled his head. "But it helps to know what's behind the music. As it is, everyone can have their own understanding and immediate interpretation. Music doesn't require the listener to learn theory, grammar, or equations. Music is ready for everyone."

Charles noted a settling down, and a sigh or two.

Master Bach bowed his head. "As I understand it, I have been resurrected to help you find the *optimum* language for our species. Not just any language or a hodgepodge of tongues, but *the* one language that best befits humans. I will do my utmost, but you must always accept our mutual premise: this optimum language must contain both mathematics and music, in addition to linguistics."

"Sharps, flats, and naturals aside," a cosmologist said, "how do we speak mathematics? And haven't we always had opera as music with language?" This man was recognized as a champion in all math genres, theoretical and applied.

Bach deferred to Charles, who gave Bach a piece of gum, one new luxury the musician and composer looked forward to in the afternoons. In the late twenty-first century, chewing gum was laced with medicinal stimulants which powered up the brain. Bach chewed, and his jowls puffed out like he was blowing the tuba.

Charles gathered himself and remembered to speak slowly. "Nanocomputers built for transmitting and receiving Mathe-Lingua-Musica will be embedded in our brains. Whatever our thoughts are can be transmitted in this optimum language, but we control the gate. If we want to keep a private thought to ourself, we can." Charles hesitated as he glanced at Master Bach who was playing on an imaginary keyboard in his lap. "As for opera, all of it is in various languages which are not optimum for humanity."

"Opera packs emotion because of the music," Bach hollered. He didn't even look up from his keyboard, and Charles could see his closed eyes. The questioner remained standing, arms akimbo. Finally he sat down.

Later, after ten hours of trying to puree mathematics with musical theory and linguistics, Charles walked beachside with Master Bach. They were on the Indonesian island Purity. Streaks of dirty clouds smeared the sky; foul odors climbed from the sea.

"I don't know why they named this island Purity," Charles said. He stepped over a human corpse and wondered if it would be removed.

"In my day, the streets reeked with horseshit. I haven't smelled that here, but I smell corpses everywhere. Is that tea you're drinking?"

"Yes." Charles saw him looking at the thermos. "Did you drink tea in Germany?"

"Not often. I preferred wine."

They watched seagulls screech and peck at the body. "Will the Council replace me?"

"I hope not. It takes a lot of energy to resurrect, or, as we say, *Lift*, and the Council had to give it much thought."

"Should they have Lifted a mathematician beyond my time—perhaps Euler?"

"He was on the list, but we wanted someone superior at music who was also gifted at math."

Bach smiled. "I revere mathematics. But I am better at music. I'm infatuated with what you call jazz. The loose harmony, the rhythms." Bach walked with his hands held behind his back. "Whatever happened to the sky? Not a trace of blue since I've been here."

"It's a long story. Master, can we perfect this language in time?"

"We had better. According to your mathematicians, it's the only way for . . ." Bach raised his hands to the sky and shook his head. "My question is, can *you* leap over everything we've done for setup? Up until now, our work has been logical but pedestrian. We must do a lot more than transliterate. We must pack different rhythms and music with expanded mathematics to generate algorithms for a unique universal alphabet and grammar."

Charles noticed Bach finger-poke his I-Trans as he struggled with the word *algorithm*. He hesitated as his German caught up. "I'm trying," Charles said.

"I insisted on a young mind. I'm learning the new types of music that came after me. There is so much. With my wisdom and your youth, we can solve this. Remember what the Council requires: *the* optimum language, for optimum communication."

Hardly a pause later, a throttling vibration shook the sand beneath them. They looked up, as the sky streaked an orange-white; any doppler effect had been reduced to a distant rumble. Something like snow afire began to descend from above them, and Charles turned to Bach. "We may have run out of time, Master."

# 2

## Four Months Earlier
## Sulawesi, Tomini Bay, Indonesia

JUANITA POPOV OPENED HER EYES AND CRAWLED OUT OF BED. TWO cockroaches twice the size of her thumb scuttled under the bed. *Damn those things, this is 2489, for Chrissake.*

Popov unzipped her body bag, threw it into the sanitizer with one hand, and selected her day's uniform with the other. After putting it on, she released her boots from the heavy-duty sanitizer and stepped into them.

Food pills and coffee constituted her breakfast. Normally, while sipping coffee, Popov would scan telecasts and listen to music. Today she did neither as she wrestled with the same thoughts that kept her awake all night—how and what to tell the people. The mathematics was clear, nothing further could be done. *Yet, maybe—no, there wasn't enough time.* But that wasn't the immediate problem. Yesterday's world status report, prepared for her by General Braun, reinforced her worst suspicions—humanity would stumble and fall.

Popov was surrounded by solid wall, but the fake windows and mirrors in the giant obelisk allowed her to digitally see outside. She watched hovers skim by her window in horizontal lanes with only fifty meters between the lanes below and above, which stretched to a dirty, clouded sky. Popov longed to take a hover to the last sea-garden on the planet.

She dumped her coffee, took a slow walk to the elevator, and expressed herself to council headquarters. The height of the obelisk above sea-level was nearly 500 meters, almost three times taller than the Washington Monument in the United States. The top was pointed, slanted on each of the four sides. The turnable center axis was re-engineered Aramid-Kevlar-steel. The inner-outside walls were covered with semi-finished marble stones. These stones covered granite and gneiss over six meters thick at the base. Outside, each side of the obelisk, shielded with plasma-enhanced carborundum, tapered downward from an upper width of 125 meters to a sea-level width of 215 meters, but the structure widened to over 300 meters as it extended down to seabed, the ocean floor.

Below seabed was the most difficult part; the immense sixty-meter-deep foundation depended on hi-tech cofferdamming of bay waters, supported by intricate and patient engineering. Nanotechnology enabled implementation of the bold plan to construct the foundation. Below the ocean floor, nanorobot and graphene swarms had built microfleets of nanomachines; nano-automation drove larger machines and tiny submersibles. Just as the Great Wall of China began with the first stone, the first reformulated metals and stone were entrenched. Nineteen years later, the giant obelisk was complete and occupied.

..................................

MS. JUANITA COLLEEN POPOV, CHAIR OF THE WCM, TOOK THREE deep breaths as she walked to the marbled podium in the packed room. Only after she put her sweaty palms on top of it did she allow her legs to shake. The five-foot-four woman stood on a hidden dais so she would appear in charge.

She looked at each of her six colleagues in the front row. On New Year's Day she had accepted the biennial position of Chairperson.

"Distinguished colleagues," Popov began, "fellow mathematicians of the First, Second, and Third Tiers, special administrators. We've assembled this meeting because humankind has an emergency. My colleagues have checked, rechecked, and checked again the simulations—if humans do not reduce wars and intra-species killing by one-third over the next fifteen months, humankind will be placed on an irreversible course to extinction." She leaned forward to her audience. "The crisis is approaching mathematical certainty." The room was engulfed by silence; nobody spoke, and nobody moved. She reached into the podium shelf and took a sip of tea.

"Yesterday morning, the Greenland-Iceland Conflict escalated to a declared war. By afternoon, Canada threatened a Controlled-Nuclear against Siberia. These four countries, not willing to meet with military tribunals, caused enough turmoil and distraction to give North America, Latin America, Africa, and Asia enough time to ally against the rest of the world. Our planet has cocked the trigger to World War IV."

At that, the dam burst. Whispers led to talking, which led to shouts and heated exchanges. Popov let the reactions run their course as she sipped tea. However, her stomach rumbled as the arguments eventually subsided.

Wang Chen De Costa, responsible for simulations and one of the seven WCM colleagues aware of the dire forecast, stood. "What Chair Popov says is true. But as mathematicians, we must find a way out." He turned to Popov. "Our Super-ICs, every one of them, have pointed to the need of a universal language, which cuts across all cultures as the only way out. I know this has been tried before, but we must try again."

..................................

TWO DAYS LATER, ALL SEVEN MEMBERS OF THE WCM MET IN POPov's office. Each of the WCM members would be offered the position of Chair for a two-year term, based on seniority. Each was expected to serve, but after their stint they would be "retired." Popov had been Chair for only two months.

De Costa, the sims quant, tried to express it simply. "First," he said, smiling as though he might have read somewhere that a smile always helps to ease another into disappointment, "I've employed the newest mathematics of fractal linguistics, which relates to some languages but not to most. Second, to enhance these simulations, I've mined social media back to when Yahoogle took over the internet two hundred years ago. I have not been able to add anything concrete. Consequently, I can't apply our newest advances for the foundation of this new language."

Popov leaned forward abruptly and brushed something off her teak-and-walnut desk. Her golden harp pendant dangled, then settled on her coffee-colored neck. She turned her head to the window screens, which stretched along the bayside wall. Her gray pantsuit and erect posture were all business. She turned back to De Costa, who was seated in front of her. "Are you certain your sims point to language as the best way out of our predicament?"

"If we can develop a species-wide language using our newest advances, sims point to ways we can penetrate across multiple disciplines and cultures in our species and check violence." He smiled again. "In time."

The idea of universal communication in a fixed tongue as a key to world peace was not new. Scattered about the globe were groups refusing to give up Esperanto. Even Solresol and Volapuk were still spoken by a few diehards. The brainy language of Lincos was used by the intelligentsia and cosmologists, but it failed across humanity because it was designed to communicate with extraterrestrials. What was new was the idea that humans had to find or create *the one optimum* language for the species across all cultures. Former attempts had been a hodgepodge—childish attempts at taking characteristics and rules from several tongues and applying them to something new.

"Most of us here hardly understand the mathematics, much less how to apply it," Popov said. "I have to ask again: How and why will a universal language stop murder? Are we not relying too much on mathematics and not enough on logic and experience?"

Gunderson stood. "Chair Popov, didn't we question ourselves like this when we were on the cusp of cancer elimination?"

"Also weather prediction in the final phases," De Costa added.

Popov's face reddened as she fondled her harp pendant. "This problem is inherent. Murder is a human trait embedded in our psyche. How can we beat this problem with math?"

Silence.

Popov continued: "It's because, throughout history, humans thought it would be foolish to try to fix this evil—an evil which is contained within each and every one of us, and manifests itself in our earliest years. Previous attempts at a world tongue did nothing to reduce violence."

"Perhaps we didn't pursue it far enough," De Costa said. "The worldwide-language failure was caused by humanity's lack of knowledge. It's been over a hundred years since we tried. With mathematical advances having occurred on all fronts, we need to try again."

"There seems to be no other solution," Reed said.

"Not if all our recursion-enhanced Super-ICs point to species-wide language," Anand said.

"Then, we have to Lift," Popov said. "We can't fix the problem ourselves. We've given it a try. Time is running out."

Five of the seven governing members of the WCM spoke in five different languages. Ear-embedded I-Translators obviated any need for a person to learn a language other than their native tongue. Modern languages, plus Greek, Hebrew, Arabic, Latin, and many others were translated within a microsecond's delay after the spoken word. But I-Translators often missed nuance and hidden meaning. Just as old-time spell-check accepted a word because it was spelled correctly, even if it made no sense in context, I-Translators missed many of the idiomatic complexities present in all tongues. But this only represented part of the communications problem: something bold, something transformational, something that would elevate understanding was sorely needed.

..................................

THE NEXT DAY, THE GOVERNING MEMBERS GATHERED IN POPOV'S conference room. De Costa—with baggy eyes—got to the point. "We ran six million sims, Cray-Quantum. We can Lift a total of nine deceased humans for up to one year." De Costa maintained the Living Earth Simulator, which modeled global governments, economies, wars and violence, and cultural trends using increasingly sophisticated algorithms.

Anand, a dark-complexioned Indian, cast his eyes over the group and said, "We need to time it so we Lift each of them at their mental peak, or when they have demonstrated significant accomplishment." He wasn't finished. The oldest of them at 116, he never rushed his thoughts or remarks, and the Board respected his wisdom. "If the seven of us, along with the greatest minds in history, can't secure a more peaceful world, we will deserve our fate."

Ms. Katherine Tuan, an Asian-Icelander, was chosen to head the committee created to decide the nine people to be Lifted, and already there was bickering.

"We must have a preponderance of mathematicians," Boucher, the youngest at twenty-seven, claimed.

Gunderson countered, "Such a preponderance will overlook acknowledged geniuses in sociology, biochemistry, philosophy—"

"We have divined that pure and applied mathematics have the best chance of ruling the planet," De Costa argued.

"We need to consider gurus and truth-seekers," Gunderson said. "And language-makers."

"We need a cross-pollination of ideas," Popov said.

"But we already consider mathematics a universal language, at least in our universe," Tuan said. "I reject your notion."

"We consider mathematics a universal truth more than a universal language. I, as Chair, have the option to veto," Popov said.

Tuan stood and glared at Popov.

"We need more insight and genius to help in other disciplines," Gunderson said.

"We must Lift Euclid and Euler," Boucher said.

"What about Gauss and Ramanujan?" Anand said.

Reed nodded. "We need the practitioners. We need the universalists, as well, such as da Vinci, and our deceased mentor, Ms. Toni Praeger."

A long, emotionally charged discussion ensued, wherein no agreements were reached. Intention of mind didn't always measure up when words were spoken. Not everyone's words were heard properly, as I-translations could be ignored. And translations missed the speaker's emotions. These missed words and faulty phrasings, followed by skewed emotions entering divergent pathways, compounded and shifted thoughts and responses in unaligned directions. As a result, what was meant was never truly said, nor ever truly heard. All this had to change.

.................................

THE NEXT MORNING, TUAN WAS IN A SOUR MOOD AS SHE PRESENTED a list of eighteen names in eight disciplines.

"We can't Lift eighteen," Popov said. She sat up straight, but her legs trembled beneath her desk. *Why has the fate of humanity chosen to fall on my watch?*

Tuan massaged an eye. "I don't see how we can Lift just nine and keep everyone happy. I don't see how we can eliminate one name. We ran the sims; if we take off any name on this list, we create an insurmountable intellectual gap."

"We'll fill the gap with our own people," Popov said.

"But nobody compares to these polymaths."

Popov perused the list and looked up. "We will choose nine. Who will lead within the Lifted group?"

"For that we need God Almighty."

But the WCM had previously tried that approach. Buddha, The Mohammed, Jesus, Moses, Allah, none of the ancient high priests or gods could be found. When one journeyed back in time, only typical *homo sapiens* were accessible. The governing mathematicians continued to argue about who could most help save humanity. The final tabulation looked like this:

Mathematics: Archimedes, Euclid, I. Newton
Chemistry and Physics: Madame Marie Curie, A. Einstein
Psychology/Medicine: S. Freud
Biology: C. Darwin
Philosophy/Logic: I. Kant
Universal: Leonardo da Vinci

"Why can't we find more women?" Tuan asked. "And why Darwin?"

"As for women, I'm sure they were out there," Gunderson, always the peacemaker, said, "but back then—"

"Spare us," Popov said. "Darwin and others," she continued, "adapted his evolution theory to linguistics, claiming languages also exhibit survival of the fittest."

"Don't we need a Saint Teresa or an Abraham Lincoln?" De Costa asked. "Someone with heart and vision?"

There was a long moment of silence.

"We've covered this," Popov said. "All our theory, all our sims point to faulty human leadership. The two noble people you mentioned also made misjudgments."

"Humans, ipso facto, can't be trusted," Anand said. "In our dilemma, we need these minds to assist us. Mathematics is the one universal truth."

"Yes," the other six said, for once all in agreement. Mathematics—the one, the only, enduring truth.

# 3

*INSOLENT*, THOUGHT POPOV. "KINDLY WATCH YOUR TONE, GENeral."

"Chair Popov, all I'm saying is we need to be ready to fight," Braun responded. "What I don't think you understand is that individual nations are ignoring world governance, and some are stacking against us."

"You must keep them in line, General."

"Then I'm ready to kick ass. With or without Plan A."

"You may do so when I give you that order, General. Until then, use other means."

"Yes, Chair Popov, but Plan A is taking too long."

Popov did not respond.

"As you wish," the General said.

But these last words by the General didn't sit well with her. *He can't wait to pull the trigger*, she thought. *Like a schoolyard bully, he is geared up, looking for trouble, eager to get it on.* She'd revealed the dire simulation that WCM was now wrestling with, but he didn't acknowledge it as he reported masses of troops in bordering nations, their threatening messages to each other, his desire to preempt. He didn't even mention droogs.

After he had left her private meeting, General Braun couldn't believe the course of events and Popov's stubbornness. *She is distracted*, thought the General. *She's conversing in a different tongue, for God's sake, with her own separate agenda. The world is at stake. She didn't even mention the droogs surrounding us. Popov is hooked on some new theory that she seems to think will preempt any military action. I'll support her, but she'll learn the hard way.*

"Set up an immediate I-Con with my top commanders," Braun instructed his aide.

*If I'm going to be hamstrung*, thought Braun, *I better prepare myself.*

# 4

DE COSTA SENSED CHARLES BEFORE HE SAW HIM PASS THE AQUARium-fashioned wall and approach the locked entryway, a vertical rectangle of louvers folded into the glass walls of the divided aquarium. De Costa turned down the music and pressed a button. Charles was the sixteen-year-old son of WCM's Wang Chen De Costa and his missing wife who, before she'd gone missing, had been moved up to Second Tier. Charles, the spawn of prodigious mathematical minds, was returning home from academy.

"What is the necessary condition for a Hadamard matrix of dimension *n* greater than 2 to exist?" asked the recorded message into an intercom controlling the lock mechanism. De Costa had programmed the lock differently for each day, thirty days out.

Charles, shuffling size-twelve feet, which he felt made him look like a clown, steadied himself and answered. "*N* must be a multiple of 4. It's now known a Hadamard matrix of dimension *n* exists for every *n* that is a multiple of 4."

Half the louvers slid up, while half slid down, and into the room walked Charles.

De Costa studied his son, who pulled a plastic plug from his ear and removed a patch from his forearm. Charles rubbed his eyes and proceeded toward his loft.

"How will you prove the Euler-Mascheroni constant is irrational?" his father asked.

Charles reached for his music mask, which hung from an ancient gargoyle mounted on the adjacent wall. "I need to think more on it, Dad." He positioned the mask to his long, thin face and angled to the stairs leading to his loft. He pulled tangles of black curly hair, uncovering his ears, one of which stuck out more than the other, and shoved on the mask.

"Just a minute," De Costa said. "If you solve the problem, you are on your way to a full scholarship at Praeger U."

Charles's face was hidden behind the mask. "Can I go now?"

De Costa stared at him. He needed to choose his words carefully. "Charles, I'm concerned about your motivation. We have struggled to find a particular problem your strengths will breach. You don't have time to waste. Any day, one of your rivals will crack the problem, and you will have to shift direction."

Charles stood at the stairs, silent as the moon.

"I'm honor-bound not to assist you. It would cost me my position. I will tell you this: I believe the approach to solution lies in nested sets and isomorphisms." His father gathered the folders and laser from his desk and placed them on the podium arching his treadmill. He brought the treadmill up to speed and got back to work.

Charles adjusted his mask and stumbled. The six-foot teen was at the age when his intended steps hadn't caught up with the growth of his legs. He recovered as his father returned to his music and simulations. Charles senior was reviewing and entering data from the Intellectual Peace Corps. It was a rite of passage for all university students to contribute their energy and insight to problems of the world for one year after graduation. Young people were hailed for retarding climate change and putting their elders on the right ramp to finally bring it to a halt, but the planet had suffered and the world was treading a fragile balance. De Costa's specialty was the behavior of complex systems and attempting to find convergence to predict outcomes. He tracked large-scale simulations every twenty-four hours.

In his loft room, Charles sat on a zebra-striped futon. He dimmed the lights by pointing his finger and, with a directorial move of the same hand, summoned music that was piped into his head via the mask. As he absorbed sounds of timpani, bongos, tabla, and zithers, and squeals from a mixed chorus, his fingers beat on a mica pad placed across his thighs. The beats projected bursts of color onto a trapezoid wall to his left while, on the wall to his right, mathematical formulae and dense convoluted equations scrolled down, one after the other. When the wall was filled, it became blank, and from the top the similar outlandish language of Praeger-calculus, Boolean algebra, topologies, and geometries began to scroll.

As Charles beat on the mica, it would appear to the casual observer that he was typing, but there were no lettered or numbered keys, and he looked more like one playing a keyboard instrument.

The center of the room was stepped up to a bed positioned between narrow end tables, all atop a platform similar to a lazy Susan. On one end table were assorted colorful masks; on the other, mica sheets and window-like panes stacked vertically as if they were old-fashioned books on a bookshelf. A bust of Euclid of Alexandria held up one end; a bust of Toni Praeger, the Black Goddess of mathematics, occupied the other end.

On the remaining two walls not projecting math or bursts of color were rich-colored paintings, looking like posters, but which flashed and disappeared and reappeared in an eccentric sequence. One of these walls contained a painting of what appeared to be an alien, looking like a human, eating the cojones of a bull it had gored—the bleeding bull with the ripped-out scrotum lay sprawled in the background. Charles watched the painting change to a live painting of the earth as seen from the moon. Blood-like veins and arteries weaved over the earth, and soon the wounded earth was a rete in blood. The painting morphed to a picture that zoomed the viewer to the South Pole, where suddenly an earthquake occurred and the ice imploded in snow, lava, blood. Charles continued to watch as the picture transformed back to a live painting of the alien matador who smiled as fanged teeth and jowls crunched to finish his meal.

On the remaining wall were seven paintings of peculiar machines, dense with sprockets, gears, wings, and bizarre, wobbly piston-driven engines enclosed by glass. As Charles focused on the first painting, an angel in a cockpit transmogrified into a growing bulbous insect, which pulled a lever. Something in the next painting in line began to move, and the third painting revealed an image of the air machine ascending. By the time Charles had followed the action and moved his eyes to the final, seventh painting, discharges from a machine gun, operated by the insect-pilot, burst and hammered into his vision. Startled, Charles covered his ears to a Doppler-roaring shriek; a greasy smell of smoke and oil stung his nostrils; he felt sweat under his arms as the floor shook. He at last looked up and saw that the paintings had reverted back to the originals.

Charles held his mica again and continued to tap at it while the mask remained strapped over his nodding and twisting head. For another ten minutes, a litany of equations, posits, diagrams, and three-dimensional objects continued to tumble down the math wall, then slowed and, in a matter of seconds, rested on a coagulation of nested sets.

Charles removed his mask.

# 5

## Several Days Later
## Tomini Bay, Indonesia—WCM

THREE HUNDRED YEARS AGO, THERE WERE OVER 17,000 ISLANDS throughout Indonesia. Of the 6,000 civilized, the rising oceans forced the inhabitants of over 4,800 of them to move to other islands as their homes disappeared under the seas. Before scientists could at last halt climate change, only 1,911 islands of the original 17,000 remained; and on the surviving islands, every hamlet became a busy town, every town a city. The days of strolling down streets conversing with friends were long past. People moved as if exiting a soccer arena after a championship game, and sellers at bazaars used megaphones in an attempt to gain the attention of passersby. At least there were no pickpockets—microchips imbedded in fingers controlled all money. Left pinkie equaled 1, all the way to right pinkie equaled 10; opposing thumbs placed side by side, pointing to a seller's wand, gave a zero.

The early-morning Tomini Bay typhoon had turned into a mid-morning tempest. The vicious morning storms were as predictable as the dirty sunrise. Any other structures bracing against two-hundred-mile-an-hour gusts would be cast into the ocean, but the giant obelisk was engineered to twist on its axis—ninety degrees clockwise or counterclockwise. Every day, the construct trimmed, and the winds slid by.

The nine Lifted thinkers have been in the present for one month. But similar to an ocean diver who is brought slowly to the surface lest they get the bends, there was not enough time to slow-Lift the thinkers through the years, and for some their abrupt emergence into the present was disorienting. Euclid and Archimedes were the most affected, because they traveled through the longest passages of time. Though they had been quarantined like the rest, Euclid and Archimedes exhibited signs of paranoia—their fragile and exacting senses slower to absorb the present. Just as historical sculptures and paintings showed, Archimedes had a large and balding head and a beard flowing from cheeks and chin. Archimedes, a former pupil of Euclid, resembled him, but Euclid had a narrower face and more hair on his head. The two hung together like twin brothers on their first day of school. They had to be spoon-fed history, new sciences, advances in medicine. When it got to be too much, Euclid removed the I-Translator from his ears and ignored everyone. Only in mathematics were they at peace, at which time Euclid replanted his I-Translator and asked astute questions spanning topology, Riemann functions, Boolean dimensions, and logic. He and Archimedes could not get enough of the advances in mathematics and begged for more, as hungry puppies beg their masters for food.

It was agreed that the Lifted, in the spirit of equality, would conform to a dress code. When the nine were assembled, in their mauve one-piece uniforms, in the obelisk's topmost quarters and told why they had been Lifted, it was Kant who asked an obvious question.

The short man, hair done up with a bun on the back of his head, looked vigorous and fit as he stood and asked, "What does mathematics have to do with the inherent and omnipresent violence of man?"

Popov smiled as she graced the podium. She wore the standard female uniform of silk-taffeta and had chosen painted butterflies for the occasion. Her flaxen hair was curled short, showing off silver dove earrings; a different harp bangle hung from a gold chain on her neck.

"We are inching closer to understanding how mathematics is a determinant of history. Our studies reveal that when mathematics is combined with linguistics, indeed when it is applied to all languages known to man, ancient and modern, it suggests a series of equations resembling fractal and catastrophe theory. These equations are similar to the mathematics portending violence. We need help in analyzing and understanding the data as it relates to all the disciplines. That's where you come in."

Popov reached into the podium for her cup of tea and took a sip. She returned the cup. "These data inquiries and setups have to be done before we can create *the* perfect language for humans."

Curie, a handsome woman displaying an air of confidence, raised her hand, but Freud stood, and Curie deferred. She sat next to Einstein, who was a longtime friend.

"I don't see how the elegant discipline of mathematics relates to the psyche of mankind," Freud said. "A beast will always be a beast."

Popov was surprised at how little and fragile the famous doctor looked. Bald, with a trimmed beard, he insisted on wearing his own glasses and declined temporary laser eye correction. He'd been refused tobacco and looked lost without his cigar.

"Yes," Popov said, "but our newest simulations indicate that a fuller understanding of the mathematics and the deeper questions beneath as related to biochemistry, physics, logic, and psychology will enable us to create the optimum language to guide our species and check violence."

"What's behind these assumptions?" asked Freud.

"Conflicts and wars have been the results of miscommunications and misunderstandings. And, I'm ashamed to say, many times these miscommunications were intentional."

"Your leaders didn't figure that out?"

Popov shuffled her feet. "It's complicated, doctor."

Freud sat down. Einstein stood up.

"Here's my question. How exactly did I and my colleagues travel through time to get here?"

Curie, sensing the moment, rose and placed her hand on Einstein's shoulder. "And what happens if the Council fails?" Curie asked.

Popov looked solemn as she nodded to De Costa, who stood to address the assembly. He was the tallest, at seven feet, and looked rangy in a gray one-piece uniform. *Thank God*, thought Popov, *he has the sense not to smile.*

"We, as a species, become extinct."

# 6

## One Month Later

GENERAL BRAUN'S HANDS WERE FIGURATIVELY TIED. HE'D JUST finished talking with Army Engineers about their progress on Plan A. The General and the world would have to wait six more months to finish. Military Plan A would enable General Braun to enforce peace anywhere on the globe. He realized the plan wouldn't be ideal for dealing with the ever-shifting droog cells, but no rogue nation or entrenched group of hostiles could put up a sufficient fight to ultimately resist it. In a heartbeat, hundreds of robotic-creeper tanks would descend to the spot and annihilate. *But until then, what . . . ?* He called Popov.

"Chair Popov, I've managed to keep the world's nations in line, as instructed, but I don't know how much longer I and my lead generals can do it."

"I know you are up to the task, General. We absolutely must prevent World War IV. If we don't, it will signify the end of our species."

"I must request a Controlled-Nuclear or the dam bursts."

"Won't that act of desperation serve to burst the dam?"

"Perhaps so. It will happen sooner or later, Chair Popov."

"Request denied. Continue on course, General."

..................................

A FEW HOURS LATER, SEVEN LEADERS OF THE WCM MET IN POPOV'S chambers to report on progress. All seven appeared tired, angry, or both.

"I will not put up with da Vinci's sexual innuendos and arrogance," Tuan screeched at Reed, the de facto leader for the nine Lifted. "I don't care if he's superior to Jesus Christ Almighty."

Popov rose again from her seat to try to calm Ms. Tuan, who looked as if she would pounce on Reed like a cougar.

Reed closed his eyes and started to say something, then closed his mouth and folded his hands on the table.

Gunderson palmed up his hands as a preacher, which his great-great-grandfather had been. "We understand how you must feel," he said, as he attempted a smile at Tuan. "Try to empathize with da Vinci—he is confused, ignorant of the current age, and we suspect he feels threatened by women."

"Then why do Euclid and Archimedes treat women with respect?" Tuan countered. She was almost as short as Popov, but her untiring energy was an even match for anyone on the Board.

De Costa raised his hand and said, "I must confess that Archimedes told me da Vinci needs a good thrashing. 'Where are your whips?' he whispered in my ear. 'I'll do it myself.'"

"Is Archimedes jealous of him?" Anand asked.

"Hardly. I believe he sees da Vinci as a spoiled brat who only cares about painting. Einstein also thinks da Vinci is arrogant and a troublemaker."

"If he continues to be a problem," Reed glanced at Popov and Tuan, "I propose we consider finding him a woman from the outside."

"Won't special treatment stir up the others?" Tuan asked.

"Of course," Reed said. "We'd have to do it secretly. I suspect the others find knowledge to be their aphrodisiac; our da Vinci displays restless hormones that knowledge alone doesn't satisfy."

"I have another theory," Boucher said. "Outrageous, but I get the feeling his capabilities don't match the others."

"Meaning?" Gunderson asked.

"He's slower to absorb. He doesn't catch on as quickly."

"If he is acting out to cover that up," Popov said, "we have a much more serious problem." It had been time for her to say something, but in truth Popov wasn't paying attention to the conversation. She'd been thinking of her talk with General Braun, and the droogs.

.................................

LATER, AFTER EACH WCM MEMBER HAD PRESENTED REPORTS RElating to each Liftee's particular disciplines, the good news was the convergence of all the mathematics appeared sound and suggested stepping stones to ongoing linguistic advances. Moreover, each Liftee, including da Vinci, understood and accepted that they had been resurrected to assist with the creation of a particular language as a way to reduce violence. The bad news was that each of them was sluggish in relating what they now learned from the underlying mathematics to their various disciplines. From a viewpoint and filter of Renaissance thinking, even the purported Renaissance man, da Vinci, with the hooded eyes and wild, unkempt beard, appeared lost.

"We are giving them as much data as possible," Gunderson said, "and they get proper sleep. The question is, are we giving them the best information? The required and appropriate knowledge? And, is our message clear?"

Tuan said, "Although we've given each Liftee their personal history, Freud claims a detailed accounting of how their discoveries have affected society through the years after their deaths would better ground and inform them. Curie complains that details about their progeny are hidden. She wants to learn of her daughters' children and is curious about a former lover. Freud wants to know about his daughter Hanna's family."

"The less personal information disclosed to them, the better," Popov said. "If they begin a personal journey down the pathway of their children, relatives, and the like, they will become distracted from our objective."

"What I'm saying is," Tuan countered, "the Liftees are aware that we have not made available certain information about their families, and they understand why this decision was made. Are we sure it is in our best interest not to divulge at least some of the information?"

It was put to vote again, and while detailed personal family information was not approved, it was decided that more information from critiques about the value of their work through the years would be provided to each of the Liftees.

.................................

AFTER RUNNING CONCURRENT SIMULATIONS BASED ON PROGRESS and options, after another two weeks of meager progress, the WCM agreed that three days of rest were now necessary. Despite imposed schedules of treadmill exercise as they worked and balanced nutrition (to include placebos packed with nanobots that monitored health, took vitals, and optimized periods of work and sleep), it wasn't enough to refresh the Liftees' brains. Arrangements were subsequently made to take them to one of several oxygen-deprived resort peaks in the Himalayas. There, the accommodations were infused with a chemically prepared oxygen-rich environment containing tinges of an LSD substrate, used by humans who could afford it and who qualified for it based on their give-back to society.

It was their first night of liberty, and the excitement among the Liftees was palpable as their oxygen-refreshed brains understood they would be "fed" music. They were assembled in soft, velvety, swiveling rocking chairs, in a modest auditorium with two lounges on a dais facing them. Five of the WCM members sat amongst the Liftees in the audience, and the other two, Boucher and Popov, approached the dais and reclined in their lounges there.

The lighting dimmed to the luminance of old-time candles, with the silence as thick as falling snow; and when at last Boucher spoke, the Liftees experienced enlargement of their mental faculties.

"We will first perform," Boucher said, "a late twenty-third-century work of minimalist reverie by our esteemed composer, Geraldo Pierre Wu. It is untitled, so you can remember it in your own way; it will always be there for you."

In the limited light, Boucher and Popov put on white helmets with inlaid face masks and fastened body straps holding them to the lounges.

They rotated their lounges so they faced each other, and the lounges raised, moved to meet, and were locked in such a way that Boucher and Popov were held vertically, directly in front of each other, close enough to kiss. Instead, they each placed their hands over the helmet of the other, inserting their fingers into orifices present in the helmets. At once, the minds of all present sensed "audio." It reminded Madame Curie of the record player in her time when the needle has been lowered onto vinyl and the music is about to begin.

"Miss Popov, are you prepared to think harp and percussion?" Boucher said.

"I am. Are you ready to think voice and all other instruments, Mr. Boucher?"

"Yes. As soon as we tune."

The pristine pitch of B minor grew and was omnipresent. And then, just as it had initially grown, the pitch folded away and faded to thickening quiet. The arpeggios of a harp came from all directions. This segued to harp-string plucking, embracing a melancholic phrase which iterated in minimalist fashion. When it became too heartfelt, oboes reversed the phrasing, timpani brushed into harp, and double bass and tablas packed into the violas while trombones bleated plangent wails of frightening remorse. Soon this competed against an organ repeating a phrase implying hope. After eight minutes, the organ's ever-repeated thrusts of individual tremolos built within each listener an urgent desire for hope to overpower remorse—all in sound, all through music. Lastly, a basso ostinato of human voice wiggled into the fray, a voice that grew and permeated and overtook the orchestra and the mind. A voice of joy, iterating for humanity. It reached a crescendo in which all instruments supported the phrasing, led by voice. Over and over the feeling of joy built, while, underneath it all, drums provided a beat—a pulse for humankind.

After the music ended, no one moved. For several minutes, the echoes of the music remained in each of their minds. When the lighting increased and Boucher and Popov removed their hands and fingers from the helmets, the musical echoes faded.

"Extraordinary," Newton said, his eyes sparkling above a long and prominent nose. A floodgate opened, releasing gushes of approval and bravos as Boucher and Popov rotated their lounges to face the standing audience, placed their hands on their hearts, and bowed. The piece had lasted eighteen minutes. Hugs and tears lasted for several more.

..................................

LATER CAME A PERFORMANCE OF MAHLER'S SECOND SYMPHONY, known as the *Resurrection Symphony*. It was requested by Einstein, in a prearranged lottery because "the name is appropriate for Liftees," he'd said. The symphony was served up from the archives by Tuan, thinking percussion, Gunderson thinking all strings and voice, and Anand leading and thinking brass and remaining instruments. At the finale, the avalanche of sound from the organ, bells, and voice crossed over into the realm of too much, too soon. Archimedes fainted, and Euclid appeared dizzy and was incoherent. Even after these two oldest Liftees were attended to, thoughtful mumblings and questions persisted.

"But how does it work?" Newton demanded, crinkling his eyebrows and running fingers through his tousled hair.

Boucher said, "The music is done by electromagnetic waves superimposed on brain waves."

"Does the sound, the music we heard, come from within the mind, or was it in this room?" Madame Curie asked. She placed her hand on Boucher's shoulder and looked into his eyes. "You must tell us."

"Both," Boucher said. "The music comes from within via brainwave entrainment thought by the performers; the sound emanates from the walls, ceiling, and floor, which are electromagnetically connected to the performers and amplified by them. That's enough for you to absorb for now."

The revived Archimedes wore fear on his face, while Euclid remained unstable, as both were wheeled to an adjacent sitting room.

Later, at an unplanned WCM meeting in a separate room, it was Popov who broke the silence.

"I erred. I allowed them too much."

The others nodded.

"Do you all still feel as I do?" Gunderson said. "And, we've circled this before. Music has always been considered a 'universal language,' this . . . this problem we are trying to solve . . ."

De Costa stood. "Yes, music has to be involved somehow. The humanity shown . . . after."

"We need to explore amalgams of mathematics, linguistics, and music in our languages," Popov said. "Where do we discover those clusters? Why do we always keep music separate?"

De Costa started to say something and stopped.

"What is it?" Popov asked.

"Some of the mathematics we ran in sim seemed connected to the math of music, as we understand it, but then the lines diverged. Yet I noticed reconnects later. It was almost as if the music part floated or hovered throughout."

"Like all of you," Popov said, "I have the feeling music should play a part as we move forward."

"You are a musician," Gunderson said.

"Right. Let's pursue it, but we can't waste time—we must put math and language first."

# 7

THE FOLLOWING MORNING, BEFORE DAWN, CHARLES WOKE TO A windshear he'd sensed from his dream. It often happened like this, and his father told him such dreams were a positive sign. Nevertheless, as he heard the ghostly rumble of the obelisk's inner gearing from its bowels deep below, he felt unsettled. It was as if his brain was attempting to align itself to a twist of the central axis as it turned on a half-circle of chromium-steeled ball bearings the size of super-inflated beach balls. It all combined in his head as a warning that a storm was brewing.

Yet, at academy, Charles received the highest score on the math exam; and because his average score finishing out the month was the highest in the class, he was awarded the opportunity to consult with one of the Liftees. He chose Euclid.

..................................

AFTER LATE-AFTERNOON ADVANCED CLASSES, CHARLES WAS LED to Euclid's study. Liftees were given separate sleeping quarters, to include a private study, below their daytime working rooms, in the obelisk. Charles focused on a sketch of the great geometer in profile, hanging on the wall above his desk.

"That is exceedingly good," Charles said.

"As it should be," Euclid said. "It was left to me, *ex voto,* by da Vinci. He wandered in here one night, established his charcoals, and sketched as I worked—took him under an hour."

"I was blown away by *The Elements,*" Charles said.

Euclid blinked several times and pointed to his I-Translator in his ear. He didn't see how "blown away" fit in with his math treatise.

"I think I get what you mean. Thank you. But what happened to my main book? My *Ruminations Mathematica.*"

Charles tilted his head. "You mean you wrote another book?"

"Dear boy, I wrote four books, although the last one was a compendium I incorporated into my *Ruminations.*"

Charles wanted to ask why Euclid blinked so much. Medical would have picked up an eye problem, he thought. Charles nodded, and his hazel eyes scanned the wall shelves of silica sheets; Euclid had already organized his personal library of mathematics. "Did you ask the WCM about it?"

"I did. Like you, they are surprised but claim more pressing matters are of immediate concern. I persisted and they revealed that although my work was written in Greek, it was lost by the Romans, yet preserved by the Egyptians, and finally passed to the world in Arabic." Euclid threw up his hands. "As if that might explain it."

"How did you learn the entire math ahead of time? I mean, who taught you?"

"I had most of it up here," Euclid pointed to his head. "No one taught me. I was poor, uneducated, but I'd learned much from personal study and, as I traveled, from long discussions with builders, tradesmen, astronomers, mariners."

"Did it take you long to write *The Elements*?"

"Not when I decided to put everything down in one place. I collected my parchments and scraps and organized them for the peoples."

"The peoples? How could the masses understand your work?"

Euclid hesitated. "We will keep this between us: dear boy, from what I can see, there has been a diminution of intellect since my time. Archimedes has also noticed it."

Charles stared at Euclid. The geometer continued to blink.

"I'm convinced it has to do with memory. No one has to remember anything in this time—your time. All knowledge is instantly available."

"Yes, but . . ." Charles looked disturbed.

"True, you all work on intricate mathematical problems, which are most interesting, yet progress is slow. You work off a vast knowledge dump. Look at your computers, your Super ICs, and all those stacked adiabatic quanta." He chuckled and shook his head. "What you need is originality and creativity to solve the fix you are in."

"Have you told this to WCM?"

"Not entirely. Let's keep it our secret. Your people in this time are trapped in a huge—what you used to call—mindset. There isn't enough time to change direction. We Liftees have discussed it. Let the computers keep working. We—in particular, me and Archimedes—hold the reins of creativity, of thinking 'outside the box,' as I heard someone say."

.................................

THAT EVENING, EUCLID AND ARCHIMEDES WANDERED TO A SEPArate conference room where they met fellow Liftees every few days to chat, brainstorm, and commiserate. After complaining about pill food, no access to tobacco, the WCM's reluctance to permit them to relax, the frantic drive for progress, the Liftees were quiet and contemplated for several minutes. Only da Vinci busied himself, as he drew on a pad he held in his lap.

"If they take away my violin, I'm going to raise holy hell," Einstein said.

Newton chuckled. "Mr. Einstein, may I paraphrase a joke I heard during my entrainment?" Before Einstein could answer, Newton asked a second question: "What did you do with all the money your parents gave you?"

Einstein looked puzzled. "What money?"

"All the money your parents provided for violin lessons."

Laughs and chuckles all around. Finally, Einstein threw in his lot and grinned.

"Okay, everyone," the great physicist said, "here's my question: All this digging for the mathematics hidden in our respective fields to provide insight and scaffolding for a unique universal language, how do we know it will work?"

Curie stood up. "Listen, all of you. They have accomplished much more than cures for cancer and heart disease."

"Agreed," said Archimedes, "but . . ."

"Hear me out. We learned that it was an unusual inductive math breakthrough that enabled them to solve Alzheimer's." She shushed the beginnings of foment. "Okay, Alzheimer's was caused by tobacco and smog; however, look at their math. Equation after equation show how and why it happened, and later equations showed how to prevent both cancer and Alzheimer's from recurring, even with pollution."

They were quiet for a spell. Da Vinci said nothing and continued to draw.

Newton said, "But what about during their World War III, when scientists and mathematicians were hunted for blood sport?"

"Why?" Einstein asked.

"Mathematicians tried to take over and govern the world too soon. Some nations rebelled against the takeover, and mathematicians were put down like cockroaches."

"We must get them this language," Curie said.

Da Vinci continued to draw images with his charcoals, even after everyone had left the room.

. . . . . . . . . . . . . . . . . . . . . . . . . . . . . . . . . . .

CHARLES AND EUCLID HIT IT OFF, AND OVER THE NEXT COUPLE OF weeks, at Euclid's request, Charles visited him in the evenings. On one of the evenings, in a daring move that risked his expulsion from academy, he showed Euclid his pending scholarship problem.

The master perused it, glanced at the ceiling for a moment, re-studied it, mumbling in Greco-Latin, and then scribbled on a pad at his side using an old-fashioned pencil. "Let me think about this," Euclid said.

Two days later, when Charles arrived at the master's study, Euclid invited him in and bolted the door after Charles had sat down. Euclid turned and said, "I have solved your problem." He crossed his arms and blinked his eyes. "Lost lemmas in my *Ruminations Mathematica* would have helped you."

Charles smiled. "Wow! That's great!"

"Not so fast. You will substantiate my theory of diminished intellect if I give the solution to you. No. You will see the solution when you move away from raw computing power, tables of data, and think using your mind."

"Sir, I do try to think of new lines of attack in all my work."

"I will admit in you I see a spark I have not seen in your elders. I'll give you three days to solve the problem; if you do, I shall request your continued personal assistance in my work here."

"Can I ask for a hint?"

"Music."

# 8

## Exam Room, 1st Tier

"YOU ARE SURE DA VINCI REVEALED THIS?" REED SAID TO EUCLID.

"Yes," Euclid said, while hunkered in his mauve jumpsuit, as if he expected to be shackled while standing before the members.

The WCM sat at an oval table of ingrained larch and beech and conferred in whispers while Euclid blinked and fidgeted. A three-dimensional chess set graced a table between two chairs in a corner of the trapezoidal room, its game pieces arrayed for combat. The top halves of the four sides of the room were covered with milk-colored sliding panels, and all the panels were covered with abstruse mathematics—equations, imaginary numbers, and topological and stellated figures of geometries. In trays at the bottom of the panels lay color-coded laser markers, as well as old-time grease markers, requested by the Liftees. Above the trays were inlaid touch screens providing mathematical tables, summaries of calculations, special determinants, higher-order matrices, and formulas. Euclid walked to one of the panels and picked up a purple marker as the whispering subsided.

"Bring da Vinci to us," said Reed.

.................................

LEONARDO STOOD BEFORE THEM, HIS UNIFORM SOILED WITH PAINT and charcoal. "There is no reason why I shouldn't be permitted to paint. Sketching and painting relax me."

"You do know what's at stake and why you are here," Popov said.

Da Vinci remained silent and sullen. As did Euclid.

Popov looked away from da Vinci's hooded eyes and folded her arms. "Do you have something you should tell us?"

Da Vinci looked at Euclid with alarm.

Euclid put a hand on his shoulder. "We can see you are an extraordinary artist. You have a God-given gift. But I had to tell them."

Da Vinci covered his reddened face with a forearm and tried not to sob as he shook. Popov noticed flecks of paint and charcoal dropping from his hair.

Gunderson rolled a chair to him and told him to sit. Glancing at Popov, Gunderson said to Euclid, "We will pursue the matter sub rosa. Please return to your work."

Euclid blinked several times, turned to da Vinci, and bowed. "*Ecce homo. Invictus.*"

Popov poured a dark red liquid into a silver cup and offered it to da Vinci. He sipped and swallowed.

"Thank you."

The room was silent as da Vinci sipped and swallowed again. He placed the cup on the floor beside him and looked downward for a moment before raising his head to stare where the ceiling edged a wall.

"*In vino veritas.* Il Pauperito," da Vinci said.

"What? Who?" asked Gunderson.

"Il Pauperito. My servant. A mathematical genius the equal of Euclid and Archimedes together."

One of the five men seated around the table banged his Qubetch-a-Sketch.

"But your books, your drawings."

"All dictated by Pauperito. I drew, I wrote; he had the mind for it and dictated everything."

Everyone sat in stunned silence.

It was Popov who unfolded her arms and looked into the artist's eyes. "You must Return, and we must Lift Pauperito."

"*Non serviam?*"

No one moved.

"As you wish," da Vinci said, looking resigned. The ruse was over.

More questions were put to da Vinci and discussed in an atmosphere of respect and admiration. Leonardo appeared to accept his fate and, for the first time since being Lifted, his countenance appeared to be without secrets. His eyes didn't flit and were opened full.

"How much of this experience will I remember?"

"Everything. But only as a dream," the WCM assured him.

"Will I change when I go back?"

"No," Anand said, "history will continue as it did, as it must. For you, all this will be a night's dream."

Just before he was led to Time Travel Control, De Costa called out, "Master da Vinci, I've always wondered: who was the Mona Lisa?"

"*Madre di Pauperito.*"

# 9

THE ACADEMY CHARLES ATTENDED WAS LOCATED IN THE HEART OF Jokowi, a former village grown into a city with a preponderance of intellectual elite. The students at this particular academy were the future of Planet Earth. Leading up to the academy, several mathetoria bordered both sides of the street. An old-fashioned bookstore, complete with handheld books, was a popular landmark, and Andrica waited by the entryway holding a Java Joe tinged with cinnamon cocoa. One shoulder was uncovered and sported a *smart* tattoo of two dolphins on her smooth, unblemished skin. Whenever Andrica rubbed the dolphins with her implanted thumb, the skin under her dolphins would vibrate as the dolphins shimmied and squeaked their unique sounds into her brain. She grabbed Charles's arm as he walked by.

"You might stop a second for me, you know."

Charles hadn't even registered her presence, and Andrica knew he was moving equations around in his skull. She envied Charles's intellectual brio, which had blossomed since his meetings with Euclid.

"Can't you take a few seconds, Charles, to reacquaint yourself with humanity?"

"Kant told Euclid he used to walk every day."

"Terrific," she said. For example, the fact that she and Charles shared the same birthday, except for year, didn't interest him, other than the math behind those odds. Charles, with condescension, explained to her the "Birthday Paradox," as if she didn't know. Even when she interrupted—"What about twins?"—he hadn't lost a beat.

". . . fascinating odds—two people in a random pool of thirty will share the same month and day . . . what did you say?"

"I said 'what about twins,' stupid. Triplets will skew the odds even worse." They were in the academy cafeteria, and she jerked her head close to his face, blinking her narrow-set eyes a bunch of times. "Riiiiiiight?"

"Yeah, okay."

"Just because you are conferring with the great Euclid doesn't get me all hot and bothered, Charrrrrlie." She doubted he even knew what she meant, but saw him bristle at "Charlie." She still wanted to slap his face.

In conics-minus 3, Andrica found the opening she'd been waiting for. At the laser board, in front of a class of fourteen students, treadmilling at their workstations, Charles was explaining a new approach to sets and quantile regression, which he thought was original. Each finger of his right hand wore a color-coded laser. A few treaders had increased their speed, inclined higher, or both as they attempted to follow Charles. Andrica stepped off her treader and folded her arms. The revered instructor, a former math prodigy, looked to her. "Yes, Andrica?"

"Lussier would not agree. Charles implies risk-reduction modules, which will impose unstable patterns on the Cucci method."

Andrica watched Charles blush and, speaking with gusto, went in for the kill. "I submit Charles's line, as described here, circles back to Lussier's admission that his recast of the Traficante-Cucci method was faulty at worst, unproven at best. In short, a paralogism."

There were no chimes indicating the end of sessions; the entire class rotated at one revolution per hour. During the time, new laser boards opened and closed. Class ended, and Charles was instructed to dig into Lussier to confirm his reasoning and address counterarguments heard in class.

After the session, Charles caught up with Andrica but didn't say anything as they walked to labs. Andrica was a head shorter than Charles and had to stretch her strides to keep up with him. After an interminable silence, she shuffled her shoulder and arm into his side as they continued to walk the academy hallway. On the walls, announcements and posters appeared only when and where one looked. Cameras recorded eye movements and translated those movements to info-space.

She was Charles's first girlfriend; he was Andrica's fourth boyfriend.

"You don't have to get all pouty, Charles." She laughed.

Charles said nothing and looked straight ahead.

"Your trouble, Charles, is you live between your ears. You're brainy, but you don't take in the big picture."

"For example?" he said, persisting in looking straight ahead.

"Oh, get over it, Charles. I can make you a lot happier than Euclid ever could," she said with a laugh. Most adults, even teenagers, would have figured out she was covering up a sensitivity and was in fact sentimental, a good offense being the best defense. Not Charles. Andrica stopped, looked at Charles, put a hand over her eyes, and peeked through her fingers. When he turned to her, she cut an angle to intersect another boy and left Charles looking like a turtle placed on top of a post sticking up from the desert—uncertain how he found himself there, and uncertain what to do about it.

But at night, alone in his bedroom, Charles had an epiphany. The strange encounter with Andrica still cascading in his mind, he didn't feel like working on his scholarship problem, nor did he feel like losing himself in related data he'd summoned from his computers. He'd allowed himself music, music of chants attributed to the time of Euclid.

After listening to boring harmonies for twenty minutes, he began to note a similarity to the Pythagorean idea as well as a descending Fibonacci sequence, both related to division of musical scale. In a burst of insight, he saw it. Charles had been heading down the wrong path in trying to solve his problem. The problem was hardly related to recursive nested sets: the equations he'd thus far developed mimicked patterns of a tonal system using chants. Starting anew and making corrections, he worked throughout the night and requested a meeting with his master, Euclid.

Charles bounded into Euclid's study and handed him four computer-scripted pages. The master took the pages of equations and perused them.

"You have solved the problem," Euclid said. "This is imaginative, but a circuitous way to solution."

Charles felt better than expected, considering he'd spent the last hours condensing his solution from six pages to four. Euclid handed the pages back to Charles. "Would you like to see a much simpler way to do it?"

..................................

THE NEXT MORNING, ON THEIR WAY TO COLLABORATED STUDY WITH other Liftees, Euclid asked Archimedes again: "What happened to Tulis? I can't find one word about him."

"As I said, I never saw any of his work, although the name is familiar."

"Pity. I've investigated; scrolls were logged into the library."

"Well, I told you about fires," Archimedes said. "Since antiquity—long before us—knowledge had been destroyed. And long after us. In their World War I, over two hundred thousand important books and manuscripts were lost in a library fire in a Belgian city called Louvain."

"His main book," Euclid continued, "is *Mathelumina*, and it discusses mathematical relationships between the Greek language and music."

"How so?"

"I confess, though I intended to read it, I never got to it. He told me his ideas would enhance the Greek language and understanding among tongues via harmony of the spheres."

Archimedes stopped and looked at Euclid. "Yes, a pity. You've found nothing?"

"Not a whit. I remember how excited Tulis was with his discoveries, how he exclaimed he had expanded *musica universalis* to override the Tower of Babel fiasco. He claimed he was trying to set up classes at the odeum to teach everyone." Euclid shook his head. "Aside from God himself, Tulis was the one."

"They should Lift him."

"No. Never. He was beheaded for raping and killing children."

# 10

POPOV CLOSED HER PALM AROUND HER HARP PENDANT ABOUT HER neck and tried to switch her thoughts to music, rhythms, the heaven which calmed her. She tapped her glasses to lower the volume as she listened to her morning update from General Braun. "We are on the brink of catastrophe," he said. "Our warring nations can cross the line with nukes at any time, but our pressing problem here is the droogs."

"What about the droogs?" she shouted.

"They are organizing, they have hierarchy, they are a different breed of combatant."

"What are you doing about it, General?"

Popov lost concentration as General Braun explained his plans for infiltration. Popov ended the update when she stifled another shout.

Popov could not believe what she was reading. It was an old-fashioned penned note from Kant. He had not been seen at meals that morning, and Security had found the note in his room.

Chair Popov,
Please don't be alarmed. I've taken walks all my life. I do my best thinking when I walk. So please allow me an occasional morning constitutional. Thank you.
Immanuel Kant

Six hours later, at three in the afternoon, WCM and Security still hadn't found him. Popov reread Kant's note. "What in heaven will be the repercussions of this?" she muttered to the Security guard. Popov thought about the asteroid from out of nowhere that had slammed into Earth.

She turned to the guard, "Sergeant, tell me again how this happened and why you can't find him."

"Kant showed Security a release, forged of course, allowing him to visit the museum—for 'Research,' it said. We've traced the hover-bus to the museum drop off, but no one has seen him. We believe he inked out his Security tattoo and compromised the implant."

"We must find him. God help us if he is harmed. Where is your Security hat?"

Sergeant Jbeetuie looked down from her eyes. "I don't know."

..................................

THE WALKING PHILOSOPHER FELT UNSHACKLED AND NOTED THE spring in his legs. Knowing he might get this chance but once, he would make his freedom last as long as possible, rather than declining this opportunity and regretting it later. With confidence, he adjusted the Security hat he had swiped from the cubicle, turned away from the museum, and headed down an alley. The alley led to a short street with closed-up shops, and he eventually emerged on a path lined with huts. *Ahh freedom.*

..................................

IT WAS SUNDAY, AND CHARLES HAD KITE-SURFED WITH TWO friends to one of the surviving Indonesian islands four miles away from the WCM obelisk. They had kite-landed on the island of Pisang with morning mists feathering the valley, and while the sun-speared shafts of copper and bronze shimmered between dormant volcanoes. Walking to the mathetorium had taken them past a stand of mango trees with clusters of unripe green mangos, and Charles found himself thinking about and missing his mother. By coincidence, a golden-mantled Racquet Tail, his mother's favorite bird, had then flown from a tree, crossing about a yard in front of Charles. He recalled asking her one time why she had a fondness for the bird. "Note the dignified beak," she'd said. "It is a distinguished bird who withholds the compulsion to explain and rant from the mouth—instead, it whistles."

Now he and his friends sat in a crowded mathetorium called the *Baswedan*, which overlooked the ocean. Aromas of grilled goat satay and peanut sauce came from a table of students next to them. Everywhere that Charles looked seaside, he saw all sizes and types of boats manned by commoners, spreading their nets and pulling up photosynthetic algae from contaminated waters. Almost one hundred fifty years ago, genetically engineered and transformed antiseptic algae became the dominant food to feed the have-nots. This breakthrough, combined with desalination, meant humans would be less likely to die of hunger and thirst.

Behind movie sunglasses, Charles and his friends sat not speaking, but from time to time they would smile together, laugh, or look solemn. Seated at other tables were other groups of young people; many were doing mathematical work or reading the temporary tattooed equations and symbols on their palms. Throughout the room, busts of famous mathematicians protruded from three-foot-long shelves. Charles sat near Toni Svea Praeger, the Black Goddess, where one could voice-activate her mathematical discoveries and proofs. The proofs were projected on a screen above the bust, as Praeger's bust explained, complete with her eye movements and arching of brows.

The movie over, Charles and his friends removed the lenses covering their glasses.

"I was surprised at the part where she stabbed Olin," Charles said. "I didn't see it coming."

Austin said, "But you knew from the beginning she adored Ringio. It was the music, remember?"

Charles said nothing as he restored the lens with built-in sonics to a pocket. In the movie, Olin had reminded Charles of himself.

"Besides," his other friend said, "when the time came, Olin couldn't get it up for her." He watched Charles blush. "Poor Olin couldn't rise to the occasion."

"Hey," Charles said, relieved to have found a reason to change the subject, "look at the vagrant over there. The guy with the bloody nose and tousled hair. You know who he looks like?" He used the prevalent Austronesian tongue of Bahasa, which they all knew, obviating the need for I-Translators.

KANT HAD GOTTEN LOST. HE REMEMBERED THE FABLE WHERE A young girl was lured deep into a forest because she saw pretty flowers, each one prettier than the last, as she kept walking. The reverse had happened here: it had gotten ugly, but he couldn't stop himself. Besides, he had the Security hat and, rather than skulk, it had emboldened him to take sure strides, attempting to look distinguished.

From the first, he was fascinated with the wooden huts with gutters the width of the retractable tubes he'd seen used as adjustable stilts. The gutters were semi-circular, having been cut lengthwise to capture water. Each hut had barrels at the end of downspouts. As he moved on, the huts became smaller and more dilapidated. Wood slabs were missing and replaced with bark, which hung askew. Tin roofs were bent, and some had partial re-roofs of cut tin.

A young lady studied Kant as he walked past, and a boy who he assumed to be her brother dipped a vessel into the barrel and drank from it. The boy gave some to his sister who, after a sip, hung the vessel on the barrel. Both of them stared at him without saying a word.

Further on, older people, stooped and covered in burlap, watched Kant silently. A few began to follow, ten to twenty yards behind him. But when he turned down a garbage-strewn dirt lane, intrigued by the grass huts on both sides, the people behind him stopped and turned away. He began to feel vulnerable, but it was a bright morning and the huts of thatch and grass called to him. He slowed as he stared at the wattled roofs and, not seeing gutters and downspouts, wondered how these people got their water. He saw no one around to ask, so he kept on.

The smells, which he couldn't place, were smoky and rotten. Kant followed the smells, determined to find their cause. Several side paths later, each path rounding a different crater, some as large as half a soccer field, he saw a group of people on the other side of a giant pit. They were hollering, dancing, and waving torches. He looked down into the crater near him and concluded from clumps of charred and cut roots, as well as the clusters of broken rocks and concrete tracing the debris-filled bottom, that a powerful explosion was likely the cause.

Kant sensed the trio of Putins streaking the sky before he looked up. The afterburn of plasma roared into his ears and smeared heaven as the manta-shaped planes disappeared over the horizon. The plasma smells drifting his way didn't erase the rancid odor regaining his nostrils as the echo from the Putins faded.

Deciding this was enough for today, Kant began to retrace his steps. He ran into his first trouble when he observed another group with torches headed his way. Kant dashed to his left and crawled into a trench. The refuse sickened him, and he used the Security hat to cover his nose. He peeked over the side of the trench and saw the painted faces of about a dozen teenagers. Half of them pushed and half pulled a beat-up cart carrying two middle-aged men who were tied and gagged. He watched as the first group he'd seen across the giant pit circled around to meet the new group. At about forty yards from Kant, the groups met. The dancing and ululating of both groups stopped. Heads were down. *Praying?*

All at once, guttural sounds turned to shrieks hollered into the sky. A girl from each of the mobs pulled the two older men out of the cart and untied them. The gags remained. There was a period of silence, followed by the same guttural sounds and shrieks. When Kant didn't think their shouts could get any louder, some of the boys anointed the two helpless victims with brushes dipped with goo. Two girls shook their torches while a trio of boys ungagged and held the victims. The unfortunate men pleaded and wailed. The two girls raised their torches high and, on some prearranged signal, torched the victims, then stepped back, forming a circle with all the others, watching the flaming torsos within. Torches and coupled hands were raised as the writhing men screamed their last and crumpled to the ground. After several more minutes, the torch-bearers from both groups kicked the smoldering bodies into the pit.

Kant had discovered the source of the smells.

He forced himself out of the trench and hunched down, the hat pulled low to his nose as he tried to find the way back. He found a familiar-looking path to his right, which bordered another pit he dared not look into. But the route took him to a cluster of craters he hadn't seen before. *There must have been a battle here*, he thought. Then he encountered a second bit of trouble. The mobs had united and were coming his way, led by the two girls, who no longer held torches. Kant put on his hat and tried not to tremble as they drew up to where he was standing.

"I say, can you tell me the way to the museum?" Kant said.

The lead girls stared at him. He realized they were twins. On each, a bold black *X* went from both sides of their foreheads, down across their noses, to the sides of their chins.

"I seem to have gotten lost," Kant said.

"Is that your hat?" one twin said.

"No."

The other twin walked up and yanked it from his head. A few of the others chuckled. "You been to the beauty salon, sweetie?" a boy said as he felt Kant's bun of hair.

"The fuck you doing with this," the second twin said, as she placed the hat on her own head. She turned around and faced her mob.

"A-Ten-HUT!"

The first twin laughed, as did the others. She took the hat from her sister's head and faced the mob.

"Paraaaade REST!"

The second twin took her hat back and faced Kant. "I asked you a question."

Kant couldn't make himself think. He was confused and stared at a red *Y* etched into the middle of a sun painted on the questioner's T-shirt. "It's my turn. Let me throat him," a boy yelled. "I get to chop him," a young girl piped up, stepping out from the group with her gilded hatchet.

The twin with the hat went up to Kant and eyed him. "Ya got two seconds to answer me."

"I beg your pardon." She had the skin of a young girl, but her nose looked broken. Kant fiddled with his fingers. "What was the question?"

She socked him in the nose. Kant went to his knees. Both hands rose to his face.

"I asked you what you are doing with this hat." She pointed to the top of her head. "Stand up and answer me." The mob gathered around Kant and the two twins.

"I snuck out of WCM, the obelisk," Kant stood. "By using the hat. I swiped it."

"Yo Yo Yi. Let's torch."

"Wait," the twins said in unison. "What do you do at the obelisk?" the hatted twin asked.

"I'm Immanuel Kant, a philosopher from Germany, in the 1800s," Kant wiped blood from his nose with his handkerchief. "I've been Lifted here to help WCM. You do know WCM is trying—"

"Torch!" a girl in the pack hollered.

"Don't fucking move," the hatted one said to Kant. Her sister searched his pockets and came up with a fountain pen, a museum ticket, and a pad of paper. The searching twin noticed a piece of paper had been torn off, but she could see indentations of a note left on the pad. The other twin looked at it and pushed it into Kant's face. "Read what it says," she demanded.

Kant said it was a note explaining his desire to walk.

"Read it."

Kant read the note word for word as he remembered writing it. The hatted twin grabbed her sister and motioned the group to follow them. They stopped a few yards away, as a few turned to keep an eye on Kant. He wiped his nose.

"Listen to us," the hatted one said to her charges, as she interlaced her fingers in her sister's hand. "We heard about the crazy new doings in the tower. Anyone think this dumb cock who walks in here on his own is from this world? Huh?"

"They have jesters up there, don't they?" someone said.

"This ain't no jester," the unhatted twin said, holding up the pen. "He's too far-out weird."

They all turned to look at him.

"We off this nut and we sign our death warrant, 'cause if he's who he says he is, they'll be all over it."

"What are we gonna do?" asked an imposing boy, banging his fists together. "I'm tired of waiting to break in over there. We got an opportunity right here."

The hatted twin said, "Want to send the shitheads at the top of the obelisk a better message? We send him back as is without his hat, pen, and paper. Let them find his museum ticket. He tells them a true story; you know he saw the torching."

"What if Greenland-Iceland had refused to wait so long in World War III?" another young man countered. "Would we be living like we are now?"

"You are the smartest guy we got here," hatted said, "and you give us rag. The bunch of us here and the bunch in Ash Town, together, wouldn't make a scratch on that vertical prick." She pointed to the obelisk reflecting sunlight at the top.

"Just saying."

"Think," the other twin said. "We need our allies from Samoa Town, Droog Island, and the South Horn. Still not enough. Until we get Jakarta's Kota and Glodok droogs, and killer-droogs from Cinder-Town, then get everyone coordinated and organized, we don't have a chance. Understood?"

"How long?" another brawler asked, matching fist bangs with the first brawler. "Kota-Glodok can get a nuke anytime."

"What's the plan after? A bunch of us are working on plans. The WCM doesn't know it, but the sharks are circling. We're further along than you think. Six months, nine at the outside. And we don't," she looked back at Kant, "breathe a word of this to anyone. Are we clear?" She and her twin raised fists. The others did the same.

"Where should we put Dumb Cock?" a girl asked

The twins stood in front of Kant. "Who do you work with in the obelisk?" the unhatted one asked.

Kant thought a second, someone from the mob kicked dirt, the other twin held up a finger.

"Most of the people I engage with are mathematicians, but we are. . . ." he faltered, and the twin's finger shot up again. "We think this new language we are creating needs . . . we may have to Lift musicians and . . ." Kant looked at the hatted twin. "Can you show me the way back, please? I'm sure they are distressed about my whereabouts."

"Did you say you work with mathematicians?" the mob guru asked.

That decided it. "We've got a place for you," the hatted twin said.

With their guru's wit and charm, knowing Kant couldn't kite-surf, they procured a hover, which they over-rode and directed to an Island mathetorium.

As Kant was about to walk up the entry ramp to the hover, the second twin, who'd watched her sister accost Kant, put on his hat and tapped him on the shoulder. When Kant turned, he heard her say, "You have to understand, Herr Kant, this is a twin thing." She walloped him in the nose, and everyone hooted as Kant crawled his way into the hover.

..................................

CHARLES AND HIS FRIENDS STARED AS THE MAN WIPED HIS NOSE with a handkerchief again and stumbled to a corner table at the end of a wall in the mathetorium.

"It's Kant," Charles said. "I saw him walk by Euclid's room the other night. He looked right at me."

One friend chuckled, saying, "Well, there you go, he just sat in front of Euclid." They glanced at the bust of Euclid staring at Kant, and the other friend laughed. "Charles, you're cuckoo, what would he be doing here?"

Charles watched Kant stare back at Euclid while he held the bloody handkerchief over his nose. "I'm sure it's him." Charles positioned his glasses and tapped them.

"Dad. What's Kant doing on Pisang?"

# 11

AFTER THEY KITE-SURFED BACK TO THE MAINLAND, CHARLES found himself alone as he stepped up to one of several bridges ending at the obelisk. He was the only one of his friends living in the secured upper floors of the obelisk. One of the others was a son of a Second-Tier mathematician and lived on lower floors restricted to Tier levels. The other boy, Austin, was orphaned but gifted, and sponsored by a Third-Tier single father. He lived closer to sea level.

Charles tried not to think about Kant. He felt sorry for him, as the bloodied gentleman looked hopeless and frightened when Security stormed inside the mathetorium, grabbed his arms, and all but carried him to the waiting hover outside. Charles's father had been summoned by Popov to an immediate WCM meeting, and Charles would hear the outcome tonight.

.................................

POPOV WAITED IN HER OFFICE FOR WCM COLLEAGUES. BEFORE turning off her window screens so everyone could focus, she took in the views. Ocean everywhere. Her office was close to the top of the obelisk on the 195th floor of 200. She looked down the length of over four soccer fields to sea level. The top floor under the apex had retracting portions of roof dedicated to telescopes. If a tele locked on to something and wanted to track it, override electronics permitted the obelisk to turn if the weather was stable. Floors 197 to 199 comprised working rooms for astronomers and astrophysicists, plus exobiologists who worked with SETI (Search for Extra Terrestrial Intelligence) and TESS (Transiting Exoplanet Survey Satellite). The floor directly above Popov was kept unoccupied, but Chairs could use the floor above as they wished. Popov dedicated those rooms to music and meditation. Floors below Tier, stretching to sea level, contained Indonesian government offices, municipal officials, and associated families. A number of gyms, spas, stores, shops, and cafeterias were included on lower floors. A well-intentioned mosque built at sea level had now emerged as a meeting place for recreational mathematicians. Popov thought about that as she shut down the window screens. Mathematics had become the true religion, everywhere. The deeper one journeyed into the winding pathways of numbers, the less religious and more spiritual one became. Transhumanism was embraced and carried the day.

Below sea level, twenty floors stretched to seabed. Government adjuncts, obelisk personnel, other workers, and Security lived there. And below seabed, straddling the foundation on all sides, space was dedicated to ocean-desalination, alga-rice food processing, and waste management—where organic waste was, with the help of microbes, turned into protein for fish farms as well as animal food. Extended foundation walls, below seabed, afforded additional space for electronics—including nano-hard-drive storage; labs for biologists and biochemists; quarters for biogerontologists and transhumanists; warehouses; and backup Security. Thousands of workers on eight-hour shifts were busy around the clock below seabed.

The entire obelisk, from top to bottom, including the levels below seabed, was protected by nano-constructed anti-ballistic shields. Engineers claimed the construct could be shaken and torqued but not destroyed. One other obelisk, two thirds the size of this one, as well built and defended, was also planted three kilometers offshore in Tomini Bay, but on the other side, off the southern coast near Bunta. Its one purpose: military. The two cities of Marisa and Bunta were separated by 120 kilometers of bay water, and these waters were patrolled constantly.

*How is it,* Popov thought, *that a civilization that is able to create this incredible construct can be so vicious and rampantly kill fellow humans?*

.................................

POPOV FACED THE WCM MEMBERS FROM BEHIND HER DESK. "KANT must be Returned. His contributions have been spotty. If his story is true, hideous as it is, he has become distracted. We almost lost him."

The Board agreed with her assessment.

"Now," Popov said, "I want to hear from each of you about something different. Tell me what you know about droogs."

.................................

KANT WAS IN HIS QUARTERS. SECURITY HAD BEEN REVAMPED. ALL ID devices had been reset. The WCM had worried that Liftees would try to escape until the Board realized that Liftees, already deracinated, feared being cast off again. Where would they go; how would they survive? They felt chosen and safe. They bonded, each appreciating the opportunity to work to save their species.

Kant had been asked to brief the WCM, and he gave his last words of advice in a drafted statement, after which he was Returned.

Popov tried to appreciate his written words, which seemed like excuses, and the more she read, the more she understood why Kant had failed as a Liftee. Though he understood the present-day language problems, he was arrogant and a loner who had little to offer in the way of solution. She filed his statement.

.................................

TWO DAYS LATER, JOHANN SEBASTIAN BACH WAS LIFTED TO REPLACE Kant. Popov referred to her notes provided by Tier: *Bach should be able to synthesize and develop ideas through previous generations. What's more, he is mathematically gifted.*

With a change in procedure, following complaints and suggestions of original Liftees, Darwin introduced Bach to the other Liftees. Darwin took his time during the introduction, and Bach and the Liftees were given time to ask and answer questions of each other. The seven Board members were impressed with this idea of formal but casual introductions, and Popov said to her colleagues: "You see how we have lost communication skills over the centuries? We never gave the first batch of Liftees proper grounding. It was rushed."

A half hour later, Darwin summed up: "Again, you have been selected to help our species get out of our predicament. We haven't much time, and we Liftees, as well as Earth's governing body—"he waved his arm to the Board seated in front of the conference room—"will drive you hard. However, I will be available to listen and take suggestions from you."

As a special welcome to Bach, some Liftees suggested his music be played. His immortal Toccata and Fugue in D minor was chosen. Transferred from a twenty-first-century recording, the master heard the organ from the walls, as did everyone else. During the rendition, the master maintained the hint of a smile. Despite his double chin and puffy waist, he appeared energetic, animated. At the conclusion, he said, "May I see the organ pipes?"

It was explained why it wasn't possible. "How did you like your music?" Madame Curie asked.

"A little faster than I'm used to. And a bit sharped, which is why I wanted to examine the pipes. Nevertheless, an admirable job by the performer."

Bach was pampered, pushed, coddled, and cajoled. He didn't contest his assignment. He was eager.

Two days after Bach's arrival, after much anguish, Popov suggested to her Board colleagues that Newton be Returned. "It comes down to this," she'd said: "we need a language maker. And Isaac, while busy, has no-ended himself in abstruse mathematics, leading us astray. He's also asked Liftees what they know about alchemy. I've looked at what we have of his ancient writings, and alchemy was a specific interest."

As a result, the Norwegian, Ivar Aasen, nineteenth-century creator of languages, was Lifted. Aasen had a random tic in his lower lip and was quiet as he was introduced by Madame Curie, who had volunteered to share Darwin's role.

.................................

IN THE EVENING, ARCHIMEDES PACED IN EUCLID'S STUDY AS Charles entered. "I need my book, *Abstracts*," Archimedes said.

"There were fires in old-time. It may have burned in Alexandria," Charles said.

"Along with my *Ruminations*," said Euclid, as Archimedes stamped a foot and left in a huff.

Euclid wiped his face with his arm. He looked at Charles again and refocused his eyes. "Okay. Where are we? What have we learned?"

Seconds later, Euclid said, "Sometimes a simple approach will enable a foothold."

Charles looked at the final tabulation of alphabet characters and understood the possibilities. Just as "e" is the most common letter in the English language, Euclid and Charles had isolated the most common letter in 746 of the main languages on Earth. Then they isolated the next most common letter (in English, "a") and the next and so on, in all 746 languages. After that, they moved on to the most frequent pairs of letters, the most common utterances, the most common words, and the most common nouns. It was busy work, but simple—almost pedestrian. Until they realized that one hundred years ago, Indonesia alone had retained 719 languages across 360 ethnic groups, whereas in modern times there were 42 languages scattered across 17 cultures of the archipelago.

"What happened to the other tongues?" asked Euclid. "Wait. Didn't you say as islands slipped under the tides the displaced natives moved to other islands?"

"I did. I'm told the disappearing languages coalesced into those we have now."

Euclid looked at him. "What we've done thus far is partial. We have yet to contend with obscure Asian languages, ideograms, and . . ."

They took the results and, based on intuition and Venn diagrams, combined linguistic universals, thus creating a new alphabet. The alphabet had 96 characters/graphemes based on letters/characters of languages that overlapped certain sounds. Charles was convinced it was a foothold. Euclid was skeptical.

"Try to look for patterns," Euclid said.

"Shouldn't we see Aasen?" Charles said.

"Let's not rush. This new alphabet changes everything; we need to study the mathematics behind it first."

But on a hunch, after hearing about Bach and his mathematical precision in fugue augmentation, Euclid showed the alphabet to Master Bach.

Bach, fascinated with the possibilities, applied inversion, transposition, and isometries. Several days later, he had worked out a series of quasi-chants based on new utterances he'd never previously heard. He'd used the electronic musical keyboard on his computer. By improvising further, his electronic chants, in their hypnotic minimalism, although at first strange and off-putting, gradually produced a calming effect in the listener.

..................................

"IT MIGHT BE BEST," EINSTEIN SAID, HIMSELF AN AMATEUR MUSIcian who adored the violin, "before one human communicates with another at an ultra-efficient level, to prepare, or get set up to converse."

"I don't understand," Reed said.

It was afternoon in the main meeting room, and all Liftees were present at the WCM's request to discuss Bach's possible breakthrough.

Aasen raised his hand. Beardless, hair pulled back to reveal a roomy forehead, he did not stand. "These strange new sound-utterances take some getting used to. Conversation, communication, won't just happen." The tic in his lip was almost as quick as Euclid's eye blinks.

"He means that, to reach the highest levels of communication, some linguistic foreplay, some verbal thrusts to reach common ground will have to be initiated," Tuan said.

"Will humans take the necessary time?" asked Popov.

De Costa raised a hand. "If we need to systematize an approach to enhanced communication as opposed to conversation, I don't think humans will have the patience for linguistic floundering."

"I don't believe it will work either," Tuan said. "To communicate means one human or group of humans finds common ground with another right away."

"Ideally, but we may have to prepare . . ." Anand said, glancing sideways, ". . . linguistic runways, if you will, offering a way into the atmosphere of true communication."

"The optimum language for homo sapiens," Gunderson said, "may need some type of omnipresent working rheostat—a biochip in the brain—which will control, allow for, and adjust or adapt the language based on gender, age, health of participants, culture gaps, intelligence, et cetera."

Darwin had been taking notes. His serious demeanor gave him the look of a poet. "'Optimum, you always say. What we are trying to find, ladies and gentlemen, is not just any unique universal language, but the optimum language."

Popov offered: "Perhaps the opening of any dialog is a preamble, a setup, a registration, a time of adjustment, before anything is communicated. Participants can listen and adjust with music, mathematics, rhythms, and chants. The notion of lingua-musica ambigrams comes to mind. I do feel communicants can't just dive in—there must be interpretive setup."

Bach stood. "I hear your underlying questions. In music, the concertmaster sets pitch and tone. We have overtures before operas, orchestral music leads into themes. Let me work on this."

But it was Gunderson and Aasen, using mathematics, who began piecing together the probability structures in the new language. It was a given that the probability of the next word or characters in any language text depended on word-data coming before it. And in this strange new tongue, the mathematical probabilities resonated sooner. They were on the right ramp.

# 12

ARCHIMEDES WORKED OVERTIME TO RECREATE HIS *ABSTRACTS Mathematica*. He told the other Liftees that he was recreating the connections needed to advance to the next stage in their mutual quest. But his secret goal was to regift humanity with what he considered to be his most important work, lost to the ages.

The great man lost sleep and deprived himself to the extent that he appeared daft and was incommunicado. No one could reach him, including Popov. The tragedy occurred when Popov had no choice but to Return him. His handlers escorted him to Time Travel Control and at the last second, in an enraged fit of despair, he deliberately broke loose, ran, and plunged headfirst into a steel retaining wall.

The next morning, an emergency meeting of the WCM was held. "This is an indescribable tragedy," Popov said. "If he doesn't survive the coma, we will have altered history, and we all know the price we paid the last time."

"The asteroid that came out of nowhere," Reed muttered.

"He must be Returned at once in his current condition," De Costa said. "We cannot risk another moment with him here."

"How did Archimedes die?" asked Tuan.

"No one knows for sure," Anand said, "but according to history, the Romans took him away as he pleaded 'Do not disturb my circles.'"

"They killed him," Reed said. "I vote we Return him at once. Can't take any more chances—at least he's alive. Get Medical to fix and stabilize him."

The vote was taken, and it was unanimous. Archimedes was treated and Returned to the juncture from where he'd been Lifted—his room, in front of circles drawn by a stick in a muddy sandbox.

At the same time, a twentieth-century polyglot and sinologist, Emil Krebs, was Lifted to replace Archimedes. This resurrection had been a fight between several WCM members requesting DeMambro, the brilliant Afro-Italian mathematician, who thirty years ago had advanced the understanding of Lie Groups to include numerically related phonemes, and those on the WCM panel who advocated Krebs.

The fact that Krebs had mastered forty-eight languages in speech and writing won the argument.

..................................

BACH WAS THE FIRST TO PLUNGE IN—HE CLAIMED HE COULD HEAR it.

"Hear what?" Curie asked him, her eyebrows arching.

"Music. Martin Luther was right. He said 'The devil does not stay where music is.'"

Euclid and Curie, working with Tuan and De Costa, along with Aasen, were the first to substantiate the mathematical scaffolding of a new language. After discussions, the WCM decided to name the new language Mathe-Lingua-Musica, or M-L-M.

..................................

POPOV FELT THE TIME PRESSURE MORE THAN ANYONE. SHE REALized the initial slate of Liftees had been faulty, at best. It was rumored Einstein, despite his best intentions, could not focus because something puzzled him about the Grand Unification Theory, which had been formulated and proven over a hundred years ago. Curie, his close friend, claimed Einstein told her that God had given him this second chance to fix it. *He has to go back*, Popov thought.

Freud and Darwin were a puzzle. They worked hard; they were opinionated. But Darwin couldn't assimilate to the task. Popov saw now, despite initial opinions, that his math wasn't exceptional, and he worked his way around the issues.

Popov considered Freud. The doctor seemed threatened by an ultimate language. He was defensive and insisted the psyche of man wouldn't change. Of late, when he spoke, he never turned his head to anyone; he expected everyone to turn to him. Both had to go, and Popov wanted to tear her hair out.

# 13

GENERAL BRAUN SUMMONED HIS AIDES AS HE REREAD THE DROOG report in front of him.

"What do you mean we can't find them? That's because they've infiltrated, right?"

"I'm afraid, Sir," said the top aide, "we are not receiving previously planned responses and checks."

"So, where the hell are they? Those two were our best men and specifically trained for droog penetration."

"There is the remote chance—"

"No! When it comes to the goddamned droogs, we don't deal with remote chances."

"We've lost our men, Sir."

"Are you implying that our people joined the droogs?"

"I believe they were found out, Sir. And have been eliminated."

Later, in his office, the General knew his aides were right. He'd become jumpy whenever he thought about droogs and couldn't understand how these thugs had grown from inconsequential disorganized nobodies to a formidable threat. *The problem is,* he thought, *trying to catch them is like trying to grab smoke.*

..................................

AASEN WAS PAIRED WITH BACH AND MADAME CURIE DURING THE day. At night, Aasen doubled his efforts alone. The task was mind-boggling. While Bach and Curie experimented with musical and mathematical patterns of new utterances, Aasen had to create a new language—M-L-M—using the ninety-six phonemes suggested by Euclid and the boy Charles.

Aasen decided to amalgamate several of the phonemes into language blocks—blocks that would deal with greetings, friendship, cooperation, and the like. He was deciding which words—utterances—one was to speak and how to speak them. He chose to invent sounds of harmony, familiarity, and integration, based on the common-ground utterances and epicene cognates of 746 languages reduced to 96 characters.

He knew "home" was considered to be one of the most comforting words in the English language. Thus, Aasen experimented with how he could establish the concept "home" using the new alphabet-language, M-L-M.

Aasen realized most educated English-speaking adults have a vocabulary of about sixty thousand words. Yet the most frequent hundred words account for 60 percent of all conversations in English. And the most common four thousand words account for 98 percent of conversations. *But what will be the most common words in Mathe-Lingua-Musica?* He would start by collecting the most common four thousand in all the 746 base languages. For the final result, which would be incorporated into M-L-M, he doubted he could use more than a quarter of everything out there. Where the rest of M-L-M would come from, he had no idea.

"Shouldn't we ignore words related to war and violence?" asked Anand, who had been assigned to work with Aasen for the next few days.

Aasen thought about Anand's question, and for the moment ignored it. He was quicksanded in another problem. The main Chinese language, Mandarin, in essence, had no alphabet. Mandarin relied on thousands of ideograms to represent each word and syllable. Two thousand or more characters had to be remembered just to read a tabloid. On top of this, voice pitch and intonation gave different meanings. Homophones in Chinese languages are very common, and different words are spelled the same. Thus, the need to distinguish by pitch.

"I . . . grammars," Aasen finally said. "We need recursion in selected grammars. And prosody."

Anand looked at him, into his eyes. Aasen was in his new world—searching.

Aasen leaned his head upward. "Syllabic information density. Mandarin contains too much." He looked again to Anand and tried to remember his question. He gave up.

.....................................

BACH HAD ALREADY DECIDED THAT ANY FORAY INTO MATHE-LINGUA-Musica would center on the perfect fifth, an interval which he and other musicians considered stable and powerful. He admitted this didn't hold in other cultures, and he was isolating a section of humanity. He avoided dissonant tritones, but allowed lower and inverted mordents.

A tinge of dissonance, Bach later decided, would serve to amplify the soothing proportions before and after. But this was based on the European ear and the seven-note scale, not the ears of Asians preferring the pentatonic scale, or the scales of Indians, Arabians, and others. Curie and Tuan were able to give him musical samples from the cultures of the 746 base languages. The master and great organist became one with his keyboard as he reached for afflatus. Bach understood that the physical and mathematical beauty of most music he was familiar with was controlled by ratios and proportions. Curie and the others also understood, but to find *the* particular musical proportions of M-L-M by investigating music from all languages and cultures and to unify them into one system was overwhelming—even for Bach.

.....................................

THEN THERE WAS WITTGENSTEIN, THE HANDSOME NINETEENTH-CENTURY philosopher-logician. "He sees around corners," Reed had said. "Now is his time." He had replaced Darwin and considered the Asian ideogrammatic languages. Wittgenstein looked to Aasen. "I'm beginning to think the idea of one universal language may be beyond humankind's capability. The mix, the jumble, this unordered macaronic mishmash of a language . . ."

Aasen countered: "Mandarin and Cantonese are tonal. A rising or dipping pitch changes a word's meaning. The Chinese culture was on the right track all along; they needed to branch further."

"I'm all for sinology, but common sense keeps telling me music and singing are culturally defined," Wittgenstein said. His full, open eyes never seemed to blink. "What we find pleasing doesn't bring the same reaction to other culture blocs, and vice versa."

Aasen stared at the floor.

"Also," Wittgenstein continued, "music doesn't prevent periphrasis. And in Switzerland, diglossia exists . . . Is there anything wrong with devising additional . . .?"

Aasen realized Bach had come by to listen, and after Bach mumbled, "My God in heaven, spare us all," the organist wandered back to his music.

Aasen toed-up to Wittgenstein as he responded loudly and curtly to the question posed: "Oh, nothing at all, except you've quintupled the work and lessened the time to complete it."

*Why didn't his lip spasm?* thought Wittgenstein.

It was the first time anyone had heard Aasen raise his voice.

# 14

IN HER OWN PRIVATE ALOOFNESS, ANDRICA FOUND PEACE AND harmony with her dolphins. City residents who could afford it contracted sea-level pools for their own enjoyment. These pools held decontaminated water and were kept covered when not in use. The floating pools, strung out like many unhitched necklaces about the obelisk, were motored and could be moved within marked channels. Andrica, who'd asked her mother for dolphins as a birthday present two years earlier, had also persuaded her to transition their pool for fishy comfort. She was an only child, with a father long gone, and a mother—working in Industrial Security—who had used much of the inheritance in efforts to satisfy her daughter. To her mother's great satisfaction, Andrica was a precocious student who had passed special exams, enabling her to attend academy.

"Dolphins calm me," she said to Charles when he asked her why the inordinate interest in the mammals.

Charles tried to contain his smile.

"They don't behave like idiots. They are comfortable with their world, playful, and exhibit enormous happiness," she said.

They were walking back from academy and Charles was aware she was envious of his exalted status now that he'd secured a "full" at Praeger U. As a full, one of four at the academy, he got to wear the academy brassard on his left arm with the words *Mathematics—The Pursuit of Truth* sewn in.

"Euclid's a pure, unadulterated genius," Charles said.

"Yes, Charles. So, my dolphins don't interest you?" She had four of them, a neutered male and three females.

Charles turned and looked at her.

"I repeat, they calm me. Isn't that what the WCM and Liftees are looking for?"

"Aasen and Bach work well together. They may be close to a breakthrough. I did the best I could to help Bach, but I'm excited to be back with Euclid."

"Jesus," Andrica said.

.................................

ANDRICA WENT TO HER DOLPHINS. SHE THOUGHT ABOUT THE PEACE and calm they offered and wondered whether it could be connected in some way to their language of squeaks and squawks. It was an obvious idea but she decided she would study their language, even though a ton of dolphin-language research already existed. She recorded their sounds above water, but also submerged herself below water and recorded. The sounds, though muted, were much richer and more varied below the surface. Knowing dolphins can hear pitches up to 200,000 Hz, way above dog frequency, which was about 45,000 Hz, she wondered if she was missing high-frequency communication. Tomorrow she would run mathe-graphics on the pitches, clicks, and pings of higher frequencies.

Two days later, she attempted to charm Charles with a bouquet of flowers.

"What's this?" He took the fresh roses and smelled them, at a loss for words.

Andrica was not surprised with his puzzlement; *the great Charles*, she thought. Charles would never notice that men gave women flowers, not the other way around.

"I need a favor, Charles. I ran some tests on my dolphins. I can't begin to understand it, but there might be something others have missed. Can you show this to Aasen for me?"

Charles took the "tiny bean," the equivalent of a high-end twenty-first-century thumb drive, and looked at it.

"It's a complete audio-vid with my notes and conclusions."

"He's kind of busy."

Andrica stared at him. She moved closer and sniffed the roses. She looked up into his face. "Charles," she whispered as she bussed his cheek, "do me this one little favor. Okay?"

Charles stuck the bean into the mini holding receptor on his glasses.

..................................

THREE DAYS LATER.

"The dolphins know," Aasen said.

The Liftees and the WCM were seated in the main briefing room. Popov encouraged the great linguist, who rarely said anything at meetings. She walked closer to him and smiled. "Please. Inform us."

"They know. They know how to do it," he sputtered.

"Know what?" Popov asked.

"They know how to calm themselves. They have done it. In their own language."

"Can we transfer, can we apply their technique to M-L-M?" De Costa queried.

"I'm not sure we can."

"So, what have you learned?" asked Popov.

"It's all in the interstices."

"Please explain," she prodded.

"They know when to be quiet. They, they . . ."

"Go on, please." She smiled.

"They know when not to speak. It's all in their—it's in the spaces and rests between."

Only later did a few remember it was at this juncture that Bach had gotten up and left the room. The same evening, Bach requested the assistance of Curie and Euclid.

"Up to now, our mathematics has been applied to the sounds and patterns of sounds. It needs to be applied to the silence between words and to the beats as well," Bach said.

"Of course," Euclid said. "How could we forget? The interstices must be assigned value."

"It appears," Curie said, "just as we know light by darkness, we shall know this language and its music by silences between notes and beats, between utterances."

# 15

WORKING WITH EUCLID IN HIS ANECHOIC CHAMBERS, CHARLES listened to dolphin-like music arranged and reconfigured by Bach to associate with the Asian musical scale. He became dreamy.

"I've noted the same feeling," Euclid said. He laid down his stylus; they were working on continuity agreements, combinatorial arguments, ways for projective geometries to communicate with algebras. They were enjoying themselves and their work, but most of all they enjoyed their personal silence, which was enhanced by the silence between sounds in these strange and bewitching rhythms. The music's inchoate communication used silences to reinforce what preceded and what followed.

"The young lady has stumbled on something revelatory," Euclid said, as he waved a hand above and around him, to the music.

Charles sat back, tilted his face to Euclid, and gave back a smile.

..................................

THE FOLLOWING MORNING, BACH AND MADAME CURIE ADDRESSED the WCM and all Liftees. "This could be a breakthrough," Popov said. For a full twenty minutes before the meeting proper, Bach's refigured dolphin music was fed to them. The minimalist squawks, with intermittent rests, and tuneful clicks drove them all to silence; it was the first time that had ever happened. The recipients were not entirely at peace—tremors and queasiness surfaced here and there—but they were quiet. No one could explain how this happened, much less why.

It was Curie who concluded the prepared report. She had ascended as the de facto leader among the Liftees. She commanded respect, whether she was analyzing data or drinking coffee. And she didn't play politics.

"... we believe, as Aasen contends, the way to develop Mathe-Lingua-Musica for our species lies in what is *not* said or heard, as well as in the words and notes themselves. We must apply all our mathematical efforts to the spaces between words, the silences between beats of music, as much as to the phrases and language architecture itself." Madame Curie stopped and sat down, and for three minutes no one said one word as the background dolphin-minimalist enfolded them. All of them listened and thought. Popov, who was familiar with the music of twentieth-century minimalists—Reich, Adams, Glass—wondered what they would have done with this.

Reed, unknowingly, paraphrased Curie's insight. "Just as dark matter throughout our universe had mystified us for centuries and then pressed to our understanding, it appears the stops and silences of language will aid our progress.

"Will the grammars allow it?" asked Tuan.

"It's our job to make it so," Aasen said. "The language will not support the grammar; the grammar will support the language."

"Godspeed," Popov said, and the meeting was adjourned.

# 16

POPOV DIRECTED HER ARM AS A WAND AND POINTED TO A 5-BY-8-meter window screen in the "Orion Lounge," the astronomers' cafeteria on the 190th floor. A screened-in balcony rose from the floor, a luxury the obelisk engineers had granted. This imitation balcony forced a three-dimensional reality into one's mind. Popov became absorbed in the moment as she looked "over" balcony railings and experienced vertigo. She walked about the balcony, saw and heard seagulls, and inhaled the day's aroma, which had been dispensed by hovers. Aromas selected were random for an entire month. Today she closed her eyes and imagined firs mixed with . . . *What was this gorgeous smell again? Canadian balsams mixed with attar of North American lilacs?* She could never remember, but wished she could open her eyes to forests and gardens as shown in her collection of *National Geographic*. Her memory of the lush pictures from old-times was strong. She imagined herself on a fervid green embankment overlooking the sea, a forest of firs behind her.

Popov felt rewarded that tangible M-L-M progress had been made, but she had no delusions of success. Although plans for implementing the new lingua franca to administrative officials and the common people were being handled by Third Tier, and she'd been pleased with their setup, something was missing in WCM's educational efforts. As part of the cross-pollination of ideas, Popov rotated private meetings with WCM members and Liftees. Today she had invited WCM member Katherine Tuan and Liftee Madame Curie for lunch and waited inside at a reserved table on the "balcony." Popov nodded to several astrophysicists and stargazers. The cafeteria near the top of the obelisk had another wall of glass screens along with inside partitions, which were divided into a series of nooks with couches, private tables, and, if one wanted, streamers of paintings—Renaissance to present age—floating into each private nook as wished.

For several minutes, Curie admired the paintings of da Vinci. All three were silent as they studied the *Mona Lisa*, after which they began lunch.

"Katherine, as one fluent in Mandarin and as one who's lived in Asian culture, are we missing an opportunity? No Asian has been Lifted or considered."

Tuan wiped her lips and held the napkin on them for a moment. "I've always believed," Tuan replied, "much like survival of the fittest, whoever breaks through to lead, whoever rises to eminence, as we have ourselves, deserves to lead and have ultimate destiny."

"Pleased you are committed and loyal," Popov said, "but I'm of the opinion that we can't succeed without also employing great minds of the Far East, India, and Mid-East lands."

"We Liftees knew this would be coming," Curie said.

"What do you mean?"

"There are others who can help us, but each of us likes the challenge and doesn't want to be replaced."

"I see," Popov said. "We have scientifically tried everything to enable more Liftees to join us. We can't do it. Simulations show instability leading to collapse of government if more than nine of you are here at one time."

"If I tell you who we need and why, will you let me stay?" Curie asked.

Popov looked at her. "Madame, for reasons I'm sure you understand, you know I can't."

Curie smiled. "Understood. We must have the Indian—Ramanujan."

Tuan leaned in toward Curie. "Einstein has also mentioned him."

Popov stared at Curie. "You knew him?"

"I didn't know him personally. I saw pages from his last notebooks, and they contained tedious but bizarre equations about theory concerning music and linguistics. No one could figure it out."

Curie pulled a notepad from her purse and quoted from notes provided by Tier:

*Ramanujan recorded his mathematical discoveries in 1919–1920. More than 100 hand-written pages contained over 600 mathematical formulas.*

"And these formulas relate to music?" Popov asked.

"Many, I believe, do."

Popov pushed herself from the table and shot up from her chair. Her face reddened. With Olympian restraint, she waited for her anguish and excitement to diminish. Tuan and Curie had never seen her so distressed, and said nothing as she finally eased down into her seat. A full minute passed.

"Ms. Tuan," she said, "find me the greatest Asian mathematician who can cross over to music and meta-linguistics. I will search the Mideast." Popov looked at Curie. "We will Lift Ramanujan." Popov picked up the silicon tray holding her bowl of tonseng, half full of goat meat in curry, and excused herself.

.................................

THE FOLLOWING DAY AT 7:00 A.M., A MEETING WAS CONVENED IN the WCM conference room. The following proclamation was distributed and read aloud by Popov.

Memorandum 27

August 23, 2489

Esteemed mathematicians, beloved Liftees:

For reasons you best understand—for it is crucial to the continuance of our species—a continual working rotation of Liftees will commence immediately. I chide myself that this was not done earlier.

Any Liftee who is quiescent and unable to contribute within one month will be Returned to their time.

Any Liftee who wants to Return, may. This Liftee must give us a detailed report on how to proceed without her or him and suggest the best-suited individual to replace same.

By vote of WCM committee, one or more Liftees will be Returned every two months. Others will be saved for the following two-month period based on their contributions.

We will never support any type of ethnocentrism.
The above rules are inviolable. Please do not feel unwanted, threatened, or solemn. This is done for one reason only: to save humanity from extinction. May the spirit of mathematics be with us all.
Juanita Colleen Popov

The Liftees were wary. They learned Second-Tier mathematicians had found ways to reduce the time to get a new Liftee up-to-speed upon entry. In an induced coma, she or he was electromagnetically mased and brain-fed the new advances in mathematics, history, and sociology, and other disciplines, from the time they died to present age, plus given detailed analyses and updated progress on the optimum language problem. Liftees surmised there would be more switching in and out. When it was later announced who was going back and who was saved, rancor ensued. But Popov brooked no dissension. She'd revised the rules and regulations for WCM Chairs and had consulted with the Board. "The terms are set," she said. "For those of you leaving us, we thank you for your valued service."

She planned on replacing Euclid, Freud, and Einstein with the Indian mathematician Srinivasa Ramanujan; Liu Hui, the great Chinese mathematician of antiquity, who had been working on musical patterns and mathematical rhythms for conversational language; and the ninth-century Persian mathematician, Muhammad al-Khwarizmi.

Popov also announced, effective immediately, that a rotating committee had been established using First-Tier mathematicians to ascertain individual Liftee contribution and to make recommendations to the WCM on who to Return.

Madame Curie did her best to calm and motivate her Liftee colleagues. She first met with them in their individual rooms, then together in the conference room. Einstein was upset when she met him privately.

"I'm almost finished with corrections to my Grand Unification Theory. There was a flaw in their supersymmetry."

"In Europe, I asked you about your GUT. You said 'I've led humanity to the right spot, they will find it if I don't.' Well, they did."

"But . . ."

"*They* will fix it, Albert. That's not why you're here."

The great man quieted as he realized he would be Returned if he didn't focus on a different problem. Later, in the larger room with the other Liftees, he still wasn't settled and sat with arms folded across his chest.

"Madame Curie," he said, "I and my colleagues appreciate your time in listening to our concerns and your offer to represent us to Ms. Popov and the WCM Board." Einstein uncrossed his legs and leaned toward Curie. "If you can plead my case and gain me another week, I can offer humanity corrections to their solution to my final theory. Their solution, as it stands, misses a hidden dimension. I have the mathematics to support my contention."

The others were silent. Someone sighed. "I'll try," Curie said.

Euclid spoke not a word, and, although nothing had been told to him or the others, he felt he would be Returned. Freud was despondent as frowns multiplied on his forehead while he stared at his notepad. He hadn't been told either, but he knew.

"We must work until the last hour," Curie said to every Liftee. "We were chosen. It is the least we can do."

Less than eleven months were left.

# 17

GENERAL BRAUN, FOR ONE OF THE FEW TIMES IN HIS LIFE, WAS flustered. He read the memo again and squinted at Farzad, his general of Security. "What do you make of this? Droogs?"

A half-opened, Army-issue, Ho-bag of killer scorpions had been found in the corner of the enlisted mess. Everyone knew it had been full of the large scorpion mutations because of the poison stench, which came from the bag. This added adaptation-mutation had first been discovered only thirty years ago, and was now prevalent in the species. On this occasion, a crippled scorpion, the width of a working man's fist, had lain hidden in the corner and injected its poison when the bag was opened by Security. If it hadn't been for the gloves worn by the guard, he would have died within a half-hour.

"How many and where are the creepies now?"

"Worst-case scenario, a maximum of twenty-five could have been transported in the bag. Or it could have only been a few. Best case, it was just the crippled one, now torched."

Braun tossed the memo back to Farzad.

"Killer bots launched?"

"Yes, Sir. But I must tell you, chem is saying that judging by the strength of the stench, ten to twelve were in the bag."

Braun reddened. "Don't ever offer a best-case scenario in situations like this again. Understood?"

When Farzad left, the General noticed the rare tremble of his own index finger. Killer scorpions were bad enough. And a warning. What caused the tremble was his growing certainty—droogs.

CHARLES AND ANDRICA WERE IN THE MATHETORIUM PLAYING mathescrab. One of sixty drones fluttering food and drinks throughout the mathetorium hovered over Charles and speakered: "Order 331—two puce lattes and asperkraut."

"Yia-yee," said Charles, and the parachute-shaped drone descended so Charles could remove two lattes attached to the sides and a breaded plate holding asperkraut hooked to the bottom. Charles touched a red light on the drone; the drone responded with a "Yia-yo," ascended, and curved away to load for the next customer.

Andrica was in high spirits. She'd been selected to work with Third Tier during free time. Third Tier was assigned the task of implementing the new language planetwide; the work was crucial and the best prospects were selected to help.

"I'm glad for you, Andrica."

"Thank you, Charles, but it still bugs me that I was never assigned to a Liftee. Like you were."

"But Euclid thinks he'll be Returned soon. I don't know what happens to me."

Because of the progress Charles had made with Euclid and Euclid's marked increase in energy whenever he worked with Charles, Popov had initiated an apprentice program for the most-gifted academy students. The students followed up with oral notes copied to WCM and First Tier, and also discussed their experience with academy teachers.

Having finished his portion of the asperkraut, Charles reached in and pinched off a piece of the breaded plate that held it and ate it. Andrica did the same as Charles. Asparagus and sauerkraut, mixed with a touch of clomiphene and hormone enhancers, was a popular aphrodisiac for young people. Charles had ordered it to impress Andrica, who was looking at him, staring into his eyes. Without changing her look, she reached for her latte and, as she sipped, winked at him from over her cup. She'd frazzled her aqua-tinted hair and dyed the wrestling ladies on her left arm blue, while boxing ladies on her right arm sported black and white prisoner stripes. These were subcutaneous tattoos surfacing after taking a pill. Unlike the dolphin tattoo, which was permanent, she could erase these or submerge them under her skin. She eyed Charles with suggestive stares. What gave her away, countering the effort of naughtiness, were her dolphin earrings.

"So, Charles, what do you have in mind?" Andrica crossed her legs and poked about Charles's shin with her foot. She smiled at his blush.

Charles broke off another piece of the breaded food plate and offered it to her. She leaned over and took it with her lips. She smiled at him as she sucked the breaded plate into her mouth.

"Oh, God, Andrica," Charles said. "That's not what I . . ." His face reddened and he peeked about him.

"Oh, Charles, what's to worry? Don't you like me?"

"You know I do."

"Tell you what." She broke off another piece of plate and offered it to him.

Charles hesitated, but after a moment he leaned over and took it with his lips. For a moment he didn't smile, and then he ordered a jumbo nepenthe-shandy . . . with two straws.

..................................

IN HER OFFICE, POPOV WAS REVIEWING REPORTS OF ACADEMY AP-prentices. From time to time, she projected charts she brought up on her screen to the white projection wall across from her workstation. She concluded that Charles's and Euclid's contributions had become unimaginative, nothing new. They were traveling familiar mathematical territory and were stuck. She put in a request to have Charles reassigned and confirmed to First Tier that Euclid would be Returned. Her request concluded with the observation that Charles's recent efforts aligned himself with the thinking of Ramanujan.

Popov reviewed her chart, which showed the Liftees planned for the next two months:

Mathematics—S. Ramanujan, D. Pauperito
Physics, Chemistry, Mathematics—M. Curie

Music/Mathematics—J. S. Bach, Liu Hui
Linguistics—E. Krebs, I. Aasen
Universal—L. Wittgenstein and Muhammad al-Khwarizmi: ninth-century Persian mathematician and teacher, who developed algorithm concepts and synthesized Greek and Indian knowledge in the House of Wisdom.

.................................

ALL ARRIVED HEALTHY, BUT LIU HUI WAS STOOPED AND HAD A PRO-nounced limp from a twisted leg. Popov had culled the best choices from a list of sixty names given to her by Tier, Board colleagues, and Liftees, to arrive at thirty-nine must-have individuals. But it couldn't be done in the time remaining. Popov had the final say and did the best she could. She felt the weight of humanity upon her and hoped for a miracle. Popov had the horrendous thought that Liftees were dragging their efforts because they liked being present in this time. *Are we missing opportunities by keeping Liftees too long?*

There was little doubt that Liftees were a definite help. A first realization of this had occurred after WCM decided the new language would be utter-chanted. The Liftees realized this was impractical and showed that important elements of music and math would be left unused or forgotten. The consensus now was to encode and decode by computer what could be useful, which meant that for communication, computers would "speak" and translate the language internally. Liftees were helping to decide what to bring and what to leave behind, and a foundation for the language was established. *But what about all the scaffolding? Accuracy? Truth? Hope? Humanity?*

Popov read through the final slate of nine Liftees one last time. *If there is a God, I need her now*, she thought.

Charles had already been assigned to Ramanujan, and tonight in her private study Popov would review and approve other academy assignments. What everyone tried to ignore was, although new Liftees could be brought up to speed within forty-eight hours, their burnout time was fast—sometimes as quick as just four to six weeks. Pauperito, an older

Liftee, was still contributing, and Popov felt he could last a few more weeks, but it had taken him two weeks to be up and ready.

Progress in gaining the universal lingua franca was at a delicate juncture. Popov visualized several amplituhedrons juggling around each other in her own brain about to become one, providing the mathematics were perfect and inviolable.

In the evening, in her special room above her offices, Popov, as she always did when she became overwhelmed, went to her harp and soothed herself with music. She changed into a sarong as she hummed an Indonesian chant. Before plucking the strings, she opened a tiny plastic etui glued to the bottom of her harp and took out two pills, one for excitation and one for relaxation. As she downed them with sips of caffeine spiked with asperkraut, she wondered why it had taken so long for her species to realize and accept how crucial music was—*had* to be—to communication, to language. True, there had always been song sung with word, and much of meaningful prose and poetry had been put to music. Everyone she knew relaxed with music—*relaxed*. Still, why did all the main languages consist of only the spoken word? Music must be commingled with language.

Popov closed her eyes, pulled and plucked the strings, and imagined Venn diagrams overlapping with music, mathematics, and meta-linguistics. *How might language relax a person? How would language deflect and attenuate moods and thoughts of violence in humans?*

She played her harp using the additional double bass and guitar pedals and soon snuck in electronic loops. In the last seventy-five years, harps had been retrofitted with such features, and Popov's custom-made harp could also mimic kettledrums and tablas. After finishing a piece she had always admired, she took note: *Minimalist, therefore iteration. Thus, should be mathematical iteration. Whatever music it is, the music must be carried and blended into language. Biochips. But how do we create and get music on the biochip? Graphene? The Neuro Responsive Simulator?*

# 18

CHARLES WAS IN EUCLID'S PRIVATE STUDY. THIS WAS HIS LAST NIGHT with the great geometer. Euclid was ready to Return after the session.

Charles turned from Euclid's eyes and said, "Tomorrow I've been scheduled to work with Ramanujan."

"Yes, I heard, and I wish you well. Last night I studied some of his work. He is brilliant—pay particular attention to how he sets up on a problem. I, too, have learned from him."

Charles smiled as he shut down his e-tab, to close off outside distractions.

Euclid said, "I have something special for you. A parting gift, shall we say."

The great man opened his notebook and took out two sheets of paper. Charles recognized a tessellated magic square.

"This scheme I remembered from my *Ruminations*. It's a musical square based on the notes of the scale and zero. You can assign any number, one through nine and zero, to the seven notes of the do-re-mi scale, providing each of the chosen digits and zero are not duplicated in the horizontal, vertical, and diagonal. This example, the most fundamental, shows the digits one through six and zero corresponding to the do-re-mi. Hum accordingly as you move digits."

"So, how . . ."

"It depends on how you assign numbers to notes."

"But what about the missing digits in this—seven, eight, and nine?"

Euclid showed him the second sheet of paper. Another square, but larger with the digits one through nine and zero along the top.

"Okay, one through nine and zero," Charles said.

"Right. But what about the missing notes?"

"Sharps and flats," Charles said.

"No. Sharps and flats have nothing to do with anything here."

"Do I get my one clue?" Charles smiled.

Euclid returned the smile. "Okay. In some cases, zero can equal the musical 'natural.'"

As he finished, two officials walked into the room for Euclid. "It's time," one of them said.

Euclid, still smiling at the boy, pulled Charles to him. "I shall wake up to a dream later. You've been a most pleasant surprise."

"Thank you."

"And I thank you."

Charles watched Euclid being led away, and, almost as if Charles had willed it, Euclid turned back to him.

"One last thought, dear boy. Try to remember: one who thinks too much is seldom happy." And with a final wave, he was gone.

..................................

IN HIS LOFT, CHARLES HUMMED AS HE MOVED DIGITS PROJECTED into squares on his projection wall. So far, nothing had presented itself, but Charles wasn't in any hurry, and he wasn't trying to solve anything—yet. He was dreaming and reminiscing about his time with Euclid. His thoughts soon turned to Andrica, and he felt himself grow. He stuck in his eye-ear piece and tapped her.

"Do you want to pill?"

"Sure."

Charles reached to a hidden spot under the bed, below the mattress springs, and pulled out a tiny box. "Tell me when you are ready."

"Okay, I'm ready."

"On the count of 'yi-yi-yo.'"

He watched her in the semi-dark. Her hair was in a bun on the left side, and she'd flaked her eyebrows. "You look pretty tonight."

"And you are beginning to look more like my stud, Charles. Oh wow, indeed."

Charles chuckled. "I suppose I should thank you for initiating me."

Andrica puckered her lips and drew in closer. "Think nothing of it, Charles. Someday we'll do it real, 'cause I want a little one. I've registered and been cleared for a baby, in case you didn't know."

"We might have to marry."

"We can work on it. Meanwhile, glad I could launch some of your pent-up hormones."

"Do you want me to satisfy you first?"

"Your seXpressions amuse me. No. Lie back, Charles." Andrica neared and spritzed her mouth.

Charles swooned as he smelled tulip and jasmine with a tinge of zinnia.

"Relax, Charles. Let yourself fall. Keep one eye open."

# 19

POPOV WAS MEETING WITH KREBS, AASEN, BACH, AND DE COSTA IN her office when she got the dreaded news from General Braun. Canada was adamant about getting a Controlled-Nuclear against Siberia, a war which had started over new minerals and oil discovered by Canadian mining engineers living in Siberia.

"What about our worldwide delicate balance?" Popov asked.

*You know the back story on this one.*

"Of course I'm aware of their long messy history. I can't allow a Controlled-Nuclear, General. We are on the cusp of things over here."

Over the years, mining technologies had enabled deeper drilling. With the newest nanotechnology, we had the means to extract elusive minerals from the depths. In this case, the Siberians had yet to mine one pound of minerals or one gallon of oil from their deepest shafts. But it could be done; and the Canadians, who had made the discovery first, demanded their rights.

Humanity knew the hatred each country harbored for the other. The WCM governed the planet and had shown and explained statistical simulations of the horrid outcomes of intra-species murder to national governments, all the way down to the precincts. Despite that, the WCM hadn't been able to hold war back any more than a city or nation hundreds of years ago could forestall a riot or a revolution.

Neither spoke for several seconds, and the silence spoke volumes. Popov thought of Aasen and his discoveries from dolphins. *Yes,* she thought—*the mathematics of silence.* Her mind reached to Aasen and Bach.

"General, I'm going to try something different. To show both sides the emergency of our species, I will invite their heads of state to my offices for a special session and will attempt to communicate with them using M-L-M."

"If we frustrate them," Braun said, "it will make our situation worse."

"I understand, General. I ask you: What else is working? I'm taking the chance, hoping by this unusual, unprecedented approach, the adversaries will come to their senses."

.................................

POPOV SHUT DOWN HER ROBO-AIDE PHONE AND PURSED HER LIPS. She stared at a space of wall between faces. Aasen, Krebs, Bach, and De Costa remained still and waited for her to say something. They were given to understand that silence ruled. She'd presented the newest emergency. She had willed them to keep quiet.

"Mister De Costa, rerun the simulations based on a Controlled-Nuclear, and bring them to me. I'm calling a meeting for six p.m." She turned to another aide, a former principal of the local math academy. "Invite all Tiers, our Liftees, and the usual administrators and officials."

.................................

AFTER A STORMY OPENING SESSION IN THE CONFERENCE ROOM, WCM members threw up their hands as if they'd been insulted by humanity—"the very idea," said one.

De Costa had presented the new simulations: thirty-one percent chance of species survival if a Controlled-Nuclear was authorized. The immediate problem was the event horizon for World War IV. If all nations toppled, humanity would surely run out of time.

After a chilling silence, it was Bach who first came to the rescue.

"Madam, my friends," he said, motioning a hand to the other eight Liftees, huddling together, "agreed, we do not have our optimal language yet, but in this case, as I understand it, we are still dealing with French-Canadian and Russian-Siberian. I submit that we have these two languages, ab ovo, converse with the other; and that we also have

French and Russian music converse, including folk music of both cultures, according to newest mathematical principles developed by Pauperito. As soon as you get me workable compilations, I and Liu Hui will work with Krebs and Aasen."

"To what end?" asked Tuan.

Hui limped up next to Bach. "I'm sure we creators will find something we can work to. I have learned European scales and have studied the music of Master Bach. It aligns to ideas I'd been working on. I must ask, though, did anyone bring my parchments, my *Analects Mathematica*? We need this." After he realized nobody knew anything about his particular work, that it was no doubt lost forever, he sat down on the floor and cried.

..................................

LATER, AASEN LOOKED DISTURBED WHEN POPOV TURNED TO HIM and said, "We don't need an entire language, Mr. Aasen, we need some phrases, bridges—yes, bridges—to understanding."

"Based on our new math," Pauperito said. "We must try."

Thus it was agreed, and computers were reprogrammed to find common ground in Russian-French languages and Russian-French music. In projected Venn diagrams for each side, they watched over the next two and a half hours as the common ground enlarged for each. When the common areas of culture-sets were projected onto each other, transformulated, blended, mixed, twisted, interchanged, and pureed—all to new mathematical principles—Bach and Liu Hui went to work.

"I understand what you mean by chords," Hui said to Bach, "but to my ears, these—chords—don't suffice."

Bach hid his disappointment. "This is what I know. How else do we do it?"

"Using chords, we must build to signature phrasing. Recognizable passages to alert and inform the listener."

Bach folded his arms, but paid attention. They were in Bach's private music room, adjacent to his quarters. A keyboard was in the middle of the room, and Liu Hui sat to Bach's right as if they were about to play a duet.

"Let's try to create a friendship passage," Liu said. He played some G-clef notes and rolled them to a minor key chord.

"Can I say . . ." Bach stopped speaking and added a few bass notes in B diminished and rolled them to chord. Liu rolled similar but then changed to *natural*. Back and forth they went. Liu Hui was quick to see possibilities, and the great organist smiled. Bach was in new country, and the unusual bass rhythms intrigued him. It became a game for both of them as they enlarged music for each other. Liu took Bach down strange pathways, and Bach would counter-demonstrate in what, for him, was familiar country. What emerged were rhythms unfamiliar to both, which suggested motifs. They were transfixed.

"So," Bach said, "do we have a peace motif, or an understanding motif?"

An hour later, Bach and Liu came up with three signature motifs: peace-friendship, understanding-resolution, and fear. These motifs could be voiced and would be augmented at called-for intervals.

"But why should we keep fear?" Bach asked.

"To all the more feel peace and understanding," Liu said.

.....................................

SIX HOURS LATER BACH, THE COMPOSER, AND LIU, THE MUSICAL mathematician, finished a piece of music, which they'd titled *Invictus*—from a poem showing fortitude in the face of adversity, they'd said. Not long after that, Krebs and Aasen submitted bridge-phrasing. Krebs looked victorious in his top hat, which he chose to wear in recognition of what he deemed as breakthroughs. The government heads of Canada and Siberia and, per Popov, three members of each staff—but no military—were on their way to the government obelisk. Meanwhile, the mathematicians endeavored to code and align new phrasing with the new music. All the day's activities were dedicated to a singular effort to enhance communication as much as possible between the two nations.

Popov set up the procedures and the agenda. Her plan, reviewed by WCM, but giving her the final say, was simple. The heads of state would be received by their current anthem. First by Siberia, which had been threatened, and then by Canada. This would be followed by four minutes of total silence, in a semi-dark room, after which a toast would be given for humanity at large.

The next twenty minutes were to be filled by the new music with bridged utterances resembling a pureed language fed to each of them in a biochip. This oral recitative, inlaid with music, could not be understood—it was more of a persistence developing in the mind; communication, reason, and wisdom were unfolding. But the singular goal of *communicating* was built via utterance and music.

..................................

THE FOLLOWING DAY, AFTER THE RESPECTIVE ANTHEMS AND FOUR minutes of silence, the room brightened. Popov made a sincere and humble request that all present take a new and different journey—right here, right now.

It began smoothly. The heads of state and their staff looked sheepish as they closed their eyes and listened to pure music followed by recitative and voiced song piped in from the walls, ceiling, and floor, similar to what was done in the Himalayas. The room wasn't hyper-oxygenated, but she begged unknown gods to fit the unique sounds into their souls. Popov began to settle. She sensed the same in the posture of the Canadian who sat next to her. The room stilled, and Popov thought they might achieve a victory.

After twenty minutes, there was stillness, and it looked like each head of state was determined not to speak first. The scene reminded Popov of something she had read long ago about an incident in World War I—*or was it in World War II?* Soldiers from two warring countries, observing a ceasefire on Christmas Day, emerged from their foxholes and took up a game of soccer. They spoke different languages, and both sides had been warring for their respective fatherlands, but each enjoyed playing soccer. After the game was over, and when the next day dawned, no one had wanted to take that first shot. But at some point a commander had ordered a soldier to fire, and the violence and slaughter returned.

Popov ambled to the podium.

"After this time of reflection, and going by alphabetical order, may I ask the Canadians to please state their differences?"

Efforts were made on both sides to come to agreement, and for a while it seemed events would mature. But soon a verbal thrust was made, followed by another, followed by counterthrusts and threats from both sides. Popov was successful in gaining a time-out of fifteen minutes, in which music-recitative was once again fed to the assembled parties. But one dignitary refused to listen on the grounds that she felt she was being brainwashed, and soon another from the opposing side stood up to contend that the music, while well-intentioned, had outlived its usefulness.

Speaking for the WCM, Popov pleaded for peace, or at least a reduction from Declared to a Conflict. She re-showed the two nations the latest simulations. Not gaining resolution, the WCM, via words of Popov, made veiled threats of their own, which served to intensify a reactionary mood in the heads of state. Popov, suffering from a lack of sleep, realized her miscalculation. Pandemonium ensued, and Popov banged her gavel to try to restore order; but although some order had finally been restored, hard feelings remained.

A short while later, the heads of the two nations left; neither agreed to a Conflict.

Back at WCM headquarters, Popov requested the WCM Board remain for a closed meeting. Tiers, Liftees, and others scuttled about, not knowing how to proceed. They were told by WCM to shut down for the night; business as usual would resume in the morning.

The Board rehashed every possible scenario, but could not decide how to avert new escalation. To the possibility of ending a different war or Conflict, they realized *that* solution was, for the moment, hopeless. After a heated discussion, which subsided, all looked at Popov.

"We have endured much and deserve better," Popov said. "We shall continue with calmness and deliberation. We will not allow a Controlled-Nuclear."

After entering the newest updates, the revised simulations revealed less than ten months were left to stop the slide of humanity into extinction.

"Mr. De Costa, are you convinced we . . ."

"Yes, Chair Popov, everything breaks apart, governments shut down, local riots arise to raid food stocks, desalination plants are sieged; the sims show it becomes every person for themself."

# 20

THE CHEF OF THE ENLISTED MESS REACHED UP FOR THE HANDLES of a stewpot. When he placed it on the range, the mighty scorpion, almost the length of the pot's diameter, jumped from within the pot and landed on the chef's bare arm. The chef screeched as the poisoned stinger punctured his arm and discharged its venom. The only acceptable news, as the chef twisted and fell to the floor, was that the spent scorpion crawled away to die. Meanwhile, the head chef turned up the exhaust fan to suck out the pungent stench.

There was still a debate in post-bio-climate change circles—did the mutated scorpions become more poisonous and odorous after they began to enlarge, or did the killer poison with stench come first?

.................................

THE FIRST ITEM CHARLES NOTED WAS THE ABACUS. RAMANUJAN was lost in thought as he stooped over it, one hand behind his back. On Ramanujan's table sat a three-screened computer, but the brown-complexioned man fingered the abacus and touched one of the computer screens with his index finger.

"Mister Ramanujan?"

"One moment, please." In a flurry of movements, using both hands, he tapped a sequence on all three screens and moved beads on the abacus, once crossing hands. He sighed and turned toward Charles.

"I have to make sure my computer programs are in tune." He patted the abacus: "When in doubt, do it the old-fashioned way."

"But certainly . . . a computer is superior to the abacus."

"Your allusions are lost on me."

"I don't understand what you did or how you did it."

"No matter. Shall we chat a bit?" The small man gestured, and they moved to what looked like an old-time card table with two chairs. They were in Ramanujan's private quarters. The furnishings were severe and bleak, almost like a prison. The mathematician sat down and faced Charles.

"Tell me what this M-L-M project is all about."

Charles was stunned. Ramanujan had been to present age for two weeks; he'd been force-fed everything, and Charles had been told the mathematician was in peak form and already contributing.

"Not to worry," Ramanujan said. "I've heard what your masters have wanted me to hear. I need to hear it from a young person, from one who hasn't been form-fitted, from one who doesn't find problems with possibilities."

Charles noted the folded hands and the nicotined index finger. The Indian math genius didn't seem to be in any hurry, but his energies appeared to be directed to the moment. There may have been some trace of humor about the eyes as he removed his glasses to wipe them, but the mouth and face looked stern. He took a sip from a cup of tea; a large lip traced the rim, a blunt nose slanted into the cup.

"Let me first allow," he said, "I understand the need for a universal language, and I will do my best to help create and develop one optimal language for humanity." Here he threw up his hands. "Where are we? Are we on the right path?"

Charles smiled with relief. Here was a person, like Euclid, who would listen. Charles found himself getting up and pacing back and forth in front of the man.

"We're taking too much time. We're trying to be too careful in what we discard. We cover the same ground a lot," Charles said. He looked at Ramanujan, who nodded and kept his hands folded. "I mean, we all know the tragic outcome if we don't fix this, but we need to approach things from new angles."

"What do you have in mind?"

"Euclid and I—" he glanced at the self-made wonder.

"I adore Euclid. Continue."

"We played with Venn diagrams. We might not be able to contrive one language, but we might be able to shift between culture blocs."

Ramanujan shot a finger to a keyboard and turned the computer screen to project on his grease board.

Charles went to the board and stared at a Venn diagram for six sets representing six culture blocs. "We may try to unify something for the Indo-European family of languages. Right now, we are concentrating on African, East Asian, Arabian, Indian, Caucasian, and Australasian. The remaining cultures are a separate group."

Ramanujan smiled and turned his head back and forth. "If we take Venn to the limit, sixteen intersections, overlapped or osculated, would it do any good?"

"I don't know," Charles admitted.

"Just as well we don't know, for now. Continue."

"WCM is trying to create the optimal language by combining common linguistic universals"—Charles pointed to overlapping ellipses in the six-set projection—"from six cultures, but in the process, we dilute or weaken the language of each. The amalgamation could even lead to more confrontation when we make careless mistakes. In our ignorance, we risk overlooking other possibilities."

"Possibilities such as?"

"My girlfriend has discovered calming tones in the language of dolphins. She's working with—"

"Yes, yes, I was entrained during entry, and I've heard the new Bach-Liu Hui. Interesting and remarkable. But how do we use it to save humanity? Can humans utter such sounds? Do we hold international meetings near a pool of dolphins?"

"We're pondering options. As you know, Sir, we are trying to develop a unique musical scale based on a new alphabet of ninety-six phonemes culled from seven culture blocs. I've added Indo-European."

Ramanujan folded his arms. "How do you see us communicating in this new tongue? Do we sing it with spoken recitative, as in opera? Are we all to take voice lessons? Why can't we rework opera—something we already have?"

"Maybe this new communication will be operatic. I don't know how it will be done. But whatever we come up with will be created using revolutionary mathematics. Maybe at important international meetings, experts in our new tongue will voice for us. But everyone needs to learn how to communicate in M-L-M. Biochips will have to be reloaded and tweaked."

"Will we do it in time to educate the commoners? Trust me when I tell you all unrest comes from the people on the streets. Every person must be trained and be able to communicate in M-L-M."

Charles sat down, deflated. He glanced at his Venn diagrams. Ramanujan said nothing, and Charles realized his new master would wait forever if necessary. He remembered—the thought coursed through him—silence speaks volumes.

"It may have to be a new type of language," Charles said. "Computers aren't finding many calming patterns in these seven blocs." Charles pointed to the grease board.

"Think," Ramanujan said. "Leap."

"We create new and unique mathematical scaffolding for M-L-M, which can be tweaked and adapted for the significant culture blocs."

"So, you don't have a true universal language; you've decided the planet will have a number of similar languages."

"I know where you're leading me," Charles said. "Does one culture care about the tweaked language of another?"

"And how do you educate all the peoples of the various blocs?"

Charles stood still. "I don't know."

"Can we get help from the dolphins? Do we have to explain and translate so much? This planet is almost three quarters water. How presumptive humanity was to call it Earth." Ramanujan smirked and raised his palms. "Perhaps water creatures large and small are the planet's true citizens."

"They were the first," Charles agreed.

Ramanujan nodded. "Take yourself out of this world. How would extraterrestrial beings solve our problem? I want you to think about everything we have talked about. For now, these are the topics I will discuss with you. Don't worry; when the time comes you will be involved in mathematics above your eyeballs."

Ramanujan stood and walked to the diagrams. He added "Dolphin" outside the circles. "Let's say Dolphinese for now."

"Do you think we can teach these cultures in time?" Charles asked.

"I don't have a clue."

"If," Charles said, "our Tiers, their work, the academy's—"

"Spare me what you've heard." He threw up his hands. "Where are we? Are we on the correct path?"

Charles looked down at his own hands as they clenched and unclenched.

"The other night I came across an opposite quest," Ramanujan said. "Did you know American Navajo Indians used their particular language in World War II to thwart the enemy? It was so difficult to penetrate, the Japanese gave up. Are we making our quest too difficult for humankind? Is there a simpler way?"

"I don't know," Charles said.

"Enough for now. Come back here with ideas, a plan, and one other thing: I want a large tin of Assam tea. Make sure it's Assam, from my country; nothing else is suitable."

# 21

CHARLES KNEW HE WAS DREAMING. WHEN HE KNEW, HE COULD sometimes nudge his dream. Archimedes had cornered him. But Archimedes had been Returned to his own time.

"Take me to your gears," Archimedes repeated.

"What?" Even in the dream, Charles was puzzled.

"We are twisting. The wind is turning us, right?"

"We turn on huge ball-bearings, not by gears," Charles said.

"Take me to your gears. I will show you something."

The dream fast-forwarded to a darkened tunnel. The noise was deafening. Charles led the way, with Archimedes behind him. They seemed to be going uphill, but the noise had stopped, and there was brighter light ahead.

The calamity of sound started again, and Archimedes brushed by him. "Gears," he hollered.

They emerged from the tunnel into a glass-enclosed cubby in front of three massive slicked balls that rolled to the right, then slowed, enabling another ball to edge into view on the left.

"These balls are taller than we are," Charles said.

Charles realized the cubby overlooked a track he thought was straight, but he could see it curve into the distance. Suddenly, enormous splashes of liquid jetted from funnels above, onto the balls in front of them. Oil odors fouled the air as the dark-green liquid covered the massive bearings and dripped to the track below. Almost like an afterthought, a dumping of what had to be grease smeared over the oil and oozed.

"Ah," yelled Archimedes. "And now you see. There."

Charles looked below the track and saw what looked like cut-off T-bar. But, pressing closer to the glass, he saw it was one giant tooth of a gear.

Archimedes kept hollering: "Below, look beneath."

Charles had to cover his ears as he watched the edge of a giant ratchet wheel turn, in sync with the gear under the massive bearings.

Archimedes smiled. "Just as I thought. Watch."

The massive ratchet wheel turned one minuscule and a giant pawl clanged down and nested between teeth of the gear.

"But," Charles said, "how will the gear move now?"

Archimedes looked at him. "Use your head, boy. How will new and different winds make a change? Who directs the winds? The winds of change are for us to control."

Charles fought in his dream to see it, but he sensed the end of his dream. He heard the last words of Archimedes: "Ancient mariners controlled their destiny by controlling the winds. Didn't you notice the counter-pawl? Without the pawls, the winds would spin us crazy."

"Are the winds a language?" Charles asked. No answer, and Charles tried to nudge the dream.

But Archimedes was gone. Back to his old-time, and Charles opened his eyes in bed—alone.

Before class, Charles queried the *obelisk specs* and found drawings. There were gears, a sprocket, a ratchet wheel, and two giant pawls below the track where the balls rolled. *How did Archimedes know this?*

.................................

CHARLES WAS IN CONICS-MINUS THREE DIMENSION IN ACADEMY, sitting next to Andrica. They were listening to new developments in Mordell's conjecture, which linked topology with number theory, and Charles couldn't concentrate because Andrica was trying to excite him with footsies and drive him off his game.

But Charles had other thoughts on his mind—yesterday's unresolved session with Ramanujan had unsettled him. As well as last night's dream, which made no sense. He'd rolled and reviewed simulations several times with his father; the math was true—societal breakdown was near. Humanity was at stake, and this was no time for him to study conics. He'd discussed his feelings with his father, who understood, but Charles was not relieved when his father claimed the education of the masses rested with Tier. His father added, if one had to second-guess Tier's dedicated support, it would serve to distract one's individual commitment. "Stay focused, Charles," he'd said.

Charles considered the plight of all those who would be left behind, like the non-gifted workers who added benefits to everyone. Many of them worked in elderly care and geriatrics. Seniors did not want androids caring for them. They insisted on humans. Tests showed human touch and companionship extended their lives. Common workers were also needed for water and food management—it was a fine balance between how much could be taken from the seas and from land. Freshwater management meant additional tunnels under mountains to lakes and reservoirs, the building of new dams, the repair and sometimes relocation of existing dams.

Charles thought of food processing and foodservice. He remembered seeing vertical farming inside greenhouses in Iceland, and he was told such greenhouses were abundant in Siberia and Greenland as well.

But it was still a war economy. Next to food processing, water management, ocean replenishment, and perhaps healthcare, most of the common people were involved with Security or Defense, and fought in Conflicts and Wars. The wounded also refused to be tended to by androids and robots. Thus, the constant need for health- and human-care workers.

Charles realized, more than anyone else, that if the new language was unlike anything heard by humanity, the world wouldn't be ready in time. *But,* he thought, *just as we force-feed Liftees to bring them up to speed in a matter of days, we can use Neuro-Linguistic Programming—*

"Charles. Charles?" the instructor repeated.

Andrica swung a foot to his shin. "Psssst, Charles."

"I'm sorry. I missed the question."

"Give me two Diophantine equations that lead to solution here," the professor said, pointing to the laser board.

Charles stared at the mess of mathematics on the board for over a minute.

"Can I give you one?"

The class roared and Andrica's laugh was the last of them all. Later, Charles realized the professor had been looking for the one and only Diophantine solution.

.................................

AT DAY'S END, CHARLES MET ANDRICA AT THE MATHETORIUM. THIS had been their new ritual Monday through Friday after classes, labs, and sometimes after Charles's sessions with a Liftee. Most young people went there in the evenings. On weekends, there were sponsored Fischer-Random chess tournaments as well as mathematical games, contests, and math-league playoffs. Even those not math-minded came to watch, much like the couch-potato athletes who went to sports bars in old-time. What was different for Charles was that he mixed with Andrica and her friends more than he did with his old gang. Some in the gang were jealous and looked away from Charles when he waved to them at the usual table.

"So, how is the genius Ramanujan?" Andrica asked, as she passed a textbook-sized magic square to her girlfriend.

Charles tried to think of an appropriate response, but words got tangled in his throat and from experience he knew that what he would utter wouldn't match what he wanted to say. He wondered about this. What humans spoke in their language approximated their inner intentions and emotions. *People write books,* he thought, *but at important meetings people don't read from books, yet they may read from prepared scripts. But during confrontation, different questions are asked, challenges made, taking one off-script. On their own, the person is thrown into the fray of approximation.*

"Earth to Charles. Do you mind, Charles?" Andrica said.

"I'm sorry."

"Think you're slumming with the riff-raff here?"

"No, not at all."

"You *are* condescending. What are you thinking about?"

"Approximations. We—humans—approximate when we try to put thought into what we verbalize."

"Some are good at verbalizing their thoughts, Charles."

Charles looked at her. "Yes: you, for example, are much better at verbalizing than I am."

Andrica cross-eyed him and put her head down on her folded arms on the table. She twisted her head, pushed her hair to one side, and peeked up at him. "You get hung up inside, Charles. You spend too much time on exact and joyless passions."

"But if I want to communicate truthfully, shouldn't I be exact?"

"The truth can hurt, Charles."

"Can we think about that? If leaders are trying to meet on common intellectual ground and are trying to avoid confrontation, they have to be truthful, don't they?"

"Maybe they don't *want* to meet on common intellectual ground. Maybe one side or sides is trying to outfox the other?"

Charles was annoyed with this; something else he'd overlooked. Casuistry.

"So . . . we use language in international meetings, or any meeting of note, to deceive, as well as to communicate?"

"You have an amazing grasp of the obvious, Charles."

"Then how can our species enhance communication?"

"Language, linguistics as we understand it, doesn't communicate all views simultaneously—never mind the so-called truthful ones."

"Exactly," Charles said.

# 22

OVER THE WEEKEND, CHARLES COMPETED IN A THREE-DIMENSIONAL Fischer-Random chess tournament. The mathetorium's bleachers on all three floors were extracted from all walls and extended. Packed full, all eyes were on the screens of each wall. Each of the four walls' screens was split: the left side showed the players in combat; the right side showed an enlarged board with positions of pieces, posting every move. Electronics muted conversations, coughs, and any extraneous sounds that might distract the chess players. Andrica and half the academy, those who had already been beaten in Fischer-Random Chess, sat to cheer on their remaining favorites. And Andrica had to admit it: she wanted Charles to win even though she expressed a different wish to her friends.

"Charles won't fight it out in the endgame; he always pursues a draw," Andrica said.

"Why are you always down on him?" Olivia asked.

"'Cause he's a wuss."

A cheer erupted as Conrad, last year's champion, created a gambit, offering a pawn to Charles. While Charles considered options, Conrad played mathescrab on his touch phone. He was playing against two Samoans and had them on the ropes. After dispatching one of the Samoans, using a little-known equation from *Boolean-Abstracted*, he touched off the phone to pay more attention to the board. Charles had declined the gambit and with an unseen riposte was attempting to force the game into the Riemann variation.

A new cheer started and gathered steam as viewers realized the move's potential.

"How about that, Andrica?!" Olivia said.

"Too little, too late." But she smiled. Charles was going to fight it out after all. Conrad meant nothing to her; she could have him anytime she wanted.

Conrad countered in what looked like a protective move—but, after a deeper look, it was a veiled attack on Charles's queenside pawn flank. It was brilliant, yet Conrad didn't turn his phone back on; his eyes remained fixed on the board.

Charles lost the game, and two days later Conrad won the championship again. Charles took a bronze. After the tournament, Charles went up to Conrad. "That pawn you offered me, was it for real?"

"No, Charles. I wanted you to think it was."

"So . . . there was no plan for it . . . if not, why did the audience cheer?"

"Stupid people don't question, they assume."

Charles looked at him.

"They would have figured it out, but not soon enough," Conrad said.

That night, Charles replayed their game, and when he came to Conrad's gambit, he studied the position. No, Charles said to himself, Conrad had made a blunder. What's more, Conrad should have lost the game—and Conrad knew this: he just wouldn't admit it.

With this insight, a lever tipped in Charles's brain. He went straight to Lussier's proofs. Even before he found the smoking gun, he realized Lussier's mathematics in support of this one obscure proof, proof of a minor point in a little-known subset, was designed to fool the reader. It wouldn't have made any difference to most quests, but this particular proof had been accepted carte blanche in the scaffolding of a mathematical alphabet used in finding the language optima.

..................................

RAMANUJAN LISTENED. "VERY INTERESTING INDEED. YOUR DIScovery may be of profound importance. I shall not deal with meta-mathematics but will notify my logician-minded colleagues. Bring this discovery to your father and have him inform Popov."

Charles consulted with his father on Lussier's proof. He wanted his father to admire him, and Charles was pleased when his father congratulated him on his discovery. Yet Charles remained unsettled. Our language, any language he knew of, did not reveal exact thoughts, just approximations, and it didn't reveal all views simultaneously—how could it? "Read between the lines" was still the adage. That had to change, but how?

"Let's review this again," Wang Chen De Costa said to his son. "Right now, the WCM and Liftees are integrating minus three-dimensional mathematics with chaos, catastrophe, and fractal mathematics. We are applying recursions to linguistics and musical theory. If Lussier's proof doesn't stand up, everything we've done is in question."

"If it doesn't stand up, we may still be right," said Charles.

..................................

POPOV LISTENED TO GENERAL BRAUN'S UPDATE ON THE CANADA-Siberia war. Since Popov's private attempt, over eighty thousand Siberians had been killed and twice as many West-Canadians. A Controlled-Nuclear was not authorized.

She glanced at the afternoon agenda. Popov had decided to meet with both Wang Chen and his son. If what she was hearing was true—she got wind of it from Ramanujan and Krebs—she wanted to meet the young man who had made the ominous discovery.

..................................

THAT AFTERNOON. "RIGHT. I UNDERSTAND," POPOV SAID TO DE Costa and Charles, "just don't ask me to Lift Lussier to get to the bottom of it."

Popov knew she was showing her agitation, her sleep-deprived pettiness. But she could see no way around the fact that Charles's deconstruction of the subset was correct: the proof was false. And it looked like a deliberate cover-up by Lussier, who was known for rigor. He'd soiled the language of mathematics. What wasn't known was whether the oversight would affect the mathematics following the faulty proof, which had been used to develop M-L-M.

"We don't need to Lift Lussier," Wang Chen De Costa said.

"Why not?"

Charles stood, but sat back down, realizing the inner sanctum they were meeting in was different from a discussion room with a Liftee. "We are running out of time," Charles said. "We are looking at new advances which would make the proof moot."

"Right. We'll press on. Maybe this will force us to leap in new directions. At the present rate, what we've achieved isn't near enough."

"We need to find a wormhole to a new language," Charles said. "We haven't found a wormhole into an alternate universe; maybe we can wormhole to an alternate way of communication."

When the meeting concluded, Popov requested Charles meet with her one-on-one every weekend, beginning the next day. She faced De Costa squarely.

"I need more perspective from our young people. I shall, from time to time, meet with the young, the creative, and I would like to start with Charles."

"I think it's a wonderful idea. Charles?" De Costa said, turning to him.

"Yes. Thank you, Ms. Popov."

That evening, after long and solemn thoughts, which wound her up, Popov closed all outside communications and went to her harp. This was the best way she could triage and manage her thoughts properly. An hour later, she decided the time had come. She'd hoped she would never have to pursue this avenue, but for the sake of humanity, she knew she had no choice. She would apprise WCM tomorrow and put it to vote.

She put on special glasses and tapped a sequence over both ears.

*The Department of Security, Division of—Oh, Chair Popov, I'm sorry . . .*

"General Braun, please."

*General Braun speaking. Yes, Chair Popov.*

"About our starship," Popov said.

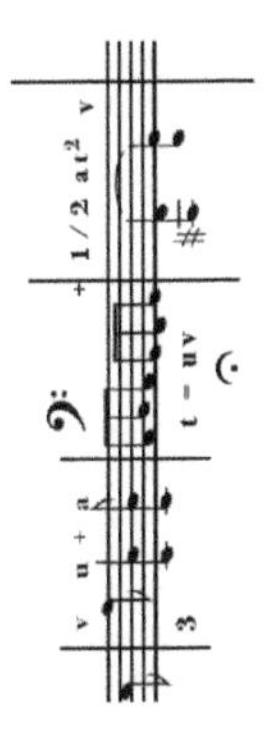

# II

Why do we seek climate warmed by another sun? Who is the man that, by fleeing, can also flee from himself?

—Horace

# 23

"OKAY," THE LEAD TWIN SAID, "THE BAG OF SCORPIONS SENT A message, but it was premature." She and her twin went up to the cell's most physical fighter and stopped two inches from his face. "From now on," the other twin said, "nothing is done without our approval. Got that?"

"Just trying to move things forward a bit," the fighter said.

The first twin turned around and mule-kicked him in the nuts, while the other twin grabbed his hair and pulled him up to his feet.

"My sister asked you a question."

.................................

THE MORNING BEGAN IN FOG AND SMOKE. A SKIRMISH IN SLUM-town, the uncontrollable ghetto, had erupted last night, and fires, not for the first time, were set in trade schools and nursing homes. The General surveyed the damage with his aide-de-camp in Military Hover-1. Sleek in design compared to bulky commercial hovers, easier to maneuver than an old-time helicopter, and shielded with carbonates, the General and his aide were safe and secure.

"Smell the stench," the General hissed. "Know what that is?"

"I hope it's not what I think, Sir."

"Smelled it every day during my duty in China-India." They both looked up at the air vents above them. "Human flesh, burnt to a crisp," the General said, "not even our perfumers could override it today, though I'm sure they tried."

General Braun pressed "infrared night vision" on his binoculars—the smoke had gotten thick—and focused on what was the slum's healthcare complex. It was still in flames.

"Can't we do something?" his aide said.

"The problem is if we help the victims, we show the droogs attention. That can actually make it worse. We've tried giving help before, and the bastards tore up the city."

"Garrison troops do their best to keep order, except for Slum-towns," the aide said. "I heard the suicide rate is over twenty-five percent here."

"In old-time, towns and villages had dumps, places for refuse. That's what Slum-town has become. They foul up like this, they gotta live with their own mess."

"But schools and aide-homes? Why do they even do it?"

"The droogs take the food and look for meds. It's become a new low," the General agreed. He focused on a white flag waved by someone in a wheelchair, and pointed for the aide.

"I see him, Sir. Shall we grab him?"

General Braun was about to okay the save when he saw the man take what looked like a blast from behind a shattered window. The wheelchair fell over; the man's legs were on fire.

Braun put down his glasses. "Won't do any good now," he said. "It's the age-old problem of the haves and the have-nots."

"But we provide alga-rice and water whenever they need it. Their vital needs are cared for."

"Some have-nots are just stupid. Many have head problems. Charities don't exist here, because no one can regulate them. People devoted to spiritual issues have disappeared and given up."

"The situation worsened when the obelisks were completed."

"Agreed," said the General. "The towers became the line in the sand."

"I wonder if we should try harder to reach the have-nots."

After a brief silence, Braun said "We have over eleven billion people on the planet. There are too many other issues." Yet Braun was convinced this domestic problem was getting worse. Droog cells were popping up everywhere. "I guess what the commoner wants is recognition, and no one has the time to give it."

Army general Roy Braun, along with his senior staff and aides, hunkered in the military obelisk on the south side of Tomini Bay. In old-time, a VIP began with full colonel; it still did, but now all officers from lieutenant on up also had to be academy-trained mathematicians. There were no exceptions. Braun and his fellow officers supported the WCM, much like military commanders in a democracy had supported a president hundreds of years earlier. Braun and his staff understood and accepted that world government was best handled by math minds. Most in the military, when pressed, admitted that if it had been left to them, the planet would have been covered with ashes decades ago. Braun's job was to contain all Conflicts, avert Declared War, and intervene anywhere in the world at the request of WCM. He had his own theory about war in present age. Too many people and too little space for all of them was the problem. But the occasional Declared War and the rest of the ongoing Conflicts resulted in fewer people, thereby leaving a bit more room for everyone. What's more, though this blasphemy was never mentioned, people lived too damn long. The average age at death in the world was north of 130.

After the conversation with Popov, the balding General Braun sat at his desk and reviewed his notes a second time. The request from Popov was more than unusual. He consulted his WMD—World Mathematics Dictionary—something of this nature he wanted to see for himself. Military VIPs had a micro-mica of WMD projected into special eyeglasses. Braun reviewed the most recent versions of Riemann-Roch and its application to catastrophe theory. He fed data into his main computer and rolled to simulation. He made some calculations and could see where the mathematics was heading, directly to singularity. Humanity was at the event horizon; the black hole was near. Not a real one, of course, but he understood the metaphor. Additional calculations indicated humanity was accelerating to breakdown. He summoned his three assistant generals for an after-hours meeting. The generals were department heads of Security, Logistics, and Defense.

After the generals were seated in the locked conference room adjacent to Braun's office near the top of the military obelisk, Braun collected all communication eyeglasses and associated electronics. His General of Security, Amin Farzad, piqued with surprise, was about to protest but acquiesced. After which, in a show of support to his General of Security, Braun removed his own electronics and pushed the combined pile to Farzad.

"Now, then," said Braun, "earlier, I received a call from Popov. Not a word was mentioned about Siberia, Western Canada, or any other battle front." He let the silence cling.

"She wishes she'd told you to be at her fancy-ass M-L-M meeting," Blackston, head of Logistics, said. "From what I heard, the meeting didn't go down too well."

Braun's countenance appeared to agree, but he waited as he stared at the top of the desk in front of him.

"We've been ordered," Braun coughed like he sometimes did when he was blindsided and began again: ". . . to scrap Plan A—and prepare Plan B—in order to ready Starship *Welkin-Alpha* for liftoff seven months from today."

"Jesus. Plan B—the starship? Which is docked at Moonbase-1," Osteen, General of Defense, said. At six-foot-two, she was one of the tallest women in the Army.

"Right."

"We're holding off World War IV so others can bail? Just how in hell can we make five shuttle trips to Moonbase within such a short time?" General Blackston, of Logistics, asked.

"Six," the General countered. "Three thousand trekkers, total. Six hundred on the first five trips. Forty-one auxiliary command, backup, and remaining supplies on the last trip."

"It can't be done," Blackston said.

"It must be. You've been updated on simulations and know what's at stake for humanity."

"I'd been told of progress and a breakthrough," General Farzad said. "Why the change?"

"Does anybody at WCM understand logistics?" General Blackston asked.

Braun sighed. "Popov says they were cutting it too close on time, and it appears some of the mathematics is based on a falsity."

Farzad threw up his hands. "What in Siri are they doing over there?"

"Now's a fine time to throw the bomb to us," Blackston said.

"Silence," Braun ordered. "Or you will, I swear, join me on a ten-mile run in full battle dress."

Braun loosened his collar. "At ease, fellow soldiers."

The other generals unbuttoned their collars; General Osteen, Defense, removed her topcoat. She strutted to a coat hook on the back of Braun's door and flung it there.

"Look," Braun said, "I don't like it either. But we are also mathematicians and trained professionals, with a long history of respect and honor. The fact that the fate of humanity requires our leadership to support WCM and get the job done should make us proud."

Braun squinted his eyes, which meant he wasn't finished. "It will be a different kind of war. Now it will be a race."

"Can I ask one question?" Farzad said.

"Of course," General Braun replied.

"Up until now, no one seemed too concerned about Plan B—Welkin-Alpha, which sits on the moon. We've put all our training and wisdom into Plan A—Orion. This change is rather abrupt. Is there another reason?"

"No. Everyone thought Military Plan A, using shuttle *Orion*, would be the final answer. Less than six months from now, with three hundred androids manning individual creepers maintained on board, we could have achieved stability and peace worldwide. Unfortunately, humanity has run out of time. The math says we have seven months, tops, before we begin an unstoppable slide to species extinction. Our engineers must disassemble major portions of the shuttle, ditch Plan A, and retrofit for Plan B."

"May I ask, General," said Osteen, permitting herself a rare smile, "which would be the more difficult: to ready *Orion* for Plan A in six months, or *Welkin-Alpha* for Plan B in seven months?"

General Braun stood and put his hands on the table. "I . . . We," he looked into the eyes of all of them, "have been ordered to ready Starship *Welkin-Alpha* for Plan B. For what it's worth, the math I've looked at indicates this is the best next step. Makes no difference. I'm following an order, and that's what *you* will do. Are we clear?"

"Yes, Sir," Osteen said, as anger flamed her cheeks.

Braun waited until they all acknowledged.

"Okay," Braun said, as he sat back down, "inform your staff and your commanders at once of"—Braun tried for humor"—the change in plans. General Farzad, this change requires the utmost security. I hereby invoke Wartime Security, Alpha 1."

"Alpha 1?" Farzad said.

"What can be more important than the preservation of our species? Alpha 1."

"Tonight," Braun continued, "review your particular instructions for Plan B and be here tomorrow at 0800. Good evening, fellow soldiers."

.....................................

TWENTY MINUTES LATER, BRAUN WAS IN THE MIDDLE OF EXERCISES in his private gym, which was attached to obelisk Security-command, at sea level. After pull-ups, squats under a 100-pound barbell, and one-handed pushups, he exited a door onto a cinder quarter-mile track built on top of the hover air hangar. He pressed a timer on an old-fashioned wristwatch his grandfather, a battle-scarred armor colonel of the last vicarious war—the Indonesian Island War—had given him, and took off. The first two laps were warm-ups, and he cruised at a 7:15-minute-a-mile pace. Then he alternated half-laps of sprints with half-laps at a 6:30-a-mile pace. After three complete miles, he walked two last laps around the track, head down like he always did when deep in thought.

As soon as he showered, he changed to battle fatigues and returned to his office. He put on glasses and tapped them once.

"You're right on time, General."

"One habit you can always count on in the military, Chair Popov."

"How did it go?"

"As I expected. Do you remember that old line about rearranging the deck chairs on the *Titanic*? It was heading in that direction."

"And?"

"Everyone is on board. You have our full support. My top people are meeting with me tomorrow to review Plan B."

"Good. Do you have any questions, General?"

"Two. The first one is, who are the people who will be leaving us?"

"They are being selected now, which no doubt leads to your second question."

"Yes. Who selects Auxiliary Command?"

"Third Tier recommends, Second Tier reviews and culls for First Tier. WCM has final approval."

"Thank you, Chair Popov."

After the conversation, Braun called his wife, who was at their home twelve kilometers away near Bunta, and told her he would be staying the night at his office. She didn't question him until he revealed that office overnights would be frequent for some time. Because of situations like the one Braun faced now, all military who worked in the obelisk kept their families separate. Braun would not brook any distractions, for himself or for officers in his command. For reasons Braun felt no explanation was necessary, his rule didn't apply to female officers. They could not reside in the obelisk. When he was pressed, "It has to do with distractions," he'd stated. "Leave it at that." He gave his love to his wife and to his son as he projected selected holograms of his family in front of him.

General Braun went to his cabinet and removed two plastic bottles. The first was labeled Stroganoff-Tonseng-Rawoon; the second was labeled Ugli-Kiwi-Berries. He removed one pill from each and put the bottles back. He went to his mini-bar and poured a Chianti-Molinari from Sardinia into a goblet and flushed down both pills, knowing the fruit pill opened when it sensed the main course was finished. He'd already pilled a Salada-DiPlacido for lunch.

He sat and watched a series of holograms from his grandfather's time, then moved ahead to his father's time. Braun's father had committed suicide soon after graduating from Powell Military Academy. Braun, who had been a baby at the time, never learned the full story until the day his grandfather chose to be medically deceased. He told Captain Braun his father was the only one who'd ever hacked Military Quantum-Security. At the arrival of quantum computing with its shifting superpositions, old-time hackers were put out of business; trying to hack disturbed the quantum states and set off alarms. Code combinations were infinite and could change in nanoseconds. When his father showed his results and methods to the military, he was arrested and quarantined. Even when his father showed the top brass how to fix the breach, he was set up for court-martial. Braun's father saw the implications for his family and knew it would be a lasting disgrace. Suicide was his way out, for himself and for his family. Braun's grandfather, moments before he passed, told his grandson "The writer Khaled Hosseini wrote, 'It is better to get hurt by the truth than be comforted by a lie.'" The General finished watching his father, in dress blues, collect the Euler for mathematics, the military's most prestigious medal, except for the Medal of Honor, at Powell graduation ceremonies.

Braun didn't feel grounded. He and his commanders, especially Osteen, were trained for Defense. Which meant offense whenever and wherever needed. Thus, Military Plan A. *Orion*. He would have gotten a fifth star, the first five-star general in family history. Now the charge was different. The crème de la crème was jumping ship. He knew he would be staying. He wanted to stay and finish the fight. The fight to keep WCM whole and to keep Indonesia the ruling empire. He would prevail on Earth, even if he was the last man standing. With this commitment, the General settled.

After he finished the wine, Braun rinsed the goblet in the mini-bar sink. He sat back at his desk, removed a framed Eunice Choi sketch from the wall behind him, and pushed a button. A section of wall expanded behind him, and a two-foot-square metal cabinet emerged. Braun put his right index finger on a marked spot and a green light blinked on, at the front of the cabinet. He waited three seconds and said, "This is General Braun, Commander and Chief, World Army—Open." He heard the click and the door opened. The General took up a thick dog-eared folder on top—Plan A, and placed it underneath another thick folder. He removed this new top folder and relocked the safe. General Braun opened the unblemished folder before him: Plan B—Starship, *Welkin-Alpha*.

# 24

WORKING ALONE IN HIS PRIVATE STUDY, RAMANUJAN WAS REVIEWing a treatise on Benford's Law, the puzzling mathematical oddity which maintains certain digits show up more than others. In Benford's Law, no matter what the set of numbers, the number 1 will appear as the first digit 30 percent of the time. The next leading digit, 2, appears 18 percent of the time; but 9 will lead off only 4.6 percent of the time. *Why?* Ramanujan wondered.

Ramanujan sat at a rectangular desk that measured one meter by one and a half meters. The desk had one middle drawer. Liftees could order their own furniture, and this is what he'd requested. The former card table was sent to storage. He'd removed wall hangings hung by Euclid, who had had the room before him. In place of da Vinci's charcoal of Euclid, he'd hung a picture of Gandhi. On his desk beside a one-eighth-inch-thick mica screen lay his abacus. His cropped black hair was combed. He was thirty-one.

Ramanujan accepted that his theoretical foray into the mathematics behind Benford's Law was a distraction from his true work at M-L-M, but these occasional efforts to solve a puzzle relaxed him, and he had a hunch that exploring the reasons for Benford's Law might show him an original approach to a new computer language. And weren't they all working on a new language? Would it be that the optimum language of *homo sapiens* was a mathematical computer language instead of an uttered one? Or, as he liked to say, a *sputtered* one.

When Charles had shown Euclid's magic musical square to Ramanujan, he thought he saw what had been niggling him about Benford's Law. After concluding his session with Charles, he went again to his simple desk to work on a different approach to a unique computer language that would involve musical and metalinguistic patterns using a modification to Benford's Law within the code.

The next day, he met with Gunderson and Tuan and showed them his newest calculations for an original computer language.

"I see what you've done," Gunderson said. "What's the underlying code here?"

Ramanujan held steady, waiting for a reply from Tuan.

"I'm not following this," Tuan said. "Are you suggesting a language that talks to itself before it communicates?"

"Yes, and more," Ramanujan said. "This language, when modified, will build upon itself and pull the listener and other communicants up to its level."

"Interesting," Gunderson said, "but what is the inner code?"

"Similar to what we have accomplished, except for modifications to Benford's Law. I've related the most common Benford numbers to the most common alphabetic letters. For this new language, fate and Benford's Law combine and advance into new dynamics of number theory, resulting in linguistic patterns not seen before, but which mimic musical patterns in Bach-Liu Hui's recent music."

"Can the language be verbalized?" Tuan asked.

"No, I don't think so. But it could be coded and communicated by computers."

"You mentioned fate," Gunderson said.

"Yes." Ramanujan crossed his hands in front of him and stared at his shoes. "Charles showed me a musical magic square Euclid had developed. Somehow, I don't understand it," he threw up his hands, "the do-re-mi scale plus the musical notations, in random patterns on this square, segue to Benford's Law in deriving algorithms for this new language."

They both looked at him like he was crazy.

"I've found algorithms relating to Bach's musical-linguistic patterns," Ramanujan said.

Tuan and Gunderson stared.

"And when I play with the square—excuse me—as I *work* at the square, other musical patterns present themselves."

"Akin to work of other composers?"

"Yes. A resemblance to their *musical* patterns, but not as keen as Bach's. What's more, I don't see or hear the other composers' linguistic elements; they are musical but not linguistic, and the resulting language is indecipherable."

A faint hum fed the air, and the obelisk turned.

"You must remember," the Indian continued, "different cultures use different pitches in their scales. In Western music, there are twelve unique pitches. In my country, musicians playing sitars and other instruments can choose among twenty-two pitches. Who knows how many pitches can be used in our new optimum language? And pitch is just one category. Different cultures have varied keys, scales, et cetera."

..................................

THE NEXT EVENING, CHARLES CAME TO RAMANUJAN'S QUARTERS for his session. The atmosphere was electric as he entered his doorway.

"My turn to show *you* something," Ramanujan said. "Come see this."

After Charles closed the door, he heard a steady hum like a koan emanating from the walls. Occasionally the hum would lurch into atonalities, but only briefly.

"Alphabets," Ramanujan said. "I've overlaid 156 of Aasen's random alphabets from world cultures, and they are talking to each other in my new computer language."

There were two short discordant bursts. "Stop," Charles said. "That's annoying."

"The computer will hold it in memory. We can listen to it later. I'm waiting to hear more musical patterns; of two earlier patterns, one mimicked the avant-garde composer Cage. The patterns appear when the Venn builds to 'common.'"

They listened to more sounds climb out of the hum—clicks, Doppler-like cymbal clashes, mewls and cat-like screeches, and another atonality Charles recognized, too brief for him to have to cover his ears. Ramanujan and Charles recorded times between discordant bursts, frequencies, associated colors as depicted by Stritchard's Prisma-sound, and tweaked the underlying math.

"Okay. Call Aasen," Ramanujan said.

Charles tapped his glasses. "Aasen says he's composing his report and would like to finish."

Ramanujan touched Charles's glasses and his own. "Aasen, please come to me in twenty minutes. It's important."

Ramanujan, with the assistance of Charles, programmed Aasen's newest amalgamated alphabet of ninety-six characters into code using Ramanujan's new algorithms. It took all of 130 seconds. Ramanujan and Charles then overlaid the result onto Venn common produced on their computer—another two minutes of work—and waited for Aasen.

"How do you know we have something substantial for Aasen?" Charles said.

Ramanujan rubbed his hands and smiled. "I'm interested in Zen. Your father found me a book about Zen and motorcycles, and I'll always remember the last sentence of the book: *You can sort of tell these things.* This," Ramanujan pointed to his computer and the walls, "I can tell."

Aasen came in a few minutes, delighting Ramanujan, who smiled and offered Aasen tea.

"Yes, please. And how are you, Charles?"

Before Charles could answer, Ramanujan said, "We three are the first of humanity to witness this. Mister Aasen, I'm using our—I should say *your*—newest alphabet. We need a new word or concept combining your and our, maybe—y'ours, with y-apostrophe?" He dimmed the lights and tapped the remote built into his glasses.

The earlier koan Charles had heard lasted a few seconds. It seemed like a place marker, an intimation of something to follow. The new sounds were of unimaginable purity but unlike any he had ever heard. An admixture of female voice, birdsong, mantra, of . . . they looked at each other, confirmed that the sounds, though they felt internal, were real. Charles, overcome with hope and glory, sat down on the floor, transfixed.

# 25

AT 0600, GENERAL BRAUN, FORTY-FIVE, THE YOUNGEST FOUR-STAR general in modern history, had completed his exercises and had popped his breakfast pills—shredded wheat-rice with spices, figs, and banana-ugli-berries. He picked up a cup of Braun-brewed coffee spiced with masala and sat at the military workstation with his aides for the daily Telecom World Briefing (TWB) compiled by his field commanders. An android with double-handed arms fluttered her twenty fingers over a console comprising mica screens, which showed field units, armaments, troop movements, weather, along with dozens of other micas showing individual commanders giving orders or listening to reports.

Braun had an interest in the Canadian-Siberian Conflict. A former academy classmate, Ingrid Resnikoff, was a field general of Canadian light infantry in Western Canada. She reported to her top commander, who'd asked her to give the TWB to Braun.

"Sir, the Conflict is intensifying," she said. "The Siberians have broken regulations twice."

"Which?" Braun asked.

"Geneva 112c, lobotomy of prisoners, and Jakarta 3a, corruption of medical supplies."

"Noted. General Injeeede, of Siberia, what do you have to say?"

"Sir, General Resnikoff is correct. My commanders have confirmed."

"Accordingly, under Rules of Conflict, I request, General Injeeede, that you deliver double new medical supplies that were corrupted and deliver replacements for double the prisoner count of those who were lobotomized, with one-third of them junior officers."

"Sir. Why officers?"

"Don't test me, General. This is the *second* infraction of Geneva 112c. Consult your Rules of Conflict."

"Yes, Sir."

The briefing concluded at 0645. Braun ordered his aide to complete the report of infractions and follow up to see that the instructions were followed.

Braun then turned his mind to the 0800 Plan B meeting.

.................................

IT WAS 0800, AND THE GENERALS, ALL IN BATTLE FATIGUES, WERE in a quandary. How to get Plan B done—in seven months. General Blackston, Logistics, pressed his main issue.

"Sir." Blackston stood. His gray hair made him look like a professor. He was lithe and agile—like a soccer coach. "No disrespect intended, Sir."

"I know," Braun said. "You think you are more emphatic if you stand. Well, go ahead." Braun leaned back in his chair and clasped his hands behind his head. His gangly arms looked like wings.

"Our supershuttle, *Orion*, has to be torn up and retrofitted. We have three smaller shuttles—"

"Request denied. Not only are the other shuttles *much* too small, requiring a dizzying number of trips; they are needed, at orbital, as is. Popov and I have agreed not to break routine."

"Sir," Osteen said, "with all due respect, shuttles for prisoners retrieving space junk aren't critical, any more than prisoner-vans for bagging roadside trash were critical three hundred years ago."

"Request denied."

"Okay. I've studied the plan, Sir," Blackston continued. "We need to re-design and dismantle guns; pull out creepers, armor, computers; and create additional space for the maximum load of six hundred people, plus *Welkin-Alpha* supplies, plus—"

"General Blackston, I don't have time for these exercises. I'm not going to listen to a laundry list of complaints."

"Okay, but, Sir, every time I review simulation updates, my storage bays are reduced. If some jerk wants to add a Ping-Pong table—for the tender loving care of the *Welkin-Alpha* android crew—I've got to ship it up there, and that jerk cuts the square footage out of my shuttle storage."

General Braun looked at him and didn't twitch a muscle. The other commanders remained silent, trying to read Braun. Braun then laughed uproariously. One by one, the other generals took up the laugh. Blackston threw up his hands and laughed with them, but Braun laughed the loudest and the longest.

"I love it when you get so upset," Braun said to Blackston. "Maybe there will be a Ping-Pong tournament, 'The Blackston Finals,' in your honor." The others chuckled.

"I challenge you, human on human, to a game on board," Farzad said.

"I accept," Blackston said as he sat back down.

General Braun took his hands from behind his head and rolled his chair close to the table.

"Generals Farzad and Blackston, who says you or any of us will be on the shuttle to *Welkin-Alpha*?"

One could have scratched the silence.

"I would think, Sir," Osteen said, "if we are to enact Plan B, we—"

"Should get a free ride?" Braun said. "You have a chance, General Osteen. For reasons understood by us, I believe you should go to represent our military, but you haven't been preselected."

She said nothing.

"I wonder, Sir, where that puts me," Blackston said.

"Right where it puts me," Braun said. "I'm needed for the fight here. You need to understand, no one has been preselected. I know what you're thinking: we do most of the work here, and then we're discarded."

"It never changes. All shit runs downhill," Blackston said.

"Enough, General. Stand up, soldiers." Braun stood up.

The others stood and knew what was coming.

"We're gonna do 7:30s."

They emerged to the cinder track and did stretches.

"You are right, Blackston," Braun said. "Some things never change, like right now. Just like the ancient Greeks, to stretch the mind we work the body."

They followed Braun to a starting line, where he set his timer. "Okay, we're off," he said.

After a mile, General Braun let them catch up and cluster about him, except for Osteen, who had matched the General stride for stride, and jogged in place with him as they waited.

"Now then, this is how we are going to proceed. I want each of you to state in one concise sentence your biggest challenge in enacting Plan B. Shove off. Jog and think; think and jog. Eight laps later, when you return to this spot, I will ask for your first three steps to solution. Clear?"

"Yes, Sir," they hollered.

Braun set his timer and ran in place. "General Blackston, we start with you."

# 26

CHARLES AND ANDRICA WERE ON AN INDONESIAN BEACH, LOOKING at novels in emojisensi-3. Charles had often wondered how a person in old-time could have read a novel word by word for entertainment. They sat facing the ocean, holding hands under individual sensi wraps, viewing through shaded emoji-loaded glasses. They had paid 180 worldos (fourteen hundred old-time Euro) each for use of a designated two-by-three-meter section of beach for one hour.

Charles was looking at the newest psycho-thriller of Ramon Bouffant, the sixteenth in a series featuring Dagmar and her female warriors riding basilisks. Charles sniffed the air—*fire*—and became alarmed as the emoji picture characters shuffled through his glasses. This often happened, and Andrica giggled as Charles calmed, knowing his sensi wrap was working well. Soon Charles was in Arctic tundra; he experienced chills, heard unrelenting gusts of wind, and smelled sweat-stinked flesh as he watched a female fatale, riding a behemoth, stab her foe with a shined golden sword. The emoji symbols fluttered by, and Charles sped them up a notch with a tap on his glasses—it was getting too cold for comfort.

Twenty minutes later came the miserable announcement: "You have ten minutes to clear the beach. Others have reserved prepaid spots and are waiting. Please be courteous to the three o'clock wave. In eight minutes, Security will fine any slackers. In ten minutes, you will be arrested if you haven't left this beach."

"Yo Yo ii Yoyo," whined Andrica. She pulled off the glasses, took off her wrap, and made an adjustment to the glasses marking her place in the book. "Can you imagine how nice it must have been to sit on a beach all afternoon in old-time?"

"You could do it all day, I think."

"Consecutive days?"

"Well, I'm not sure about that."

The planet contained eleven billion people. And beach lovers and claustrophobic madness were everywhere. We did indeed evolve from the ocean, thought Charles. As they squeezed their way to hover platforms, Charles wondered what it must have been like two hundred years ago when there were still cemeteries and places to stroll. For a number of years, people insisting on burial were buried vertically in an attempt to save space. The cemeteries remaining were a few military ones, and they were under siege—more space, any space, was needed. No more burials—bodies were cremated and the cremains scattered into the ocean. The irony was that many cemeteries, in particular those of churches and towns, had been dug up and replaced by nursing facilities.

Prisons had been the next to go. Lifers were sent to orbital space stations, where their main job was to retrieve swarf and space junk. Prisoners were incarcerated in off-world docking orbits that, in a final humiliation, were controlled by androids working with cobots. Lifers had a choice—either retrieve the space junk, or they would *become* space junk. Less egregious prisoners were shunted under the world's oceans and seas to neutralize plastic waste. Several swirls of plastic waste and detritus three hundred years ago had been nearly the size of Italy. On the planet now, over fourteen ocean-debris swirls exceeded Italy's size. Laser-fitted submarines had reduced plastic waste by a third. The subs were monitored and controlled by port authorities, who could disable any sub in case of mutiny.

Charles grabbed Andrica's hand as they stepped up to the platform. The hover's AI sensed their approach and lowered. A retractable ramp emerged from the ball, and when neighboring hovers had finished separate loadings and maneuvers, Charles and Andrica were allowed entry. "We can go to my place. My father is working at the mathelab."

"No, we can pill tonight. I'm behind with my mammals."

"Can I help?"

"Not really. It would take a while to get you up to speed." She glanced at him. "Don't take it personally, Charles. I accept I'm not in your league, but . . ."

"What kind of new stuff are you doing?"

Andrica didn't answer, and Charles didn't pursue.

In the auto-guided hover, they punched in their respective locations, put on wraps, and refastened their emojisensi glasses. But Charles didn't pay attention to the minicons. He thought about his next meeting with Popov and her request for him to link across mathematical fields with the newest updates in M-L-M. She'd said his strength was as a universalist. He tried to see further into applications of Euclid's magic squares, which had eluded him when Euclid told him of a pleasant surprise, to the new work of Ramanujan. *Was this what Euclid had alluded to when I last saw him?* Charles reconnected his thoughts to Benford's Law and attempted to fit the math to all that he knew. But he couldn't get a foothold and gave up. He was to meet Popov in two days, and he'd hoped to produce something substantial.

After kissing Andrica goodbye, Charles decided not to go home and reset his route to a less-familiar mathetorium. He returned the hover to a sky-hangar and thumbed his approval to the bill. At the mathetorium entrance, Charles grabbed the first balloon he saw, not realizing a classmate, Holly, was also trotting to it. He waited for her to squeeze the other grab-hold beside him and released the helium-filled balloon.

"Charles," she said, "you must be slumming. We never see you here."

Charles smiled and felt himself blush as the balloon rose to third balcony, which was reserved for academy students. Holly arched her back and frog-kicked her legs, directing the blue-and-citron-starred ball—docking lights blinking—to a section of the balcony where he saw acquaintances and classmates, including Conrad, the chess champ.

"Well, well," Conrad said, "look what the mongoose snagged. And where is Miss Andrica?"

Charles waited until Holly stepped off. Even if she released too soon, the balloon wouldn't drop her—sensors from the balloon's hangar talked to her implanted ID, and magnetic holds prevented anyone from releasing too early.

Holly wrapped her arms around Conrad and kissed him on the cheek. She whispered something in his ear, and he smiled. "Really?" he said, looking right at Charles.

"How you doing with the Sicilian-Riemann?" Conrad said.

"I haven't played chess since my last game with you," Charles countered.

"Maybe Charles is up for a little matheblitz," Conrad said.

"Now, that's *supe*," Holly said. "Mark off."

Charles stepped in place and put his hands behind his back. He felt pushed, manipulated. Conrad faced him at three yards, and his alligator sandals, scorched with yellow-painted lightning bolts, annoyed Charles. Holly removed their glasses.

"You're the visitor, Charles. You may start first," Conrad said. Holly put on special glasses and tapped them while their friends, five girls and six boys, all attending the same local math academy, moved in closer to the contestants.

Charles gushed: "8 squared, plus 8 cubed, minus 19, plus 1, divided by 2 squared, times 2."

"Two hundred seventy-nine," Conrad said.

"Challenge?" Holly said.

"No," Charles said. "Correct."

Conrad rushed words: "Cube root 531,441, minus 80, minus 1 cubed, times 1 squared."

"I protest," Charles said, "and accuse you of pre-calculating."

Conrad smiled. "I accept the protest." Conrad knew Holly could tap a lie detector built into her game glasses while taking his pulse. He turned to Holly: "Award Charles the point."

"Before Holly does," Charles said to Conrad, "what is the answer?"

"For me to know; for you to find out, Charles."

"Maybe you don't know the answer."

"The answer is the difference between 2 cubed and 4 doubled—or zero."

And so it went, back and forth as the contestants advanced to random math selections read by Holly. If the contestant answered right without challenge, he received a point; if still right with a challenge, two points. If a contestant answered wrong, he was docked a point, and the other was awarded two points if he correctly answered the same math run.

Charles had been behind by one point, and he'd just been challenged; Conrad won the challenge, and Charles, behind in time, conceded the match. Nevertheless he was applauded, and the group accepted him. Except for Conrad.

"You'd be better off re-studying the Sicilian," Conrad said.

"Yio Yio," Charles said.

"Touchy, Yi Yi, testy," Conrad said.

Holly glanced at Conrad and walked away.

"How's Andrica doing with her birds?" Conrad asked. He appeared to be interested.

"The birds are macaws. Nothing to report yet."

Conrad, feeling good that he'd shown his mettle, relaxed and offered Charles a cup of Loose—spices tinged with a substrate of LSD. Before Charles had even agreed, Conrad ladled some from the group's punch bowl into a cup and handed it to Charles.

"Thanks."

For the last two hundred years, all drugs, opiates, and liquor were legal. At age fourteen, parental agreement was required. From the age of sixteen onward, no parental agreement was required. From the age of sixteen onward, no parental agreement was required since sixteen was the age they became adults in the eyes of the law. It was not the same for tobacco. Anyone, no matter what age, caught using any form of tobacco, was kicked out of school or released from employment. For a second offense, the person was sent under the ocean to "neutralize" for ten years. When whistleblowers forced tobacco companies to release hidden data, it became a public outrage, and the companies were shut down for good. Studies showed that the damage of tobacco and secondary smoke was rampant; and when the damage was connected to early-onset Alzheimer's, there were riots. A Nobel-awarded biochemist had re-formulated a strain of heroin, which was successful in reversing some of this damage. Ever since, old-time opiate laws had been revised.

"I heard Andrica is doing superb work," Conrad said.

"She may be on to something. But the math doesn't check."

"That's where we come in, Charles." He took a swig of Loose. "I'm told you are meeting with Ramanujan. What's he like?"

Charles sipped the Loose and popped a vodka capsule into his mouth. He pulled another out of his pocket and offered it to Conrad, who took it.

"He listens a lot and spends a huge amount of time setting up."

Conrad leaned in toward Charles's ear, eyes flitting to and fro: "He was seen with a cigarette."

# 27

GENERAL BRAUN SAT FACING CHAIR POPOV IN HER PRIVATE OFfice. A tinged atmosphere of bio-formed Z-orchids from Lembang wafted in from outside. He looked up at the ceiling vents. He hadn't realized, although his office in the military obelisk was also in the bay, the rotation of atmosphere aromas on this side was also scheduled at random, as this morning he remembered cinnamon and vanilla orchid aromas, familiar to him as a teenager growing up in West Malesia. His electronics had been removed and sealed upon entering Popov's office. Only a high emergency could override the sensors. Popov's inner sanctum, like all others, contained a wall of sliding laser boards.

Popov was the world's leading expert in number theory, and Braun studied notations on the board beside him while Popov, who'd apologized for being tied up extra moments, tapped her glasses. He followed her initial notations, became lost, found his way again, gave up when he realized she was using an urelement.

"General, you've come in battle dress."

"Absolutely. Your wishes are my duty."

"Expected. Nevertheless, appreciated."

They stared at each other a few minutes.

"Still working your field, I see," Braun said, gesturing to the wall board.

"Yes. The work keeps my mind sharp; after almost a year, I'm closing to solution of Singer's conjecture."

"No wonder I lost you there." Braun stared at the loopy equations.

"General, update me on the droog situation."

Braun nodded. "Droogs are responsible for the killer scorpions. Cobot AI claims to have eliminated all but one, which they can't find."

"Yes, but the droogs. How bad is it?"

"One of them managed to get inside our tower to send this obvious message of infiltration. And the droogs' guerrilla tactics have become more than simply vicious. They are training their leaders as they expand."

Popov waited.

"Truthfully, I am concerned. They sense the end of the world as we know it. In my view, they are building and preparing to conquer territory in the likelihood of World War IV."

Popov shook her head as she eyed the General. "This infiltration message, which I choose to call a threat, couldn't come at a worse time, General."

Braun said nothing, but shifted in his chair as he faced Popov.

"As you know, General, many of your distinguished colleagues feel that Earth's violence is related to the number of people the planet supports. Further, they wish for Conflict and agitate, stirring up trouble, even creating an occasional *casus bello* as a way to reduce populations in turbulent spots. This allows them to test new weapons and schemes. Am I right, General?"

Braun nodded. "I feel compelled to add, Chair Popov, most of your colleagues at WCM over the years have looked the other way during these slaughters. I'm of the opinion, up to now, you and your people have supported the old German excuse—Lebensraum."

"I won't contest the point, General."

"Today we can't even slow the slaughter, never mind stop it, and, all of a sudden, we face—"

"General. Whether you sympathize with my approach or not doesn't concern me. You have followed orders; I have no complaints."

Popov sipped from a cup. "May I get you a cup of tea, General?"

"Yes, please, Lime with Spices." Braun watched her step to the minibar. He had to admit, she was in charge. "If the WCM is convinced the best way to reduce violence is with an optimal language—"

"Excuse me, General: *the* optimal language."

"Right. My staff and I are in full support. What's the newest time frame?"

"About seven months."

"And you, the WCM, won't find this lingua franca in time?"

"Mathe-Lingua-Musica."

Braun nodded. "Yes. M-L-M."

"We are making progress, and I do feel we will develop the language; but we won't be able to deliver it to the peoples of our planet in time. It will not have a chance to be absorbed."

"What about a massive inoculation, using virtual?"

"We've considered it. Our Tiers are working together on a tele-con, but we don't have the final product, which will have to be vetted, tweaked, adjusted—you know what the process is like. Simulations reveal we will be beyond singularity; by that time, we won't be able to turn back the clock and save ourselves."

"Chair Popov, does the language have to be perfect? Can't we inoculate with what we have?"

"We have wrestled with this. The calibrations of amalgamated musical theory, meta-linguistics, and mathematics are so sensitive that simulations which reveal any slight variation can have opposite effects."

"How so?"

"We aim at truth, but this inchoate language still works around it, yet our fractals are closing in. We are trying to reach precisions. The right rhythms, the right music, is needed."

The General rubbed his cheek and muttered incoherently.

"This new language will be much different from anything imaginable," Popov added.

"I don't understand."

"Our experts and polyglots tell us most languages build within by patterns and inherent linguistic universals. When that happens, there is room to move around in the language. But those languages are not interdependent on music theory and mathematics. This language *is*. We thought we could *find* the optimum language by taking selected utterances from all tongues—ancient and modern, human and mammal—in the world. Turns out we have to *create* the optimum language by using what little we've found to be useful, and by discarding everything else."

"Maybe we don't need music and—"

Popov fisted her hands. "Mozart wrote that to create a language without music is to never have painted with color."

"I'm sorry." Braun smiled. "I'm aware of the Mozart effect."

"We are certain that in order to communicate with calm, deliberation, wisdom, and respect, this best possible language needs to incorporate some type of music with mathematical linguistics."

"How will we know we have found *the* optimal language?"

"That's the question I expected from you. Just as music can be an anodyne to grief, we will witness our optimum language subdue animosity. But the answer you are looking for is this: updated simulations will guide us; mathematics will prove it."

"Are all significant cultures behind this?"

"Yes. As it stands now, the world's different cultures realize they don't 'hear' each other because they communicate in non-optimal languages."

"So, what's the breakthrough?"

"You might want to take another sip of tea and ready your mind."

Braun stood and approached the mini-bar. "May I?"

"Yes. And I'll take a Ginger with Licorice, please.

"General," she continued, "we have isolated calming phonemes in dolphins and birdsong. When combined with certain musical patterns, the calming effect and the readiness to communicate are palpable. We are on the second or third rung of an extensive ladder."

Braun took a sip and stared at her. "I'm sure you know what I'm thinking: how in hell do we speak birdsong-dolphinese?"

It was Popov's turn to stare over her cup. She looked at her wall board of number theory, turned back, and took a sip of tea.

"I have no idea, other than to pipe such music into Neuro Responsive Simulators—nano-biochips, located in particular spots of the brain. The music could then be decoded and serve to complement and reinforce oral speech."

Braun nodded.

"I believe the problem is connected to why we can't update and fill present brains with new histories like we can do with the brains of Liftees. Yet even Liftees don't absorb M-L-M any better than we do."

"I'm assuming WCM and Tier mathematicians will be leaving for a world unknown?"

"Don't assume, General. Many premier mathematicians will take the journey, obviously. Along with top specialists in other fields—linguistics, music, statistics, medicine, psychiatry—but the emphasis will be on math universalists, and everyone, without exception, must be conversant in the newest M-L-M. Special I-Translators will have to be programmed for M-L-M; there will be no fallback to another language."

"What else can you tell me?"

"You've read the file."

"Absolutely; I know we are—excuse me—I know *Welkin-Alpha* will be auto-piloted to Kepler-1649c and Cryopreservation has scheduled the sleeps. Plasma-physics has engineered fusion-based rocket propulsion, yada, yada, yada." He pursed his lips. "Chair Popov, where is your Defense?"

"Think, General."

Braun flushed, and threw up his hands. "It is the nature of humankind to conquer." He knew he was headed for a cliff but roared ahead. "It's still survival of the strongest as well as the fittest, wouldn't you say?"

"No, I would not say." Popov straightened and placed both her palms on the table. "Look, General, I respect you for your military professionalism. I can imagine how you must feel about this. But those on board will journey without any type of military support—"

"What about Security?"

"Please don't interrupt me. M-L-M is being designed without any reference—not one word—to violence. For example, the word *kill* will not exist in this new language."

Braun stared at her.

"The nature of Mathe-Lingua-Musica, the extraordinary purpose of this mission—not merely a journey, mind you—the unprecedented nature of the trek shows, by mathematical simulation as well as by common sense, that the future of humanity lies in optimal communication, not in aggression; and not in continual defense. Defense, I might add, which serves to embolden aggressors."

"Common sense, you said."

"General, I once heard you quote America's George Washington telling one of his commanders 'We must bear up and make the best of mankind as they are, since we cannot have them as we wish.' General, I submit to you that we are now on the trajectory to have humankind as we wish."

"By your account," Braun said.

Popov ignored his parry. "It's on the line for humanity, General. Mathematical histories confirm humankind as their own worst enemy. Benjamin Franklin was on the right track when he said, "There was never a good war or a bad peace." Humankind has had one too many wars. The India-Pakistan war, after five bloody years, ended in a stalemate. Three million lives lost, for what? And now, five years later, the same hatred continues. We've forced our species into a corner. There is no escape for those remaining on Earth. As you know, General, we dare not go back to try to change our misfortunes. As we go forward, we do so under the exact rules and orders keyed to Plan B—Starship *Welkin-Alpha*. Are we clear, General?"

"Oh, yes, I am clear, Chair Popov. But what if you are wrong?"

"General. Do I have your full support?"

"Yes, of course. Please don't ask me if I agree."

"General, there will be no communication with our starship after liftoff."

Braun felt dizzy. Uncomprehending. "The trekkers won't be in Cryopreservation forever."

"Our species has a virus, General. Thus, *tabula rasa* for the starship. We will quarantine ourselves here on Earth from *Welkin-Alpha*."

"Forever?"

"Yes. WCM is in total agreement. We are all virulent, General. If a few of humanity have never been evil in thought, word, or deed, good for them. But if only one of us keeps this virus, we shall never engage with the ship."

She took another sip and kept the General locked in her gaze.

"Consider the possibility, General, that advanced civilizations never had the concept of war, violence, mayhem, destruction—or they have eradicated those concepts to the extent that such notions are alien to them. Consider there are no words in their languages for any of that."

Braun forced a sigh and rubbed his nose.

"We can't take the chance of infecting this voyage, this *escape*," she continued. "Good intentions aren't enough here. We shall give humanity every extra chance by leaving this starship alone."

"So, no one from the military will make this journey?"

"Correct. General, the captain of our starship is a former Academy First who was selected from Tier several years ago. His executive officer and his engineers were all waitlisted at Tier and have been re-vetted."

Popov saw and felt the General's struggle. She stayed silent and sipped her tea.

"Okay, then," he said. "I will stay quiet and keep a close eye on my staff in case someone would like to join the voyagers. I don't expect a problem. Truth be known, and I feel I can speak for us soldiers, we wouldn't know what to do on your ship. We'll fight to the last here on Earth."

Popov forced herself to silence as the General pouted. *One wrong word*, she thought, *and I could lose his support.*

"General, we were both wrong."

Braun looked up at her.

"The WCM thought as you did a decade ago," Popov said. "If we could get through one last war, if we could stabilize one last Conflict, we could begin to terraform Mars."

The General nodded. "We ran out of time on the Mars opportunity."

Popov felt some relief. "You realize, General, you can beat the odds if you can end a Conflict or demote a Declared."

Braun put up his hand and smiled. "Notice, Chair Popov, I haven't interrupted you."

"Continue." She smiled and took a sip of tea.

"I wanted to say, under Plan A, we could have saved the planet. Now—"

"And now, General, I must interrupt you. First, I'm glad you used the past tense. I trust you fully.

Popov sipped her tea and continued. "It comes down to this: Plan A, if carried out in time, would be a temporary solution. Other aggressors—soldiers like you—would figure a way to deactivate the ship's retaliatory devices and forge a crusade that would continue wars and violence, as history has shown us time and time again. With Plan B, we leap into the unknown, pure. A new start, *tabula rasa*, for our species."

Braun stared at a wall. "Time and time again, you say. I wonder why?"

"Since Cain killed Abel, our species has had this virus. My colleagues and I contend that in this universe, our universe, there must be other species, similar to us, who have never intentionally killed another member, much less a brother."

"Interesting notion."

When Popov stood to adjourn, they both received the override alert on their emergency implants. To Braun it seemed like Popov had activated the override as she stood. They locked eyes. Iceland and Greenland had each requested a Controlled-Nuclear against the other.

# 28

LATE THAT SAME AFTERNOON, CHARLES ARRIVED AT POPOV'S quarters for their meeting. He was distraught. The opportunity of a lifetime—just being in the great mathematician's office—and he hadn't been able to come up with any worthwhile connections related to mathematics, linguistics, or music, as she'd requested.

Charles gave her this news. He watched her peek at him over the rim of her cup as she took a sip of tea. He had declined a beverage and wondered whether he was trying to punish himself.

"I mean," he said, "I didn't come up with anything substantial leading to follow-up."

She watched him. "I understand fully. Just because one like you holds promise doesn't mean a creative stream of nuggets can be turned on at will, like a spigot."

The kind remark didn't relax Charles. He was still pushing the inner passageways of his brain, seeking.

"The last time you were here, our first meeting, you devoured my board of equations and showed an understanding that impressed me. Do not worry about this, Charles."

"Ramanujan says he sees more in Benford's Law that should connect to M-L-M. He's working out the mathematics, but is stuck."

"He's already accomplished much for us. I get all Liftee reports and Tier compilations, which are prepared for me. But they are summarized and watered down. I'm more interested in out-of-the-box ideas. Which brings me . . . would you like to hear some harp music?"

"Oh, yes. Please."

"I have something new, from Bach and Liu Hui. It's . . ." she drew Charles into a hexagonal sitting room, "well, you'll see. Excuse me for a moment."

Charles gazed at five walls of micas. The sixth wall was a doorway, but above the door frame was another shelf of micas. Three of five walls were covered in purple-brown micas, the chosen color for mathematics. He grabbed one mica and slid it out, *Markovian properties of Mathematical Linguistics*. He replaced it and removed another, *Bouba-Kiki, the Mathematics Behind Sound-Shapes*. She must have everything, he thought.

Charles did a double-take as Popov emerged through the doorway, rolling her harp. She'd changed out of uniform into a body-form of blue-green satin, with matching slippers. He noticed a new pendant of opal scarabs. She was beautiful, and he watched her close the door with calm. Charles felt special and that something unique was about to happen.

"We'll keep this between us, Charles."

"Okay."

"I learned long ago that I play best when I style myself to the music." She looked to him as she positioned herself at her harp. "Remove your sport coat, Charles, and your shoes. I want you to lean back in the chair, close your eyes, and count to thirty."

Charles did as instructed.

The arpeggios seemed like warmups, and he was surprised at their repetition. First, she played in one key, *C major*? This was followed by other keys, then back to the first key, and then she skipped a key, but kept playing arpeggios. *Is she tuning?* Charles squinted an eye open and watched her. She had closed her eyes, and her jaw was set. Charles closed his eyes again and waited. He began to hear accents, which became more pronounced. The accent moved about the scale in no particular pattern; once the accented string was thrummed thrice, in rapid succession, before the accent gained volume and pitch, like it had been set to a new level by the rapid thrum.

The music wasn't melodic, nor was it relaxing. It was edgy, but it held his attention as he followed from pattern to pattern. If this music was meant to calm, it had the opposite effect on Charles. *What is she doing?*

He watched through squinted eyes again, and Popov had tilted her head sideways. She frowned and looked like she might be grinding her teeth. Charles closed his eyes and made a supreme effort to understand; he had a distinct feeling the music was trying to speak.

After a few more minutes, Charles lost the pattern, but the music became more tuneful. A moment later, when he felt more relaxed, the pattern emerged—but it was different. It coalesced into a pattern of triplets he pictured going up, down, under, and through—continuing to repeat the pattern. He couldn't understand what was happening when the music became discordant and burst in new directions. He fidgeted his toes and rubbed his shoulders. He couldn't discern any pattern in the plucking atonality, and when he could no longer stand the abrasive sounds he covered his ears and leaned forward.

Popov stopped at once, and Charles looked at her.

"Well, you lasted longer than I did," she said.

Charles was speechless, his head echoing with turbulent dissonances. "What *was* that?"

"Phrasing by me, taken from computer-composed and computer-generated. You'll have to ask Bach to learn more, something about the 'dubstep doesn't match the reverb,' says he."

Popov directed Charles back to her office and slid back a wall board, revealing the one behind; it was the same one full of equations he'd studied at their last meeting. He recognized patterns, the same as in the music just played. He looked at Popov, who was smiling at him.

"But—"

"Look again," Popov said.

Charles began to build. The first set of equations, without exponents, had to be akin to C major—there were no patterns. The second set of equations in the same designated category had exponents to the second power and showed a pattern similar to what he'd initially heard. He moved to later sets of the same category and recognized patterns that, with a stretch, mimicked what he'd just heard, which brought him to the end of the board, as it had last week.

Popov slid the board aside, revealing a final board, one he'd not seen before.

Charles couldn't make heads or tails out of the mess on the final board, but, without thinking, he announced "New Category—Atonal."

"Right. What do you see?"

Charles strained. He could almost feel his brain pump. He took up a laser and integrated, differentiated, transposed, combined, inverted; he flushed with hesitation and anger—there was something there, but he couldn't find it.

"I know an answer is there." He turned to her. "I just don't see it."

Popov put her hand on his shoulder as Charles flustered. "The math breaks down at this point, but I too know it's there, Charles. I can't find it either."

# 29

WHEN GENERAL OSTEEN HEARD THE NEWS IN GENERAL BRAUN'S office—that no military personnel would make the trek to exoplanet Kepler-1649c—she clamped down her jaws behind pursed lips and stifled her rage. She looked to a picture on the wall next to Braun. It showed his army-general grandfather pinning lieutenant bars on Braun's shoulder at Powell Military Academy graduation ceremonies. PMA, in Sulawesi, Indonesia, was the world's supreme military academy. It had grown from the West Point tradition, after the Point was demolished in the USA's second civil war. Years later, the area on the Hudson had become a backwater, like much of the USA, and West Point remained a memory. She read the caption on the photograph, hand-written by his grandfather: *To serve is an honor—welcome to the Braun tradition.*

Braun's grandfather had been a hero. Knowing Indonesia was losing hundreds of islands every year due to the final stages of climate change, it had been decided to have other warring countries settle their differences on abandoned, soon-to-disappear, Indonesian islands. Undeclareds, or Conflicts, were brought to the islands, and the round-the-clock coverage turned into quasi-sporting events. Mascots represented sides, commoners placed bets and lost money. Debtors, criminals, deplorables were sent to fight and die in raging Conflicts that seemed to never end. Some saw this as a vicarious physical and mental release, which would be beneficial for society, and also serve as a way to stem ever more people from populating the planet. The entire enterprise became corrupt after Braun's grandfather had exposed senior commanders who bet against their own side and who instigated other battles around the globe to be settled on Indonesian islands. The ruse and profit-taking were soon over. Hordes of commoners who had lost substantial sums were outraged, and the droogs were born. The abused relicts who called themselves droogs retaliated everywhere, and the vicious violence increased yet again.

In present day, organized droog cells were popping up everywhere, changing color like chameleons and persevering like ticks and cockroaches. This created a growing alarm in the military and fear in the hearts of many soldiers. Braun was one of these soldiers.

Although he was successful in getting Iceland and Greenland to come to their senses and withdraw their request, he, his staff, and the military were getting blamed for increasing droog chaos.

"I'm not surprised," Osteen said. "For most of my career, the military has been the scapegoat every time something goes wrong. Look at India-Pakistan. Was it all our fault? Now, it seems, we are blamed for the decline and fall of humanity."

She watched Braun eye her. She knew she was being vetted.

"Do you resent it, like I do, General Osteen?"

"Truthfully? No. I don't. If I were on WCM, I'd feel as they do. When you look at history, I can't blame them."

She expected Braun to reread her file, in particular the parts about her rape by a martial arts master in Okinawa. She'd been told several times, once by Braun, to dial it down when competing with men.

"But you're pissed, General Osteen."

"Okay, I'm pissed. Who wouldn't be? Like you, General Braun, I'm a soldier; always have been, always will be."

She watched Braun sit back and put his hands behind his head. She'd seen this body language before and knew the next exchange would be critical.

"General Osteen, I've been thinking." Braun looked to the picture of the uniformed soldier on his desk. "For the benefit of humanity, I like the idea of someone or two, maybe three, with our training on—"

"General!" Osteen shot up out of her seat. "If this is your way of checking my mental state and commitment, I resent it." She leaned in over the desk and all but hissed, "And if you are serious, which I hope the fuck you aren't, I'll run you right up the flag."

Braun arched a brow and smiled. "Okay, then."

.................................

IN HER BACHELORETTE QUARTERS, AFTER EXERCISES IN HER PRIvate gym, an hour of mathematics—*Riemann, Revised for Minus 3 Dimension*—along with a cold shower and a sensi-wrapped session in her sauna, Osteen contacted her close friend Ginger Pompadoux, Colonel of Tactics, World Army.

The following night, on a civilian section of Indonesian beach, which she'd cleared of electronics and surveillance by faking an atmospheric problem, she met with Ginger. They'd been talking an hour.

"The point is, Ginger, man has fucked up this planet. You mentioned Joan D' Arc, an isolated case, an anomaly. Maybe man had to kill to survive initially, but all the Wars and subsequent Conflicts have been led by men."

"General, what about us?"

"We still do his fighting."

"What would you do differently?"

"It's about time you brought that up, Ginger. You know, I know, and if there is one," she pointed heavenward, "the man upstairs knows it was with reluctance by men that glass ceilings for women were breached. From the right to vote—to VOTE," she hollered, "to where we are today has been a constant struggle, and I'll be goddamned if I'm going to sit around to watch men board this ship and escape Armageddon when it is men who fucked up our planet."

Ginger pulled her knees up tighter. "As I said, women are also leaving on the starship. Give me some time to think about this."

.................................

TWO NIGHTS LATER, ON THE SAME STRIP OF BEACH, OSTEEN SAID, "Ginger, you are my trusted ally. What have you decided?"

Ginger folded her knees up. "Doesn't it seem a bit rash, General?"

Osteen stared at her. Ginger wouldn't meet her eyes. Osteen waited.

Finally, Ginger said, "I don't think . . . I don't know."

"We don't have time, Ginger. I need to know: Are you with me, or against me?"

Ginger glanced away and spoke, not looking at Osteen. "We've been friends since Powell. I treasure you, General." She turned to Osteen and said in a lower, measured voice, "I'm not with you. I can't be. Janice, I don't want to go against you." Ginger took Osteen's hand. "Janice, I want you to rethink what you've asked of me. Will you do that for me?"

"Don't you want to be on the starship, Ginger? Why must we women be left behind?"

"Yes. I'd like to go on the journey, but I can't."

"Ginger, I'm asking you to join me."

"No."

"What will you do about this?"

"General Osteen, don't make me say it, if you will not change your mind."

"Are you going to report me?"

"General, with all due respect, I'm asking *you* to change your mind."

"I see. You would report me?"

"I must, General, if I can't persuade you to change your mind."

Osteen nodded and leaned in closer. "Oh, Ginger," she whispered, as she whipped her hands to the sides of Ginger's face and then lifted, twisted, and broke her neck. "Why did you make me . . .?"

She didn't look at the rolled-up eyes, but grabbed the stashed surfboard, which she'd often used at night, under the stars, alone. She laid Ginger's now-dead body on top of it and, straddling her and the board, paddled out to the undertow. *Get over it,* she thought. *She would have reported you. You couldn't trust her; she wasn't going to come around. You did your best.* She pushed the body into choppy foam and, by moonlight, watched it float southeast for several seconds and then disappear.

*I had no choice. There wasn't an alternative. Steady. Brace.*

.................................

LATER, BACK AT HER QUARTERS, SHE FELT BETTER. SHE'D KNOWN after the first night on the beach that Ginger was a maybe. A formidable danger to her plans had been eliminated. Tomorrow would be a new day. What's more, two other women she knew were ready and eager to join her cause.

.................................

GENERAL BRAUN HAD JUST FINISHED A PRIVATE INTERVIEW WITH General Blackston. He'd saved Blackston for last, and although Blackston had given his support, he wasn't in agreement with WCM and had reservations about their methods. Blackston would have to be watched. Braun made notes and, by tapping special glasses, he set up appropriate checks and Security measures. The truth was Braun felt as Blackston did, and he wondered whether Popov was setting up on him as well.

Braun was disgusted. Yet, he was a professional; always had been. He looked at his grandfather's picture again. *To the last*, he told himself. *To the last.*

He would have liked to conduct one more round of questioning with his staff, but the Canada-Siberia War was bleeding his energies. A Controlled-Nuclear was again requested. Further vetting would have to wait, and he closed staff files knowing he'd never get to do it. He reported his staff cleared for Plan B and gave orders for them to vet their top commanders and on down the chain.

He checked his glasses and winced when he saw he had just forty minutes to prepare for the Canada-Siberia meeting he had scheduled. The two national commanders would be arriving to meet him in the Nelson Mandela room. He'd be reporting results of the meeting to Popov. He tapped his glasses and reviewed the Regs for declared war.

In present age, missile-carried nuclear bombs were forbidden in wars on Earth. Mutually Assured Destruction (MAD) had kept humanity from Armageddon. The WCM controlled the stockpiles of each major country, and the missiles were quarantined for one use only—defense of the planet. The one nuclear exception was the one he reviewed now: Controlled-Nuclear—Communication Impasse.

He finished studying the Regs and consulted his aides' briefs one more time. He reviewed calculated simulations and verbal-saved his notes. Five minutes before the appointed meeting time, he called in his administrative aide.

"Do not send anything to my generals or Popov until I've reviewed all conversation," he instructed his aide.

"Yes, Sir," the aide said.

The aide was a backup translator, fluent in Canadian-French and Russian. Protocol required backups in all meetings of declared war, in case of a communications breakdown in I-Translation.

General Braun faced his aide. "After everyone departs, I want you to provide me with your own written translation of everything said, including conversation before and after the official meeting. Pay particular attention to what is said and what you think is meant between the lines." This translator was new, and Braun pressed the issue. "It's been my experience, when matters escalate in any kind of war, there is a lot of smoke and mirrors at meetings like this, and people don't, or won't, understand the other. Your job today is to give me the truest intention of each side present, as you understand it."

"I will do my best, Sir."

"Call them in. I'll be there in a few minutes."

Braun set the tempo. The more important the meeting, the later he arrived. Let them sit, let them fret. Let them know who's in charge.

General Braun wasted no time. "This is a bad time to even consider a CN," Braun said. "For everyone." He let that fester. "I'm up to my neck in droog shit, and much of my time is shifting to those thugs."

"We've heard the scuttlebutt," the Canadian general said. "Can you enlighten us?"

"I know what you've heard, and it's all true. The bastards are expanding everywhere." He took a sip of tea, but didn't offer drinks to any of the others.

"On another subject, has WCM decided who will travel and who will stay?" the Siberian general asked.

"That matter will not be discussed here. But I will tell you this—you've made their main charge of limiting violence much harder." Without looking at his aide, General Braun held out a hand to him. Like magic, a half-sized mica rested in General Braun's hand, and Braun put on special glasses.

"We can make this simple," Braun said. "I will grant a WCM board request for one Controlled-Nuclear for detonation in Western British Columbia and one Controlled-Nuclear for detonation in Central Siberia—within Andropov coordinates only."

"You know that accomplishes nothing for either of us," the Canadian said.

"You are dragging out this war," the Russian said.

Braun removed his glasses and took another sip of tea. Although he had expected their reaction, he saw and felt the inane futility of it all. He wished in another lifetime he could escape on *Welkin-Alpha* and journey to exoplanet Kepler-1649c. He didn't like the odds of human survival.

"I don't give a fuck about either of you pogues or your goddamned war."

Braun wanted to flush them with hot tea from his cup, and before he rejected the thought, the cup handle snapped off the cup. He stabilized the cup in time, but tea dribbled in front of him and toward the generals seated at the table.

His aide rushed over to assist. "Sir . . ."

Braun watched his aide mop up the dribbles on the table, and sighed.

Braun held up the broken cup handle in his hand. "This sums up how I feel right now. Don't you see," he faced the opposing generals, "nothing will ever get resolved if the two of you continue your nonsense."

"Sir." The Russian general stood and stuck his chin out.

Braun threw the broken cup handle at him and watched it bounce off the Russian's belly and land in the Canadian's lap.

"Get out of here. Everyone. OUT!"

# 30

HEAD DROOGS FROM FOURTEEN CELLS WERE MEETING IN A HIDDEN basement in Slum-town. The X-marked twins chaired the meeting and sat on two scratched, squeaky, and upright wooden chairs in front of thirty-two chiefs; eleven were women, twenty-one were men. Not one of them was older than twenty-one.

The twins, along with their designated guru, pressed their point: "If we screw up, there is no second time," a twin said. "We must do everything right the first time," her sister said.

The guru, sitting on the floor beside the twins, rose to his feet. Unthinking, he patted his groin area and winced. "The plans we are all working on are becoming more impressive every day, especially the recruiting of new blood and our ramped-up training. We are building a war machine that is going to blindside the bastards in both vertical pricks. But we need the right moment to strike. We must stifle our impulse to literally go off half-cocked." There were the usual groans, but he held firm as the twins got up and stood beside him. One twin said, "Your work on these post-nuke plans is shaping up. Refine your linkup plans with all your assigned droogs and we'll meet again in one week."

.................................

"SO, BIRDS AND OTHER MAMMALS AREN'T ABLE TO DEVELOP THEIR own language? We have nothing to learn from them?" Andrica said.

"Sharks have lived on this planet for over four hundred million years," Krebs said, "and their brains are still the size of a golf ball. So yes, that's part of it. I haven't a clue as to why their intelligence hasn't evolved."

Andrica crossed her arms.

"What we have taken from the dolphins may be all there is," Krebs, the Liftee who spoke forty-eight languages, added.

Krebs, thanks to the help of Charles and his father, met Andrica at her place; at the moment, the two of them were watching her dolphins and listening to them communicate. Communicate with whom, they didn't know, but they were convinced the strange clicks and sounds were definitive phonemes of communication.

"Strange patterns in the clicks," Krebs said. He had a wattle under his chin, which he rubbed with his thumb and index finger.

"Yes, I'd noticed it right away," Andrica said.

Krebs pondered the unique sounds while now rubbing his chin whiskers, pulling the whiskers and chin into prominence.

"Do the dolphins communicate with the macaws?" Krebs bent closer to two macaws, which hung in a cage overlooking the pool.

"No. I tried."

"What did you do, specifically?"

"First, I recorded any sounds that seemed like phonemes of both species and transmitted them to each other under controlled conditions. No reaction. I employed computer-drawn utterance overlays using all other sounds to try to syncretize the different inflectional forms. There was a minor overlap, which amounted to nothing."

"Well, if we can't get a foothold in either language, how am I to work here?"

"In present time," Andrica said, "all of us, no matter what our field or interest, are updated in mathematics."

"Yes, I know," he said. "Tell me what else you've done."

"I've isolated the mathematics and two possible musical patterns. I overlaid the mathematics with computer-drawn randoms of M-L-M, and the results point to some type of computer code."

"Some type of computer code . . ." Krebs repeated. "Can't anything we don't recognize be some type of computer code?"

"The musical patterns are unique, interlarded, and atonal, so the code appears corrupt; nevertheless, all the math points to a viable language," Andrica said.

"A viable language for computers," Krebs said. "What are we to do with it?"

Andrica offered Krebs a reclining lounge and dimmed the lights. "What I've managed to extract might be of use."

Krebs stared at the lounge and finally sat down. Andrica said,"Please listen, and give your opinion."

It was the cacophony that bothered Krebs. Discordant, unfinished, repugnant sounds that had no place in anything else he heard. It was like the scratch sounds on an old-fashioned slate, mixed with off-key viola squawking, on top of out-of-rhythm tom-toms. The "everything else" he did hear with Andrica was mysterious, unmelodic, and erratic, but did display at least an attempt at structure and organization. At the end, Krebs said he couldn't reach an opinion other than he hated the sounds. While downloading a copy into his glasses, he took a last look at the macaws.

He pointed at the one sitting alone in a private cage—he'd been separated because he chased and fought with the two females. "You, young fella, need to make yourself understood. Look at you." The macaw cocked his head and eyed Krebs. "You have the same problem as humanity: no one understands you, which is why you sit in your swing all alone, looking discombobulated, sexually undernourished, and perplexed."

The macaw, seeming to understand Krebs, delivered a few shrill *acks* and snapped his wings. Krebs looked on silently. He pointed again at the macaw. "What's that you say?"

As if on cue, the macaw *acked* again, but didn't flutter his wings.

"Well, young fella, I don't understand, but thanks for repeating."

"So, what about my dolphins?" Andrica said.

"What about them? You're further along with your fish than we are here," he said, nodding to the birds. "And my hunch is we are missing something with these birds. Good afternoon, young fella," he said to the bird.

When Krebs had departed, after they'd closed the door, his "young fella" *acked* a different series of utterances—longer in duration and lower in scale. Andrica's audio-video cam hooked to the outside of the birdcage recorded it all, including the slight difference in the bird's snap of wings.

# 31

IN A CHANGE OF VENUE THIS AFTERNOON, WCM MET IN THE BASEment of the obelisk, sixteen floors below sea level. With a sensitive agenda, Popov felt a need to relax her charges using a different setting. The chosen location included a reinforced aquarium wall with an electronically displayed real ocean, teeming with aquatic life, imbued with sensor-heightened colors. The forty-square-meter room displayed peaceful décor, with subtle lighting that projected varied Calabi-Yau manifolds throughout. An octagonal-shaped teak table rested amid eight high-backed rolling chairs, on a rug that was bamboo-felt. Recessed dimmers and selected background soundscapes rounded out the atmosphere.

One of the tasks in the basement was to select those who would make the journey to exoplanet Kepler-1649c. Those selected would be computer-taught and inculcated with Mathe-Lingua-Musica. To make it possible, exabytes of M-L-M were being updated every day and readied for biochips and neural nanobot implants.

It was decided Cryopreservation would freeze a cross-mixture of math-gifted men and women, and the most promising young adults. Two mathematicians would initially navigate the ship after liftoff, assisted by robots. In three Earth days, robots would take over completely. When they neared their new home, preset computers would first awaken the navigators from Cryopreservation. Within two Earth days, everyone else would be awakened.

Meanwhile, before the ark's launch from Moonbase 1, military personnel, including engineers, prepared the Earth-to-moon shuttle, *Orion*.

After everyone was seated around the table, Boucher, the chair apparent, stood.

“Chair Popov, esteemed colleagues, we need special medical people now, who will prepare the travelers, confirm their health, and see that they are properly inculcated with M-L-M via neuroprosthetics.”

“You are right,” Popov said. “This is too important to leave to computers and remote systems. We need a trained physician to lead this effort.”

“Yes,” De Costa said. “We may have to Lift. Not many school-trained doctors are left. None capable of the task here.”

In the end, it was agreed Popov would find and Lift the best person who could prepare the travelers. In an adapted scheme, this Liftee would work with Tier mathematicians responsible for traveler preparation.

“Good,” Popov said. “Mister Boucher, colleagues, here is our present slate of Liftees. One of these Liftees will be replaced. She tapped her glasses and the list appeared on everyone’s eyewear:

D. Pauperito
J. S. Bach
E. Krebs
I. Aasen
Liu Hui
L. Wittgenstein

“It is integral,” Popov continued, “that this list also show our newest Liftees, which include: Toni Svea Praeger, math-linguist and computer-language specialist.

“Armando Petitjean, master of mathematical languages and phonologist versed in psycho- and socio-linguistics.

“And Sean Bromsky, twentieth- to twenty-first-century linguist and scholar.”

.................................

AFTER ANOTHER NINETY MINUTES, THE GROUP TOOK A WELL-NEEDED recess of half an hour. They used restrooms and listened to prerecorded soundscapes in their glasses, which matched the changing scenes in the aquarium. After random periods of ten to twenty seconds, the background lighting inside the aquarium would glow a different hue. Each hue locked on a different key in the musical scale, and the music, with occasional recitative, changed in everyone's glasses. The music was relaxing and communicative in the spirit of critical thinking, decision-making. The music, though a humble effort, had been a workable test of M-L-M.

Back at the table, Popov said they would, at a later date, choose the final twenty humans to travel—those preeminent mathematicians who would govern the travelers on the new planet. Meanwhile, they hashed out additional details associated with each of the proposed travelers.

"Do we need teachers?" Popov asked.

"Not many," Boucher said. "Our young will have been inculcated or, as some say, inoculated. Some of our young people are Academy Firsts."

"Well, if I'm selected to travel, I'll head up the teachers," Gunderson said.

The others chose to ignore Gunderson's subtle plea. The conversations and attempts at communication became drawn and testy as each of them began to think about their place and how much they yearned to go on humanity's greatest adventure. The thoughts of being left behind became trenchant, and the resulting silences became longer and distinct. It didn't take too long before everyone stopped, and, one by one, they looked at Popov.

"I hear your thoughts," she said. "It hasn't been decided who among the WCM Board will travel. I don't know if I'm going myself."

"Who decides?" Anand asked.

"We all do. But I have the final approval and the right to veto. It falls under Emergency Contingency in the bylaws."

"Let's decide we eight travel together," Anand said.

"No. I can't allow that."

"Why?" asked Boucher and Tuan, at the same time.

"Listen to me, please. Together, we approve travelers aboard our starship, including Auxiliary Command. These approvals are based on recommendations from Third Tier, which lead to review by Second Tier, and to final selections by First Tier. That's the process, and I won't be pressured into anything further at this juncture."

# 32

GENERAL OSTEEN EXPRESSED DISMAY OVER THE REPORT OF MISSing officer Colonel Ginger Pompadoux and told her staff to keep her updated on the case. She felt a troubling surge in her abdomen whenever she thought about her friend. But this surge was muted to a twinge as she thought about Brigadier General Constance Malone, of Security, and Major Maryann Troy, of Logistics, who had both empathized with Osteen's view and who supported her. They too had had enough and wanted out and away from an Earth destined to ashes. An Earth compromised and wrecked by mankind.

General Osteen would never reveal to them what had happened to Ginger, and the fact that she outranked Constance and Maryann would help her if any coverup was needed. In her meetings with each of them, on different sections of beach, she'd laid out preliminary next steps. The first was to isolate and keep secret any and all communication among the three of them. Osteen was to provide special glasses for them to communicate with each other, and this she'd already accomplished.

The second step was to procure regular updates on M-L-M. If they were to board *Welkin-Alpha*, never mind communicating on the ship and at destination, all three had to be conversant in and understand the newest improvements to M-L-M. General Malone would use special contacts to accomplish this.

The third step was to find three of the most anonymous travelers they could replace. How they intended to replace them without detection would come later.

Major Maryann Troy was to provide the self-contained shuttle's designs and details. Osteen already knew much about the shuttle-ship,

*Orion*, because of her MOS, Defense. Unlike old-time, where a shuttle would piggy-back a separate launch, this huge shuttle was self-contained. In Plan B, limited fuel hoisted it two-thirds loaded from Earth. It was refueled and further loaded at one of two orbital space stations, before landing at Moonbase. It had been designed with retractable wings and fins, in accordance with Plan A.

To the credit of the WCM, they had persisted in a backup plan. As humanity's survival prospects worsened, humankind needed a way out. Survivors couldn't be packed like sardines onto the moon; they would destroy that too. The gargantuan starship, *Welkin-Alpha*, had been the planned escape for the future of humankind. And the Earth-to-moon shuttle, the retrofitted *Orion*, was the first step of Plan B.

.................................

IN THE WEE HOURS OF MORNING, AT HER BACHELORETTE ADOBE ON the outskirts of Bunta—sitting in her attached forty-meter-square roofed lanai which contained her personal gym and dojo—Osteen thought out how she and her cohorts would escape. After reps on her abs machine, before curling free weights, she considered her final challenge. To emerge as stowaways on the interstellar ark was out of the question—WCM would inspect every inch of the shuttle, and there would be no extra cryo-capsules. Three selectees would have to be eliminated. Osteen needed the others' help to make the switches seamless. Osteen accepted that aggression on board the starship-ark, ipso facto, had no place. Once boarded, the occupants of *Welkin-Alpha* communicated in M-L-M and worked together until Cryopreservation and launch. She intended to be a passenger and would conform to passivity and agreement. But not before; not during her time on Earth. *We will neutralize to create our own spots on* Welkin-Alpha.

The main problem she saw was her immediate superior, General Braun. Aside from being a first-class mathematician, he was committed and uncanny. She'd often wondered if he'd found a way to implant sight on the back of his head. She would have to use every subterfuge she knew of while maintaining an aura of strained obedience.

Osteen thought of something else. From all she understood, there was still the outside chance humans on Earth could be saved, that M-L-M could be developed in time. Especially if the Canada-Siberia war could be contained and brought back to a Conflict. If so, Braun would eventually get to the bottom of the Pompadoux case. Thus, another reason she had to escape, aside from her main reason—she'd been taken advantage of all her life, her rape being the worst of it. She would take charge of the rest of it, on *her* terms.

.................................

LATER, WORKING OUT OF HER MILITARY OFFICE, SHE RECEIVED A call from General Braun.

"I'm making you my first confidante in Canada-Siberia. Plan on working with me."

"Yes, Sir."

"I don't detect much enthusiasm."

"What about my Plan B role?"

"I need you here."

"Is there an under-message you want to convey, Sir?"

She noted his hesitation.

"Popov has made changes. Some Plan B assignments have been eliminated."

"And this relates to me how?"

"I don't need to spell this out, General Osteen. I'm sure you get the drift. You already knew you weren't traveling. I've decided there is more need for a Defense MOS here, regarding Canada-Siberia."

"Thank you for being truthful. I look forward to my new assignment, General."

Well, there it was. She hadn't expected to continue as General of Defense, Plan B—perhaps they should promote some goddamned Chaplain, but working with the General on the Canada-Siberia War would make her other plans difficult at best. *Nothing's ever easy*, she thought. Yet there was relief in knowing for sure how the situation stood. Escape was fixed in her mind.

..................................

THE NEXT EVENING, ON THE BEACH, OSTEEN MET WITH GENERAL Malone and Major Troy. Moonlight pooled and shimmered on the ocean as she led them along the strand. It was hushed, an atmosphere thick with secrets. The day's aromas had worn off, and the hovers had yet to cover the Tomini coast with mists of aromas planned for tomorrow, which accounted for the pungent odors of filth and rot.

Osteen recounted to Malone and Troy her conversation with General Braun.

"How can you plan our escape when you are right under his thumb?" Malone asked.

"I've thought about it all day. Major Troy, will you be my aide for my work with Braun on the Declared? I'll shift you to my quarters." She'd said "Major" to let Troy know a senior officer was making a request; but by phrasing it as a question, she was giving Troy respect.

"Of course. But won't we both be under his thumb?"

"It's a sound idea," Malone said. "It allows General Osteen more freedom, and with both of you working the War, you can also keep extra eyes on Braun."

"When I have to accompany the General on trips, you'll be right there, in the vortex; you'll be my eyes and ears as we further our own scheme," Osteen said to Major Troy.

"I agree," Troy said. "We'll turn a potential negative into a positive."

..................................

"I DON'T HAVE A PROBLEM WITH IT," GENERAL BRAUN ALLOWED, when contacted by Osteen the next morning. "Does she have enough math?"

"In spades," Osteen said. "She was an Academy Third, and competes regularly."

Braun knew, by her nature, Osteen would never choose a man, even if she could boss him around. Her rape in Okinawa prevented it. "Okay, then. Bring her on."

Osteen was comforted as she relayed the official news to Major Troy. Her reassignment was to be effective immediately. The General had intimated that a strong showing by Troy would clear her way to being promoted to Lieutenant Colonel. Osteen, re-invigorated, thought ahead; there was much to do.

# 33

ADJOINING THE OBELISK AUDITORIUM, THE MAIN ROOM WHERE THE WCM met in conjunction with Liftees and Tiers, four hallways led to separate labs and conference rooms where groups of people could convene and workshop ideas. By now, some Liftees had established partners. For example, under the guidance of Tier and approvals from WCM, Curie and Petitjean collaborated. Liu Hui and Krebs collaborated, as did Aasen and Bach.

The other Liftees continued to work on their own, following earlier paths they had forged. Even though Pauperito and Praeger were apprised of new developments in M-L-M, they insisted on following particular lines. They realized, under the rules of Popov, if they didn't contribute something substantial within the next week, they would be Returned. They did have one supporter, however: Wittgenstein.

Wittgenstein, gloomy with lips curving downward, looked lost, as if he'd been locked up and was looking for the man with the key. Yet he'd been brought up to speed quicker than any previous Liftee. The WCM thought they might have omitted something as they fed him all the histories from the day he'd died to the newest updates of yesterday. Wittgenstein absorbed the exabytes of information containing anthropology, astronomy, musical theory, metalinguistics, all mathematical genres, world politics, sociology, et cetera. Liftees, on receiving these data, didn't experience an expansion of the brain; the data were implanted and available when they awoke. Yet some Liftees took a while to get to the point where they could wield the information. In Wittgenstein's case, he wore new knowledge like a favorite pair of gloves. The more he learned, the more he absorbed, and the more curious he became.

Wittgenstein was a proponent of dissimilar musical scales, including twelve-tone serialism, speaking to each other, and he supported Pauperito's and Praeger's work. He worked with them on assigning sundry alphabets to all dissimilar musical scales, which corresponded to various equations he'd worked out with Toni Praeger. Wittgenstein was enamored with Aasen's unique alphabet, to be sure, but he still investigated possibilities in over five hundred languages in extant cultures. He even went so far as to have symphonies and other forms of music talk to each other using these modified musical scales based on different alphabets, which were aligned by Pauperito-Praeger-Wittgenstein mathematics.

At the moment, Wittgenstein was in his private quarters, listening to mash-up, an amalgamation of Mahler and Sibelius. When Tuan had asked why Wittgenstein preferred nineteenth- and twentieth-century classical music as opposed to other cultures, he did not hesitate.

"You must remember that my preference is from the European tradition and our seven-note scale, which at the time I was part of, and which was dominant everywhere. Yes, sinologists counter that Asian musical traditions employing their pentatonic scale were listened to by more people, but that was *their* people. The Asians didn't promulgate or spread their tradition. Perhaps if they had, my preference would be different."

Tuan, glancing around the room as they talked, appeared puzzled by a broom standing in a corner, standing in a dustpan.

"I begin each day by sweeping up my workspace," Wittgenstein said. "A clean workspace helps clear the mind and focus it. Which is why I admire Ramanujan."

Supine on his cot, dressed in Liftee uniform, praying hands placed over his lower abdomen, Wittgenstein listened to the usual discordance of sound mixed with a few unusual harmonies. He recognized dissonances he'd heard from Aasen's earlier experiments. It was the same discordance he'd also heard from Krebs.

He called Pauperito and Praeger to his quarters. When they arrived, he began to explain his experiment.

"Listen."

He restarted Mahler's Eighth Symphony with Sibelius's Fifth. Discord emanated from the walls. When the specific atonals grew from the walls, Pauperito and Praeger, with her round face and pinched nostrils, looked at him.

"There they are again," Pauperito said.

"Why do they keep showing up?" Toni Praeger asked. Her sleeves were always rolled up, and one wondered whether she hung her garments in the same fashion. Her rich blackness emphasized her smile of perfect white teeth, while her stoic elegance contributed to her presence.

"Let's overlay another piece," Wittgenstein suggested. He coded Beethoven's Third and added it. Three symphonies "mashed" with each other.

The result was harsh and frightening. "Stop," said Praeger, "the mathematics can't hold."

"We must let it stabilize," Wittgenstein said.

Pauperito paced as if he'd been whacked in the ears. "Praeger's right," he said. "We don't have that kind of mathematical scaffolding."

They shut down and discussed the dissonances for over an hour. They could not understand what the familiar discordants signified. The odds of such sound randomly occurring in any two pieces of music, under the mathematical-linguistic scales they'd used, were astronomical. Yet they'd heard those same sounds in three separate pieces of music.

Later, Wittgenstein fell asleep on his couch. He woke up around three a.m., and something made him search for Shostakovich's Fifth, which he subsequently encoded. Using updated mathematics, he overlaid the code with Beethoven's Third, the same symphony of Beethoven that he'd used earlier. Nothing resulted but the usual mish-mash and a few peculiar harmonies he hadn't heard before. He was about to turn everything off and go to bed when the same atonalities as before grew from the walls. However, rather than what he heard, what bothered Wittgenstein was that *something* had made him search and select Shostakovich's Fifth. But he didn't know what.

THE NEXT MORNING, INSTEAD OF PLUNGING INTO HIS WORK, WITTgenstein went to other groups and watched what they were doing. To help cross-pollinate, any Liftee could consult with any other, but time was precious and meeting requests were scheduled by aides in Third Tier. If Third-Tier members thought the request would be a distraction to overall progress, they would refuse it; if the Liftee persisted, Tier would attempt a simulation of expected output, and get approval from Second Tier. But oftentimes, like a kibitzer in chess, a Liftee would take a break from isolated work and observe others.

Wittgenstein watched Pauperito and Praeger pull out equations from Venn common, which had been further overlaid with alphabets, musical scales, scale-step enrichments, and atonalities. The closest tie between mathematics and music was patterns. They studied the pure and gripping soundscapes Ramanujan had created with his overlays and listened for patterns.

Praeger said, "This set is from differentials corresponding to B-minor twelve-tone, aligned with Aasen's new alphabet. And this set is from integrals of A-minor twelve-tone, same alphabet. Why is this particular combinatorial overlay producing harmony and no dissonance?"

"Harmony, as you and I understand it," Wittgenstein interjected, "becomes enhanced by new musical grammars as *you* interpret them. To sapient aliens or to any different species, our so-called *harmony* supported with your grammars could be chaotic rubbish."

Praeger, for the moment, ignored him. Pauperito stood, thinking. "I don't think anything—harmonic sound, or otherwise—is rubbish," Pauperito said. "It's some type of code; and instead of looking for harmonies or dissonances, we should be looking for unique code."

"Code," Wittgenstein echoed. "Atonals make a funny type of code. But if you're right, isn't that the place where we can find more code?"

"I think we still need to search for structure and harmony," Praeger said. "We've played with scales built from logarithmic structures, created tonal scales based on primes, et cetera, and found nothing useful, but we must still seek structure with harmony. I'm convinced we will find this by creating sophisticated, more meaningful musical equations."

Wittgenstein, perturbed, went to observe Bromsky, who in a separated room was lecturing Krebs and Aasen. Wittgenstein sat down in back and heard the great twenty-first-century linguist mention something about the Kabbalah and segue into his own classification of formal languages. "Kabbalah" rushed into Wittgenstein's brain like a burst dam. It brought his mind to Helena Kosovsky, his former pupil and, later, unofficial partner. She had done her best work, she claimed, by refitting the Kabbalah.

Over the next thirty-six hours, Wittgenstein was at a loss in his work and felt the direction taken by the WCM and Liftees was bent and untrue. When he could no longer stand the confusion around him and his own mounting frustration, he went straight to Popov's quarters without even notifying her office.

# 34

OVER THE NEXT THREE DAYS, THE MONSOONS TOOK OVER. EACH afternoon, a forty-minute storm with powerful shifting winds and slanting downpours became an enforced siesta for the minions and commoners. Huddled under their carts, empty baskets, or corrugated tin, they would cringe until it was over. The lucky few who were inside some type of edifice watched as the afternoon storms bent palm trees and scattered rubbish. But this was different. Weather patterns had shown anomalies, and although ocean warming and subsequent ocean rising had been stopped, scientists reported that the damage done hundreds of years ago continued to produce aftereffects.

In Tomini Bay, several miles away from shore, the storms were violent. The obelisk twisted one way, then the other, and the turns became quicker. The occupants living below sea level claimed they smelled the extra oil and grease jetted into the bearings. On the top floors, one could hear the Kevlar-enhanced beams bear new stresses as I-bars and T-bars torqued and flexed. The chopped-up bay waves accumulated and built. The rain and gusts became incessant.

And Helena Kosovsky was rebirthed.

.................................

HELENA KOSOVSKY'S BRILLIANCE APPEARED INDISPUTABLE, AND it was gallant of Wittgenstein to alert the WCM of her work in combining mathematics, music, and metalinguistics. At first, WCM thought Wittgenstein had been in love with her, and this was why he'd requested she be Lifted. But when he suggested that Helena Kosovsky replace him, the WCM began to pay attention.

The problem was, nothing written or recorded could be found, and nobody seemed to know anything about her. It was as if she had never existed. Wittgenstein insisted that was the case because of her work, which elevated Hebrew, Chaldean, and Slavic languages. He claimed her work had attracted the attention of Nazi sympathizers in the late 1930s, offering that she'd been arrested and sent to Dachau. Wittgenstein said that all of her writings, workbooks, and notes had been confiscated and burned with other Jewish thought and achievements. Despite it all, her insights, consistency of method, and dogged work habits were God-given.

"We need her here now," Wittgenstein said.

"How did you meet her?" Popov asked.

Wittgenstein chuckled. "I'd taught grade school in the countryside, and she was one of my pupils. She didn't come to school often—she had to help her extended family who worked as boarders on a farm. She was advanced but appeared sickly; I think she came to school to rest. She often fell asleep at her desk, and I didn't disturb her."

He rubbed his cheek. "I met her again some years later when I revisited the area. She reached out to me, actually. I didn't recognize her behind her glasses and a scarf, still working on her family's farm. She'd matured, as had her conversation. Her grasp of language was extraordinary. It turned out she'd read most tomes in the nearest library and had become fluent in eight languages. At the time, she couldn't have been more than seventeen.

"I offered to let her help me with my *Praxis*." He looked at Popov. "At first, I thought she might assist me; help organize my thoughts. But . . ." Wittgenstein became quiet. "Soon she began to correct my mistakes—she reorganized my logic and discovered mistakes I didn't know I'd made. She did this in ways that were foreign to me; she'd created new mathematics I'd thought at the time was faulty, but now it appears I had misunderstood. It's true, she rewrote most of my *Praxis*, but she didn't seem to care that I took all the credit.

"Her leaps of brilliance began to frighten me. I couldn't measure up. I became unstable and went to Norway. When I found out she'd been arrested—her cousin wrote to me—when I found out she'd been exposed, all her work destroyed . . . I've never been the same since." Wittgenstein coughed, apologized. "You must Lift her. You can send me back. Kosovsky will be my lasting legacy. She always has been, and always will be."

So, they did. She was Lifted out of Dachau on November 11, 1942, and Replaced Wittgenstein.

It took much longer to bring her up to speed. To Popov, this was a sign of her true gifts. Popov didn't like to make the comparison, but she reasoned that whereas animals developed as soon as they were born—standing, teetering, and shuffling—humans remained incubated as if still in the womb—vulnerable and feeble. They needed extra time, and in the case of Helena Kosovsky, her immense gifts required special incubation and protection. Popov treated her like her own child and believed from the first—"woman's intuition"—she'd said, that Kosovsky was special.

It was true. Although disappointed to not see her friend and partner Wittgenstein, she divined her real purpose—they were struggling to find a breakthrough, they were running out of time, they needed direction. At once she put all distractions aside and plunged into her work.

She had one admitted vice: the need of tobacco.

"With respect," Popov said, "haven't you been weaned of it? Dachau and all?" They were in Popov's office.

"No. And the questions are proper. I missed tobacco dreadfully, and I always did my best work with it."

"You are not the only Liftee who has asked about this. I cannot meet your need. Our rules are strict and enforced in this matter."

Popov saw the nicotine stain on her left index finger. "Aren't you right-handed?"

"I smoked using my left, while I wrote using my right."

Popov sighed and thought. *I could give her scented denims, they don't absorb . . . but others will want different uniforms.*

"We will make this our little secret. I will have tobacco delivered to you for use at your personal quarters only. You must disguise your breath before coming here, wear special laundered uniforms delivered to you each morning, and wash your hair every day. Under no circumstances will you use tobacco, in any form, on these premises or in public. Are we clear?"

"Perfectly. Thank you."

Popov nodded. "Make sure you don't breathe a word of this to anyone, especially Ramanujan."

..................................

WITHIN TWO WEEKS, KOSOVSKY HAD ACCUMULATED, ABSORBED, and prioritized the latest thought and progress of WCM. It was then that Popov, first, and others later, recognized her true genius, her ability to absorb mountainous collections of mathematical information across multiple fields and organize it. Further, the mental act of doing that cleared her mind and energized her thoughts in new directions. Her method was rigid and inviolate: she absorbed and organized during the day; at night she did her own work. Everyone wondered when she slept.

As a result of her efforts, she found the mother-lode code for atonality. She hadn't broken the code, but showed everyone how she thought it could be done—"start with alphabetic-numeric math pangrams," she'd said—and gave the paths to be taken. Popov, Reed, Gunderson, and the Liftees Pauperito and Bach all shouted approvals. "Yes. Why hadn't we seen that?" Liu Hui stood and had almost straightened his spine. Popov remembered his words: "My friends, this is the direction I'd turned to in my lost *Analects*."

"Much remains to be done," Kosovsky cautioned. "The musical keys change randomly—you will need to refigure."

Popov looked to Kosovsky, puzzled. "Sounds like we still need your guidance," she said.

Thus it was a shock to all when the next day, after a month of collaboration, Helena Kosovsky requested to be Returned.

Popov leaned over her desk, the better to reach Kosovsky's eyes with her own. "You can't leave us now. Humanity needs you."

"My work is done here," Kosovsky said.

"Helena. Helena, please. Why would you want to leave here and go back to a concentration camp?"

"I'm unable to explain it. It's time for me to leave."

"You can confide in me. Has something happened I'm not aware of?"

"No. As I say, I'm unable to explain it. My work is finished here."

"The newest simulations have put us ahead of schedule, thanks to you. Humanity may be saved after all, but it doesn't mean *we* are finished."

"Right. I've given Pauperito algorithms to redirect atonal phonemes." Kosovsky sat rigidly. Her mind was made up.

Popov tried silence, but gave up. "I will honor your request. May we delay for a quick celebration this evening?"

"Good of you. But I best be going."

Popov winced. She wanted to probe further. "As you wish," Popov said as she tapped her special glasses and made the arrangements.

"Regulations require me to meet with WCM senior staff before conducting an actual Return. No need to worry, however; your request will be honored." Popov removed her glasses and wiped her eyes with a tissue. She blew her nose, feeling like her own child was abandoning her.

"I am sorry, Ms. Popov. Please forgive me."

"Certainly. Helena, on behalf of everyone here, and on . . . for . . ."

Popov came around her desk; Kosovsky stood, and they hugged.

"Helena, thank you."

"And thank you. You are doing a fine job."

"I need more like you, Helena. Helena, where are the other brave and brilliant women from your time?"

"They remain unnoticed. I'm not sure who they are. Many are accomplished hidden gems who have chosen not to make an issue of their plight. However, this is not all man's fault. True, it is much more difficult for women in my era to be noticed. But we women could have bonded more and come farther. Yes, we should have."

"Our Tiers are still male-dominant, but we're about thirty-eight percent and improving," Popov said.

"You will make it; and you, Chair Popov, will finish Mathe-Lingua-Musica. It will come down to neuro-linguistic programs."

"Is there anything else you can offer me?"

"I believe you should focus on a modulus. Modules of prosody and fluxion, I think. Think of poetry and how the poets build structure to deliver more than the sum of its parts. It's the age-old problem of finding the hidden structure in a language. And knowing what to discard."

.................................

WHEN POPOV ANNOUNCED TO THE WCM KOSOVSKY'S REQUEST FOR Return, there were mixed feelings and one clear protest. Not a protest that she would be Returned—everyone agreed to support her wish, according to the proclamation enacted by Popov. But why back to Dachau? It was Popov, herself, who protested the location and countered all arguments.

"I'm aware," Popov said, "of the mistake made with Hitler, but that was a much larger and more far-reaching issue we'd disturbed. This is a simple one-person humane decision."

"We must not take the chance," Reed said. "You already refused da Vinci when he begged you for a mere extra twenty-four hours to make a minor change which would have allowed him to avoid a simple mistake. Why would you take a chance now? Why risk another asteroid slamming into Earth?"

Popov said nothing.

Knowing how the decision would fall, Reed raised his hand. "Let's take a vote."

Popov said, "I can't believe Returning Helena after Victory in Europe (VE) Day World War II will cause any type of commotion in present time."

"Let's remember," De Costa said, "Ms. Kosovsky requested to Return. This was her idea."

"I don't like this dilemma either," Tuan said. "We are taking a risk if we don't Return her properly, but I support the decision to try and save her."

"If we are going to mess with the time frame, shouldn't we consider going back earlier to save her former papers that were destroyed?" Boucher asked.

Popov considered the trilemma—return her to precise retrieval time, send her later, or send her back before Dachau.

"Mr. Boucher, if we Return her to before Dachau, we take a large risk, plus she may still die a cruel and inhumane death. Let's Return Helena to Dachau the day the camp is liberated."

After her remark, Popov called a vote. Seven voted for Kosovsky's return on the same day and time she'd been Lifted. Only Tuan had sided with Popov.

"I'm glad that's been resolved," said Reed.

"I veto," Popov said.

Her veto was followed by more protests. Reed rolled back his chair, slamming the wall, and stormed out. Even Tuan shook her head, looking like she wanted to change her vote. It wouldn't have mattered. Resolute, Popov stared at the table in front of her and waited until they all departed. Tuan was the last to leave. She stood at the door, looking at Popov, who was still staring at the table in front of her. Tuan started to say something, went through the doorway, and closed the door.

A last thought occurred to Popov. The time traveler selected by Time Travel Control was to leave in one hour to Return Kosovsky and Lift Pemberton, a recent biophysicist and former musical prodigy, who was next in line on the Liftee list maintained by First Tier. She rushed to Time Travel Control on a lower level to make the request in person.

"Abort Pemberton," she ordered. "Do I make myself clear? Return Kosovsky to the changed time as instructed. Return without Pemberton."

She waited right where she was, comforted by the hope that her idea of aborting Pemberton would neutralize—at least mute—any possible retribution.

De Costa decided to investigate simulations regarding Kosovsky. From all he could intuit, in normal time she didn't survive Dachau. But he couldn't get a mathematical foothold if she were to be Returned on the day Dachau was liberated, per Popov's instructions. He ended simulations. Of course, De Costa had no idea that if she was Returned later, at the new time insisted upon by Popov, Kosovsky would outsmart a woman who was studying medicine with the result that this woman would not gain a position of her first choice in Europe, but a lower position in a country across the Atlantic, with the added result that Jonas Salk, the curer of polio, would have never existed.

Popov allowed herself to relax a constricted lower abdomen when within the next hour the traveler Returned without Pemberton, and when Popov was convinced that her instructions had been carried out as ordered.

..................................

THAT NIGHT, WHILE PLAYING A PIECE BY HANDEL ON HER HARP, with hope circulating in her heart, she felt a tremor grow to vibrations. She wondered if it might be the other experimental music that she'd reduced in volume but forgotten to mute from the walls. At once she was thrown to the floor, her harp on top of her. If Popov had been allowed to look outside, she would have witnessed an impossible tsunami, from out of nowhere, washing up the sides of the obelisk.

# 35

POPOV CAME TO AND CRAWLED FROM UNDER HER HARP. SHE WAS bruised and felt wretched—not from bruises, but from the tumbles in her gut. *No*, she thought, *this has to be an ugly coincidence.*

The obelisk withstood the tsunami. But a tsunami without an earthquake? It was precisely for that reason that engineers had insisted on Tomini Bay: it lay protected, alee from the ocean. When a third of the Maldives had been covered over by water two hundred years before, planners had fixed these obelisks for long-term. Yet the massive wave roared inland and destroyed everything in its path. The roaring tsunami *had* to be the result of an earthquake, Popov thought. She checked a different TweetV channel. Not the slightest tremor had been recorded. Popov watched live TweetV pictures of the devastation and projected them onto the ceiling, as she lay prone to be treated by Tele-medicine. "Take the pills prescribed and remain at rest for at least twenty minutes," the voice from her glasses said. Popov stood up after twelve when she could no longer stand seeing the massive destruction videoed by solar drones. "The tragedy occurred minutes ago when many beachside inhabitants were asleep. Deaths are estimated to be close to a million," the reporter said.

There was more bad news.

"Yes, General Braun."

"I trust you are okay. Nothing happened here on my side."

"I am." Popov rubbed her reddened arm and looked at bandaged fingers.

"Chair Popov, there was another tsunami, in the Atlantic, which slammed into the USA. Miami, Florida."

Popov stifled a wail. With Olympian restraint, she managed to ask "At what time?"

"The exact same time as this one. Eleven-forty p.m., our time."

.................................

POPOV SAT ALONE IN HER OFFICE AS SHE AWAITED HER COLleagues for an emergency meeting. Boucher had concussed his head and couldn't attend.

Reed—*Well, I hope you're satisfied*—declined.

"Dr. Reed, I want you at this meeting. I order it."

*I've broken my foot; I'm not up to it.*

"Then come on crutches!"

Popov opted to have the meeting in her office to show she was in charge. She didn't feel in charge at the moment, but she prepared her thoughts, her demeanor. She looked at the conference table where they would sit and where her electronics had already been placed at one end. She would not fortify herself with any pills, just a cup of Assam tea with pinches of oxtail and two filtered grains of stable amyl nitrite. At the last minute, she secreted a jujube under her tongue and let it dissolve.

.................................

"WELL, WHAT DO YOU HAVE TO SAY FOR YOURSELF?" REED INquired.

Popov noticed he hadn't brought crutches and walked with a mere limp. *He always looks entitled, because he's the first of us to be born on the moon*, she figured.

"Nothing I say about the decision I made yesterday is going to change anything that happened last night. As a mathematician, I would expect you to know that, Mr. Reed."

"Your tone surprises me and is offensive," Reed said.

Popov looked at him like she would a filthy sock. *You disgust me.* "Enough of your gloat rage. If you are looking for me to wallow in pity and ask for your personal forgiveness, Mr. Reed, I won't do it."

She turned to the others. "I've ordered Time Travel Control to retrieve Helena Kosovsky and Return her to original." Reed burned her a look. Tuan brushed something from her sleeve. The others said nothing. "We have work to do. Let's get down to business."

She took a swallow of tea and waited ten seconds. "I didn't Lift Pemberton. I decided not to, hoping it might neutralize or mute any retribution. I was wrong."

Reed continued to glare at her.

She continued: "We have fixed the Kosovsky situation."

"'We,'" said Reed under his breath.

Popov ignored the aside.

"Is Pemberton coming back?" Gunderson asked.

"No. Time Travel Control is awaiting instruction; the traveler is in suspension."

"This has gone on far enough," Reed said. He looked to Tuan and several others. "I propose a recess. I want to talk with my colleagues, alone."

"Mr. Reed. Look at me and listen to me. If you want to try to impeach me, you will do so following procedure." Reed got half a word out—"Spare me your philippic, Mr. Reed. Either shut up, or excuse yourself from this community and go somewhere else."

Anand looked at Reed. "Sir," he said, "this is not the time for private discussion. Chair Popov is correct, there are procedures to follow."

"I have to agree," Tuan said. She looked at Popov. "Why do we not Lift Pemberton?"

"That's what I want to discuss. First, let me say I have requested another be assigned to Pemberton's place. Second, I've studied this most of the night: we do not need Pemberton at this particular juncture. We'll need him later. Third, as a courtesy to all of you," she looked at Reed, "I wanted to explain why I have done this."

"So, you . . . it's going to change without our input?" De Costa said.

Popov felt trapped. "'A courtesy,'" Reed snapped.

"Let's settle down," Gunderson said. "Proceed, Chair Popov."

Popov thought about the saying her father had placed under the glass top of his work desk: *I can't give you the formula for success, but I can give you the formula for failure: Try to please everybody.*

"In my last meeting with Helena, I was convinced that we have enough mathematics to decode and to complete M-L-M. We can do it thanks to the path she's given us."

She swallowed some tea while Reed made a puerile show of putting his hands over his face. She felt like telling him to put his head down on the table and disappear.

"It comes down to this," Popov said. "Our starship preparation is critical and must be done on time."

Tuan said, "You are intimating that we need someone who can best find the way to prepare each and every human. In time."

"Yes," Popov said.

"We discussed this at preselection, in the basement," Tuan continued. "This same Liftee has to confirm all selected travelers are maximized with M-L-M."

"Exactly. The person I've selected is not only a skilled physician, but a first-class administrator."

"Elyssus Bogoljubov," Anand said.

"He had been at the top of my list, but I changed it. Jonas Salk, the discoverer of the polio vaccine, is the best person for the task in my opinion."

There was surprise and consternation. "You've made a total sham of this," Reed hollered. He stood up and shook his finger at Popov. "And, yes—"

"Spare me your peroration, Mr. Reed."

"I'm leaving to protest, and I intend to file for your impeachment."

Having put his quietus on the debate, Popov noticed he stormed out without the slightest gimp.

The next morning, at the WCM briefing—Popov had decided not to change timing or routines, despite the uproarious effects of the tsunamis, the droog riots, and associated problems—she announced that she had replaced Reed. All eyes turned to the empty chair, including Boucher's—one black and blue, below his bandaged head.

"I feel Joiacham has become hostile, and he will impede our progress. I summoned him last night, and I regret to say we could not come to agreement. I have removed him."

"Isn't there a bylaw for that, before formal impeachment?" Tuan asked.

"No. There isn't. And since there is no guidance in the matter, I acted on my own and have submitted a new bylaw." She let that sink in while trying to keep her legs from shaking. "I lauded Joiacham for his valuable time and contributions."

"Where is he now?" De Costa asked.

"Mr. Reed is being detained. I do not feel satisfied, which may surprise some of you. He is a talented individual, and I shall always regret that I was unsuccessful in appeasing him."

Popov stood and walked to the sideboard for more tea. She took her time and, after filling her cup, walked to the door with deliberate poise and opened it.

"Please come in, Thaddeus. Fellow colleagues, it gives me great pleasure to re-introduce you to Thaddeus Smith, who is, *was*," she smiled at the tall Black man, "next in line after Pemberton."

Everyone at WCM knew the distinguished graduate of Howard University and Oxford, who was considered the leading expert in the Theory of Categories, Sets, and related mathematics. Popov was delighted to see how warmly Thaddeus was welcomed. At the conclusion of the meeting, she noticed looks darting to her and, with discretion, said, "Thaddeus, thank you for joining us this morning. I'll see you, as planned, this afternoon." Popov sat back down after he left, as did the others.

Popov scrolled her eyes over the Board members' faces. She sipped her tea as the silence thickened. "What is on your minds?" Popov asked. She placed the teacup in front of her.

"You should know," Tuan said, looking at Popov. "Reed's filing for impeachment has been granted by judiciary. He's called us to meet with him at his quarters this afternoon."

# 36

GENERAL BRAUN SAT IN HIS OFFICE, LOOKING DISHEVELED. HE hadn't shaved for three days and was feeling the effects of juggling too many balls with too little sleep. The Canadian-Siberian War was turning ugly; Canada was on the verge of ignoring nuclear Regs. Braun had been down the same road before, eleven years ago, in the Turkey-Greece War. Neither side would conform to Regs, and both nations had had to be neutralized per orders from the WCM. The problem here was the vast expanse of the areas and the critical oil and mineral deposits vital to the rest of the world. Canada and Siberia were both aware of this, and Canada was threatening the use of extra nukes, calculating that it wouldn't be neutralized.

Another ball to be juggled was the aftermath of the two tsunamis. The tsunami damage was catastrophic, with deaths in Miami over 800,000. Looting and rioting were becoming unmanageable for the General and his commanders. Ordinary criminals in neighboring areas where the damage had been sustainable joined the droogs, which served to offset droogs killed in the tsunamis. The General was shocked that the droogs in Miami were as organized as the droogs in Indonesia, which confirmed his nightmare that expanded droog cells had proliferated—deceptively and independently—worldwide. This combined force rushed into damaged zones to loot, threaten, and convert young people to their cause. Victims of lost homes from both oceans—enraged and droog-led—looted and killed indiscriminately. Fitter droogs moved up in their chain of command, while everyone ignored the law. Reports from Braun's commanders confirmed droog-coordinated guerilla attacks—stick and run—occurring around the clock everywhere. The result was that Braun's military couldn't tell the innocent victims from the droogs—everyone was a lawbreaker. The tsunamis had provided the droogs with an open season.

The third ball was Starship *Welkin-Alpha*—Plan B, and this pissed off the General most of all. No one saw Plan B coming. Plan A could have been the world's final authority. "But, no," the WCM said, "it is a new optimum language the world needs, a language of universal calm, deliberation, wisdom."

"Bullshit!" the General hollered to himself.

In this frame of mind, he looked up at his senior aide standing in his office doorway.

"What is it?" Braun growled.

"Sir, Chair Popov's come to see you."

Braun looked at him.

"She came unannounced."

The General buttoned the top button of his shirt, frowned as he felt whiskers, put on his coat of medals, and shuffled a few items on his desk. He marched to the sitting room, aware of the chain of command—he reported to Popov.

Braun saw at once Popov was distraught. Her arm was bruised and swollen; her hand was bandaged. "Chair Popov. Please, come with me."

They settled in his office. He served her a shot of brandy and waited.

"General, I've made a terrible miscalculation, and I've come to you for counsel."

Braun didn't meet her eye. "The tsunamis."

"I screwed up."

General Braun surprised himself by not feeling puffed up that she would expose herself to him and ask for his counsel. Instead, he felt a tinge of terror. *When society fails,* he thought to himself, *when everyone is vulnerable, the world veers toward collapse, for the rudder on a great ship is busted.*

When she was through explaining her concerns, the consequence of her colossal mistake, she told General Braun how she'd like to contain the fallout, and asked for advice. The General remained thoughtful out of respect, and a touch of wisdom began to seep into him. His previous thoughts, before her visit, had been rash. *No,* he thought, *she is on the right side of humanity.*

"As much as I admire your truthfulness, Chair Popov, I can't counsel you to reveal your miscalculation to everyone. You will lay yourself wide open to all kinds of attacks. No. I wouldn't do it."

"I need to purge myself of this, General."

"You have. We all make mistakes. You've confided in me, and I will support you."

"I shall think about it. This talk with you has helped me to understand my intentions better. I appreciate your listening to me."

When Popov left his office, General Braun considered the possible outcomes of her admission. Although she was clueless in military affairs, he was a military man, and he would see that his commander in chief was protected. That Popov had done wrong, he accepted—a grave mistake—but she had owned up. That meant a lot to the General. He contacted his naval commander.

"Have you replaced the submersible drone damaged by the tsunami at Government side? Good. I want you to add two more submersibles, one to follow at 180 degrees, the other to patrol in an expanded circle, in the opposite direction. And do the same here. Report back when all drones are in place."

Braun rubbed his eyes. He looked through office blinds at the track behind him. From experience, he knew his tiredness was mental, so he changed his clothes and charged out onto his private track. He was outside running for thirty-five minutes and revisited his desk after taking a cold-hot-cold shower. Feeling refreshed, and wearing a fresh set of battle fatigues, he poured himself an iced tea.

"Bring me General Osteen," he told his aide.

"Good afternoon, General," Osteen said as she walked in, also in battle fatigues. A subordinate officer would salute their superior when summoned to a meeting, but his top commanders were also four-star generals, and Braun had relaxed the courtesy.

After General Osteen's update, Braun got down to business.

"General Osteen, in view of the runaway escalation in Canada-Siberia, and due to the continuing riotous aftermath of the tsunamis, I'm placing you, for now, in charge of Plan B. I don't like moving away from it, but I need the brief separation to stabilize other crises. I leave at noon tomorrow for Siberia; the day after, I go to USA-Florida. My aides will update you on Plan B. I'll make myself available as much as I can. Do you have any questions, General?"

"No, Sir. It's my honor to serve you, General."

# 37

"EXCELLENT!" BOTH TWINS SAID AT ONCE.

A representative from each of the ten largest cells in a twenty-square-kilometer area sat in front of the droog twins in Slum-town.

"We will keep this bomb here for safekeeping," the other twin said.

"How long?" the rep from Cinder-Town asked. She'd brought and unpacked the nuke seconds ago.

"Until we are absolutely ready. Until all cells are synced, to power through to gain more territory, arms, and recruits. We have suffered some organizational damage but are using the tsunami tragedy to our advantage. And with this"—she pointed to the nuke, which could fit in a bowling-ball bag—"we will blindside them more than any tsunami."

Both twins stood and held hands above their heads, which was a signal for all to stand and join hands.

The twins, as if in stereo, said, "Our mission, our goals, are on the horizon. We won't have to wait much longer."

.................................

CHAIRPERSON JUANITA COLLEEN POPOV ARRANGED A *PRIORITY one* meeting for the following morning. The turbulence within WCM, the tsunamis and subsequent riots, the wars, and the newest simulations revealing humankind being further behind in its quest for saving itself had upset and distracted everyone. Attentions were scattered; her charges had lost focus. She was responsible.

Seated before her in the auditorium were the entire First, Second, and Third Tiers, the WCM, the current slate of Liftees, special administrators, and General Braun. Popov looked game and had managed to get a satisfactory night's sleep, but she hoped she could camouflage her emotional angst.

"Good morning, everyone. This meeting is for us and for the benefit of everyone on our world. This isn't the time to be covert. I will share with you what I know. Following my remarks, I'll be glad to field questions."

Popov took a sip of lemon water. "Our world is sick. What began as pandemic terror has ripened into an uncontrollable virus. A virus of violence. We are in the throes of a terrible and terminating disease caused by animosity and cultural hatreds. We humans are the culprits and always have been. There are eleven billion humans on our planet, but there is little humanity. The newest simulation before me, completed twenty minutes ago, reveals we have a less than thirty-percent chance of survival as a species.

Popov took another sip of water for what was coming next. She looked several members of the audience in the eye, including General Braun. "I know your first questions. Did WCM err? Were the tsunamis caused by a misjudgment from me? Have the tsunamis contributed to the dire simulation I shared with you?" Popov hesitated. "Yes, to the first question. Yes, to the second. Most likely, yes, to the third." She let the murmurs settle.

"Let's reground. We all see the need of creating the optimum language for our species—it's so everyone can communicate and elevate understanding. Our mathematics, our calculations, in the creation of this optimum lingua franca always point to, or circle back to, musical algorithms and patterns. And when we listen to some of these patterns intermixed with linguistics, our species experiences undeniable calming effects. In summary, mathematics is to provide the scaffolding for M-L-M. Mathematics will combine music and metalinguistics."

Popov reached into the lectern for an aqua tissue to moisten her lips. She wore a stoat wrap and took it off; an aide went up to retrieve it. A harp dangled from her necklace, and miniature harps dangled from her bracelet. She was dressed in a beige pantsuit and blended in with everyone except the general who remained in uniform.

"Everybody you see here is entrusted with the task of saving our species and civilized world before we are sucked into that black hole of violence and oblivion. Most of you know about Plan A, which was to design an off-planet Defense system to keep peace on our world. No army on Earth, in its present stage, could defend against it. Many of us, including me, had doubts it would be effective for long. The point is moot; our mathematics and our simulations tell us we don't have the time to complete that plan."

A few people looked at General Braun, who said nothing. He sat in battle fatigues, a frown building on his forehead, with each hand clamped to the side of his chair.

"If we did anything right, we had designed and have built a multi-generation starship, an interstellar 'ark,' to save some of our species should we fail here on Earth. Much of this starship relies on modules already built and tested by our engineers. Starship *Welkin-Alpha* is our Plan B, our backup for saving enough of our species to enable humanity to reproduce elsewhere. Maybe in our hearts we had known Plan B was coming. We may or may not save our species and our civilization here on Earth, but three thousand humans will travel to Kepler-1649c, where transmission spectroscopy has confirmed water, air, clear skies, and abiding temps. This ship will be ready in time. And even if we beat the odds here on Earth, which we will try with all our efforts to do, our ark will still make its journey to a new world."

Popov stopped talking and looked at everyone.

"Now, here is what I need to tell you. Our progress in developing and refining M-L-M is at a standstill. We have made discoveries, we see directions to pursue, we know what the end result must be, but we can't find or agree on the next best steps to reach the goal. And I think I know why. We, including me, have lost our focus." She took a breath and came out from behind the lectern. She came as close as possible to the sixty-odd people in attendance, near enough for many to see the tiny microphone pinned to her chest. "If we are to create this language, we need everyone's absolute focus. We don't need gossip, we don't need hidden agendas, we don't need accusations and the pointing of fingers. We need your best work, now. Your diligence, your focus, today. To save ourselves as well as to seed us in a new star system.

"Okay, I'll try to answer your questions."

"Kopaneau from Third Tier, here. Will you or someone warn us if we reach singularity, if we run out of time?"

"No. You must give of yourself to the last. Can you tell me why?"

"There is always the chance we'll beat the odds," Kopaneau said.

Popov, for the first time, smiled. "Exactly."

A woman from Second Tier next asked, "Will some of us making the journey be accepted by lottery?"

"No. Everyone is preselected."

The woman followed up her initial question by asking, "Is the selection process complete?"

"I'm not here to discuss that, but I will tell you the selections are being finalized."

There were some murmurs and shaking of heads.

"I see Mr. Magnuson of First Tier," Popov said.

"You say progress is at a standstill. Where exactly are we? Can you elaborate?"

"I'll try. With the help of electronics, we can think music telepathically. We have never been able to do that with conversational language. It seems that because we have to enunciate, to articulate, to use our mouth, tongue, lips, and vocal cords, we deny telepathic word, except, to some extent, when we have journeyed back in time. But here in present time, just as when we play an instrument and we cannot telepathically transmit that sound right then, when we utter words, we can't telepathically transmit on the spot. You ask why can't we think words later, telepathically, as we do music? We don't know. Despite efforts for years, we can't. Our main challenge is to develop M-L-M suitable for everyone, or at least the mathematical scaffolding which can be adapted for the largest blocs of people and to prepare this foundation for every human in time. Right now, we don't have this complete language; what's more, we are not sure of the best way to teach it or to impart it to the rest of us. Our plan is to take the best language we arrive at by a specific date, so we have time to disseminate it worldwide."

Jonas Salk stood. He was never without glasses and had requested a second pair. After his first day, he'd contacted Popov, requesting a white lab coat, saying he simply couldn't work without one.

"I'm the new guy on the block, and I'd promised myself to stay quiet, but I can't. We don't have the time to teach anyone this language. Our polyglots and linguists could learn it in time and teach the rest of us in an ideal situation, but not while the selected are frozen and not while the rest of us battle for survival here on Earth. Even if the rest of us who remain here did learn and communicate in M-L-M, it would be too late. No. We must inculcate by graphene biochips in the brain, or find a different way of disseminating the language. I will throw myself at this," he said, and sat back down, removing a pen and notebook from his lab coat.

A woman in the Second Tier raised her hand and waved it back and forth until she was recognized. She looked harsh, and her voice matched her looks. "I could focus on my work, if I knew I'd been selected," she said. "If I don't know, how can I focus?"

"I feel the same way," announced a man in Third Tier.

At this point, Popov watched Anand and Gunderson rise from their seats. She swallowed in consternation and anger as everyone else in WCM stood up. Tuan spoke: "As do we," she said to Popov.

Popov, at a loss for words, managed to say, "Right now, this second, I could use our new language." She hoped for a few smiles. There were none.

Salk offered, "I remember what Karl Popper said: 'In our infinite ignorance, we are all equals.'"

"I will not cast a stone," Popov said.

General Braun shot up and strode in front of the WCM like a pissed-off attorney would approach a defiant witness. He scrutinized the WCM and snickered. "So, these confreres seated before us are the best we have to govern our planet. Here's my question: If you are not selected, would you focus then?"

"General, please," Popov said, "sit back down. I've put myself in a corner; I'll deal with it."

It took a while for the General to sit, but he did.

"I hadn't thought this through," Popov said. "I didn't realize." She pursed her lips. "I shall offer you this. I will not be taking the journey; I've removed myself." The audience murmured.

"It is right that some of us stay and attempt to govern our world as long as possible. All of us here can't expect to leave it. I agree you have the right to know who will remain. If I'm making a mistake in telling you, I hold myself accountable."

General Braun stood up again. "Chair Popov," he said.

"It's okay, General. Please." She turned to her WCM colleagues. "Our esteemed Liftees know they will be Returned. General Braun already knows he is not going on the journey. Nobody in our military will make this journey. I will not announce or display the names of anybody not here in this room. For the rest of you here with me this morning, I will inform each of you at four p.m. this afternoon. This meeting is adjourned. Thank you."

General Braun walked up to Popov as the others exited.

"When did you remove yourself?" he whispered.

"When I left your office yesterday morning. And I re-confirmed it to myself three minutes ago."

General Braun removed his hat and nodded. "You needn't have done that."

"I believe I had to, General. Besides, I've always done my best work when the odds were stacked against me."

"I regret I have further news making those odds worse: Canada has gone renegade; Siberia will follow."

# 38

CHARLES, ANDRICA, AND SEVERAL OF THEIR ACADEMY FRIENDS listened to and watched "Rona," the new jazz sensation whose burst from the Jakarta slums was unprecedented. With her attitude-spiked-afro, she looked ready to change the world. Half of the mathetorium had been converted to a semicircular stage, and the facing half comprised a seat-filled floor and three balconies of cheering students. By custom, the leading mathematicians and winners of prizes and contests sat in first balcony. There wasn't confusion or annoyance about this, as everyone was aware of the rankings, and premier math minds were accorded the respect and esteem of old-time professional athletes. Exceptions were made for guests of first balcony. Thus Andrica, who belonged in second balcony, sat with Charles as his guest at the matinee.

"I heard she had trouble with calculus and matrices," Andrica said of Rona into Charles's ear.

The chocolate-skinned Rona took up a cello. At all of seventeen, molded into a body-tight red satin mini-dress, she hugged the instrument and clamped her legs around the bottom of it. With soul and passion, she closed her eyes and belted out her signature piece, a love song, Sumatran in nature, which had been her first mega-hit. She had prerecorded tabla rhythms as backup, and, with mature bow artistry on the instrument, she brought the entire mathetorium to silence. Her left hand on occasion plucked and strummed strings, but she pressed and vibrated her fingers, while with her right hand she drew the bow and, by unique twisting motions with it, was able to draw loss and melancholy, as well as tinges of joy and hope.

Charles watched her hug the instrument closer and ply her left fingers. "I wish I was her cello," Charles whispered aloud, drawing nods and chuckles from two boys in front of them.

Andrica's foot banged Charles's shin, but as he glanced at her he noticed Andrica was taken, enraptured. Seconds later, they held hands and leaned back in their seats. Both of them, as if on cue, squeezed and un-squeezed their hands during expressive passages as Rona sang and played. Charles felt rhythms of loneliness, keened by an unyielding sexual pulse. He and Andrica had heard the song many times before, and while Charles liked it and Andrica would sometimes hum parts of it, at this moment in the mathetorium the two were overcome. Andrica laid her head on Charles's shoulder and wiped her eyes. Charles bleared but refused to let on, hoping his eyes would dry before the lights brightened. The emotionally fraught lyrics jostled his rigid perspectives, which wasn't the reaction he'd expected. Neither he nor Andrica had taken any sex pills—they were expensive—and there was always the fear they might hinder mathematical performance. But these sounds, this feeling he had right now . . . he would love Andrica forever.

Later, they sat in the hover and programmed a longer, scenic way back to the obelisk, as they stared at tiny ocean islands and dots of gulls diving into the water for food. They clamped hands, and as they basked within a prismatic view spilling different hues, a tinge of orange, a purpled heaven, Charles turned down the piped-in minimalist music Andrica had requested.

"Andrica," Charles said, "everyone knows the powerful effects music has on people, on the soul. We heard it with Rona today. I know we are on the right track with M-L-M."

"But why can't others feel what we do?" she asked.

"I think they do; at different times, in different cultures. We aren't synced. But how come the effect fades so fast? Tomorrow, tonight even, her song will be a nice memory, but the effect will be muted. In a few days it will be forgotten and ignored."

"You can't capture music in a bottle," she said.

"Why not? Why can't we capture and keep it somehow?"

Andrica pantomimed uncapping a bottle and sniffing from it, looked at Charles with hooded eyes, put her hand on his crotch, tongued his ear, and whispered, "I want it now, Charles. Oh, stick me."

Charles felt his stiffness under her hand before she laughed and shook her head. "Later, Romeo, later. If the world could harness *that*," she said.

Before they pilled, in their separate, private bedrooms, Charles brought the subject up again.

"When we try to communicate across cultures, each culture loses something. We try to paste in created music within a created language. But if a culture could bring some of their established music—yes, in a bottle, or something—and if we could bring ours, if we could exchange samples on the spot, might we not find common ground?"

"I have to admit it is a grand idea. But it'll never be simple, like bottles."

"No. I guess not," he said. "But we are on the right track with music."

"When Rona sang those hot jazz numbers, I felt I could jump off roofs and embrace everyone. She made me jealous and showed me how boring I am."

"I teared up during 'I've Gone, Darling,'" Charles said.

"Everyone did."

"I told you about Popov's harp."

"Yes, Charles, you did. Gobs of times."

"And the other night with Ramanujan—the effect was extraordinary. I can't even begin to explain it."

"Let's pill," Andrica said.

Charles could hear her move under a sensi-wrap in her bedroom. "Okay. And let me try an experiment. I'm going to background us with some of the new music I heard at Ramanujan's."

Charles played the musical sounds he'd recorded from the other night and moved back to his loft bed. He pulled his sensi-wrap up to his chin and closed his eyes. Once again, the purity and hold of the sounds was ineffable. Buoyed by the music, Charles and Andrica went to work, for that's what it seemed like as they tried to focus on sex during the sounds.

"Charles, these sounds are incredible, but they are too much for me right now."

"Let me turn them down." But it didn't help. One couldn't extract one's mind from the music. Charles had to agree: he couldn't think of anything else while in the throes of the sounds. He turned them off.

"Andrica? Andrica, are you there?"

"Yes. But I don't want to pill. Sorry."

"That's okay. I feel different about it too. What just happened?"

"I don't know, Charles. I want to hear those sounds again. They are unreal and not from this Earth. But I'm not ready to hear them right now."

"The music may have affected you more than it affected me. Ramanujan has changed. I hope I haven't changed."

"No. You haven't."

"So, what happened here?"

"I think the sounds were wrong for the occasion," Andrica said.

"Could that be all it was?"

"I don't know. Charles, I have to sleep now. Thank you, love, for a wonderful evening."

# 39

POPOV LOOKED AT CHARLES FROM ACROSS A WORKTABLE SHE'D set up in her reading room. Her harp, damaged and looking lost, sat out by the bedroom door. Micas were spread on a couch under a window screen with an ocean view. Charles could smell traces of rubbing alcohol and unguent. They both drank Tai Chiang Mai coffee during this week's meeting, and she'd just listened to Charles's story of Rona's concert and the effect the music had on him and Andrica. Popov felt more than twinges of jealousy.

"Tell me more about what happened after," she said. "I don't know what you mean about the music not being right for the occasion."

Charles flushed, as she expected.

"Charles, excuse me, I'm not prying," she said, smiling. "I'm trying, like you, to figure out why the music didn't work its charms on either of you."

"We were talking . . . romantically . . . from our separate rooms. I thought Ramanujan's music as background would enhance the moment."

"A special moment? I'm guessing."

She watched Charles move his feet and how he avoided her eyes. *Why am I doing this?* She couldn't stop herself and felt giddy as they continued.

"Okay, I believe I understand better. It's important that I see what you mean. You both were anticipating a higher experience, but the musical sounds caused you both to lose focus. The music became a hindrance."

"Yes. We said a few more words . . . we were surprised . . . the sounds affected her more than me."

"Andrica said the sounds were too much for her?"

"At that particular time, they were. She wants to hear them again . . . she said they were incredible, and not from this Earth."

Popov looked at Charles, and a seed began to develop within her. She couldn't believe what she was thinking. And this was Wang De Costa's son, no less.

"Do you enjoy vicarious sex with Andrica?" She put on her smile of wisdom.

"Yes."

"I'm glad you do." She reached out and touched his wrist. "You have discovered something and learned something. We have to find a way to channel M-L-M music, Charles."

"Will we be able to think it?"

"I hope so, but we haven't found the instruments or the right mix of instrumentation and orchestration to play it. At least not for Ramanujan's newest."

"Why?"

"The music is too mathematical. It's computer-initiated and computer-enhanced. We've never been able to telepathically transmit computer music. We see the math behind the musical language in our brains, but it doesn't lend itself telepathically. The receiving brain has to translate the math back into sounds."

She watched Charles pick up on this. "If we do succeed, the re-translated sounds may not come out as pure," he said.

"Right. We'll try. We've captured the frequencies and most of the pitches, it's the individual matrix of sounds we can't get at. In the few instances where we have been able to copy a sound, it's not the same. The larger effects aren't there."

She nudged his foot. "Sorry," she said. "Looking ahead, we'll need to channel the right music for international occasions."

"By thinking it?"

"Perhaps for one-on-one. For meetings of many, we'll use electronics in walls, floor, and ceiling like we do now."

They talked more, and Popov smiled more. She even giggled once and watched Charles grin. Popov loved how he was brainy, though he lacked poise, which she attributed to an absent mother and a father who was too reserved and studious. She felt satisfaction bloom within her as she gave a woman's wisdom and tenderness.

She also liked to see him blush; and after giving him his next assignment and leading him out, she grabbed his arm and pecked him on the cheek. "Now, do give my best to Andrica," she said.

After he left, Popov shut down her electronics and went to her harp. She massaged the dent on the metal side and made a few adjustments to the strings, before tilting her harp in tender hands. She'd decided to compose a piece of music for Charles—for that particular occasion.

# 40

GENERAL OSTEEN RETURNED HER NEWEST AIDE'S SALUTE AND OFfered Major Troy the chair in front of her. They were inside Osteen's office, a rather sterile workplace, with a spotless desk except for one folder. Not one mica or notebook showed from the desk or any wall shelf. It was as if General Osteen wanted to remain ambiguous, if not anonymous. She sat with perfect posture in combat fatigues. Two pictures graced the wall next to Troy. One was a photo of Osteen and her twin sister. They looked like young teens and were identical, each in matching bathing suits, arms around each other, smiling for the camera. The other was a photo of Osteen holding her award for seventh-degree black belt. She was in Karate Gi, alone in a dojo, and displayed no grin.

General Braun was on his way to the United States of America: Miami, Florida. His grandfather was born in New York state, near West Point, the former military academy.

"At ease, Major." Osteen smiled and leaned back in her chair. She tapped her glasses and said, "No disturbances. I'm shutting down for one half hour." She removed her glasses and centered the desk folder.

"Thank you," Troy said.

Osteen noted the major's look and tone. This was the first day in Major Troy's new assignment, and she was eager to please.

"General, I'm impressed with how you've managed this."

"It took some effort," Osteen lied. "I will let nothing get in the way of our success. We're meeting General Malone this evening."

"Connie? You aren't wasting any time, General."

"The three of us need to make every minute count. Keep in mind, it isn't a given the shuttle will be ready in time."

"It has to be. We'll make it be."

"Here's your first assignment, Major," said Osteen as she pushed the closed folder on her desk to her. "I want you to select for my review, *our review*, ten individuals from this boarding roster who we can best replace. The three of us will select three of those ten and replace those people." Osteen would figure out the steps to accomplish the physical transfers later.

"Okay, General. Has everyone here on this roster been selected?"

"Yes. And not one person is military. But that is to change. Right, Major?"

"Indeed, General. Maybe I can have this assignment done by to-night."

"We're meeting General Malone at her office at 1800 hours. If you can, Major," Osteen said, glancing at the folder.

When Major Troy left, Osteen wondered how her commanding officer, General Braun, was handling the snub from WCM. He'd said he didn't have time to think about it and would not second-guess WCM. Osteen had wanted to say, "But what if the ship runs into alien hostiles on the way? What if Kepler-1649c is inhabited by savages? Or intelligent hostiles? Of what use would M-L-M be then?"

She didn't know, and told herself *she* could help save humanity. She was as fit as any man on the street and as fit as most men in the armed forces. General Braun could perhaps outrun her, but she would more than hold her own, and she was superior in physical combat. She reminded herself, it's human nature to fight, dominate, and control. Nothing is going to change. Her time had come. She would be ready.

.................................

GENERAL BRAUN, IN BATTLE FATIGUES, WAS VIEWING ESCALATING riots and looting via Yahoogle-TweetV from his heliohover. Two aides sat beside him, his pilot sat in front, and the mayor of Miami sat behind him. Four gatling-gunners were placed in nodules about the hover—locked and loaded. As an extra precaution, two World Air Force Putins, sensor-fitted, escorted the General's hover, one ahead, one behind.

"The worst area is up ahead," the mayor said to the General, "behind the beach, or what can be taken as beach."

Braun looked at unbelievable devastation from the tsunami. All the high-rise resort buildings and condos, some that had been over 150 stories high, had imploded and collapsed to piles of extended, winding rubble lasting for over two miles along the shores of a calm ocean.

"Over nine hundred thousand are confirmed dead. Almost six hundred thousand injured. Another fifty-five thousand unaccounted for and presumed dead," the mayor said. "We keep finding them under rubble, in the ocean . . ."

"How many have been killed by droog rioters?" Braun asked.

The mayor hesitated. "I must get you an update, General."

"I want an answer before I leave." *Good luck with that*, he thought.

Braun switched off the TweetV. News had been unreliable for centuries. He shut his eyes thinking about when the historical tipping point was, of fake information becoming the accepted news. Telecasters and professional news anchors had all but led nations to arm and fight in World War III. These women and men created worst-case scenarios for viewers, which served to push nations into a "prepare to defend" mode before they could even negotiate. Like tactical experts, newspeople asked experienced experts: What happens if the United States does this? How can Canada respond to that? All internal secrets of nations were leaked in pseudo discussions by rival personalities on competing networks. The language of negotiation went underground. Governments told lies to cover up real intentions. Nobody knew what the course would be, so newsmen created their own versions and threw it out there for the masses. Revolts led to revolutions. Wars commenced.

"Okay, let's see for ourselves," the General said.

The hover dipped and turned toward Route 1 and came back along the west side of the Intracoastal Waterway. The General spotted what looked like fortifications and had his pilot circle. Sure enough, he could see armed men scurry with their rifles and disappear into makeshift bunkers. An orange warning light flashed in the hover's cabin. "Brace for 'possible,'" a gunner said. But the light didn't change to red as the rear Putin dove down and at the last minute arced to level and released tear-gas. As the gas clouded the area, the General permitted a smile. "That'll annoy the bastards."

Braun turned nasty. This was Popov's fault. The tsunami aftermath in Indonesia and their riots and murders were just as atrocious. Perhaps he should have insisted that Popov accompany him to see both disasters. The mayor said something, but Braun ignored him. The world has become too dangerous, he thought—the danger was palpable. Braun, an experienced battlefield-soldier, could feel it down to his innermost core. Canada-Siberia and the other Declareds were not Popov's fault. But the tsunamis had tipped the balance. A balance had also been tipped in the General's mind. For the first time in many years, he was worried. He wondered how in hell "birdsong-dolphinese" could stop growing cells of droogs comprised of individuals who were becoming trained marauders with weapons. He thought of the droogs behind him who were already out in the streets killing, making plans to gain the next foothold, and organizing. He had no idea how to stop the geometric cell growth. Over half his military infiltrators had disappeared, and he wondered how many of them had become droogs. What concerned the General was that the droogs were patient. They were a festering wound, and trying to treat it no longer seemed possible. They'd infiltrated the enlisted military, commandeered hi-tech equipment, and removed themselves to infiltrate elsewhere. Droogs that were killed seemed to be replaced effortlessly. If they were captured, they instantly committed suicide with a poison tablet given to each of them on initiation.

The General thought about his son, an excellent mathematician, who was in his first year at Powell Military. He was the tail end of four generations of military officers in Braun's family. *What kind of world, assuming it wasn't torched and they'd self-corrected in time, would his son—and his expected grandchildren—inherit?* The General thought about Popov again. He admired her forthrightness, and he honored the sacrifice she'd made. But she would need every ounce of her wisdom and luck to accomplish a fix. What she was coordinating, he couldn't understand. He would have to trust her. She was one of the seven best mathematicians on the planet, and the General believed in mathematics. He couldn't question the WCM, for he no longer had a solution. All paths from his line of sight led to more wars and violence. All he could do was protect her.

After reviewing data collected by the Miami mayor, receiving a final briefing by his ground commander and aides, and issuing his own orders and instructions, General Braun prepared to leave for Canada. He had nearly an hour to himself, but before using the time to review files on the Canada-Siberia Declared, he made a call to General Osteen.

"Everything is in order, General," Osteen said.

"Are you getting full support from General Blackston?"

"Yes. There hasn't been any trouble. He and I have served together on other commands. We've always gotten along."

"Good. Glad to hear it. How is your Major doing? I forget her name."

"Major Troy has settled in, thank you. She's been a big help already."

"Doing what?"

General Braun noted the hesitation. His antenna went up.

"Oh, thank you," he heard her say to someone. "I beg your pardon, General, that was her now. She's prioritizing my night work and has been tracking progress versus completion dates, that sort of thing."

It was the General who hesitated. Deliberately. "Okay. Keep me updated."

When they disconnected, General Braun felt a ripple run through him. Perhaps she was just piqued at his "doing what?" Her hesitation was her way of displaying annoyance at him. *Yes, that's what it was,* he concluded. *I'd feel the same way.*

# 41

WHEN GENERAL OSTEEN REMOVED HER GLASSES AND CLOSED THE door, she thought about her conversation with General Braun. She'd heard suspicion in his voice. She'd regained herself, she thought, with the fake "thank you" to Troy, but was irritated by his nosy inquiry regarding her aide. She decided to assign other legitimate projects to Troy, enabling Osteen to explain what Troy was doing at any time. She would brief Troy and alert her to probable probing from Braun.

Osteen was in General Braun's fishbowl. She feared he might have found information about the death of Colonel Ginger Pompadoux and had set her up here to make a mistake, to reveal herself. She knew what she had to do—protect her flank. She retrieved the General's file on Pompadoux and went behind closed doors.

After reviewing Braun's file, Osteen concluded he would have no reason to suspect foul play; but she felt uncomfortable that the General had flagged the file for updates. He didn't think Pompadoux had disappeared on her own. She tapped her glasses, making a note to review the file once a week, and made a reminder to tell another aide to inform her whenever the file was otherwise reviewed, and by whom. She thought about Troy. Osteen would use Troy's eyes and ears to find Braun's weakness.

..................................

AFTER HOURS, OSTEEN SCOURED BRAUN'S OFFICE. SHE WOULD make no attempt to gain entry to the recessed safe she discovered when she removed the painting. She held the painting for a second but rehung it, knowing a new fingerprint on the outside of the metal box would send an electronic alert to the General. But she sat down in the desk chair and went through his drawers.

The next morning, she summoned Troy.

"See if you can find the digital key to the General's middle desk drawer. Be cautious."

Two hours later, Troy went into Osteen's office, closed the door, and palmed what appeared to be a half-stick of gum offered to Osteen. "I fished it out of Samantha's jacket and had a duplicate made. The original's back in her coat."

.................................

AFTER NORMAL HOURS, OSTEEN UNLOCKED THE MIDDLE DRAWER IN General Braun's desk. She grabbed a journal and read over recent entries until she realized it was devoted to family. But then she found something useful. A full page devoted to his son, dated three days ago. Braun wanted him out of Powell Military and onto *Welkin-Alpha*. The last line on the page, handwritten in ink, said it all: *Roy, Jr., not selected; must be on* Welkin-Alpha. *How do I accomplish that?*

# 42

DR. JONAS SALK STUDIED HOW TIME TRAVEL CONTROL SCIENTISTS imparted updated histories to new Liftees. Via computer with nanocable six hundred times thinner than spooled thread, the new information was condensed to qubits. Zettabytes of data slipped into several nano-biochips imbedded in the brain, and the data spread through the brain like filtered gas filling up a tank. When the Liftee Returned, TTC shut down the nano-chips. Knowledge and dream faded away.

A Liftee born three hundred years ago was now brought up to speed within eighteen hours without any aftereffect. They absorbed everything new to them, including updates in M-L-M. But here the system balked. M-L-M mathematics, associated lingua, and musical brainwave entrainment, such as it was, could be fed into the brain, but the brain could not combine them into an incipient language.

Salk took it personally. What should have been an easy task became the mammoth in the room. He knew the proper track was neuroprosthetics, biochips placed in the brain, but what good was this new language if it could be entrained but not learned and used? Was it because M-L-M in thought, word, and deed was so pure that the soul of this new language protected it from all Earth history to avoid contamination? Did the soul itself reject the use of M-L-M on account of humanity's virus of evil? Was this why, up to now, the brain only absorbed it when a human learned M-L-M by trial and error with his own soul, in his own time, using his own brain cells?

Salk posed these questions to Conrad, the young man before him. Like Charles, the gifted Conrad was awarded the chance to meet with a Liftee, and he'd chosen the physician.

"I've read somewhere 'the soul of the world is language,' or maybe it was 'language is the soul of the world,'" Conrad said.

"Same difference," Salk said, testing.

"Not according to Aasen. Krebs too."

"Quite right. Krebs might allow those statements in English. Aasen would disallow. 'If it won't fly in all languages, it can't be allowed in any,' sayeth he."

Conrad smiled. "There has to be another reason M-L-M can't be force-fed."

"Give me a reason."

"I'm thinking about mathematics. Pure mathematics. Our brains can be fed *that* purity."

"I'm listening. The point?"

"Mathematicians work by trial and error. It doesn't come easy . . . sometimes . . ."

Conrad stood in front of Salk's mica-filled shelf. Salk watched him peruse the shelf, like everyone else did, and continue without missing a beat in what he was saying. *Wish I was his age again*, Salk thought.

"We humans," Conrad turned to Salk, "work pure and applied mathematics using our own brain cells. And we are contaminated with false starts and false proofs, the illogical conjecture. We've made false progress to purity here with M-L-M. So my point would be, we keep trying. There is no reason why the brain can't be fed when M-L-M is pure."

"Okay," Salk said. "What did you just say, pure and what mathematics?"

"Applied."

"Yes. That's what I heard you say."

In the evening, long after Conrad had left, Salk boiled a pot of milk and water to brew himself *cafe au lait* for the rest of the night. He looked around at his work-lab cum bedroom quarters. He remembered once again his decision not to patent his polio vaccine, because that would have made it immediately unaffordable to millions of the poor and destitute. Salk had forfeited over a billion dollars and wondered, not for the first time, how his life would have changed.

He Yahoogled the newest research on teratoma, those unusual body tumors, and began reading. He proceeded on the notion that if the human brain would not accept M-L-M directly, there would be another way to apply and funnel it.

Four hours later, Salk had absorbed a week-old medical paper on teratomas. He thought there might be a way to feed M-L-M to them—or, better yet, through them—if they could be connected to the spinal cord and thence to the brain. Salk realized teratomas, though much more common in this new age, were not prevalent. He didn't have the time to research why they were more common, but expected it had to do with atmospheric impurities ascribed to fossil fuels, which had peaked 250 years ago. Salk thought the people without them could be engrafted with one. It would be a routine operation, and with Telemedicine it could be done. If the human brain couldn't or wouldn't take to M-L-M with its music, this would be a way to tease the brain by implanting—by *applying*—M-L-M elsewhere. *We plant a seed into something unique, which will metastasize and grow.* Salk sighed and massaged worn eyes. M-L-M—so much more than an uttered-chanted lingua franca. It was looking more like a concept to be planted, cultivated, and birthed.

..................................

THE NEXT AFTERNOON, SALK PERFORMED HIS FIRST TERATOMA graft. A death-row convict was selected and fastened electromagnetically to the operating table. This convict would be spared her life if she agreed to the procedure, and she'd done so. The graft was taken from her lower abdomen and attached below the neck. Salk was successful in connecting the graft to her spinal column. He waited one day, to the hour, and was convinced the graft had taken. Salk, first, fed electrical pulses to the graft, which were picked up by the spinal column. Salk and a present-age physician detected concomitant electrical pulses in the brain, the woman herself responded: "I feel that."

Salk was ecstatic but waited several more hours while cable was prepared and links were made to the imposed teratoma and computers.

The result was unexpected. She absorbed none of the music and just some of the language. What's more, M-L-M took too long—sometimes a full minute—for her brain to translate. *These types of experiments never change*, he thought, as he considered options. A graft connected to the brain was out of the question. It was too chancy.

The problem of her not absorbing any type of M-L-M musical pattern remained. When prompted, she could not utter in M-L-M. Salk ordered a check on the M-L-M program; the data engineers confirmed that this version of M-L-M was complete, up to the newest tweaks to the language. Salk retraced his steps and tried again, yielding the same results. He concluded that the graft had to grow and mature before it could be fed properly. But who had time for that? No one did.

.................................

"THAT'S WHERE WE STAND, CONRAD," SAID SALK. "I HAD A TENSE meeting with Popov and her people today. While it appears humans can begin to absorb the lingua, there is no trace of musical absorption."

"Do you think it will take longer to grow M-L-M into the teratoma than it will take to learn the language outright?"

"For where we are now, someone like Krebs or Aasen can learn the linguistics quicker on their own. Not so for the rest of us."

"And we still haven't figured out the music part," Conrad said.

Salk drank from his *café au lait* and combed his hair with his fingers. "You have a reputation of thinking out of the box," Salk said. "We could use that now."

"When will you test her again?"

"We will test her every eight hours. She needs sleep and recovery time. There has been no change in the last sixteen hours."

"Are you playing her the musical patterns?"

"Yes."

"Including dissonance?"

"Yes. Everything."

He watched Conrad shake his head, bewildered. "Think on it," Salk said, "and I'd like to meet with you again the day after tomorrow." He knew the effect this would have on Conrad, and he watched him puff up.

"It will be a pleasure. Thank you," Conrad said.

*Good*, he thought. *I need all the help I can get.*

# 43

THE NEXT DAY, CONRAD WAITED FOR CHARLES IN ORDER TO TELL him the news.

"Salk wants to see me again, tomorrow."

"Sounds like a breakthrough."

"We hope," Conrad allowed. "We're trying to figure out why the results are inconclusive."

"Lacking, I heard," Andrica piped up, as she shifted her weight to the other leg and brushed an imaginary speck off her dolphin tattoo.

Charles saw how this dampened Conrad's ebullience. Charles knew what that felt like. It had taken him a while to realize Andrica treated everyone equally. He remembered how jubilant she had been when her dolphin pool was one of a dozen saved after the tsunami. The two bollards on her pool, which held the ropes connected to the obelisk pier, had torn away, but the pool was found the same day, adrift. She'd told Charles she could visualize her pool with her dolphins, cresting with the tsunami in glee and plunging down as the giant wave continued on its way. *So why was she moody?*

Charles saw Conrad looking at him. "What's the crux of the problem?" Charles asked.

At first, Conrad wanted to keep his information to himself. He'd been scrounging to come up with his own ideas. But he and Charles were drifting together more.

"There are two. She, or her graft, won't admit or register the new music. And she can't utter one iota of M-L-M, along with being ignorant of two thirds of the linguistics."

He thought Charles would smirk, like Andrica did; laugh, even. But Charles didn't. He was considering the problems; Conrad could feel him think, as Charles half-closed his eyes, like he always did when he pondered a chess combination.

"I learned a new word the other day," Charles said. "*Aphesis*."

Conrad, without realizing it, copped Salk's favorite retort: "I'm listening."

"It's defined as the loss of an unstressed vowel or syllable, as in the formation of the word 'slant' from 'aslant.'" Charles had ignored Andrica, and noticed her strutting away in a pout. "See ya," he said.

"Anyway," Charles continued, "I've been . . . Popov played some weird stuff on her harp . . . I don't think she understood the music either, but it occurred to me that like the loss of the initial 'a' in slant, maybe we could have lost something in scale-step enrichments as well?"

"Interesting. Aphesis as applied to music. Who will take credit for this, Charles? I might steal your idea."

Charles looked at him. "Conrad, why . . .? You are the stronger chess player. I accept that."

Conrad looked at Charles squarely. "A little better, maybe. I might be holding back." He smiled.

"And your math," Charles continued, "when you find your second, simpler solution to the Riemann hypothesis, we will all genuflect before you."

"I must tell you, Charles, I would never have expected you to say that."

"Conrad. I'm thinking . . . we should work together more."

"Now this is getting interesting. Since when have you ever shown any interest in me, let alone working with me?"

Charles grimaced. "But . . . I . . ." Pushing himself, he reached for the fruit of insight. "See, this is what I always thought about you. Right here is the trouble with our language. This has to be—you and me—about faulty communication. Conrad, how is it that we both have the same lopsided feelings about each other?"

Thus began their partnership. Did they totally trust each other? No. Did they agree on how they would work together? Not yet. But they breached a wall, and, as they took a step ahead together, Charles and Conrad peeked into the possible.

The next morning, before classes, Andrica was puzzled when she spotted Charles and Conrad talking and smiling at a less-frequented cafeteria table neither of them had sought before. She circled the table, doing her best to ignore Charles, and was beyond annoyed when he didn't notice her.

Conrad was to meet with Salk that afternoon and, with Charles's help, was trying to get a fix, something to help Salk address the M-L-M problems with his patient. "I need more, Charles. You've covered solid ground with me, but Salk has gone over the same ground."

"I'm sorry I can't give you more ideas."

"Don't be. For us to nail this, just like that," Conrad filliped his fingers, "would be like winning an old-time lottery."

"My great-great-grandfather won a lottery once. Before they were outlawed."

"Really?"

"He'd turned ten, the legal age back then to participate, and won a million dollars."

"What did he do?"

"Spent it all on compu-games. The money was gone in six weeks. His gambling addiction, which developed from that huge initial win, clung to him for years. He amounted to nothing."

"When do you meet Popov?"

"Tomorrow afternoon."

"Okay. We'll meet here same time tomorrow. I'm going to pummel you with questions about your assignment. Later!"

"Later," Charles said to him, as Andrica drew up and bumped Charles.

..................................

"WE'VE NOTED IMPROVEMENTS," SALK SAID. "THE GRAFTING IS sure."

Ramanujan and Conrad stood next to Salk who, in his special lab, continued to monitor his patient. His lab consisted of a quarantined forty-square-meter room with two patient beds, one of which Salk used for sleeping. Liftees respected his privacy and left him alone to concentrate on M-L-M preparations. Salk, though he was impressed by two available androids who diagnosed and performed operations, had insisted on twentieth-century equipment for his lab. "I'm flat out more comfortable with it," he'd said. Ramanujan stared at a table of handheld instruments and blinked at the CAT-scanner. Beyond the table, a floor-to-ceiling bookcase of medical books and journals graced the wall. On the top shelf were updated micas given to him by WCM.

Ramanujan folded his arms in front of himself. "Expressing my ignorance, doctor, why can't you connect to the thigh, or skin under the arms, or something similar, and avoid engrafting?"

"We've tried. Other than the brain, non-grafted areas don't absorb data of any type."

"Why?" Conrad asked.

"Other established body areas already perform a function. Even excessive skin under your arms and inner thighs has been mated to the body and accepted. M-L-M disrupts this mating and connection. Anything foreign does, from poison ivy to cancer."

"Anything else happen?" Ramanujan asked.

"Where we had hoped for calming effects with the music and/or the language, there is an opposite effect. M-L-M, as it stands now, is a horrid macaronic mishmash."

# 44

WHEN POPOV WOKE FROM THE MOST VIVID DREAM SHE'D EVER HAD in her life, she found herself out of bed and facedown on the floor. Realizing the experience was a once-in-a-lifetime event, she turned herself over and sat up. The dream returned to her in pieces. She'd found herself in heaven, or at least that's what she thought it was. It was still; she was alone, walking a sandy beach. There was a slight breeze, and there were seagulls—it reminded her of a beach she'd been to in Greece with her father when she was an adolescent.

Popov went to her bed and sat amidst tangled, damp sheets. She saw herself again on the beach, striding toward the ocean with purpose. She heard a hum, or someone saying "Come." She didn't see anyone, but the hum or beckoning emanated from the sky in front of her, above the ocean. She watched the sky evolve from blue to a soft yellow, which soon segued into an orange-red-purple. She focused as the mass of color—the purest she'd ever seen—coalesced to a smaller section of sky. She watched the color become a circle, and she saw what had to be a colossal planet rotating slowly. It was a gigantic globe hung in the sky, marked with what looked to her like oceans. Popov brought her hands to her head. It was as if someone had told her to cup her ears.

In the dream, sounds entered, but she couldn't quite gather them into her head as she sat in tangles of sheets. She remembered her dream. The sounds were a kind of music-language, soul-like, from within; at least in the dream she was given to think so; and she'd marveled, while in her dream, how their efforts had been on the right track all along. The sounds built, growing stronger and purer. The musical patterns were similar to M-L-M, but more distinguished. Yet the atonals—they were a match. She had approached them with her harp and had heard them in Liftee experiments. She remembered the dream again, how the sky and planet colors purified to a higher level with the music, how the sound patterns built and embellished upon themselves to reveal hope, communication, and love, all into one, all by music-language. *Yes*, she'd thought, *this is what we're striving for.*

Popov rushed through breakfast and thought of new ideas, angles, approaches—as she'd been able to do as a teenager. The dream, the memory of it became an elixir, a mental aphrodisiac—anything is possible, she thought. She swore she could feel the rush and bounce of exhausted and worn neurons re-traveling brain pathways. She couldn't wait to tell her colleagues.

Radiant with a smile, she took the elevator to the WCM offices. She was early, and was surprised to see Tuan already in the conference room, pacing about, having an animated discussion with herself. Popov waved her hand and was about to reveal her dream.

"Juanita," Tuan said, "I've been waiting for you, for everyone. I must tell you about the most incredible dream I had last night."

.....................................

IT TURNED OUT THE ENTIRE WCM, PLUS ALL THREE TIERS, ALL NOW in the auditorium, had experienced the exact same dream as Popov and Tuan. The same colors, the same music-recitative, the same atonals, the same details. Someone, somewhere, was reaching out to the World Congress of Mathematicians and Tier. There could be no other explanation. However, none of the Liftees experienced the dream, nor did Charles, Andrica, or any others.

Popov, for obvious reasons, found it hard to keep order. She had to discipline herself to listen and not engage in all the wild speculations, to consider and wait before throwing herself and her own ideas into the mix. Something unprecedented was happening, and she opted to let ideas, shouts, and ramblings play out. She sipped tea and attempted to let one person at a time speak, but soon other voices would cut in, some groups in the Tiers huddled, and she let the free-for-all continue.

When, like an old-time outboard motor powering a boat, the motor coughed and showed signs of running out of gas, and the boat slowed and stopped, all eyes turned to Popov.

She rose and once again stood before the podium.

"What is the one category we have not coded for SETI transmission?"

A half second later, Magnuson of First Tier shouted, "Discordance!"

"Correct," Popov said. "We all thought static-free pure sounds, without the scratchy, ear-assaulting mishmash, were the proper ones for transmission."

Popov looked at the faces before her; they knew what was coming and weren't buying; she heard murmurs of discontent.

"I hope and pray those catcalls aren't part of a language," someone said. "How would we speak it?" said another. "At least give us euphony."

.................................

IN A LAST-MINUTE SURPRISE, PAUPERITO REQUESTED TO BE RE-turned. Although his contributions were measured and less frequent, his mathematics was on the verge of another breakthrough. He missed da Vinci, he'd said, and he'd become unfocused. The WCM heard gossip of his growing disgust for humanity, that he was so broken by the path history had taken that he didn't want to be part of what he thought would soon be the end. "While the WCM plays music, Earth burns," he'd said. What they didn't know, and what Curie inferred, was that Pauperito was suicidal. "I'm afraid to go back and too scared to stay," he'd said.

Ms. Toni Praeger consumed herself with Pauperito's newest lines. Within thirty-six hours, under her leadership, Liftees built a mathematical platform for the atonals, which enabled them to pick the dissonances apart, frequency by frequency, amplitude by amplitude, wave by wave. The more they explored within these mathematical shells, the more mathematics they found. There appeared to be some kind of math-code overlay—a glue—organizing and grouping the hideous sounds.

Praeger put in an urgent call for Pauperito; she keyed in on something he had been working on and requested WCM delay Pauperito's Return, at least enough so he could examine what Toni had done.

Pauperito had agreed to stay to meet a last time with Praeger, whom he had often worked with. When she entered his quarters, Pauperito was already wearing his old-time clothes. He had before him a plate of what he said was his favorite meal—sausage, goat cheese, and figs. She watched him eat and let him finish.

"Sir," Praeger said, "if you—"

Pauperito put a finger to his lips while extending the other hand. "I must first study what you have," Pauperito said. "You know how I work. I can't be led down a predetermined path; I need to find it myself."

She handed Pauperito a sheaf of papers, and Pauperito, looking careworn with crinkled brows, slid his finger over equations and mathematical expressions. He went to a second paper and back to the first, thought for a moment, then studied the second sheet.

"I look at this and I say to myself, 'How come we haven't developed our own wings?' You have entered a doorway and crossed a threshold," Pauperito said, handing back the papers. He sighed. "We ourselves can't fly; we haven't even gotten our gills back. One of eight million species on this planet. And we think *we* are special. Sad, sad, oh, so sad."

# 45

THE UNBELIEVABLE HAPPENS.

Without reluctance, but with bemusement, SETI transmitted anew, and this time with the atonals. Within thirteen hours, humanity received a strong patterned signal. It was an unmistakable pulse repeating the same pattern after every ninety-six beats.

Popov and her colleagues were ecstatic, knowing M-L-M contained ninety-six alphabet characters and the signal did not vary in its ninety-six-pulse pattern. This was history. Although the pattern made no sense.

SETI determined the signal came from Kepler-186f, another planet from a habitable zone in the same galaxy. While everyone at WCM was trying to figure out whether the pattern contained a message, two other signals were received by SETI. Everyone thought the new signals would provide answers, or that perhaps the first signal had been an acknowledgement of Earth's signal that had been sent with the atonals. However, that idea was shattered when SETI realized the new signals came from two separate star systems. One from one side of the galaxy, the other from an opposite side, as though from two separate oceans.

There had been three extraterrestrial contacts within twenty-four hours, and the rest of the world took notice. For a brief moment, all battles and wars stopped, as everyone wondered what to make of the signals. Was it a WCM trick?

No. It was not a ruse, and WCM could not make anything out of the two new signals either. Both of the new signals pulsed regular thirty-one times, then transmitted ninety-six separate and different patterns; the signal reverted to thirty-one pulses, then the similar, but unique, patterns all over again, and repeated.

Astonishment built when it was confirmed that for the two newer signals, the unique patterns of each signal were identical, even though they originated from opposite sides of the galaxy! One signal was stronger than the other, but neither was as strong as the first, which kept up its continual, steady pulse-pattern.

Two hours after SETI received the second and third signals, a strange new signal appeared. It was convoluted and seemed to pulse within itself until a SETI engineer realized he had three different signals wobbling around the same frequency, each one a little off from the other, which had caused the confusion. He was able to separate them, and SETI was astounded to learn that two of the signals came from two exoplanets in a double star system, while the third signal emanated from outside the galaxy.

The WCM was overwhelmed. The three newest signals each transmitted a pattern that started out simply but added an extra pulse to each following pattern, which was varied until the ninety-sixth pattern was reached. The huge string of patterns then started from the beginning and continued all over again. All three of the newest signals repeated the same exact patterns, extra pulse and all, with one important difference: the extragalactic signal—now that it was separated—repeated its patterns after a delay of π, 3.14159 seconds. Also—and this shook heads—each of these three signals transmitted different patterns from the first three signals from the other planets. The computers and charts had recorded it all; there it was in black and white, and the greatest minds on Earth, ancient and present, couldn't make heads or tails out of the six alien signals. Only the extragalactic maintained a delay of π seconds before repeating its pattern. Then its pulses arrived every second until the transmission finished, before starting again. There was no delay with any of the other patterns; pulses ranged from every half-second to every two seconds.

Finding no obvious answer to the conundrum, the rest of the world soon lost interest, and battles and wars resumed. A few excellent mathematicians, serving in other careers, people like General Braun and General Osteen, were absorbed and mystified—General Osteen played with the mathematics for an entire morning—but after tangling with the intelligent randomness of the signals and associated difficulties, she, like the others, moved back to her own matters.

It was too much for Pauperito. He was about to flatline if he tried to absorb any more. Before Returning as he'd requested, two days earlier, he reviewed the mathematics on his eraser-walls for the last time and put a final report together for the WCM. Popov read his concluding paragraph to her six WCM colleagues.

*I've reached a mathematical cliff; I don't know how to continue. I'm caught in the middle of* 'to understand is to begin; to begin is to understand.' *Young minds are needed. The foregoing mathematics has turned on me and become strange to me. The laws remain the same, but I question how I derived these equations and what brought me to this point of indecision. This I do know: you will find the answer to these signals in the atonality of Mathe-Lingua-Musica. You must isolate every dissonance you find, including those we've seen in Bach-Liu Hui, as well as everything from Ramanujan and others. Isolate them, tear them apart, examine them, figure out their mathematics, and wield a new math. Tempus fugit. Good luck.*

Within the next twenty-four hours, SETI received six new alien signals. Each was different from the other six signals, and were tracked to six separate new worlds, one of which was Kepler-1649c. Bingo! This was the exoplanet everyone at WCM had in their hearts, ever since water had been confirmed. It was still the most-similar-to-Earth Exo discovered, and even General Braun pumped a fist when he heard the news. When Kepler-1649c was announced, the WCM and all Tiers erupted. They'd done that one right. Yet the newest signals revealed nothing. Their individual patterns were similar but different from the other five newest signals and different but similar to all the others. $\pi$ did not show itself. Mathematicians locked into Kepler-1649c's signal and re-studied the pulses. They came in groups—shells?—and ninety-six shells were counted before a string of unique patterns recontinued.

By the end of one week, a total of thirty-one separate alien signals had been received, recorded, and locked in by SETI. Each one pointed to a different world, thirty of which were located in their galaxy. No further sign of $\pi$, but everyone wondered if the transmissions were indicating, or solving, strings of equations. All of these separate signals were unmistakable pulses attempting to speak with Earth, for they all were related to the number ninety-six, the number of separate utterances in M-L-M, which had been transmitted via SETI. All Earth could do was resend refigured pangrams, using the ninety-six alphabetic characters and discordants, back to each of them as had been first done on receiving each alien signal. It was decided that before repeating the pangram, SETI would delay $\pi$ seconds. After argument, it was also decided not to mimic any of the alien patterns. For one, there were too many of them; and two, Earth had no understanding of them.

The atonals had opened the floodgate, but humanity was no closer to understanding the numinous alien communications than when the first signal had arrived a week before.

"Here's my question," Popov said to the WCM and Tier at a closed meeting. "If aliens can reach us in dreams, why do they resort to using and sending these confusing signals?"

There was no answer. No one had the slightest idea.

Even the WCM became jaded. It was like catching too many fish on one hook. It was too much bliss, too much in a one-week span versus the billions of years past. The most able mathematicians had headaches and threw up their hands as their thoughts and their mathematics tumbled to chaos.

"We will shut down and rest for forty-eight hours," Popov said, sending a dictum. "No exceptions. Too much has happened. You are to take this time to relax, sleep, and recover."

# 46

"WHY A CRYPTOLOGIST AND PUZZLE INVENTOR FROM THE 1930S?" Popov asked. It was several days later, and she was meeting with the new head of First Tier, Magnuson, and with a newer Liftee, the phonologist Armando Petitjean, whom she'd summoned. "No one on Tier has heard of him, except for you, Armando."

"That's not at all surprising," Armando said. He faced Popov in her office. Magnuson, who had arrived from Bangkalan, Indonesia, as winner of the Mathematics Olympiad, which was used to adjust Tier levels, sat beside him. "At a great loss to mathematics, this Russian peasant was purged by Stalin in that most unfortunate era."

"This year," Magnuson said, "an extant copy of his notebook was found. He'd made a concise copy, in his own hand, of all his thoughts and work. I'd put it aside, not examining it fully, but these alien signals reminded me of something in it." Magnuson, flustered, deferred to Petitjean.

"I devoured his notebook, finishing it yesterday. Chair Popov, how fortunate you are that following the Return of Pauperito, you can Lift Lobashevsky. Veced Lobashevsky is a talent, equally blessed."

Popov looked back to Magnuson. "He'd donated everything," Magnuson said, "all his notes plus compilations of his calculations, to the Hermitage in St. Petersburg. He must have had an acquaintance there who agreed to accept his unusual gift. I suspect some clerk tucked it away and it's lain in the same box for centuries."

"How did you get it?" Popov asked Magnuson.

"My Finnish relative works at the Museum, or what's left of it, and he discovered the box. Knowing of my profession, he was able to send it to me two months ago. I'd been tied up with other matters, as you well know, and didn't appreciate what I had. During your requested forty-eight-hour shutdown, I picked it up again and examined it more thoroughly. This notebook is . . . extraordinary . . ." He deferred back to Petitjean.

Petitjean nodded. "One can only imagine, or try to imagine, the other individual losses out there to humanity. But we have discovered an individual who can help us understand these baffling alien transmissions."

Popov signed off on Lobashevsky; he was scheduled for Lift that evening.

...................................

POPOV THOUGHT ABOUT THE RUSSIAN PEASANT AS SHE PLAYED HER harp and waited for Charles. It was evening, and she sensed an alignment. Her harp meanderings segued to a tone poem composed on the spot for Charles, her, and Lobashevsky. She imbued it with music from the last piece she'd composed just for Charles, after she kissed his cheek and watched him go out her door. Why she connected these three individuals, she had no idea, but the alignment seemed right, and she followed her instincts. She traveled her harp as she'd done many times and tried to reach the atonalities she'd played from the newest renderings of Bach-Liu Hui. She bent close to the dissonance, but drifted away whenever she felt she could plunge to it. The closer she came to cacophony, the more upset her stomach became. Not tonight, she thought. No, not tonight.

...................................

"CHARLES, YOU APPEAR DOWN. IT MUST BE ANDRICA," POPOV said, as she ushered him in and offered him his usual tea.

"How did you know?"

"A woman perceives such, Charles. But I shouldn't pry." She watched Charles sip his tea and felt her belly subside. "You do know I established myself in primes with my proof of the Andrica—the *other* Andrica—conjecture?"

"I've been thinking about an aphesis related to music," Charles said. "Oh, yes, I knew you had proved the Andrica conjecture. When I told *my* Andrica, she didn't even know about it." Charging ahead, "I've also discovered what *syncope* means—the contraction of a word by omitting one or more sounds from the middle."

Popov listened to him explain his thoughts. He was becoming a handsome lad. He lacked social graces; but when he became animated, as he was now, nothing distracted him, and he pursued his ideas with vigor and passion, which elevated him. Popov thought about his father, the talented Wang De Costa, and how she never noticed him. His father could be alone in the same room with her, and it wouldn't register. So, why then . . .

She nodded. "This is informative, Charles. Take me further."

"Thereby, an aphesis affecting part of the musical scale . . ."

Popov heard words and observed him. His mother had been lost at sea when she'd gone kite-surfing offshore. But the gossip said she'd landed in a forest, on a predetermined isle, and was picked up by her lover. In any event, she was never found, and no one had seen or heard from her in over ten years. Wang never talked about it, and Popov suspected he lived with it and had written her off. *This boy, all alone*, she thought.

Charles had stopped and was looking at her.

"You have cornered something which could be important," Popov said. "I will bring the idea to Bach." She adjusted her skirt, a kelly-green satin painted with morning glories. The yellow and blue bursts of flower matched how she felt at the moment.

"I said I shouldn't pry, Charles, but you are free to talk with me about Andrica." She hesitated. "If you wish."

"We had a fight."

Popov gave a knowing smile. "Haven't we all, at one time or another."

"Ms. Popov, were you ever . . .?"

"No. I've not been married, if that's what you are wondering. And it's been a while since I've had anything close to a lover. My time isn't my own anymore, Charles." She smiled.

"Your features, facially, remind me of Andrica."

"Your father mentioned that. Andrica's a spunky girl."

"Yes."

"You said 'facially.'" Popov smiled and watched him blush. "Do I look old to you?"

"No, not at all. I meant, like—your smile is similar."

"Oh, not to worry, Charles. I know what you meant." She smiled again. "And what you might not have meant."

She watched Charles endure the silence.

"Did you know that centuries ago, Russian music played by an American pianist brought both countries together for a while?" Popov continued. "They were in an intractable cold war. The pianist was Van Cliburn . . . Oh, it doesn't matter here, right now, I guess. But the power of music."

They sipped tea.

"Would you like me to play you the harp, Charles?"

Charles smiled. "Yes."

Charles said nothing when she took him to a different sitting room outside her bedroom. Popov dimmed the light and lit two jasmine-scented candles. Charles sat in an armchair labeled Pierre Jeanneret.

"Charles, remove your blazer and shoes, and give yourself to—peace."

While Popov untied her neck fichu and set up her harp, Charles looked at paintings and pictures on her walls. He looked at a picture taken when she must have been a teenager, with the Oslo Symphony Orchestra. The albino female conductor was shaking her hand; all the musicians were standing, many smiling. She resembled Andrica. Fastened on an opposite wall, Charles read from a handwritten poster:

Then, give me a harp of epic song,
Which Homer's finger thrilled along;
But tear away the sanguine string,
For war is not the theme I sing.
—Anacreon

"I've been working on something honoring you, me, and our newest Liftee, Veced Lobashevsky."

"May I ask who the painting is of, the one hanging next to you?"

"My great-grandfather. He was a full colonel and mathematics adviser in the Bahamas-Florida Keys Declared. Florida lost, and my great-grandmother lost her colonel."

Charles faced her from his chair, about three meters away. Popov was aware of him watching her. She snuggled up to the harp and plucked a few strings. She made minor tuning adjustments to several strings, flicked her head and hair to the side, and removed her shoes. After putting on the slippers lying next to her, she looked straight at Charles, smiled, and blew him a kiss. She noticed Charles didn't blush.

The music began. It lured, and Charles opened. He picked out three recurring themes and wondered if a separate theme pointed to her, him, or Lobashevsky. He decided the themes called to all three as one. The themes swarmed, flew, inverted, disappeared, and appeared again in a different key, in different pitches, and in different harmonies. The themes disappeared and troubling sounds took their place. Charles couldn't absorb the music. His mind rejected it. However, Popov looked absorbed in it, and she played with her eyes closed.

Charles closed his eyes and tried to open his heart. This music was to honor him, she'd said. He no longer tried to follow the music; he let the music follow him as he thought about Popov, his father, Andrica. And for the first time in a long while, he thought about his mother. She'd left his life when he was seven years old, but he remembered her. It was her singing that had come back to him. Her melodies had no resemblance to the music being played before him. He looked through squinted eyes; Popov had hugged the harp closer to her, eyes still closed.

As Popov played, strange new harmonies entered not his mind but his heart. He accepted the music without reservation. As Popov closed in and feathered atonalities, Charles didn't cringe at the discordance; he accepted all of it. He saw his mother, his father, and himself as a child. One by one, the original themes of Popov's music came back. Stronger. Purified. He couldn't believe these same themes played a short while ago were now infused with an ineffable richness. His spirit soared. He felt his maturity ripen. The music built to a flourish, and he glimpsed into a future, his future, one intimating stability and competence.

When Popov finished, they were both overcome and unable to speak. Charles looked into Popov's eyes; he tried to find his voice. They both gave up and let the last vestiges of the music say it for them.

Without realizing it, Charles stood and went to Popov. She rose up from her harp and kissed him. Without a word, her music permeated his soul. Charles picked her up and carried her into her bedroom. He laid her on the bed and, eyes closed, they kissed again. Charles got off the bed and went to her bedroom door. He closed it from the inside and shut down the light.

# 47

THE NEXT EVENING, CHARLES WORKED WITH RAMANUJAN.

"I'd sure like a Cuban cigar right now," Ramanujan said.

Charles smiled. "Is that why you are fidgety tonight?"

"I think it might be my appendix. I've got a continual stitch in my side."

"You should have it checked."

"People here don't realize the right tobacco is a proper stimulant." Ramanujan gave himself a last rub. "Anyway, let's continue. If we mersennate this expression with the mathematics behind the previous alien signals, where will it bring us?"

They worked together for another hour before Ramanujan decided he'd had enough for the night. "We've made progress," he said. "I feel we're on to something. See you next time."

.................................

THE NEXT MORNING, CHARLES SAT AGAIN WITH CONRAD. THEY DIScussed their individual projects and Conrad brought him up to date about his time with Salk.

As they did this, Andrica pranced by and snubbed Charles, kicking his foot. She then leaned over and whispered something into the ear of one of his rivals.

"What's up with that?" Conrad said.

Charles frowned. "I don't know. She says I've been ignoring her."

"So, how did it go with Ramanujan?"

"Not bad. He's complaining about his appendix. I told him he should have it checked."

"Appendix?"

"He's surprised that after all this time, other than a few studies and explanations, no one truly knows what our appendix is for."

Conrad stared at Charles. "Yo-Yo Yi. Yi." Conrad stood.

"What is it? Conrad, are you nuts?"

"Charles." Conrad laughed. "I could kiss you."

"Now I know you're nuts."

"Listen, tell the heads I couldn't make class today. And cover for me in lab. I'll make it up to you. I promise." And off he went.

"What should I tell them in lab?" Charles hollered.

Conrad did a 180 and smiled. "Tell 'em it's my appendix." He completed the 360 and hustled off.

..................................

SALK SAW CONRAD WAVING TO HIM. *STRANGE HE SHOULD BE HERE now,* Salk thought. The boy flashed a smile as Salk left the conference room, where he'd been listening to advances and updates from the other Liftees. Anand was monitoring the session, and, as Salk had already spoken, Anand said nothing when Salk left.

"You should be in academy," Salk said.

"Yes, but, Dr. Salk, remember how you said a graft takes too long to mate with the body for M-L-M, and a functioning part of the body doesn't work for M-L-M, and all parts of the body have purpose and function?"

"Yes."

"What about the appendix?"

Salk stared at him. "Hook up the appendix as the actual graft." He offered a smile. "It's worth a try."

..................................

"ABSOLUTELY NOT," SAID POPOV. THEY WERE IN HER OFFICE. "IT'S a splendid idea, but any such procedure on Conrad or anyone else here is forbidden."

"I mention it," Salk said, "because we need to continue tests and monitoring of the convict as she is, with her graft. We don't want to disrupt that experiment."

"I want him to use me. I offer myself," Conrad said.

"Good of you, Conrad. Right now, I want you to go back to academy."

Conrad pursed his lips and glanced at Salk.

"Chair Popov is right, son." He put his hand on Conrad's shoulder. "Go. But come see me tonight. Okay?"

Conrad got up from the chair, nodded to Popov, said, "Thank you," and left.

"As for Ramanujan," Popov said, "we have another problem."

"I can remove his appendix," Salk said.

"That's the problem. We can't touch him—what if the operation led to complication? He's being sent back lest we disturb a timeframe, which may lead to repercussions."

"Do you think it possible?"

"Based on my own error of judgment—I do. And you've learned about the asteroid from nowhere slamming into Earth. Ramanujan understands what's at stake and has agreed to it. He leaves this afternoon. He will be replaced by biophysicist and former musical prodigy Professor Ignace Pemberton, who was after your time."

Salk looked as if he were recalculating. "Conrad said his mother is working with a group on a complete brain transplant. How far along are they?"

"They have completed a partial brain transplant. We aren't ready for a full."

"I see."

"I'll have another convict delivered to you for test purposes."

.....................................

AS A COURTESY TO CONRAD'S INSPIRATION, SALK WAITED THE FEW minutes for him to arrive. The convict, a young man of twenty, had been prepared and was resting.

"What is your crime?" Salk asked.

"Murder. I killed a contestant in a math jamb."

"Why?"

"He cheated. He got answers piped into his anus."

"What? How did that help him?"

"Just four possible answers: A, B, C, or D. The right answer was a vibration of 1, 2, 3, or 4 times."

Salk sat down and observed him. He looked much younger than twenty; Salk had thought he was a juvenile. He was connected to the operating table, and, as with other cons, his head was shaved. He was dressed in an orange jumpsuit, and Salk had the feeling the eyes looking at him belied a huge intelligence.

"How did you kill him?"

"I electrocuted him. With modifications to his cheating device. Which I showed him before electrocution."

"Do you . . . would you do it again?"

"No," he rasped, and looked away. "I entered the orphanage at six and left at sixteen. I'd been wait-listed at academy, but was never taken. Two years ago, I could have gone to Uppsala University, Sweden, if I'd won the jamb; it was sponsored by Uppsala, and I competed there. It was the last round."

Salk winced. "But if they knew of his cheating—they found out, right?"

"Too late. Another contestant, who'd also been defeated earlier, sussed out his suspicions, stole the device, and told me. I'd taken some pills and went berserk."

"So you were put on death row?"

"The person I murdered was a nephew of the king of Norway. I didn't know that."

"Well, you are no longer on death row. And I'll do what I can to plead your case."

"Oh, sure. I've heard that all my life." He looked to one side of the room, sighed, and looked to the other side before looking back at Salk. "Nevertheless . . . I hope I can help you, Doctor."

Conrad arrived. "Dr. Salk, I have my friend, Charles, if that's okay. He was here to say goodbye to Ramanujan."

"Sure. Say hello to . . . excuse me, I didn't get your name," he said to the prisoner.

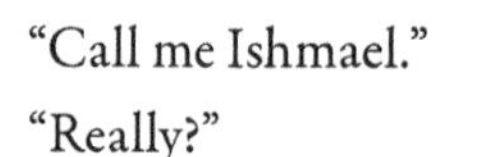

"Call me Ishmael."

"Really?"

"Really."

..................................

THAT EVENING, WITH CHARLES AND CONRAD ASSISTING, SALK readied for the first test via the patient's appendix with accompanying recombinant bio-feed to the brain. He confirmed the patient's well-being after transmitting simple neural electrical pulses.

"Yes, I feel all of that," Ishmael said.

"Good. Get ready to absorb the next feed. Please don't say or reveal anything until I tell you this feed has been completed. It will take about eight minutes."

Salk dimmed the overhead light and watched the prisoner close his eyes. Ishmael had pulled the sheet up to his neck and, if you didn't know, you'd think you were looking at either a dead boy or a sleeping angel. Salk wanted to take his stethoscope to the heart, but resisted.

Charles, Conrad, and Salk waited out the silence. Conrad pumped a fist when they spotted a tiny twitch at the corner of Ishmael's mouth. *Thank the Lord*, Salk thought. He tapped his glasses. *Five minutes down, three minutes to go.*

But at nine minutes, the feed continued. Salk rechecked everything and put a finger to his lips. Another twitch from Ishmael, same spot, and two minutes after that the feed still continued. At thirteen minutes the feed was complete.

Ishmael opened his eyes, initially looking puzzled, and then smiled up at the three of them.

"Charles, before anything further, be good enough to collect Aasen and Krebs. I feel positive about this," Salk said.

..................................

KREBS UTTERED TO ISHMAEL IN M-L-M. ISHMAEL UTTERED BACK.

Aasen selected a posterboard from a pile and held it up for Ishmael to read. It was covered with Swedish, a language understood by both

Aasen and Ishmael: *Translate what you see here to M-L-M. After, explain to me, in M-L-M, as best you can, the grammar vitals used.*

*Our father who art in heaven . . .*

Ishmael's translation of the prayer wasn't perfect, but it was about as good as Krebs and Aasen would do. He tripped on explaining some of the grammar. "He's about eighty percent, maybe a bit more," Aasen estimated. "He hasn't distinguished all the sound changes between phonemes, which vary from language to language. He has created, I believe, two neologisms, and his VOT—voice-onset-time—is off.

Krebs uttered again in M-L-M and Ishmael, without significant pauses, replied in M-L-M. "He's missing some of the vitals," Krebs said, "and he relies too much on onomatopoeia, but this is impressive. My congratulations to you, Doctor Salk."

Conrad looked to Charles and pumped his hand. "I owe you one."

"And now," Salk said, "one more test. An example of what might be termed 'mental biomimicry.'" As far as Salk knew, Ishmael had already been fed data for music into the appendix and into the biochips in his brain. He replayed the associated M-L-M musical patterns into Ishmael's appendix, which again traveled to his brain. They waited for him to connect the musical patterns to numbers and words.

Ishmael looked at them, clueless. "What? Am I supposed to do something?"

Salk played the patterns into the walls, ceiling, and floor. And waited.

"I hear this," Ishmael said, looking up and around. "I don't see the connection."

"Do you understand any of it?" Salk asked.

Ishmael listened while Salk confirmed the convict was registering the patterns, every sound. Salk was certain all the data for M-L-M, including music, had been transmitted.

Ishmael put his hands over his ears and closed his eyes, trying to concentrate. "I can't make much out of it," Ishmael said. "Most of the sounds are strange to me. I don't get what you want me to do."

"It's okay," Salk said. "You have done more than enough already."

"Yes," Charles said, feeling a bit sorry for the con, "you've helped us big-time."

Later, Salk sipped lime water and chewed on processed oats at his private quarters. *I included all dissonances into the feeds for Ishmael,* he thought. *Did I miss some? Am I deficient in cybernetics? I'm told, as an uttered language, M-L-M is not effective. It communicates better than most tongues. But not near well enough. We must have the music, say they. We can conquer this in time—151 days left, five months—if we can get the music.*

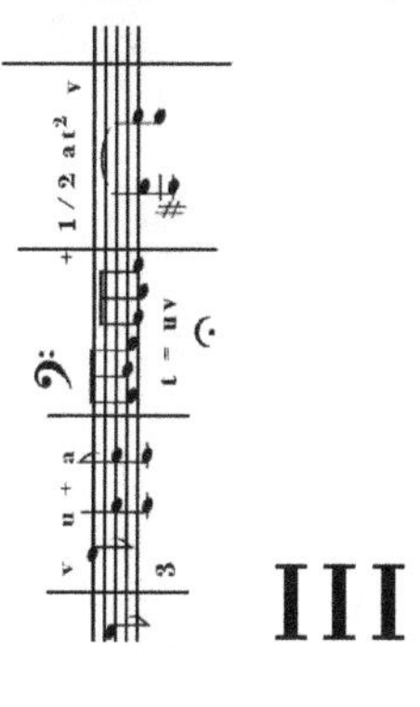

# III

Language is the most intrinsic product of any culture; you can't comprehend the language till you've understood the culture—and how do you understand a culture till you know its language?

—Brian W. Aldiss, "The Failed Men"

# 48

FROM THE BEGINNING, VECED LOBASHEVSKY WAS A HANDFUL. AS soon as he awoke, he was unstable and paranoid. Instead of awestruck ignorance, as with all the other Liftees, he grappled and attacked his handlers, trying to escape. It took three people to hold him and administer a sedative during his frantic hoots and hollers.

He awoke a second time, withdrawn and silent. His large eyes looked but didn't trust; instead of speaking, he squealed if anyone tried to approach him. Time Travel Control called WCM, asking if his brain should be "fed" under these conditions.

Magnuson was summoned, and he brought the entire wicker box containing the man's notebooks and papers, which kicked Lobashevsky into renewed frenzy. Magnuson drew up the cover of the box and reached in while Lobashevsky squealed, covered his eyes, and turned away. In Swedish, Finnish, and peasant Russian, Magnuson spoke to him about the summary binder he was holding in front of Lobashevsky.

Lobashevsky opened an eye between fingers and put down his hands. He stared at the tattered notebook which Magnuson placed into his grasp. In Russian, Magnuson tried to soothe him; he whispered and smiled. Lobashevsky opened his notebook and scanned pages. He didn't smile and didn't utter a sound. After a few minutes, he closed the notebook and clasped it with folded arms to his chest. Magnuson couldn't get through to him in any of the three languages. It was obvious Lobashevsky wouldn't give up his book without a fight; his scrawny hands clamped the notebook as a drowning man clamps a lifesaver.

In the end, they opted to wait on feeding his brain. Magnuson stayed while Lobashevsky remained under sedation and went to sleep, all the while holding the notebook. Four hours later, while in sedated sleep, his brain was fed. Twenty-four hours after, the longest for any recent Liftee, the feed was complete, and he woke up. Lobashevsky still held the notebook.

"Where are the guards?" Lobashevsky said to Magnuson.

"We don't have guards here. You're at a new place."

Lobashevsky didn't believe him and sneaked his eyes around the room he'd been rolled to. He looked at the drawn curtains; and when Magnuson drew them open, revealing a window screen, Lobashevsky glanced at Magnuson and surveyed the room again.

"Here, let me help you out of your wheelchair."

But when Magnuson came near, Lobashevsky pulled his notebook closer and gave him a wild-eyed warning look.

"As you wish, but you should look at the view out there." They were on floor 156 of the obelisk. Special arrangements had been made to quarantine Lobashevsky in the prearranged suite that consisted of an efficiency kitchen, a bedroom with adjoining bath, a common room with desk, and bare walls. Salk cautioned it would be best if he did not share the suite with another Liftee, at least for the time being, as the experiences thus far had overloaded him. Popov had further suggested Lobashevsky would become grounded when he met Liftees whose work he was familiar with.

Magnuson feigned opening the one window, and a breeze wafted in. Seagulls barked below. A hovercraft buzzed by, and Lobashevsky froze. Magnuson watched him. The new Liftee pointed as the hover buzzed back at window-screen level and hovered.

"Guards," Lobashevsky said. "Guards. Da." His finger shook.

Magnuson realized the hover was checking the quarantine. In a way, Lobashevsky was right. He decided not to counter him as the hover angled away and the sound of its rotors diminished.

A veil withdrew from the cryptologist's eyes. It was as if connections were validating within him, and he squinted, took himself to the fake window, and attempted to look outside. He fingered the screen's edges, and his shoulders stiffened as he realized the ruse. Magnuson tried to explain what it was, and what he was seeing, while the "prisoner" scowled at him. However, his first words of protest were not about the fake window.

"How did you get my notebook?"

Magnuson told him to sit down and he would explain. He offered him something to drink, and Lobashevsky, although Magnuson knew he had to be thirsty, refused. So, instead, Magnuson drank from the glass he'd offered. He offered it yet again, but still the Liftee hesitated. Magnuson showed him the bottle marked "Aqua" and poured himself more of the liquid, and drank. He placed the bottle and a glass beside Lobashevsky and sat before him to tell the complete story.

Thirty minutes later, Lobashevsky asked his second question. "So, this is a modern gulag?"

"No. A million times no. You have been Lifted—resurrected, you might say—because we recognize your genius and seek your help."

The WCM's newest Liftee sat there looking at Magnuson and, at last, poured himself some water. "And if I refuse?"

Magnuson shifted his legs and body; he'd become uncomfortable. He was bored and had lost zest for this misanthrope.

"If they throw me in prison, I don't care."

"Veced. You're not in Russia. It's 2490. You're in Indonesia."

"What happened to me—in Russia?"

"You, like most others, I suspect, would have died of hunger in the purge, during the reign of Stalin. You were selected to travel forward in time to come here; you were taken from a field at the gulag; you traveled, and we brought you to this spot."

"My notes, all my prison notes were destroyed. I was whipped. I'll die in the gulag."

"The box contains everything we found. It is late, Veced. We are both tired. Get some sleep; I'll come back tomorrow."

"So, I can't leave?"

"Well, no. We will keep you here. But you are free to pursue your work."

"Then I am in a prison. I'm not at all free. You want me to help you, so you've locked me up here. I'm not going to help you. Go ahead—kill me."

"You have it all wrong. Tomorrow, I will introduce you to another colleague who has been Lifted here just as you have. And no, I won't take your notebook or confiscate your other notes in the box. It is all yours. We give it back to you. Good night, Veced."

..................................

THE NEXT DAY, MAGNUSON BROUGHT PETITJEAN.

"So, you've brought another to try to break me. Don't think for a minute I'm fooled by this shift in technique—coming to me instead of me being dragged to you in shackles. The nice surroundings. Plenty of water. No, it's all the same, and I won't be fooled."

Petitjean was shocked. "What have we done to this man?"

"Nothing. He thinks this is the new Russian gulag." Magnuson looked at the empty water bottle beside the half-full new one. Prepared food had been left untouched. Magnuson knew the uselessness of offering pill food, and offered a suggestion. "While Mr. Petitjean tries to answer your questions, I'm going to cook us dinner. Here's my question, Veced. Would you like grilled salmon, or smoked eels with caviar?"

"And here's my answer. I don't care. I'll eat something after you both eat from the same plate first, and I get to wait ten minutes."

While Magnuson prepared the meal, Armando Petitjean did everything he could to draw out Lobashevsky.

Getting nowhere and becoming distracted by long-lost odors of kitchen-cooked food, including Indonesian rendang, which he'd brought for himself and asked Magnuson to reheat, Petitjean sat back and put his feet up on the coffee table between them.

"Mr. Lobashevsky, ask me a question. Anything."

"In these situations, it is you who asks questions. I'm supposed to give answers." Magnuson had dropped a pan, rattling Petitjean and Lobashevsky, but their eyes remained locked.

"I'm wondering whether I have the right person in front of me," Petitjean said. "If so, I was humbled by your notebook—I've read it word for word, equation by equation."

Lobashevsky watched him.

"In your notebook, you solved Lie Group E11. We didn't know of your solution. We finally solved that quest with a supercomputer in the third millennium." Petitjean smiled at him. Lobashevsky stared back.

"What I don't understand is, given that the solution describes the symmetries of a 301-dimensional object that can be rotated in 448 ways, what made you select dimension 301 for solution?"

Lobashevsky rubbed his chin with a finger and kept staring.

"Mr. Lobashevsky—may I call you Veced? It's simpler for me. Veced," Petitjean whispered to him, "how did you know to reach for the 301st dimension?"

Veced glanced behind Petitjean, as Petitjean realized Magnuson had walked up behind him. The newest Liftee said nothing.

They ate in silence. Veced ignored them and seemed to take delight in chewing with his mouth open and slurping water.

"Would you like another helping, Veced?" Magnuson said, platter raised.

Veced stuck out his plate, refused to look at either of them, and said nothing.

After dinner, Petitjean, under the eyes of Veced, pulled from a wrap a bottle of vodka he'd bought. He tore off the top seal while Magnuson found a bottle opener. Petitjean poured into three glasses, feeling a pressure from the eyes of Veced.

"So, the real interrogation begins," Veced said. "Wined, dined, and satisfied, you think I'll open up and talk."

All Petitjean and Magnuson could do was shake their heads.

"If it's to be like this, you might as well offer me a cigarette."

"They don't allow tobacco," Petitjean said.

Magnuson winced, and put up a hand too late.

"'Allow.' And you tell me this isn't a prison. You think you are speaking to an idiot?"

They got nowhere as Lobashevsky withdrew again. He pushed his vodka to the center of the table, got up, and sat away from the card table in his former chair. He refused to utter a word and wouldn't look at them.

"We may have Lifted the wrong person," Petitjean said at last to Magnuson.

They gave up; but as they approached the door to leave, Lobashevsky said, "If you had properly understood my notes, you would have realized I didn't guess by reaching for dimension 301. It was clear from Lie E9 and E10 that only dimension 301 would lead to solution. It's in my notes on 'contained category sets.'"

Petitjean and Magnuson turned around and began to walk back to him.

"No. Please, get out. Thank you for dinner. Now, get out."

# 49

PETITJEAN AND MAGNUSON WENT TO WCM FILES AND RECORDS AND retrieved duplicated copies of Lobashevsky's work. They paged to his solution of Lie 8, and found an asterisk referring to the index he'd written, in cramped hand. Both remembered how they'd ignored this asterisk during their initial reading. Now that they were aware of the meaning, the index notes referred them to his work on category sets. They found it and followed his unique approach, equation by equation. They applied his original method to Lie E11 and, behold, there it was, plain as day. The solution led to dimension 301.

"This is our man. No question about it," Petitjean said. "What a talent."

But it wasn't easy. Magnuson and Petitjean, assigned to Lobashevsky, were losing precious time. When they showed him composites of alien transmissions and played him the recorded pulses, he refused to look at the patterns and covered his ears, persisting with the idea that he was a prisoner, that as soon as he revealed anything, they would lock him up in the gulag for good and melt the key. They left him. Magnuson went to his punching bag and, while pummeling the crap out of it, hit on an idea.

"I don't like your idea," Popov said. "It sets a precedent."

"True," Magnuson said. "But we've been unable to reach him, and Petitjean and I have reviewed his work. His unique approach, his depth, is uncanny. We are convinced he is the right person at the right time to help us."

"It seems like a waste of everyone's time, but I'll agree to it, providing you take him alone. I can't give up Petitjean too."

Magnuson went to Lobashevsky the following morning and tweaked his idea.

"Veced. We have learned that aside from being a mathematician and cryptologist, you are a master puzzle-solver. Am I right?"

Veced didn't nod or shake his head. He looked like he knew what was coming next, and said, "You are going to disguise what you want from me in the form of a puzzle."

"No. Not at all. Despite your gifts, some don't think you can solve what we need help with. I'm offering you an opportunity to travel with me to your homeland to see what it looks like centuries later. If you don't want to take a look at your roots, you can travel with me to any place in the world—your choice."

Lobashevsky stared at him.

"How does that sound?"

"It sounds like a trick."

"It's an offer—no strings attached. You have my word as a Scandinavian with ties to Old-Finland and your land. My paternal grandparents are from Turku."

"*Old*-Finland?"

Magnuson ignored Veced's question. "My maternal great-grandfather had pictures of his relatives from way back, as laborers, building the first Trans-Siberian Railroad."

Lobashevsky stared, uncomprehending.

"The world is a changed place since your time, Veced. Mother Russia of your time has been cut up into, at last count, twenty-nine separate countries, each with their own administrative governments."

"Why should I travel with you?"

"You don't have to. It's your choice, Veced. I'm making the offer. But for me to carry it out, you need to solve three difficult puzzles. These puzzles have been solved before. We aren't looking for information here."

"And if I refuse to solve them?"

Magnuson stared at him. He folded his hands and stared, waiting him out.

"Let me see the puzzles," he said.

Magnuson gave him a bag of puzzles. "Assuming you prefer to work with paper and pencil, they are also in the bag."

Veced peeked into the bag and glanced at one of the puzzles.

"They are from a world puzzle championship," Magnuson said, "that took place in Old-Poland in 2010."

"Can you wait outside? I work better alone."

"Veced. I was planning to come back tomorrow morning."

Veced took up the three puzzles and read the instructions. He took a cursory glance at each puzzle and mumbled something unintelligible. "Come back in an hour. I'll have them for you."

Shocked, Magnuson could only shake his head. "Veced, there's something I've been meaning to ask you. You remain paranoid about my intention to help you. Have you absorbed the new histories we fed you, after you first arrived?"

"That's a trick question. We both know I was brainwashed."

"Not brainwashed, Veced—"

"What do you mean, 'not brainwashed'? You just admitted my brain was fed." He threw the puzzles and bag at Magnuson. "Get out."

Magnuson watched him close his eyes. He picked up the strewn paper puzzles and the bag and laid them on the coffee table. Lobashevsky had covered his face with his hands and rested his elbows on his knees.

"Please forgive me, Veced. It was a poor choice of words on my part. I understand why you think the way you do. I apologize." Magnuson went to the door. "I'll come back in two hours to check on you."

Magnuson spent the time at the nearest beach, if it could still be called a beach. He'd hovered down, paid for a spot, and sat looking at ocean. The sea was choppy. The devastation behind him was sickening. The tsunami had rolled up a mish-mash of island shacks, broken boats, dead fish, and parts of human bodies still decomposing. A shift of wind blew the stench toward him, and he turned away from the eruption of filth. He didn't want to look behind him and was glad the area he'd chosen on the beach was guarded and policed. Rioting and looting were rampant east of him; he could hear shots and saw hovers laser-gatling, but behind him it was, for the moment, quiet. He looked at the ocean. Surfers by the hundreds paddled in search of the next good curl. They looked like orcas, with their fastened tail fins, the imposing strapped-on back-fin, and hand fins extending from outstretched arms. Old-fashioned surfboards were no longer needed. At first, decades ago, a few complained something had been lost without the board. But as the fins and the back-fin were tweaked, they became human orcas and surfboards were discarded for good. The last one he'd seen was in a museum.

Magnuson looked to the murky horizon and wondered what it must have been like to watch a sunset, a gorgeous one like he'd seen pictures of, where the sun melted into ocean. Sunrises in current times were snagged in smog-filled clouds. He felt he should be thankful climate change had stopped, but he still couldn't compose himself. He needed a place more isolated, which meant he should find an island remnant that had been abandoned during climate change. He had time and, before long, as he hovered low, he saw some shacks sticking up from the sea on stilts. He maneuvered until he saw a clump of palms, and landed. He found a place under a palm and sat, looking like a cartoon character from a comic where a survivor was stranded on a clump of sand next to a palm tree in the middle of an ocean.

A half-mile away he could see a grass house, its roof made from wattles and built on retractable stilts. He could tell that the stilts were completely extended because the extension tubes were skinny and had pushed the shack up the last few feet out of the water, humankind's way to fool nature. *Ha.* Magnuson understood that at first, the stilts of many shacks were retracted, but as the waters rose year after year, the stilts—made of hydraulic telescoping tubes—were extended. After the siege from an expanding ocean, the few remaining homes on this isle stuck up just inches from drifts of mud and sand, or puddles from ocean waters. It had been a long goodbye for the Federated States of Micronesia. *Where did these families go?*

Magnuson was frustrated. Lobashevsky was driving him nuts. He hoped it would be worth it in the end.

Two hours later, Magnuson walked in to find Lobashevsky sitting in the same chair. His eyes were open, but he didn't look at him, he just stared at the window screen and projected sky in front of him. There wasn't any sign of either the puzzles or the bag, and Magnuson didn't ask. He sat down and backed his chair at an angle not interrupting Lobashevsky's view and said nothing. It had worked before. He'd try again to wait him out.

A full twenty minutes went by, and neither said a word. To Magnuson it seemed like a lifetime, yet he felt closer to Veced. He divined communication of an unknown sort between them. It was when Magnuson, without moving his head, examined the floor in front of Lobashevsky and noticed tiny bits of something which might have come from a pencil eraser, that his heart lurched.

"Next time . . . you say your name is Magnuson?"

"Yes."

"Next time, Mr. Magnuson, I hope you will give me a bit more of a challenge."

For the first time, Lobashevsky showed the hint of a smile from the corner of his mouth.

"Are you suggesting . . . no, you couldn't have."

Lobashevsky reached under the frilled hem of the chair and took out the bag. He handed the bag to Magnuson. "As I say, I was expecting something more complex. Nevertheless, thank you."

Magnuson inspected the completed puzzles, the first being the Pentomino, considered the most difficult. It lay on top. All twelve given shapes resided properly in the grid. None touched, not even at the corner. Magnuson put it aside and looked at the Poker puzzle. It was perfect, the twelve named poker hands appearing in each row, column, and diagonal. He slipped the puzzle underneath and looked at the Number Tree. The numbers 1 to 21 were placed in the proper circles so that for each branch of the tree, the bottom number was the sum of all connected numbers above it.

Magnuson looked up. "Where would you like to go, Veced?"

# 50

FROM TIME IMMEMORIAL, ONE OF THE MORE INDECENT COURSES A human could take was to ignore another. Man and woman, even as they coped with the world's violence and existential fears of the present age, still craved recognition. Charles had immersed himself more and more in mathematics and was flexing his mind with Conrad. But Andrica, even in the mornings, on walks to academy, couldn't impress Charles and was frustrated as the hip Conrad and loopy Charles laughed and synced in mysterious intellectual discussions. She felt cast off. She was adrift. And beyond pissed. Her friends noticed how Charles engaged with Andrica less. Andrica had done all she could to bring Charles back. She hadn't seen him attracted to anyone else, had tried one last time to take him from Conrad, and failed. She'd had enough.

Andrica challenged Charles to a boxing brawl, and copied their mutual friends and acquaintances on the challenge invite. There was no way out for Charles. The refereed slugfest was scheduled for the next evening at the mathetorium's Ringside.

Although variations of the martial arts were popular in Asia, some things never changed, and brawling was still the way to settle disputes. Two combatants, holding a grudge against the other, untrained in the art of self-defense, continued to settle their differences as they had in schoolyards for millennia. Courage, toughness, the will to go the distance and settle the problem was all that was needed. It helped, of course, if you knew how to move and had tussled with others.

"Yi Yi Yo, Charles," said Conrad, at their next morning's meeting, "what did you do to Andrica?"

Charles didn't look happy. "She says . . . something about I don't respect her."

"Did she pay for the brawl and set it up too?"

Charles nodded. "She even sent an invitation to Popov."

"Yikes. She must be jealous, Charles."

"Popov already told me she's not coming."

"When do you select?"

"Let's scrub our session? I need to go."

"Go. I owe you a cover."

As Charles turned to leave, Andrica strutted by and burned him a look. "You're gonna be sorry," she hissed.

....................................

RINGSIDE WAS PACKED. FACES WERE PAINTED, WAR CHANTS WERE whooped by girls and boys, martial arts music scored with grunts and shrieks boomed from the walls, containers of Loose were passed. A face-slap contest of two girls enthralled a bunch of academy mathematicians in front of the roped, lit ring. War and violence permeated the air and built upon itself as cliques batuqued with mean and shifty eyes.

Security locked all doors, and an announcer took the prefab stage.

"Good evening, everyone. Welcome to Brawwwwwlllllll."

The over-adrenalized crowd erupted and roared for a full minute. From every quarter one could hear martial war calls—hands quickly covering and uncovering mouths to ululate mincing screams and screeches from throats—the plethora of sound cresting to monster-like emanations, which flooded the arena in a final sonic blast.

The lights around the ring dimmed and a square cubicle was lowered by cables from the ceiling above. Inside, Charles and Andrica faced each other behind separate consoles, which contained four knob-ended levers—two for the left hand, two for the right, at each console. These levers controlled the upper body. Legs and feet were controlled by foot pedals. The cubicle rested twenty feet above ring center.

Two professional cyborg fighters, a man and a woman selected by the combatants, entered the ring below from opposite sides. The man's trunks spelled "Charles"; the woman's trunks, "Andrica."

The announcer referred to his notes. "Representing Charles Wang De Costa, and wearing yellow trunks, is Crusher, cyborg 217-Z." The crowd cheered and pumped fists as Crusher stood motionless. The announcer, looking perplexed, took a few steps and looked to the control cubicle above. He waved a hand and Charles, to his chagrin, had been focused on Andrica's tawdry demeanor—spiked hair, fight tattoos covering her arms, an indecent perfume drifting to his nostrils. Andrica, and the hussy in the ring with Andrica's name on her trunks, stuck her tongue out at him. Charles grabbed a lever and Crusher raised his hand and closed a fist. The roar of the crowd went up a notch.

"Wearing green trunks and chest guard, representing Andrica Jennifer Saint-Saens, Annihilator, cyborg 216-X1." As the crowd screamed, the cyborg did leaps around Crusher, ending in a backflip with fisted hands raised. The crowd loved it, and the girls and women at Ringside stomped their feet in unison as they shouted, "Stomp the Crusher, Stomp the Crusher, stomp, stomp, stomp." Over and over again they repeated the words and stomped their feet as Annihilator smiled. Crusher, unsmiling, looked straight ahead.

The announcer stuttered the lights and the crowd stilled.

"This will be a twelve-round match, five minutes per round. The cyborgs are lobotomized and move their arms, fingers, legs, and feet via levers in the control consoles above them. Those are the limbs controlled. These cyborgs can, independently, move their heads and jaws, twist their bodies, bend, and maintain control of their facials. And," the announcer hesitated for effect, "they feel everything." He held up a finger as the shouting subsided. "By pre-agreement," again hesitating for effect, "Charles and Andrica will feel twenty percent brawler pain. Ladies and gentlemen, let's brawwwwwlllllll."

More chants and stomping as the lights dimmed a final time around the ring, and brightened within it. Both the male and female cyborgs showed taut and powerful physiques, and, by regulation, they weighed within three pounds of the other. The man looked heavier; the woman sleeker and quicker. They wore gloves around their wrists and lower part of the hand, but their fingers were free. Both had competed for several years, and both were class champions. This was the first time they'd competed against each other. The ring referee drew them close, said a few mumbled words, had them touch hands, and then he withdrew.

In the glass-walled cubicle above, according to custom, Charles stood and bowed to the challenger.

"May the truer person win, Charles," Andrica said. "And, Charles, it's just twenty percent personal."

*I don't think she's as upset as she wants me to believe,* Charles thought. *But I am: this is bullshit, and I'm going to put a quick end to it.*

The first couple of rounds were uncoordinated and brutal. As Crusher and Annihilator whacked on each other, they learned how to react to the amateurish antics of their controllers above. At one point in the second round, Crusher arched a brow that seemed to apologize to his opponent as he rolled an eye to Charles in the cage above. But in that instant, Andrica head-butted Charles, knocking him sideways into the ropes. "You bitch," the real Charles yelled, grabbing his head.

Andrica closed in, smothering Charles with blows and kicks as Charles thrashed and struggled to get away from the ropes. Just as the bell sounded, Charles, before he could catch himself, kicked Andrica in the groin.

"OW!" the real Andrica said.

"Sorry," Charles said.

"You prick. You're gonna pay." Andrica hugged her lower body.

The crowd went wild.

The referee stepped in and ordered a point deducted from Charles, and awarded it to Andrica.

In the corners, handlers Q-tipped cuts, swabbed bruises, tipped water bottles into open mouths, and plastered water-sopped cloths over sweaty heads.

Rounds three through five intensified. The contestants were in the fight of their lives, and everyone knew it. Where they had telegraphed roundhouse rights before, now they brawled. "Stomp the Crusher, stomp the Crusher, stomp, stomp, stomp," the women shouted—including General Osteen, who led a group stomp of her own in a middle bleacher.

In the cubicle above the ring, Charles and Andrica endured bruises and pain, which was becoming unbearable, and they were doing their best to end the match. Charles had no time to wonder how Crusher took the beating he did, for he, Charles, ached all over, and, in a pissed-off sweat, stood yanking the controls, yelling to Crusher, "Kick the bitch! Pummel her!"

Andrica flurried at the levers. "OUCH! You fucking bastard. Tear his eyes out. Bite the prick."

In the eighth round Andrica thrust her hands below Charles's crotch and squeezed. Charles at once dropped his hands and yelped. Andrica, sensing a kill, squeezed with every ounce of her strength and shook her hand while doing it, promising no matter what, she would not let go.

Crusher jumped, twisted, bent, leaped, and screamed. General Osteen, in battle fatigues, put on her military-issue binocs and focused on Charles. She watched the boy flail at levers with one hand as he screeched. She smiled, knowing where the other hand was.

Charles knew it was over. He saw Andrica's bug eyes watching him, and that's when, in the dim recesses of his mind, he thought of one last chance. With a jerk of a lever, he knobbed it to thrust a hand straight to her eyes. The cyborg knew what to do; with a last knob-jostle by Charles, Crusher shot out his second and third fingers, which penetrated her eye sockets. Andrica let go.

Crusher fell to the ring floor, flat on his back, both hands covering his balls. Annihilator covered her eyes and walked in a daze around the ring, collapsing to her knees. In the booth above, Charles stood, turned from Andrica, and leaned his head on the wall, his hands covering his cojones. Next to him, through hand-covered eyes, Andrica was attempting to cry.

The crowd grew silent as handlers came into the ring. Both cyborgs were given spinal shots, put on stretchers, and removed. The announcer stepped forward.

"Ladies and gentlemen, this brawl has been declared a draw. Our best wishes to Charles De Costa, Andrica Saint-Saens, and to our brave cyborgs. Good evening."

# 51

BEFORE MEETING WITH LOBASHEVSKY, MAGNUSON TROLLED THROUGH WCM World News. Separate newscasts direct from individual countries were suspect. Each year, exaggerations increased, more lies were told, and veiled threats accumulated from nations "between the lines" in their newscasts. Thus, Magnuson ignored a report of a stolen nuke in South Africa's guarded arsenal, which the announcer said had been transported to Indonesia under veiled circumstances. The simple souls, common workers and providers, listened to these broadcasts and defended their turfs much like local fans supported their soccer teams. However, WCM World News, via Tier, vetted all news from everywhere to try to give an honest but useless fix on news of the planet.

Magnuson got updates:

*Canada and Siberia have taken a hard line and have rejected efforts by General Braun and WCM Chair Popov to de-escalate their war to a Conflict. Popov in a last-minute . . .*

WCM reporter Helmut Breen had this to say about the growing tensions between Denmark and Greenland:

*. . . Greenland says the statute of limitations on mineral rights in Denmark expired thirty-two years ago. Greenland Premier Otto Di Marcela orders Denmark to cease all threats and innuendos. "We will not be bullied."*

*The two recent tsunamis remain an embarrassment for WCM. Word has it that more is behind the story. Two leading journalists, who wish to remain unidentified, question the remarkable coincidence in time of impact and question how this could have happened. WCM Chair Popov claims . . .*

*In other news, amateur astronomers have noted new activity at Moonbase-1. And reporters have noted additional security at Indonesia's Orion Launch. When asked about possible new developments, General Braun was circumspect. "When the time comes, you will all be apprised," he'd said.*

Droogs, if tuned at all to WCM World News, listened with half an ear. They'd been jaded long ago with unkept promises, like better housing. Elder inhabitants in villages produced enough wares to survive, but their offspring joined gangs who scavenged and stole for sustenance beyond the ubiquitous alga-rice. They were convinced everything on WCM World News was a hoax. People were fighting and dying around them, others had been lost in storms and earthquakes, and the rumor of some type of upcoming inoculation, to prevent a rampant virus, was interpreted as another ruse. What possible virus could it be if medicines had already cured everything? Besides, the privileged who sat in obelisks and thought they knew everything had no idea what it was like to fight off immigrants pouring in from the next island, looters from changed local regimes, and droogs who confiscated their property in the middle of the night. No, individual voices were not heard. If so, they were ignored. Old-fashioned newspapers were nonexistent. Not everyone could be a soccer star and escape; few showed the mathematical ability required to contend or be admitted to academy. The droogs had coalesced and even turned against trusted commoners. The hordes knew the droogs were up to something—it was just a matter of time—and common people let them reign and stayed out of their way.

Just before shutting down WCM-WN, Magnuson heard an alert about a group of twenty-odd teenaged droogs, who shook down a legitimate food mart in Samoa Town, killed the owner and his two daughters, and dispersed, their backpacks crammed with gourmet food and spices.

..................................

LOBASHEVSKY ANSWERED MAGNUSON BEFORE HE EVEN ASKED THE question. "I was born near Kiev. Take me there."

"It has changed since your time, Veced."

"Show me."

Magnuson excused himself while getting clearance from Popov, who had to alert General Braun. Braun confirmed danger in the area but ordered Putin escorts for the shielded military hover. The hover would pick up Magnuson and Lobashevsky in two hours, and two of Braun's aides would accompany them in the hover.

As Veced entered the hover, he panicked. "Why do the guards strap me in?"

"Veced, these aren't . . . they are more like aides," Magnuson said.

Veced stared at him.

"Hasn't everything I've told you thus far been true? You can trust me."

Veced said nothing, and Magnuson hoped the fear in his face would soften.

To prepare him, after getting clearance from Popov and the General, Magnuson had programmed the hover for a slower, low-altitude route. "I don't want him to think only his old-Russia has the problem," Magnuson had said.

"Can you see?" Magnuson asked Veced.

He nodded, but Magnuson increased the telescopic view from the glass-like viewing pane covering the hover's floor.

"What's that?" Veced asked, as they flew over a ten-mile-long by three-mile-wide floating city.

"It's called Javina-Three. One of three floating cities built to accommodate inhabitants who lost their islands."

"It moves?"

"Yes, to allow for waste management and resupply. We also have a military hover base there."

Veced rubbed his eyes and had to look again. Magnuson called for someone to loosen their straps. Veced said nothing, but his bulging eyes looked disbelieving. He turned to Magnuson. "I've learned about movie screens, is that what this is?" He pointed to the viewing pane beneath them.

"No, Veced. What you see is real. Everything you will see on this journey is real, true, and not artifice."

"What happened here?" Veced asked, as they flew over a devastated island showing skeleton structures and tumbles of blasted concrete.

"The Indonesian civil war," Magnuson said. "This island took a direct nuclear hit."

"Are those people I see?"

"Your eyes do not betray you." Magnuson saw people emerging like ants from an anthill.

"Spears? They carry spears?"

"Indeed. This particular island has been forgotten. People there live under mob rule. They've built dugouts to scrounge nearby islands for food, and no one dares to stop them. They are vicious people, Veced. We sometimes joke that if we don't follow the rules at WCM, we might be dropped by parachute into Cinder-Town."

"Why not bomb it again?"

"We drop in prisoners—crippled-lifers and the criminally insane—from time to time. Sociologists track them and study the outcomes. The Military infiltrates other droog-infested islands and observes."

Later, while crossing the South China Sea, they saw a navy hovercraft, carriers, and warships. Approaching Viet Nam, they witnessed new devastation. Judging by the smoke and scattered fires, it was recent.

"What you see here happened less than twenty-four hours ago." Magnuson increased the magnification to focus on armed soldiers scattered amongst the ruins. "The soldiers are from World Army's Light Infantry Division. They are rooting out gangs. Nomads and droogs."

The devastation got worse as the hover angled north-northwest toward old Russia. What were giant 150-floor buildings had been smashed by incendiary bombs and toppled into massive disarray, as if an earthquake-tsunami had overrun the area. But this particular area was inland, the heart of an abandoned Conflict between Laos and Thailand.

"Who lives there now?" Veced asked.

"I'm told subterranean tunnels have been rebuilt under rubble. We hear horror stories of wounded survivors who have resorted to cannibalism. It's a wasteland, and no one ventures there." *The Conflict should have been upgraded to a Declared, so they could have nuked it*, Magnuson thought.

"What happened to all the other islands out there?" Veced pointed to a cockpit window. "My mind, loaded with all the new garbage you brainwashed into me, asks the question."

Magnuson answered, "The water table rose. Island cities sank. Earth—terra firma—weakened and disappeared everywhere."

Veced caught sight of what he thought might be Kiev, and strained against his harness as he tried to get a better look. Magnuson pantomimed to the aide, and Veced's belt was released. They flew over some mountains, and Lobashevsky pointed with his index finger but said nothing. When the hover crossed over a dozen creeper-tanks and artillery bastions, with more sighted ahead, he pointed again.

"Is this real?"

"I'm afraid so. But fighting has been suspended for you and me, Veced."

Battle smoke and a stench Veced recognized entered the hover's vent. Veced sniffed. "Flesh. I know the smell from pogroms."

Magnuson put an arm on his shoulder.

Lobashevsky looked on devastation unlike anything he'd ever seen. "This is worse than World War II, which you brainwashed me with. Where is Kiev?"

Magnuson ignored the brainwash comment. "You're looking at it." Magnuson patted Veced's shoulder and Veced pushed him off.

"What happened?"

"It's a long story. Since your time, Canada has become a major—"

Suddenly, the hover was hit and shook and yawed before geeing true. Veced had tumbled and banged into the floor console as the aides and Magnuson released their harnesses and tried to grab him.

Veced fought them off and thought he was fighting for his life. One bloodied aide tried to answer an incoming emergency, but his glasses were yanked off by Lobashevsky. When they had him contained, the hover was hit again. All four occupants were flung starboard and banged into the aerodynamic curvature, as the hover stopped shaking and hawed true.

Magnuson, looking through one eye while covering another, saw Veced below him sprawled on the viewing pane, not moving. He shouted to the aides, and they managed to buckle Veced into his seat. While one aide retrieved his glasses and another got medicines, Magnuson felt for Veced's pulse. "Thank God," Magnuson said.

The voice in Magnuson's ear was so loud, he looked for the hover's intercom. He tapped his glasses.

"Yes. I'm here, Chair Popov."

*There has been a breach in protocol. The Canadians have ignored the temporary truce and have attacked the Siberians. Come back. Bring back Lobashevsky. I repeat, bring back Lobashevsky at once.*

..................................

AFTER ALL MEDICAL TESTS ON LOBASHEVSKY HAD BEEN COMpleted, after Magnuson had convinced Popov the worst had passed—"He's recovering nicely and on the cusp of discovery"—Magnuson and Petitjean were allowed to deliver the Liftee to his quarters.

"It's been quite a day," Magnuson said to Veced.

The bandaged-wrapped head of Veced nodded. He tried to say something and coughed up more phlegm mixed with blood.

"Sleep, Veced. You need to sleep."

# 52

"GENERAL, I WANT A COMPLETE EXPLANATION," POPOV COMMANDED into her headpiece.

Braun wanted to give her the bad news first, but wasn't going to risk trying to skirt what she thought was the real emergency.

"Russian-Siberia claims Canada cheated on the imposed forty-eight-hour *ceasefire* of last week, in which the Red Cross evacuated the wounded and delivered medicines."

"Is that true?"

"Yes, but the time cheated was one hour."

"Are you telling me, General, because of one hour last week, your truce was ignored today?"

"Yes. Chair Popov, I—"

"Listen to me, General. What happened today was unconscionable. If you cannot impose a suspension of arms and have it followed, I have every right to—"

"Have me relieved. I need to hand you my resignation."

Her silence spoke to him.

"I have terrible news," he said. "Another low in our species has been reached."

He could hear her breaths, and he forced himself to continue. Legs wound around the other, frowns crinkling his forehead, he closed his eyes.

"Chair Popov, I've just learned Javina-Three has been nuked and sunk. We will search for survivors, but over 340,000 are presumed dead."

His glasses lost contact. *Can't blame her*, he thought. General Braun felt momentary relief. He hadn't wanted to give her the details of what he was learning, much less tell her who he believed was responsible.

.................................

THE NEXT MORNING, AFTER POPOV REFUSED HIS OFFER TO RESIGN, General Braun was investigating the Javina-Three tragedy. He'd put his glasses to *message*, and one caller was insistent. Upon retrieving the messages, Braun learned that in response to Siberia's breaking an imposed truce, the Canadians had bombed over half of Siberia's vertical-farming greenhouses.

The puzzle in Braun's head shifted. Javina-Three had nothing to do with the rancor of nations. Braun's initial thoughts had been correct—Javina-Three was carried out by droogs, and that froze him to the core. Indonesian droogs had initially developed in Indonesia, but at that time the military didn't take them seriously. Later, it was too late to merely strike in a few locales and wipe them out. When droogs learned to disengage and emerge elsewhere, droog cells proliferated and expanded. Now they were nowhere and everywhere, with established hierarchy and levels of command.

.................................

MAGNUSON STEPPED INTO LOBASHEVSKY'S ROOM.

For the second time, a corner of Veced's mouth turned up to a half-hearted smile. But it looked cockeyed under the bandages wrapped around his head.

"I have questions," Lobashevsky rasped.

"I'll answer whatever I can."

"Are Russian guards behind all this?"

"No!"

"Who is behind this?"

Magnuson explained everything all over again, like he and Petitjean had done before, and moved on to the ET signals.

"Nobody in this so-called present-age can figure them out?" Veced asked.

"As I say, we've made progress with M-L-M. We haven't gotten to square one in trying to decipher the alien signals, which we are convinced were prompted when we transmitted M-L-M to outer space."

It was Veced who got up and looked at the window screen. He tried putting his hands on the sill as he stared at the ocean. "I admit this prison is a palace compared to where I've been. But these contraptions"—he pointed at the screen—"will never fool me."

Magnuson said nothing.

"Okay. I'll look at what you have, under two conditions. One, I work here at this location, alone. I don't care if you bring Petitjean with you from time to time, but no one else. Two, I need polar-coordinate graph paper, in abundance, two gross of eraser pencils along with a pencil sharpener, a compass, and an engineer's ruler."

"Consider it done."

Magnuson came back later with several bags. He'd had to hover into a hamlet in United Viet Nam to gather everything Lobashevsky wanted. He heard deep snoring as he entered and saw from a peek into the bedroom that Lobashevsky was asleep on the bed. He was on his back, one arm covering his eyes. The overhead was dimmed, and Magnuson shut it down. He pulled the door and saw the note taped to it. *Please do not disturb. Come back in two days.*

.................................

TWO DAYS LATER, MAGNUSON ARRIVED WITH PETITJEAN, WHO'D brought another bottle of vodka. Magnuson carried what looked like an old-time Etch-a-Sketch. Lobashevsky had said he didn't trust any type of computer, but Magnuson had a hunch he'd accept a memory-enhanced Qubetch-a-Sketch. Magnuson knocked and no one answered. He knocked again and walked in.

"I'll be with you in a minute," Lobashevsky said. "Come in if you must, but give me a minute."

Magnuson put the bags into the kitchen and peeked around the corner. Veced was in underpants overlapped with a T-shirt. Magnuson watched as Veced measured something on polar graph paper using a compass, and then referred to some scribbled notes, after which he penciled a point.

"Step in, gentlemen."

"How did you know I brought Armando?" Magnuson asked.

Without looking up, Veced pointed the index finger of his other hand to the half-covered window screen. "Saw the reflection."

Magnuson and Petitjean walked to where there were taped graphs on a side wall. Some of the graphs had pencil markings throughout, while other graphs were blank. The opposite side wall contained 8-by-11 sheets of unlined paper full of equations and strange-looking mathematics. On either side of them, blank unlined sheets were taped.

Magnuson and Petitjean walked back toward Veced, anxious but eager to ask their main question.

"I can hear your minds, gentlemen. Please sit down."

Lobashevsky put down his compass, blew on some erasures, and held the graphed paper up in front of him to examine it closely. He stood still for a moment, looking at the paper, and then went to the graph wall and taped it with the others.

"Your question is, what have I found?"

Magnuson and Petitjean waited.

"First, I must tell you, Mr. Magnuson, when I said I'd expected more of a challenge, I didn't think you would take it so personally." And for the first time, both corners of Veced's mouth turned upward.

Magnuson slapped his knee and let out a long belly laugh. He looked at Petitjean, whose grin went from ear to ear.

"Veced, how about a shot of vodka?" Petitjean said.

"Indeed. I'm putting my implements in their right place." He adjusted work papers and his notebook from the original box. He laid his compass, ruler, and pencil aside. "I have a compulsive-obsessive methodology with my papers and instruments, driving even me batty, which is why I'd asked to be left here, to work alone." He shifted everything to one side, making sure the items were aligned with each other and with the table-side in front of him. He'd been working at the low coffee table while sitting on the floor.

"How come you work on the table from the floor?" Petitjean asked, stepping up with vodkas.

"Funny, I'd meant to use the card table, but once I started thinking, one thought led to another, and I'd forgotten all about it. Why, excuse me, gentlemen." He looked down at his briefs.

"It's okay," Magnuson said.

Petitjean smiled. "Don't bother."

Veced left them and went to his bedroom. Magnuson and Petitjean turned to each other big-eyed, not saying a word.

"Hello-like. Peace-like. Music," Lobashevsky said, as he walked around the corner in pants.

Magnuson and Petitjean stared.

Veced took a sip of vodka. "Those are the two expressions and the one word I've decoded thus far: 'Hello-like. Peace-like. Music.' But those three—and you can take it to the bank—appear in all but one of the alien transmissions. Thirty out of thirty-one."

"Which one doesn't contain them?"

"The transmission outside of our galaxy."

They listened to a group of gulls soaring by the window. Satisfied at last that no one was spying on him, Veced walked over and unfurled the curtain, and, digitally, a heady mix of salt air wafted into the room.

"Here's my first piece of advice," Veced said. "Drop all investigation of the out-of-galaxy signal. And I'll tell you why." He took another sip and set the glass down. "That signal, let me refer to it from here on as 'the devil,' is comprised of a different set of mathematics that is unique. And trying to decipher it—forget about π—will destabilize your mind."

Magnuson glanced at Petitjean.

"As you know," Lobashevsky continued, "in language, the probability of the next word or characters depends on prior data." Lobashevsky peered at a polar-coordinate blank on his wall. "Except for that extragalactic," he shouted and pointed. "Do not fear, I pulled back in time. I didn't realize how it was luring me in and twisting me, until it was almost too late. It is 'the devil,'" he shouted. "I will not entertain it further under any circumstances." He went to the polar-coordinate chart, which was unmarked, and removed it from the wall. "Here, take it," he said, handing it to Magnuson.

"But, Veced, is this the right chart? It's blank."

Veced took it back and looked at it. In a burst of rage, he tore the unmarked polar graph paper in half and into quarters and threw the pieces "out" the window. "See what I mean?" he said.

.................................

TWO HOURS LATER, LOBASHEVSKY WAS STILL EXPLAINING TO MAGnuson and Petitjean the mathematics behind the other charts, and they followed about half of what he said. They were elementary-school pupils who'd learned their number tables and were listening to a PhD explain higher mathematics.

"Veced, take me through your charts again," Petitjean said.

"I thought we'd covered that."

"I need another review too," Magnuson said.

"It will become clear when I build to prime."

It hit Petitjean like a thunderbolt. "You mean Mersenne prime?"

"Of course. What did you think I meant?"

Now Magnuson's comprehension leaped to about 80 percent. He looked sideways to Petitjean. "We've got to take this to Popov." He turned to Lobashevsky. "Primes are her specialty. Popov is going to love this."

"Yes," Petitjean said. "But look, Veced, in all of this high-end discussion, I've missed something else: How do we account for the near-instantaneous response from civilizations light-years away?"

"Ah," Lobashevsky said, "that's connected to an indescribable beauty I'm finding in these patterns." Lobashevsky drained his glass. "You see, these aliens have known about us for a long time, and the advancements in their communications and in their mathematics point to a signal that reveals itself when we properly wrap around it."

"Do you imply," Petitjean asked, "while their signals have been in our midst, it's only now that we could wrap around them?"

"Yes. And we three know why. I like your man Pauperito; how did he say it?"

"Pauperito said 'It all comes back to dissonance,'" Magnuson said.

"Exactly."

"Okay," Petitjean said, "we have wrapped. Have they heard us come back to them?"

"Oh, they've heard us; and I suspect, based on their advancement, and from all I see here," Lobashevsky motioned to his charts on the walls, "they have comprehended us, or will soon. The aliens control the wraps." Lobashevsky smiled as a professor who has grounded his class. "We'll know the answer to comprehension as soon as their patterns change."

# 53

WHEN GENERAL OSTEEN LEFT RINGSIDE AND RETURNED TO HER quarters, she switched from battle fatigues to her karate gi. She tightened the belt as she walked into her private dojo, removed her slippers before stepping onto the mat, which she kneeled on with bowed head, and repeated aloud her promise:

*In the way of Karate-do, I will destroy any man who touches me with lascivious intent. I will not be violated again. Ever.*

She stood and stretched in front of the mirrored wall. Ever so slowly, Osteen widened the distance between her legs and gradually slid down to a split. From there, she arched her feet and flexed her toes. She arched her back and threw her neck back as she looked straight up at the ceiling. She raised her arms to the ceiling, extending her fingers and stretching body ligaments, while still in the split. She then repeated her personal promise aloud one more time.

Osteen practiced her moves. She curled into a ball on the mat and exploded like shrapnel. Each time she burst forth, her body leaped above the mat. She did this a dozen times. Next, without resting, Osteen twisted, arched, angled, bounded, and leaped about the mat. She became an uncontrollable force, a deadly weapon, a promise of annihilation.

Fifty minutes later, Osteen sat in her private sauna and thought about her identical twin, Olivia, who eight years ago had been raped and murdered in front of her. The two beasts holding Osteen made her watch while a third mounted her screaming sister. One of the hooligans, not worth the powder to blow him up, had whispered in Osteen's ear, "Watch, cunt-face, you're next."

Osteen adjusted the temperature and laid her head back on the sauna's inside cedar wall. She remembered how the smelly, obese excuse of a human lay on top of poor Olivia, smothering her. She remembered hearing sirens and the three thugs running away. She rushed to Olivia, who wasn't moving and was no longer breathing. Osteen did everything she could, but when medics got there, Olivia was dead.

Both sweat and tears blurred the eyes of Osteen as she sat in her sauna. They never found the thugs, who could still be in Australia, but Osteen had taken action and redressed her vulnerability. She'd been promoted to colonel; and, because of the tragedy and her own escape, she had asked for, and received, a six-month leave. She vowed that she would become a martial-arts expert, a fighter. All her inquiries, all her readings on the subject pointed to Okinawa, which after hundreds of years was still considered the best place on Earth to learn, practice, and fight in the martial arts.

After six months' leave with pay, she asked for a six-month extension without pay and was surprised when it was granted. Osteen had the chance to learn from established masters who, when not competing, taught the best and most promising students. Almost all these advanced students were men. The fact that she was the one female in her class warmed her. She'd arrived.

Osteen had honed her body and mind to precision. She had placed first in her class and became the incarnation of the female warrior. She'd earned a seventh-degree black belt and bowed to her sensei. After the brief graduation ceremony, she'd been approached by the reigning karate champion and sensei who sometimes taught but often came to watch advanced students. She was invited to his home. No one refused the master anything, and she was delighted to go, for it was a special honor. No one else had been asked.

..................................

UPON ARRIVAL, OSTEEN HAD REMOVED HER SHOES AND STEPPED into the champion's modest home, which afforded a panoramic view of the ocean. He offered her tea, and a young boy brought it to her. She noticed the champion was dressed in a traditional karate gi, which meant he'd been practicing or was about to participate in a match somewhere. He appeared relaxed as he asked her questions about her homeland, her religion—she had none, not since . . . she didn't tell him. At the conclusion of tea, the sensei stood.

"You did not know this, for it's our custom to reveal it only to first-place students of karate, but I have a last kata for you to learn." The champion said this in a forthright manner and directed Osteen to a mat in an inner room.

Osteen, with trepidation, stepped before the mat and looked at the master.

"Karate-ga, go to my bath and cleanse your hands. Choose karate gi from the closet. I'll wait for you here."

Osteen looked at him. She'd been led to believe her training was finished at the conclusion of ceremonies that afternoon.

"Do not be alarmed. You will not fight me. I am here to teach you."

Osteen, realizing she was on her way to advancing to an eighth-degree black belt, reappeared and stepped before the mat. The master stood on the mat as a statue. She stepped to the mat and bowed to the sensei. She had no sooner raised her head and was reopening her eyes when the champion dove for her legs, pinned her to the mat, and chopped a blow to her forehead, paralyzing her.

"This is the lesson you will learn," the master said, as he removed his trunks and entered her.

She felt him thrust and, as she came to life, he chopped her again on the side of her head, on the ear. Although she was lying supine, Osteen felt she'd lost her balance and shook her head, trying to clear it of rings and thrumming from the ear. She witnessed his smile and looked on two broken teeth as the tea-smelled mouth hovered above her. As he neared orgasm, she felt him bounce on her and say something foreign. When he finished, he shouted the strange words again and chopped her a last time on the head.

When she came to, she found herself bound and gagged in the back seat of a vehicle. Two men she didn't recognize were in front, driving her somewhere. They soon reached an airport and she was transferred to a taxi. They'd relieved her of the bindings and gag, but she was sure she'd been drugged. She couldn't speak without slurring, and she walked lopsided. She was transferred to the front passenger seat of another taxi, and the two men climbed in back. She recognized the driver as her earliest instructor from her first dojo. The taxi stopped in front of two waiting policemen. A few muffled words were exchanged, and the taxi disappeared while she was escorted to a flight leaving for New Zealand in fifteen minutes.

The next day, in New Zealand, a country she hadn't been to since elementary school, she tried to lodge a protest at the Australian embassy. She didn't get far, and when several hours later the Australian magistrate explained the Okinawans were piqued that their decorated champion, one of their most admired countrymen, a master who was above reproach, had been disrespected, the magistrate laid it on the line to Osteen: "We have no recourse here."

..................................

OSTEEN SHUT DOWN THE SAUNA AND TOWELED OFF.

The next morning, she had Major Troy contact the administrator of Ringside to ask for Ms. Saint-Saen's address. "Tell Ringside I'm an ardent fan," she ordered. A few minutes later, Osteen reviewed the information in front of her.

"Good," she said to Major Troy. "Call Andrica and tell her I'd like to meet her."

# 54

CHARLES WAS EXHILARATED THAT POPOV HERSELF HAD CONTACTED him. He felt his crotch and wondered whether he would be able to . . . he hurt all over, but with expanded telemedicine he would make himself ready.

"It's not what you think, Charles. We have M-L-M to discuss, although there is something else we will talk about when you get here."

It had been two full days since he'd seen Andrica. Neither had called the other. His father had heard about the Ringside brawl, and they'd had a discussion about it the following morning when Charles announced he was too sick to attend academy. His father said Charles's involvement in the tiresome mess was shameful. Charles took meds and had stayed in his room all day. Chair Popov had reached out to him, and the thought of her playing the song on her harp, dedicated to him, made his groin tingle, causing him to lurch with excitement and pain. He took a pill to alleviate the discomfort, and took another pill to build his testosterone.

"Good to see you, Charles," Popov said, eyeing him and glancing at his crotch. He knows that I know, she thought.

"There will be no harp music today," she said. "You and I are behind in our work, which is, speaking for myself, unforgivable."

They discussed M-L-M at length. Most of the information that Charles imparted, Popov already knew; but she drew out more, even learning more about Conrad. Almost as punishment for them both, she had Charles re-posit to her everything relating to mathematics, music, and linguistics she could think of.

Charles stopped, and Popov nodded. "You will begin sessions with Professor Pemberton, our newest Liftee. I'll set up a first meeting tomorrow evening."

"I'm going to miss Ramanujan."

"That reminds me. Just before he was Returned, Ramanujan handed this to Security." Popov handed Charles a sealed envelope with "Charles" scribbled on it. "During my final meeting with Ramanujan, he told me how much he'd enjoyed working with you. He feels you will distinguish yourself."

Charles held the envelope. "Thank you."

"You can read it later. We'll meet again five days from now. Pemberton has been assigned work on musical aspects of M-L-M, as well as musical aspects of the alien signals, as suggested by Lobashevsky. When we meet here next, I want to hear, in your own words, three advances you and Pemberton have made."

"Okay, but . . . doesn't my strength lie in mathematics?"

"It does, which is why I've placed you with Pemberton. I'm looking for the two of you to complement and coalesce, discover something new. Something which will close the gap in our race against time."

"I admire Professor Pemberton, three-time winner of the World Gamescom. Conrad says Pemberton financed his entire education by hacking. Whenever he found a post-launch system bug, he sold it with the corrected fix back to the manufacturer."

"How is Andrica?" She watched him tighten. "I know all about it. Ashamed to say I watched the video."

"I'm sorry I shamed you."

"You are missing the point. Or perhaps you choose to ignore the point, which is worse." She watched him and could see his cheek muscles twitch as he ground his teeth.

"Here we are," she continued, "you and I and WCM, trying to improve communication on our planet; and the two of you resort to violence. Haven't you learned anything here?"

"It was her idea."

Popov slapped the table. "Don't make me throw you out of here, Charles. You are young, but you are not stupid. What an opportunity you missed to communicate with the person you love and who loves you."

She watched him tear up and left him while she went to her cooler. She came back with a dish of halvahs, two glasses of iced water with lemons, and pinches of lemongrass.

"Charles. Look at me. Listen to me." She waited. "I did a terrible disservice to you the last time you were here. Our bonding, our act of love was wonderful, but I took advantage of you, and I shall always regret it. I apologize for my mistake."

"Does it have to be a mistake? I loved every minute of it."

"Thank you, Charles. Your words mean the world to me. But yes, it was a mistake—an example of communication—music and all—for deceptive purposes. Blasphemous, and my fault."

"So it's over?"

Popov smiled. "That part is. M-L-M is not over. I need your help."

She watched him pout.

"The fact that you always speak in Portuguese and I in English, Andrica in French, your other friends in an assortment of languages, has chipped away and diluted something in all of us. What tongue does Conrad speak, by the way?"

"A combination of Farsi-Urdu. He also speaks Bantu."

"There you are. I read his qasida that won the prize, though one critic claimed visuals were distorted in translation."

Charles nodded. "He doesn't like the I-Translation."

"I-Translators try, but we keep missing and never catch up. When we do, others create neologisms and find other ways to hide their real intentions. Study the language behind Siberia versus Canada and see how governments quasi-communicate and sneak around issues."

They both took sips of iced water.

"I see your lips part as you speak," Popov said. "Sometimes I see the tip of your tongue when you round your lips as if you are readying to blow out a candle. But your words as spoken mean nothing to me. Every sound you utter is overridden in volume and translated into my English, for my ears. God, how we need to be grounded in one tongue."

"We will keep trying with M-L-M," Charles said.

Popov didn't miss a beat. "How many times have you heard expressions like 'that's not what I meant to say,' 'that came out wrong, what I mean is,' 'what are you trying to tell me?' 'what do you really mean?' 'you misunderstood me,' 'you should have said,' 'you read too much into what I say,' 'I misunderstood,' 'it's too late to say sorry'? Plus all the usual circumlocution. But my favorite one is 'we don't have a word for that in my language.'"

Charles nodded.

"We've got to illuminate these misunderstandings and fix them, Charles. All of them. Straight away."

Charles nodded again.

"Andrica loves you. Do you love Andrica?"

"Yes."

"Here's what I want you to do. We've finished for today; go out the door and go straight to Andrica."

Charles looked up.

"You heard me correctly. And before you hover over to her—"

"She might not be there now."

"Wait for her. Don't tell her you're coming, just go. I was about to say 'flowers.' Yes, say it with flowers. D' Jeerlings is good, Sukarno-town, next to SonySung."

She stood and smiled. "Go to her, Charles, and tell her you love her."

Charles stood and started to say something, but she drew him to the door, pecked him on the cheek, and with a smile gave him a gentle push as she patted him on the back. "And don't forget about Pemberton."

..................................

CHARLES DID AS HE'D BEEN TOLD. HE PICKED OUT A SWEET-SMELLING bouquet of red and yellow gardenias at D' Jeerlings and was anxious to see Andrica. *Yes, of course I love her. Why am I blinded sometimes?* He had much he wanted to tell her.

"Looks nice," Charles said, pointing to the bouquet the attendant water-wrapped for him. Her eyes landed on his with a stare that seemed to say "So what?"

A young man bolted in from the street-side door. He carried a worn canvas bag and hollered words at a curtain behind the girl, words that Charles didn't understand. The man was covered in combat tattoos showing spears and clubs, and had red Xs marked over his eye sockets and on his nose. He placed the bag on the counter. Each thumb rubbed a tattooed snake on the opposite forearm and his face flushed red as his eyes squinted. A similar-looking man parted the curtain.

"Fill up the bag; don't forget the ammo," the first droog ordered.

Charles had heard about droog gangs in this part of town and assumed this was a droog cell Popov hadn't known about. Charles's father had told him these cells were expanding everywhere, many into legitimate businesses like this flower shop, and local law enforcement had given up trying to control them. Both young men gave Charles the same stare as the sales girl had.

"You coming to the meeting tonight, right?" the first droog said to the girl.

She nodded. "Of course."

He sidled over to Charles, making him nervous. "You look like a preppy. Whatcha doing over here?"

"My girlfriend . . . need flowers," Charles squeaked out.

"Really. Ain't that sweet." He eyed the girl. "Maybe we should invite Preppy to our meeting."

"Ha. Good one." She looked at Charles and with a straight face said, "You can come with me while my Danny and Cyrus here screw your bitch."

"Now, that's a super idea. You up for that, Preppy?" the second droog said.

Charles pointed trembling fingers to the monitor, attempting to pay.

"I asked you a question, Preppy."

Any words Charles thought of were stuck in his throat. He looked to the door, wondering how he would get to it, hoping another customer would come in.

"Sorry," he said.

Droog number two came closer. "Well?"

"She's . . . my girlfriend . . . I hurt her down below . . . which is why," Charles looked at the flowers. "Thanks for the flowers."

The girl burst into laughter, which ignited laughs from the droogs. Charles stood there, unable to decide what he should do or say next.

Droog number one held up a hand to the others. He supplanted droog two and, as subtle as a battleship, stood inches from Charles's face.

"You know, Preppy, I actually believe you. But I bet you consider yourself supermundane." Charles remained helpless. "If I told you I could have gone to academy, would you believe me?"

"Yes. I would."

"Of course you would—the safe answer. Do you think all of us over here are sub-optimal? Troglodytes?"

"No. Not at all."

"We are going to prove ourselves, Preppy. You don't think we can big-time insurrect? You don't think we have long-term plans?" He thumbed behind him. "You think those towers control everything?"

"I . . . don't know," Charles said.

The droog stood up on tiptoes and hollered into Charles's face, "Get the fuck out of here."

On the way out, the girl said, "I should kick you in the balls, Preppy, to pay back your little sweetie."

The first droog said, "We've got bigger fish to fry," as Charles slid out the doorway.

.................................

THE CLOSER HE GOT TO THE EIGHTY-EIGHTH FLOOR IN HER HIGH-rise, where she lived with her mother, the more he gushed with love for her. After a brief wrong turn down the hallway, he reoriented himself, found the correct unit, and knocked on the door. Once he passed a Security test, the door opened to clangs of windchimes and to a middle-aged woman with Andrica's nose and Andrica's close-set eyes on a narrow face.

"You must have the wrong address," she said to Charles, staring at the gardenias.

Charles looked up from her sarong. "Are you Andrica's mother?"

"Oh, these flowers must be for Andrica. Okay, you may step in."

"Yes, these are for Andrica." Door-attached windchimes to his left and right bangled Indonesian-like clings as she shut the door.

"I'm afraid she's out tonight."

"Is it okay, Ms. Saint-Saens, if I wait here for her?"

"Well, I suppose." She looked at him. "She received a call. Some Army General wanted to meet with her."

# 55

LATER, AFTER SHE BROUGHT HIM TEA, MS. SAINT-SAENS EXCUSED herself while Charles sat on a bench next to a coat rack. Charles learned she worked for Humint, "Human Intelligence," she explained, "which involves codes and industrial espionage. I don't know what this General would want with my Andrica," she added.

"Your work sounds interesting," Charles said.

"After everyone got implanted and wired into the Cloud, we noticed strange, coded messages on the internet."

"What type of codes?"

She looked at him. "We have the expression 'if we tell you, we'll have to kill you.'" She patted the top of his head and left.

An hour later, Charles was sitting rock-still with his flowers in an anteroom in the hall, when Andrica walked in.

"I told my mother to send you home," she blustered. "Why the fuck are you still here?"

Charles looked at her as she rolled up bloodshot eyes. "I bought you some flowers."

"Isn't that peachy. Get out of here. You're the last person I want to see right now."

"Can't we—"

"No, we can't. Get out."

.................................

THE NEXT MORNING, HE TRIED TO CORRAL HER AT SCHOOL, BUT SHE always seemed to be a step away, or was heading off in a different direction. She didn't sit near him in any classes, and he did not see her in the cafeteria during lunch. Several of her friends looked at him and turned their faces away with knowing smiles.

"It may take a while," Conrad said. "Give her time."

"All I want to do is apologize in person, so she can see I mean it. Then she can take all the time she wants."

Conrad scratched his head and looked around him. "Word has it, Charles, the groin kick you gave her, after the bell, has disrupted her system."

"'Disrupted'? What do you mean?"

"I don't know details, but someone said she may not be able to have children."

"That's not true. It's someone's idea of a cruel joke."

"I hope so, Charles."

More than ever, Charles had to speak with Andrica. He left their last class early and hovered to her dolphin labs, where he knew she'd be going. As she was about to enter the labs, Charles popped out of nowhere.

"I owe you a huge apology. Tell me it's not true you can't have a baby. If it is true, I'll kill myself."

Andrica was startled but recovered. "I can't talk right now; I have work to do."

"Just tell me, Andrica. You owe me that at least."

"I don't owe you anything. I said I can't talk right now." She pushed open the door and Charles held it.

"When can you talk?"

"Call me tonight. I don't want to see you." She started to walk in.

"Are you okay? Tell me you can still have a child. I know you want one."

"Hear me, Charles: if you don't get away from me this fucking instant, I'm going to call Security and issue an EX4 pickup."

Charles found himself walking away, but didn't remember it later when he hovered downtown. He knew his father would be pissed at the no-show and would attempt to contact him. He wanted to contact Popov for advice, but felt ashamed to ask. There was Conrad, and he thought about contacting him; but at the last second he exited the hover and meandered to the heart of the city. He had three hours to kill before calling Andrica.

After shots of Loose at a teenage hangout, roaming the mica stores, glancing at the groins of busty women and regretting his sinful mistake—and feeling sick about it—Charles tapped his glasses. Still an hour to go. He window-shopped, and the reflection from a window showed a trio emerging from a lounge behind him across the street. He took a furtive glance and concluded, based on their swagger, they were droogs. He heard an overhead siren and watched the droogs beat it into an alley. One ducked into a low doorway, while the other two kept running. Charles went to his hover and locked himself inside. Twenty more minutes and he'd call Andrica. He sat with his eyes open in the semi-dark, watching, seeing nothing but the beige curved wall in front of him, and his brain repeating the phrase "after the bell."

Charles tapped for Andrica, once, twice, thrice. Five minutes later, he tapped his glasses again. Nothing. Ten minutes later, he repeated the pattern. She'd blocked him; he couldn't even leave a message. With an upset stomach, Charles hovered home.

Andrica avoided him in class. When she refused to speak to him at lunch, he stared at her as if he was reading a proof he couldn't understand. She ignored his attempts to converse after academy, and she continued to shut him down at night.

"Why, Andrica? You told me to call. I have."

She pursed her lips and refused to respond.

He added, "Maybe there's been damage done to me as well. I'm not feeling so good down below either."

She finally responded.

"I'll answer your original question: I don't know. Time will tell."

"So . . ."

"So, that's how it stands. I've been damaged. The damage may heal; it may not."

"Andrica, I am so sorry."

Andrica tsked. "Sure." Charles heard her chuff a sob.

"What I did was terrible. I apologize."

"It's too late. I never stomped you after the bell, even in the later rounds when it crossed my mind."

Charles did what he could to stifle his emotion. "I didn't . . . your mother is a nice person."

"Don't grab at straws with me."

"Can I—"

"Oh, sure, maybe we can fuck and find out if we'll have a normal kid in nine months. No, I don't want to see you, Charles. Please don't call me any more."

Charles went to his loft, ignoring and covering the projection on his wall sent from his father—all in capitals, ending in two exclamation points. He spent the night researching psychosomatic illness. Could it be the situation here? Pray it's all in her mind, he repeated to himself. He studied the effects of vicarious bruises from physical games like Brawl. But again, he noted the warnings: *Any contestant who opts to receive a percentage of real punishment will, in all instances, physically receive and absorb actual punishment, complete with lingering pain and possible lifetime bruising. There are no exceptions, and there can be no reversals of outcome.*

While asleep, during a fit of nasty dreams, something Andrica had said broke through. Charles woke from a dream, thought about it, and tried to go back to sleep.

..................................

"CONRAD, I ALMOST CALLED YOU LAST NIGHT IN THE MIDDLE OF A dream." They were meeting before class, as usual. "Remember when Salk said the appendix is an improvement, but a growing graft is better?"

"I do."

"The time is way too long, but . . . when you told me about Andrica."

Conrad, for the second time in two weeks, dashed off.

# 56

BRAUN WAS ENRAGED. HE LOOKED AT HIS CHIEF OF SECURITY. "Tell me again why you think three of our top intel soldiers, vetted by you, infiltrated the droogs and now have gone over to their side."

Farzad looked weak as he sighed and frowned. "All I can say, Sir, is that there is a remote possibility they were murdered, but the commo channel we used showed their secret codes, which only they knew, and then was shut down. It was their last message."

"These traitors wanted us to know?"

"It appears that way."

Braun had too much, as well as nothing to say. He continued to stare at Farzad.

.................................

IGNACE PEMBERTON HAD THE SHORTEST RECOVERY TIME OF ANY Liftee to date. He'd left present-age just thirty years earlier, his death a tragic blow to the world of mathematics.

He was a mathematics professor, Lifted from a university penthouse dorm many years prior to his death. After three hours, his brain had been equalized to present-time.

"I need my micas," were the first words he said when revived.

"You have all of them and new ones as well," Time Travel Control assured him.

"Where are they?"

"In your head; and if you insist, they will be placed in your quarters."

"See to it," he said. Pemberton looked about him and asked the arrived Liftee's usual first question. "Where am I?"

.................................

THE NEXT DAY, AFTER BEING BRIEFED BY POPOV AND HER SIX ASsociates at WCM, Pemberton was introduced to First Tier and to his fellow Liftees. He inquired about his aunt and two uncles of Tier members, and asked several additional questions.

"Has any type of musical pattern been discerned within the alien signals?"

"Patterns, yes, but they don't appear to be musical."

"How so?"

"There are similarities, but even that's stretching it."

"Have we transmitted our music to them?"

"Yes. But the choices in selection are endless," someone said.

"Let me get to work. And thank you for finding Galileo."

.................................

THE FOLLOWING EVENING, CHARLES MET PEMBERTON FOR THE first time. He'd seen pictures of him at academy, but didn't realize how blond his hair was on a balding head. Charles stared at the foot-long iguana on his shoulder.

"Meet Galileo," Pemberton said.

Charles smiled. "Galileo?"

"Why, yes. I believe these creatures exist on some of the worlds that the ancient astronomer discovered. He's rather handsome, don't you think?"

"If you say so, professor."

"Popov told me about you."

"We use your micas at academy."

"You are attending my alma mater. How goes it there?"

"They are building a new mathetorium—it's to be called 'Pemberton.'"

His smile showed his upper gums. Pemberton pinched the tiny sac below his ear lobe. "Portuguese to Polish has always been a weak spot for my I-Translator. You'd think after thirty years, they would have . . . you studied with Ramanujan?"

"Yes."

"Which puts a good deal of pressure on me. Has anyone told you of my interest in recreational mathematics?"

"Yes. And mathematics is my forte; Chair Popov put me with you, hoping—"

"She told me. She wants to hear, firsthand, of advances you and I make."

Charles said nothing.

Pemberton asked, "Can one get TDCS here? In this time?"

"I've heard of that," Charles said. "Transcranial Directed . . ."

"Current Stimulation," Pemberton finished. "Brain zapper. Doesn't matter; it was even before my time."

"The concept's been superseded. Why do you ask?"

Pemberton patted Galileo, and his eyes glazed in memory. "Sometimes did my best work with it. Drove my parents crazy one time. I used too many electrodes and the montage, aided by marijuana-laced oral stimulants, blindsided all thought and consciousness. Physicians told me later it took over sixty hours in isolation for me to retro-reset."

He gave Galileo a final pat and put him down in a corner.

"Did you know I was instrumental in solving TSP, the 'traveling salesman problem'?"

"No, I didn't." Charles smiled. "That's where a salesman has to find the lowest travel cost and the shortest distance between a bunch of cities, right?"

"Right, and the cities are all over the world. We need to get started here, but the methodology used in solving TSP can, with modification, be transferred to the challenge of finding *the* optimum language."

"I don't understand TSP complexity theory," Charles said.

"Few do. Even after the thirty years I've been gone. We first need to apply linear programming in our searches, so we assign fractions of probability to junctions we arrive at."

"We cut up the salesman."

"Exactly. And when we meet further obstacles, we assign fractions of fractions."

"Is that what you contributed?"

"In a way, yes."

Charles smiled. "We can designate an infinite number of fractions."

"That's where we run into difficulties. For what we are trying to do here, there may be computational limits, and time is running out."

"Then how—"

"We focus on music. Which I believe is the real reason I've been Lifted."

"That's where I'm weak. I don't even play an instrument."

"But you listen to music."

"Very often."

"Why?"

"I like rhythms."

"And patterns?"

"Not as much as rhythms. What instruments did you play, Professor Pemberton?"

"Keyboard. Any type of keyboard."

"How come you stopped? You were once a prodigy."

Pemberton smiled. "The pressure and the practice. Competition was keen."

"But I've heard you were tops, along with a few others."

"The pressure started early. My first name, Ignace, was taken from a famous nineteenth- and twentieth-century Polish pianist and statesman. And, I'll be truthful, the reason I stopped had little to do with practice, but much to do with pressure I put on myself—I had to have perfection. I never found perfection when I performed in public."

"Do you still play?"

"Only in my mind. I no longer go to a keyboard, and don't plan to."

"I hope I can help you, Sir. You mentioned Ramanujan. He left me some notes I somewhat understand, but he knew you were coming. He says, in a cover note, to show them to you when I think the time is right."

"I'm honored. He knew I was coming because, as I understand it, my trip here was delayed a while."

Charles pulled out the envelope he'd placed under his shirt.

"Do *you* think the time is right for me to see them?" Pemberton said.

"I don't know. I don't understand the purpose Ramanujan had in mind. And the mathematics, though I recognize some of this, isn't clear to me."

"Well, let me take a look."

Charles noticed an ocular flutter when Pemberton first fixed his eyes on the paper. Pemberton paced his room back and forth several times, reading the notes and working his fingers over the mathematics. Galileo was back on his shoulder and had his eyes closed as if he'd been rocked to sleep. Pemberton hadn't removed Gandhi from the wall, and the picture hung askew, seeming to reinforce the blatant untidiness. Pemberton took an Evergreen Mint from a tin, popped it into his mouth, and began crunching it. He reached the end of the third sheet and went back to the beginning. This time he took twice as long to finish.

Pemberton looked up and stabbed an index finger at the papers as he said, "It's clear to me Ramanujan has found another unique way to solve the traveling salesman problem." He off-loaded Galileo. "And between his solution and mine, we have a head start."

# 57

SALK WAS HUDDLED WITH SEVERAL OTHERS, STUDYING PROJECTIONS and charts, when in walked Conrad, the urgency of the moment written all over his face.

All Salk could do was smile. "Do you like skipping academy?"

"This may be too important."

"You could've tapped your crazy glasses. Saved yourself some trouble."

"Yes, but . . . Doctor Salk, what is the one graft on a human that grows from seed to full-term?"

Salk smiled. "Fetus."

"Yes!"

"From embryo to the human fetus." Salk nodded his head. "I admit I hadn't thought of it."

...................................

SALK AND CONRAD SAT BEFORE POPOV IN HER OFFICE.

"Thank you for seeing us," Salk said, as he glanced sideways to Conrad. "On short notice. The feed through the appendix, as you know, has not been complete. Conrad has hit upon a marvelous idea."

"Please explain."

"The human embryo. This is the ultimate graft: the clean slate, if you will. I'm convinced M-L-M can, and will, be absorbed in toto over term."

"Hmmm. Are you suggesting . . .?"

"We need to select pregnant women," Salk said. "As many as possible for the starship."

"Can I say *shit*?" Popov held her forehead in her palms as she stared at folders on her desk. "Most of the preselection has been completed. And now I reject previously selected trekkers to admit pregnant women? Yet I agree, the idea is magnificent."

"We have sperm banks," Conrad said, "for those . . ."

Popov looked at Salk.

"We can insert embryos," he said. "During the long sleep, the embryo can be fed organized bits and pieces of M-L-M. When these women are revived, the M-L-M feed will be complete."

"Well, that helps. Most women can stay selected. And," she smiled, "a complete and unadulterated *tabula rasa* for the baby."

Conrad smiled.

"The baby," Popov said, "will have absorbed Mathe-Lingua-Musica, a language which, by design, contains no word or expression for violence, war, murder, and the like."

"With no such words or expressions, any type of violence will be alien, and an outrage, to humans of the new humanity," Salk said.

"Yet it goes against everything we know. We could be throwing the poor angels to the lions," Popov said.

"Or the new world, out near a different star, would accept them because they *are* pure and not a virus built from evil," Salk said.

"No alien civilization had ever contacted us," Conrad said. "We changed our language, which cleansed it of any vestige of aggression, replaced evil with music, and thirty-one worlds contacted us."

"All within a week," added Salk.

"It's fortuitous that we have only allowed the best candidates to donate sperm," she said. "This is something we must accomplish." Popov smiled at Conrad and pointed a finger. "But I'm asking you, Conrad, not to leave academy again." She turned to Salk. "We won't have time to fix everyone on Earth at the present rate of violence. But we might be able to beat the odds stacking against us by the day if we can attenuate violence via the infusion of M-L-M. In either case, the idea of feeding M-L-M to expectant mothers will be taken up in earnest here. And, of course, on *Welkin-Alpha*."

"Thank you for seeing us, and now I must get back to work," Salk said. "When we beat those odds, I want us to be ready."

"Conrad, stay here a minute," she said, as Salk went to the elevator. She busied herself with papers on her desk.

She began: "Charles has mentioned Andrica to me; and I followed her initial work with dolphins—with interest, I might add. How are they getting along?"

"Not well. She doesn't want to see him."

Popov looked up from her papers. "I admit I watched most of the Ringside video. Wretched. I told Charles to bring her flowers."

"A lot of good that did."

"I see." Popov shuffled her papers. "I shall not press if you don't want me to, and I don't mind if you tell Charles or Andrica about this discussion. I'm trying to protect needed talent, as I'd do for you." She put her papers aside. "Is there anything else you can tell me?"

"I heard she might not be able to get pregnant. The kick in the groin, after the bell."

"I'm sorry to hear this—for both of them. She's seen a doctor?"

"My girlfriend says she did."

"Charles knows about this?"

Conrad nodded.

Popov concentrated her features and became still, hands placed on top of her desk. "That poor girl. Charles is going through hell."

"Charles is still trying to see her, to at least contact her, but my girlfriend says she hasn't been around much anyway."

"Why?"

"According to Katerina, my girlfriend, she's been meeting with some Army general."

"I'd like, in confidence, to learn the name of this general. Get back to me, Conrad."

..................................

POPOV'S AIDE TRACKED DOWN ANDRICA'S DOCTOR. THE ANDROID Primary referred the aide to a gynecologist.

Popov tapped her glasses. "Yes, Doctor, thank you for reaching back. What can you tell me about Andrica's injury?

"There is damage."

"I see. I'm sorry to learn that. I gather it will be much harder for Andrica to become pregnant. Doctor, if an embryo was transferred to her womb, would her chances of maturing to full-term improve?"

After a moment for the doctor to give his brief reply, Popov said, "Thank you!" She then became as still as a painting after she shut down her phone.

When Popov removed her glasses and let them hang from her neck, her secretary rushed into her office.

"Excuse me?" Popov said.

"I'm sorry I didn't knock," he said. "I . . . just . . ." He handed Popov a letter and walked out, closing the door.

It was from the head of Jurisprudence, First Tier. The letter contained an announcement of formal Impeachment Proceedings. She was to meet for a "Hearing and Declaration" the following day at 4 p.m.

..................................

THAT EVENING, CONRAD CONTACTED POPOV. "REGARDING ANdrica, it's a General Osteen, from World Army."

Popov tapped her glasses and waited, too long, she thought.

*My apologies, Chair Popov. I'm up to my neck in alligators. I'm sorry for the wait.*

"What can you tell me about General Osteen?"

# 58

"ANDRICA," GENERAL OSTEEN SAID, "YOU MUST THINK OF YOUR future. Right now, the odds are you will remain on Earth."

They were having their third private meeting, and once again Osteen was leading Andrica along a strand of beach. When moonbeams glinted off broken glass, Osteen took Andrica's elbow and led her around. The bay was motionless as Andrica traced moonbeams back to the moon before the orb was snagged by a cloud. Andrica liked it when birds flew across the moon, and she hoped she would see that tonight, as it had been a good omen for her in the past. Up to the left, Andrica found the Little Dipper handle and Polaris, and from there tried to imagine where the constellation Cygnus would be, home for the star controlling the orbit of Kepler-1649c, which could be her new home.

"I can't imagine what the future would hold for me up there," Andrica said.

"But you're not happy here."

"No." She rubbed her lower belly and realized she'd forgotten to bring her prescription pills. "I don't know what I want."

"You remind me of myself at your age. I didn't know either until . . ."

"Until your sister's rape, or until Okinawa?"

"I couldn't prioritize anything when my sister died. She was my twin, born two minutes after me. We did everything together. I was depressed to the extent . . ." She stopped. Caught her breath. "I took a proactive approach, went to Okinawa, like I told you; and after that, I knew."

"To control your own destiny."

"Yes. And to hold any man under a magnifying glass. Andrica, I don't trust them. And they never will have a hand in my fate."

"WCM Chair Popov is a woman."

"Right. But they had to bump up a woman eventually. Look at all the men before her and the fix those men have put us in. Popov is the first woman, and she is trying, but she takes advice and shit from men every day, all day. Let me tell you something. I report to General Braun, who reports to Popov. He's a snake who comes to life when he directs war and the murder of people."

Andrica looked at Osteen, and Osteen read her thoughts.

"Andrica, I'm Braun's lone female staff-general. He's required to have at least one female general on his immediate staff. It's a sham. He tolerates me."

"Can I ask you a question, General Osteen?"

Osteen stopped walking and faced Andrica.

"World Army is seventy percent men. Why are you still in the Army?"

"One, I had already begun my career in the military and was doing well. Two, to leave would announce to myself another defeat in the face of men. Andrica, I worked at my profession harder than ever as soon as I came back from Okinawa, and it's paid off."

They continued to walk.

Andrica took a tissue from her pocket and dabbed at her eyes.

"You are lucky he didn't blind you," Osteen said. "How bad do your eyes hurt?"

"My eyes are getting better." She dabbed at them again and pocketed the tissue. "I don't know about down below."

"The cyborg woman had to have both her eyes replaced. Did you know?"

"No. It's complicated, but I may still love Charles."

"Even after what he did to you?"

"I'm aware it doesn't make sense, but I know he does care for me. In that moment in the brawl, he reacted too quickly, which is unusual for him. He's wounded too, you know."

Osteen continued walking and stayed silent.

"What are you trying to offer me?" Andrica asked.

"Your life. Your future."

"I guess I'm not sure why you are being nice to me."

"I've learned your father used to beat your mother."

"True."

"Men have not responded to some of your requests at academy. Requests which were later granted to boys, you said."

"In some cases, yes."

"From what you tell me, you've been able to connect with other women, but Krebs dismisses you."

Andrica said nothing.

"I'm sure there have been other incidents. And the whole debacle with Charles."

"The Brawl was my idea. I initiated it."

"Don't you see? You were pissed off at being ignored and not respected. He had no time for you except for sex. Other than being a sex object, how important do you think you are to any man?" Osteen stopped and put her arms around Andrica.

Andrica, sobbing for the first time since the Brawl, felt a warm tear course down her cheek. She shook under Osteen's arms and buried her face in Osteen's chest, close enough to hear Osteen's heartbeat.

"Walk with me a little farther," Osteen said into her ear. "I want you to meet someone."

Ten minutes later, Andrica was introduced to Major Troy.

"It is good to meet you, Andrica. I've been wanting to tell you that my great-grandmother did academic work with Atlantic spotted dolphins and later with bottlenose dolphins, many years ago."

"I may know of her work. What was her name?"

"Denise Herzing. *National Geographic* did an article about her work."

"Oh, yes. She was the first to use a two-way strategy based on dolphins' love of play."

Osteen sat down facing the moon, which glimmered on the surface of the ocean. Andrica sat beside her. Troy sat across from them, and Andrica brought Troy up to speed on her dolphin-language studies. When they became quiet, it was Osteen's turn.

"We don't know if there are dolphins on Kepler-1649c—though I suspect there are, with all the water we've confirmed. What I do know is that Major Troy and I, and a few others, are going to find out, personally."

"You guys have been selected?" Andrica said.

"Let's just say MaryAnn and I and some others are going."

"I'm not sure I understand," Andrica said.

Major Troy gave Andrica a warm smile. "You've been given the opportunity to at least listen."

"And, as a fellow woman, we trust you to keep what we say here private," Osteen said.

"I will."

"Until seven weeks ago, I had a strong chance of being selected."

"Why would that change?"

"Why? Although I'm a skilled mathematician, men appear to possess superior mathematical skills. Why? My career has been military, but my knowledge of Defense seems to have been a colossal waste, and I'm no longer needed. Andrica, I could give you a hundred reasons why, which would amount to discrimination for me, MaryAnn, and a host of other professional women. The reasons translate to 'Shut up. Someone else will decide your fate—not you.'"

Andrica was thinking. She looked at the moon and struggled with implications about all said.

"What are you looking for from me?" Andrica asked.

"Your commitment. MaryAnn and I, and another woman whom you haven't met yet, have created additional openings for off-the-charts smart, determined, and yes—wronged—women to board the starship. We have no desire for aggression or retribution. Not our purpose. Our purpose is to bond and to control our own destiny on this starship."

"We preselect ourselves," MaryAnn added.

Andrica looked up again and saw a lone bird stroke across the moon. *Where is it going? Is it important?*

"Count me in," Andrica said. "I want to go."

# 59

CHAIR POPOV TOOK A COMFORT PILL TO ALLEVIATE A GROWING malaise, which she feared had more to do with her state of mind than physical discomfort. The pill contained a booster to help improve her nasty mood. She was in her WCM office and thought about her harp, which she knew would elevate her disposition, but she had no time.

Ever since she had released the names of Tier selectees who would trek aboard *Welkin-Alpha*, Popov had been snubbed, screamed at—and, in one case, slapped—by ones not selected. General Braun had warned her about this, and she should have listened, but it was too late now; the smiles and clubby comments of those selected, she also detested. Several advanced members of First Tier had not been selected and had screamed "foul." When Popov explained it wasn't personal, that it was separate, individual votes amongst the WCM based on tests, competitions, and contributions, their protests became all the more heated—"I never test well"; "I had a miserable headache during the last competition"; "I lost both parents and was in mourning"; and on and on. She listened, oh how she listened, but in the end she had to tell them again, "There is nothing I can do. I can't even try to imagine how you must feel, but I can't change anything. You, on the other hand, still have the opportunity to help save our world—and I'm staying here to work hand in hand with you." Some were able to stifle shouts, but most left in tears.

What heartened her was the positive reaction among WCM board members not selected. Only Gunderson, Tuan, and Anand were selected to make the trek. Boucher did not complain, as he was next in line to chair WCM. De Costa and Thaddeus Smith accepted their fate, perhaps knowing Boucher needed their help.

The good news was when preselected non-pregnant women were told of their need to be pregnant, only two refused. Popov gave them a choice—become pregnant with a provided fertilized embryo, if not naturally; or stay on Earth. Both opted to stay.

There was also the matter of former WCM Reed and the impeachment. Although Reed had been selected, he, forever the martyr, announced that he had removed himself from the roster as a protest to the gross negligence and mismanagement of Chair Popov. Popov had booted him out of WCM, but she'd agreed when he'd been recommended for the travel roster.

What worried Popov most was the inability of her mathematicians to solve the content of the alien signals. *If we can't decipher any of the thirty-one communications, which by every indication are alien messages, will the signals go away? Will planet Earth be considered a faulty, disenchanted anthill and be forgotten?* Magnuson and Petitjean were keen on Lobashevsky—she was too, after reviewing his work—but time was running out. Three months remained.

In twenty minutes, Popov would chair WCM's weekly progress meeting. Popov walked to the side wall in her office and slid back two laser boards, revealing a third. She'd worked the entire night at this board, and spent the few remaining minutes reviewing her equations.

Popov conducted WCM's progress meetings in her private conference room. At the last minute, she decided to include Magnuson and Petitjean. At the meeting, Popov revealed the newest simulation. The odds of saving the human species had dropped to 39 percent, and they had three months to improve the odds. As the remaining time predicted by simulations became less, the odds of extinction increased. There was dead silence as she quoted "thirty-nine percent."

"For our second order of business, I want to review the slate of Liftees and announce changes."

"I'm struck by this change in procedure," Tuan said. "Don't we review individual Liftee progress reports together and submit it to a vote?"

"Yes. And if I were sitting where you are and heard you or anyone else say what I just said, I'd question it."

"So, why the change?" Anand asked.

"Do you remember learning about how a Professor Wiles, in the late twentieth century, led a room of distinguished mathematicians on an unknown journey to the solution of Fermat's last theorem? They had no idea until toward the end what was happening. I'm using a similar approach, but this way we will have saved valuable time."

"By your account," Boucher said.

"At the end of this meeting I will demonstrate why I made the changes."

"We should go over it now," De Costa said.

"Okay, perhaps you are right. Let's do it now, but let me build to it."

Popov reviewed the latest progress, as she understood it, and noted their satisfaction, for she had absorbed the newest updates in their specialties, and in Liftee disciplines. Meeting with Charles, meeting with individual WCM members as well as with Liftees, examining reports from special committees, plus Tier reviews, had prepared Popov to give WCM members an elevated understanding.

Popov stopped and took a sip of lemon water; she'd been addressing her colleagues for almost an hour.

"I've arrived at some conclusions," she said.

"May I interrupt a second?" Magnuson asked.

"Yes; and after, let's break for ten minutes."

"I feel compelled to say . . . I hope you are planning to keep Lobashevsky."

Popov smiled. "Indeed. I pray his progress will continue."

...................................

AFTER THE BREAK, THE MEETING RESUMED. POPOV FELT CONFIdent, but understood the jury was waiting.

"Most of you know about my work on Singer's Conjecture, which led to patterns of far-ending primes. It wasn't until I aligned my shortcomings and dead-ends with Lobashevsky's work on primes—and all of that to musical breakdowns we are having with M-L-M—that I regained solid footing. The breakdowns in securing the optimum language for our species all relate to music. I know everyone here accepts music as one of three legs on a three-legged stool, the other two being mathematics and linguistics. At the start, we didn't consider music, and now we've tried to give the legs equal importance. But we've skewed our thinking to mathematics first, linguistics second, music last. This has been a mistake—it's looking more and more like music is first in order of importance."

Popov let her remark settle.

"It always comes back to atonality," Popov continued after a few seconds, "the discords, the dissonances. Liftees suggested that the random mishmashes of static, when separated from the alien signals, might be the alien equivalent to our musical cacophony."

"Lobashevsky had mentioned it," offered Petitjean.

"We must integrate these discords in such a way that they reveal what? Alien rhythms? Information? Messages?"

Popov projected her mathematics onto the wall. "Here's what I've found. The equations on the left side represent discordants I've achieved with my harp. The equations in the middle represent atonals composed by Bach and Liu Hui. The equations here, on the right," she stood next to them, "are my own, and also come from the alien transmissions."

She waited. "I can see you are looking for linkage. I couldn't find any, not even between mine and Bach-Liu Hui, nor could several others who reviewed them with me. I've worked this math until my brain shook, and still I found nothing. I've allowed that music on its own can be aleatory, but there should be no room for chance in Mathe-Lingua-Musica's final rendering."

Popov tapped her glasses and moved the projection to another wall. "Now, I want you to take a look at something new.

"As you know," she glanced at Magnuson and Petitjean, "my research and achievements have been in primes. And I admit to you that our Veced Lobashevsky knows as much about primes as I ever will. It's his recent notes I've been working with." She pointed to the new mathematics. "I didn't see purpose here, it wasn't a burst of inspiration; I was playing around with what Lobashevsky had given us, for the love of primes. As you can see, I made some innocuous substitutions of Mersenne arrays where the asterisks show. I redid the formulations which brought me to here," she pointed to her lower right. Thaddeus, Gunderson, and Anand tapped their glasses and kept looking up to the laser board and sideways as they tapped. Boucher took something from his pocket and studied it.

Popov gave them time—not a word was said. "If we consider each alien mishmash not as some type of atmospheric abnormality but as a marker or a collection spot, and expand the idea to an atonality which builds upon itself, we arrive at this." She projected a third set of mathematical renderings on the wall, and the links were perceived.

"Wow," Tuan said.

"Wow, indeed," De Costa said.

"I'm convinced that different forms of messaging lie in atonals. These discordants here from our galactic friends show the potential linkage to Mathe-Lingua-Musica messaging. I don't understand *how* it works, but what I submit to you is this: all thirty alien transmissions in our galaxy build upon preceding atonals according to Mersenne primes."

There was much talk back and forth about Popov's discovery. Magnuson and Petitjean looked at each other smiling, and nodded. Lobashevsky had already known this and had moved ahead.

"Your conversations remind me of the decision I'd come to."

It became still as the six looked at the walls of Popov's mathematics for a last time before refocusing on her.

"We are missing something because we are deficient in music. We need an ethno-musicologist versed in computational musicology to work in tandem with structural linguists to solve this problem."

"Based on what you've shown us, I can't say I disagree," Tuan said.

"Thank you. I've had First and Second Tier review everything, twice over, and Bach, despite his enormous help to us, has fallen off in contribution. I'd like to keep him longer, but we've got to replace him in light of what you see here."

Popov listened to agreeable silence. "We've isolated discordants and can see how they build to message. We must decipher those messages not only to understand these sapient aliens but—and for us this is more important—to be able to blend their *music* into our M-L-M."

“I concur,” Boucher said.

“Bach departs this evening. Tier has found the best replacement, a late twenty-fourth-century computational-musicologist right from our own Banda Sea—a displaced Samoan, Teuila Sefo Malala, who died less than a year ago. Aside from being a skilled mathematician, she is versed in exobiology and meta-psychonomics.”

“Splendid,” Magnuson said.

“I’m taking the newest improvements and latest results of M-L-M public. General Braun, although he doesn’t know it yet, and I will coordinate with Canada-Siberia, starting tomorrow, and do our utmost to have their top commanders experience, and communicate in, M-L-M.” Popov hesitated. “For this important reason, I’m requesting impeachment proceedings be suspended while General Braun and I throw ourselves to this task. It is my sincere hope that a thaw in that wretched Armageddon up north will help in some measure to make up for those unfortunates . . . lost to us in . . . Thank you.”

# 60

CHARLES FOUND THE DIFFERENCE IN METHOD BETWEEN PEMBERton and Ramanujan striking. Even Pemberton's room décor was chaotic, if not unusual. While he waited for Pemberton, who'd pinned a note to the door—*Be back in half-hour* (begging the question, what time had he left?), Charles stared at what looked like a zither on the floor next to a table and thought, *Pemberton had said his interest and expertise was "all keyboard." How will that help?*

The room, missing Ramanujan's little table, looked odd because Pemberton, for some unknown reason, had slanted his worktable at an angle at odds to the obvious contour of the room. *This had to be deliberate,* Charles thought, as the rug beneath it had also been taken up and more or less aligned with the table. The room would have driven Ramanujan nuts. The top of the table contained crumples of paper, popcorn droppings, several sets of eyeglasses—another one had dropped to the floor near a mat on which Galileo lay—and a hodge-podge of micas, different sizes, different colors, strewn every which way. Charles looked at the iguana again and wondered if it ate popcorn and why Pemberton loved the lizard.

Charles smiled as he thought of Ramanujan's one table fixed in its exact position, with a spotless surface except for the one or two items Ramanujan needed. He remembered how Ramanujan cleaned his one pair of eyeglasses on the hour, every hour, and how he kept his computer glasses zipped in a special pocket. "Most pathways to solution arrive from proper setup," he'd said. "Prepare your folders and mark them: Newest Research, Older Research, Alternate Approaches, et cetera. Always know where your documents are," he'd said.

Pemberton stormed in. "There you are. I've come from Thaddeus. He's worked out interesting methods of moving forward."

Charles looked at his goofy smile, showing uneven teeth. "Do you play the zither too?"

"No. But the sounds interest me. Kind of eerie and haunting, don't you think?"

"I guess so. Chair Popov wants a report on our advances. But I know little about music."

Pemberton scratched his head. "I can't teach you overnight."

"But you know math. How are they connected?"

"Your real question is: How do they conjoin to language."

"Yes. Can't we start with math and music first? I know even less about language."

Pemberton laughed. "Can't we jump into the Pacific here and swim to the Atlantic?"

"Just give me the necessary elements of music relating to math."

"Just tell me how to compose a new symphony, or tell me how to speak Swahili."

"Tell me something," Charles pleaded.

"Two plus two equals four. Three squared equals nine."

"In our galaxy," Charles said. "Is this certain beyond our galaxy? We haven't a clue about the extragalactic signal."

Pemberton cocked his head and gave a nod. "I also spent time with Aasen. Krebs was there, and I asked them to loan me the layered alphabetic music—the beautiful music Ramanujan played the night you told me about."

"I'll never forget it," Charles said. "I had to sit down on the floor; I was in a trance."

"Let's listen to it again." Pemberton pressed a wall button and tapped his glasses. Charles put on his glasses, and they listened.

"The female voice mixed with birdsong," Pemberton said, "gorgeous, as you say. I have everything recorded from that evening, including your earlier request to Ramanujan to 'Stop,' and Ramanujan's reply, 'The computer will hold it in memory.'"

"We never went back to dissonance," Charles said.

"We will now. The new buzz around here is Mersenne atonals."

They listened to another section, a spot where mishmash preceded birdsong-voice. "Okay, stop."

"Good. You and I,"—Pemberton pulled out the Ramanujan envelope and papers Charles had given him the last time and handed them to Charles—"are going to break apart these screwed-up sounds, get underneath them, and understand them, even if it takes us all night. I won't allow anything kludgy. I will allow subroutines, but they better be connected to bigger and better."

Charles smiled.

"I have something else." Pemberton held up several sheets of paper and grinned. "The last and final notations from Pauperito, steeped in Bayesian probability, before he reached his 'mathematical cliff' and gave up. We must connect this with what we've learned from Thaddeus."

"Let's hope we have everything we need."

"Mersenne primes may have clinched it. But what do the atonals say? We could have entire worlds of mathematics to work with, but of what use if we can't comprehend and reverse-communicate?"

The eager student nodded.

"First, why do these—let's call them anomalies—show up here and not in other spots? What difference can it make? Second, in which ways are the anomalies the same and different from each other in this particular piece? Which leads to the third question: Is there anything here in these particular anomalies we can find in other anomalies elsewhere?"

"From what I see," Charles said, "when the computer system imports these recorded new sounds and transforms them into a sequence of numbers, the numbers can't be decoded, because nothing in annals recognizes the sounds, or in this case the sequenced patterns."

"So? We build to new annals."

"Yes, but . . ."

"Go on."

"Unlike our computer programs that can deconstruct paintings and works of art into sets of numbers and patterns we recognize, we can't do it here."

"Why not?" Pemberton asked.

"There isn't a bank to draw on. We would create yet another new language rather than decipher this one."

"How can an atonality, an anomaly, be a new language?"

"Unless . . ." But Charles grew silent.

Back and forth throughout the night. Down one thought tunnel that twisted to another, reversed itself, and morphed to something else.

At 5:30 a.m., Pemberton looked at Charles. "I've kept you up all night. Even my Galileo looks tired." The mathematician stooped, picked Galileo up from the mat, and, after tickling the reptile's wattle, placed him on his shoulder.

"It's okay. We've eliminated a bunch of possibilities. We're closing in," Charles said.

"Yes. A disappointment here, but in an upside-down way we've made progress."

Charles collected his belongings and was about to go.

"If you can arrange it, come back tomorrow night," Pemberton said.

# 61

GENERAL BRAUN HAD BEEN ASLEEP FOR THREE HOURS WHEN HE GOT the news from his aide that he had been ordered to set up a meeting of the Canadian and Siberian heads of state with their commanders. A meeting to be conducted in M-L-M. *Haven't we already tried that?* he thought as he rubbed exhausted eyes. The world was falling apart; sterner measures were needed than sitting in a room conversing in a strange language—if you could even call it a language. Plus, there was the mystery with Osteen, which Popov had called him about. That had prevented the General from getting to sleep in the first place. He'd suspected something untoward was up with Osteen, but to snare her meant he had to set a sly and careful trap.

He called Popov at 0600. "Am I hearing right? You want another meeting in M-L-M set up with these clowns? Do you think it will help? Okay, okay." General Braun tapped down the volume. "Sorry. I'm still looking into Osteen. I need to be cautious; I'll—"

But Popov said she had another call waiting and dropped him. *It's certainly not like the old days,* he mused. *What would his great-grandfather have thought?*

He set up the meeting for that evening, at a protected, in-town, neutral location. Popov was due in four hours. He secured the meeting room and reviewed the electronics with his engineer.

...................................

"GENERAL," POPOV SAID. "I WAS SHORT WITH YOU THIS MORNING. I know you are dealing with a number of pressing matters."

General Braun saluted and shook her hand. "Not as much as you. And being overloaded is in my job description."

The General saw to her physical comfort. They were the first ones to grace the meeting room. The engineer could be seen in an alcove on the far side.

"Your reports, General, say rioting, looting, and killing from the tsunami have diminished, but you feel the problems will escalate. Why?"

"From what we have learned, several destructive groups have become new cells of droogs. What were formerly just looters are becoming trained droogs. These new cells are not entrenched in a particular place. They can disband quickly. It appears droogs had been looking for an opportunity to organize and wreak havoc, and the tsunamis offered it."

The General caught himself. "Chair Popov, my comments are not meant as a touché."

"I understand."

"My cadres of light infantry no sooner eliminate one cell than another takes its place."

"Have you been able to infiltrate?"

"A bit. It goes too slowly. These new droogs we are encountering have secret codes of some sort. I've lost superior men who were sure they had infiltrated, only to be carted off and torched alive. We've found separate individual dental fragments in the bottoms of pits. But area droogs disappeared or entered companion cells."

They attempted pleasantries, and in the minutes remaining before the meeting discussed progress on Plan B.

"I can tell you *Orion* will be ready. I'm taking the project back from Osteen, as soon as I get back."

"You've been satisfied with her work?"

"Yes. I get updated every day. She's done an excellent job—all I'd hoped for, frankly."

"Let's stand, General: here they come."

After the Canadian and Siberian heads of state and their commanders were seated around the table, and had been given an assortment of teas and confected mints, General Braun introduced Chair Popov and went back to his seat.

Popov took time to smile and extend the silence.

"Distinguished heads of state, commanders. My words this afternoon will be few. What I want to say is this: humanity is trying to save our species and thus our civilized world. Everyone here is humanity." Popov looked into their eyes. "With this thought in mind, I entreat everyone here, including myself and General Braun, to listen, to absorb, and, most of all, to communicate. Thank you."

The lights dimmed. All external sounds had been muted. The nine men and three women around the table took up prepared eyeglasses and, coached by Braun's engineer, waved them over an electronic junction on the table in front of them, then put on the special eye-sound-sensitized glasses, loaded with M-L-M. The engineer told them to lean back in their chairs. Following M-L-M-coded instructions, the engineer waited until each of the twelve participants *registered* their understanding and their commitment. It took several minutes before everyone was on board, the last ones being two military commanders of the warring nations.

Birdsong. And the hush and panorama of a sun-filled morning washed over the eyepieces of those assembled. Hay smells and timothy mixed with sea airs circling landward. Wafts of honeysuckle-jasmine and aromas of other flora native to both Siberia and Canada were accompanied by distant music from birds inhabiting both countries and neighboring seas. These were soon joined by incidental music composed on mixed native folk music and song.

An incipient female voice emerged with birdsong from the countryside, contrapuntal, a voice rising to such purity that Popov looked heavenward, imagining an angel. There ensued an entering of soft, kind, deliberate basso ostinato, antiphonal, building in the background. Another voice uttered strains of M-L-M, or intimations of M-L-M which, although sometimes discordant, continued in heartfelt purity for several minutes, rising in volume to thrums and rhythms, finishing with feelings of plea.

Everyone, conscious of the serious effort made for them, absorbed thankfulness and goodwill, as did Popov and Braun. It was evident in everyone's eyes as each heard it in their individual implanted M-L-M.

In his absorbed, imbued M-L-M, General Braun said, "Friends of humanity, let us begin anew."

One hour later, the heads of state and their commanders agreed to ameliorate the Declared War back to a Conflict.

...................................

ALTHOUGH POPOV WAS THANKFUL FOR THIS BIT OF PROGRESS, SHE harbored disappointment. "We were close to establishing full peace, General, if only . . ." but she couldn't add *we had more time.* That may have been the problem. As the effects of the music wore off and as they dug deeper and took longer to mediate details for the cessation of hostilities—and as they pushed away from M-L-M— the sides became testy.

Popov had been the first to realize it and caught the moment.

"Ladies and gentlemen, it's time; in the best interest of humanity, let's put it to a vote."

"I haven't finished," the Siberian commander said. "I demand to be heard." He'd spoken in Russian, and everyone re-engaged their I-Translators.

Popov, trying to control her emotions, reverted to English in her answer to the Siberian general. She stood and faced him, and General Braun stood beside her.

"And I demand, Sir, that you respect our rules," she said.

The Siberian general looked insulted. In his interpretation of Popov's words, he *was* insulted. He said nothing further; the vote was taken; and, though cessation of all hostilities was not agreed to, both sides agreed to reduce the Declared to a Conflict.

After documents were signed and after everyone had left, General Braun faced Popov and put a hand on her shoulder.

"Be grateful, Chair Popov. You called this meeting and, as you know, I had my doubts. What you accomplished here is extraordinary."

"But we left something back there. What the hell happened, General?"

"I'm not sure what you mean."

"Wait." Popov gob-smacked her forehead.

"It was my word *our*: yes, the Siberian commander misinterpreted *our*." She looked at General Braun. "When I said 'respect *our* rules.'"

"Okay, so you reminded them. At these meetings, we have certain rules, and we've all agreed to abide by them."

"And there it is, General. That's what *I* meant and what you understood when I said *our rules,* but the Siberian general didn't take it that way."

The General's brain shifted, and he saw the problem. "I need to sit down a moment."

"When I spoke to the Siberian general and said 'And I demand you respect our rules,' I'd meant *our mutual* rules; I wish I'd said to him '*your rules and mine.*' He watched you stand beside me, and he interpreted *our rules* as *'your'* she looked at the General *'and my rules,* Braun and Popov's rules.'"

"Yes. I see. But for the sake of one word, one syllable, we have this . . . this gap in understanding?"

"I'm convinced that's what we witnessed back there. M-L-M won't allow these kinds of miscommunication."

General Braun was at a loss for words.

"Thank you, General, for your support today." Popov preceded Braun out the door and turned to him. "Watch the Conflict closely. I will send an explanation of my ignorance and confusing choice of words to all in attendance. I want everyone to come back here two weeks from today."

# 62

FOR ONE OF THE FEW TIMES IN HIS LIFE, GENERAL BRAUN WASN'T looking forward to going back to his office. He had a sinking feeling about Osteen; his sixth sense had saved him many times, and it told him turbulence lay ahead. One didn't come this far in a military career by ducking issues. A lesser person would have waited for events to unfold, for new evidence to present itself, for Osteen to make an obvious mistake, and then pounce. But Braun was not a lesser person; he would dig to the bottom of her plot, and he would do so immediately.

But that wasn't all that bothered him. He wanted his son, Roy Jr., his one child and legacy, on that interstellar ark. Braun couldn't stand the thought of the family line ending on Earth in Armageddon. He wanted his offspring to seed the stars. Not many spaces were left on the ship. The best way for Braun to accomplish this objective would be to take Roy out of military academy. But he held hope that the military would turn the tide on Earth. Plan A was gone, yet there was still a chance to beat the odds. His comrades had already maneuvered their children out of military academy onto an ever-lengthening starship waiting list. The practice became so prevalent that Braun had circulated a "cease and desist" throughout his command. Braun couldn't go against his own order. Despite a marked improvement today with Canada-Siberia, it was too late. He should have removed his son earlier.

As the General's private military hover—Popov had departed in her own—circled the World Army obelisk, waiting to be led by Security choppers to the landing port, Braun tried to think of the best way to sneak up on Osteen. Using her new aide, Major Troy, he knew was out of the question. He'd have to tiptoe around her too. There must be someone else. *Perhaps General Constance Malone?* Braun knew she was close to Osteen because he'd met Osteen and Malone several times at officers' clubs, and he was one of three generals who'd reviewed Malone's qualifications for promotion to Brigadier General. What's more, Malone knew that. *Yes, that's the ticket.* General Braun arranged to meet her for lunch the next day. He'd told Malone the lunch was to be kept confidential, in civilian dress, and downtown.

..................................

THE NEXT MORNING, AFTER OSTEEN HAD UPDATED HIM ON PLAN B, Braun complimented her on her work, and she'd returned the compliment.

"Congratulations on Canada-Siberia. Excellent."

"Thank you, but it's due more to Popov and our newest M-L-M than to me."

"Still . . . What's the newest simulation?" Osteen asked.

"We're back up to forty-eight percent. She's waiting to set up Denmark-Greenland, but I've got my doubts. Their animosities go back too far. They are entrenched."

"Which is why she is waiting for the next M-L-M improvements."

Braun saw her glance again at his civilian clothes. "I'm meeting my wife in town. She gets tired of the uniform."

"Special day?" Osteen smiled.

"Very." And with that, the General left her.

Osteen congratulated herself. Since Andrica had signed on, plans were shaping up. In the recesses of Osteen's mind, it was not lost on her that Andrica would be a perfect hostage. If a problem arose to thwart her plans, Andrica would be her up-the-sleeve ace. She was expendable, and Osteen would find a way to take her place on the starship if need be. Osteen also knew about the two preselected women who refused to be impregnated, and more possibilities crossed her mind.

..................................

LATER THE SAME DAY, AFTER CATCHING UP OVER LUNCH, IT WAS Malone who got down to business. "How can I help you, General?"

Braun squinted at her and smiled. "That's what I like about you. One of the reasons I pushed for your promotion. No bullshit."

He summoned the Euro-Asian waiter, who took their orders, spice-laced rawon for Malone, oxtail consommé for Braun, and sent him off. "I want you to keep this meeting and our discussion here confidential. Okay, General?"

"Understood."

Braun hesitated.

"I mean, yes. Okay."

"Good. Do you know why General Osteen would be meeting with a young lady from academy?"

"Can you tell me more, General? Maybe I know the girl."

"Her name is Andrica."

"Oh," Malone smiled, "she's the one who brawled with her boyfriend."

Braun waited.

"You do know of Osteen's interest in martial arts." Malone looked him in the eye.

"I do."

Malone crinkled her forehead. "General, I'm not quite sure what you're trying to get at. I suspect she took a liking to the girl who fought like a sex-starved ibex, from what I've been told."

"So why doesn't she meet her in public, let people know about it, kind of adopt her?"

"Maybe the girl is shy."

"Did you know about Osteen contacting her?"

"Yes, I did, General. I can tell you it all goes back to Okinawa, and no doubt Australia before that. She told me she felt sorry for the girl and wanted to help her."

Their food arrived, and they both held their conversation until the server was clear of the table and out of earshot.

"You knew about their secret meetings," Braun continued.

"Sir, I didn't take it as secret meetings. General Osteen told me she'd met her a couple of times and was mentoring her, or trying to."

"'Trying to'?"

"As I understand it, the girl has been in a quandary ever since the brawl. Janice said the girl may still love her boyfriend, the one she brawled with."

Braun became silent, and they both began to eat.

"General Braun, why are you asking me all this? Doesn't Osteen have a right to reach out and help a person?"

"You're right. I can see I'm out of line here. I've become paranoid. This happens when I'm overworked and overwhelmed. I speak confidentially."

"You can trust me, General. I don't know how anyone can keep on track, managing all the responsibilities you have."

A short while later, Braun watched Malone leave. He wasn't satisfied. His sixth sense told him she was covering for Osteen. This is why he'd met her in person. To look in her eyes, hear her live voice, to suss it out. Both she and Osteen were hiding something. He'd now tipped his hand to Osteen, so it wouldn't make any difference if he proceeded to check up on Major Troy—she had to be in on it too. *At least Canada-Siberia will now take less time for me*, he thought. That was his only relief.

# 63

THE DAY SHE LUNCHED WITH BRAUN, MALONE CONTACTED OSTEEN.

"He's on to us. Don't breathe a word of this; General Braun met me for a confidential lunch today, and all he discussed was you and what you are up to with Andrica."

"I bet he lunched in mufti."

"He did. I wouldn't be casual about this, General."

"Believe me, I won't. It's not at all what I wanted to hear right now. But thank God we know—right?"

"Right. What about Major Troy?"

"My next question. Did he mention her?"

"No."

"He suspects she's involved also. Otherwise, he would have gone to her first."

"He suspects her," Malone said, "because you asked him to sign off on Troy coming to work for you."

"Right. I'll handle this with Major Troy."

"What are we going to do?"

"How did he leave it with you?"

"Nothing was asked of me. He said he's become paranoid with overwork and had read into something."

"Do you believe him?"

"No. I think he'll continue to dig around."

"Ditto. Thanks for the update. Keep it business as usual."

Osteen contacted Major Troy. She first asked Troy tangential questions in the remote chance General Braun may have already contacted her. When she was convinced otherwise, Osteen described her office meeting with Braun.

"I glimpsed him in mufti, but I'm not certain he had lunch with her. I don't often see him."

Osteen remained silent.

"You do trust me, I hope."

"Of course, but we must be careful, and I had to be sure."

"Well, you . . . okay, you had to vet me one more time."

"I know you are on board, MaryAnn, but I'd wondered if Braun had returned this afternoon to ask you questions."

"No, I didn't see him—did he come back?"

"Yes. I'm *glassing* to alert you; be on guard. He may come to you still."

"Okay."

"Next. Andrica's father, the louse who beat her mother, was former government Security. Get me the complete files on him—everything."

Osteen took time to consider her goal. Why take a chance to force her way onto a starship? Aside from the ultimate adventure—a new star system—it was the once-in-a-lifetime opportunity to start over. The ark provided adventure, which she'd always reached for, and a clean slate. At last, she'd be able to put the past behind her. Other than a distant second cousin whom she never saw, she had no relatives. Battles and command?—been there, done that. To stay on this rotten planet fighting for her life—she'd studied the simulations and the math—was a no-win. The species was destined to fire and ashes, particularly if M-L-M was ill-conceived. And if hostile aliens waited for them? *By Jesus, I'll be ready.* One way or another, she would be on the ark.

# 64

SINCE JAVINA-THREE, THE OTHER TWO FLOATING CITIES WERE SURrounded with protection. Combat subs patrolled constantly, hover flyovers occurred regularly, and droogs proliferated. Their excitement was palpable as they disrupted anywhere and everywhere. Cell droogs snipe-killed and threatened, then their cells broke into parts and re-emerged elsewhere. The droogs had started with their usual rants of having rights and demands. But now that they were on new ground, they stopped their arguments and rants. They had arrived.

The educated haves knew the system had failed the have-nots and turned them into helpless savages. For years, the military thought they'd be able to contain them, that they would keep to themselves. But instead they grew and were organizing, possibly in an attempt to take over. The WCM thought of them as cockroaches, and, with all the other problems associated with eleven billion people, so-called luminaries pushed them out of their minds. The hard truth was that it was too late to fix the ever-growing equality problem. With the tragedy of Javina-Three, the droogs had overreached, and nobody would ever lift a finger on their behalf.

Recent days brought substantial threats, increased looting, and, for the first time, cluster-bombing throughout the night. It was non-nuclear, for now. But for how long? The odds for extinction continued to build, and sims showed that the violence and destruction from droog cells would become as bad as an additional declared war. There were cells active on all inhabited Indonesian islands, comprised of leaders who operated in the background and remained out of sight. What originally had begun as a thorn-like annoyance—compared to battling nations—had now, with the sinking of Javina-Three, escalated to an uncontrollable monster with countless tentacles emerging in all nations. What's more, rumor had it that the leading droogs—those with a plan and connections—were setting up for another major strike. No one knew where, but the general assumption was Javina one or Javina two.

Meanwhile, Popov forged ahead and tangled with other emergencies. Aware of the risk of destabilizing an already Declared War further, she ordered General Braun to set up a meeting with Greenland and Denmark like he'd done with Canada-Siberia. The General had advised against it, as he'd advised her in other matters where she hadn't listened, only to regret it later. But this time, fresh from a minor victory, she was determined to try. She was ecstatic when Lobashevsky's newest notes on Mersennes reached her; his private work indicated that another breakthrough was imminent, and she'd told the General to arrange a meeting in three days. Popov got M-L-M updates every day, and, one way or another, she was going with the newest M-L-M advances to these most trenchant of adversaries.

She wondered how Charles and Pemberton were doing. She was due reports from both of them, and was disappointed to learn from Pemberton later in the day that all they'd accomplished was to eliminate possibilities.

Popov rubbed her stomach. The thought of Charles prompted another call. "Good afternoon, Doctor, it's Juanita Popov. I haven't heard back on . . . I'll wait."

A minute later. "Are you sure?

"One hundred percent sure?

"Thank you."

..................................

JUANITA POPOV WENT TO HER HARP. SHE THOUGHT ABOUT HER LIFE and how it had brought her to this point. She didn't look for discordants tonight as she thrummed, and when she neared them, when she recognized they were right around the corner, she segued to other music—more relaxing music, music which would allow her mind to drift and soar.

After Popov played her harp and decompressed, she showered, poured herself a glass of white retsina, and prepared a vegetable-sushi salad. While eating, she shut down her electronics except for Afro-Indonesian rhythms emanating from the walls, floor, and ceiling. After swallowing the last of the wine in the goblet, Popov finished up her evening meal with a couple of figs. She avoided evening pill-meals: food pills were too quick and didn't give her time to think.

Popov left her kitchen table and went straight to her work room. She slid back the two largest wall boards and examined her work appearing on the third board behind, which was half covered with primes, mathematical arrays, and equations. Popov picked up a laser, hesitated as she placed her other hand on her belly, and put the laser back down. She went to her bed and lay supine. Popov turned up the music, advanced the ceiling glow, and stared at the constellations she'd projected onto her ceiling. She tried to see between stars. Somewhere out there, she thought, is Kepler-1649c. After an hour, she went back to her boards, but, before retiring, made herself one more drink, a nepenthean shandy for the purpose of easing her into pleasurable dreams.

# 65

WITH CLICHÉS RUNNING THROUGH HIS HEAD SUCH AS *IF YOU CAN'T stand the heat, get out of the kitchen* and *this is what you get paid for*, General Braun marched into his private elevator, taking him to the joint-command suite near the top of the military obelisk. There was no track behind this office, no gym either, but he felt it was the proper place to conduct special inquiries and to pronounce judgments. Plus, he would throw Osteen off her guard and off her game.

General Braun had pieced everything together, and he knew he was right. Ostensibly, he'd called this meeting to announce Major Troy's promotion to lieutenant colonel. He had invited Osteen and General Constance Malone, who were told by the general's aide of the pending announcement. What the three women didn't know was that he'd also invited a polygraph expert, three undercover Military Police agents, a legal adviser, and several other aides and administrators. They would be there now, waiting in an adjacent office—in an area called the wonk room—and would be summoned at the General's command.

The General walked into the adjoining suite, calculating he had about twenty minutes. He used the time to go over his notes while sipping his usual spiced coffee. General Braun soon found himself shaking his head at the stellar career Osteen had had, up to present day. Like himself, Osteen was a skilled mathematician who could have gone into academia and ended up in Third, or maybe even Second Tier. Now, she was a threat. Braun checked the glow on his watch—0800 hours.

At 0815 hours, General Braun knew this day would be a complete disaster, as well as an embarrassment to him, the Army, and, by extension, the WCM. Osteen, Troy, and Malone were nowhere to be found. They had removed their electronics—communication and location were blocked—and gone AWOL. General Braun, tail between his legs, sent his waiting operatives back to their duties and called Popov.

"They didn't show. They've gone AWOL," Braun said.

*This confirms a conspiracy. Where do you think they are, General?*

"It hurts like hell to admit it, but I don't have any idea. They could be anywhere."

*Do you have suspicions about any others who could have joined them?*

"Other than the girl Andrica, no."

*Hold on a moment.*

Braun knew what Popov was doing and held back a grunt. He could have at least made that call himself.

*Andrica is at academy—in class as we speak.*

"I wanted to tell you of the situation right away. Chair Popov, I will examine every—"

*Yes, I know you will. I'm having Andrica brought to me direct from academy. I'll talk to you later, General.*

Braun threw off his glasses and stood up. Without so much as a "good morning" to the rest of his staff, he stormed into Osteen's open office. From the outside, it looked like it had looked last night, when he'd nodded her a good evening. Braun pulled out empty desk drawers and yanked open doors to empty cabinets, searching every nook and cranny, and found nothing. He marched into Troy's office and did the same. Nothing. Braun's mind probed and reached to other matters gone awry. *Pompadoux.* He wondered. He asked his secretary to pull the Pompadoux file.

"It appears to be missing," she said.

"Who signed for it last?"

"General Osteen, Sir."

The General took the elevator down to his private gym and changed into his jogging clothes. He needed to think—hard—and emerged onto his oval track. He was determined not to stop rounding the oval until he developed a plan.

AT A CHIPPED AND LOPSIDED CEMENT PICNIC TABLE IN MARISA'S "slum-dog" ghetto, a woman sat in a painter's cap marking up her sketch board with charcoal. At least she appeared to be a woman, but it was hard to tell; no hair fell from under the hat, her hands didn't look delicate, she wore no jewelry or makeup; and yet for some reason there was an overall assumption that the person was a woman.

Twenty minutes later, a little man showed up and sat at the cement table, across from the painter. At least the person looked like a man, but again it was hard to tell. The person wore sneaker-shoes, carried a canvas tote full of hand tools, carpenter's laser-level sticking out, and wore sunglasses.

"Janice, when did you cut all your hair?" the person asked the artist.

"This morning, before leaving. When did you dye yours?" Osteen asked.

"Last night," Troy said. "I had to circle this block twice to make sure it was you."

"I saw you, MaryAnn. I didn't want to take the chance of making contact in case anyone is watching us."

"Which begs the question," Troy said.

"No. I'm quite sure no one is watching."

"Are we set for Malone?"

"In a few minutes—don't look—we will walk across the street into the ruined building behind you."

"The tsunami wrecked this place," Troy said. "I saw the mess as I reconnoitered. The bodies have been removed, but the stench—is it from all the draping seaweed? It's stuck everywhere and covered with all type of shit. They need to truck this crap out of here."

"The good news for us," Osteen said, "is everything of value here has been looted except for hidden supplies in the building behind you, which Connie has arranged."

"We'll be safe here?"

"Rioters have left this area. A few people are trying to build again and re-establish themselves amongst the ruins. We are to look like them, act the part."

Troy glanced at her tote of tools. "We might even need to use some of these tools." She pulled out a hammer and stuck it back in.

"Keep that hammer near you at night," Osteen said.

..................................

GENERAL CONSTANCE MALONE OPENED THE STEPLADDER AND WENT up three steps. "Hold the ladder," she said. As Troy and Osteen held the sides, Malone pushed back a damaged ceiling panel and reached in. Malone looked the part. She wore a toolbelt over a painter's jumpsuit and had, "by design," she'd said, spotted herself with assorted colors of paint, caulk, and whatnot. Osteen didn't seem to mind Malone's taking charge, temporarily.

"These are for each of you," Malone said. She handed fingerprint keylocks to each of them, along with new electronic IDs and the newest M-L-M-loaded computer glasses. "I also have backup tablets with false IDs synced to Tier to provide M-L-M updates—too late for them to suss out."

"Neat," Osteen said. "Let's work together every night to gain understanding in M-L-M. It's a must for our Starship."

"The IDs have been preloaded. You have everything you need," Malone said. She showed where each of them would sleep—adjoining rooms, community bath and kitchen, and a crushed-in den that was empty from apparent looting.

Osteen looked around and turned on a faucet. "Still the main problem," Malone said. "There is no running water. But," she held up old-fashioned keys, "over here is what was once a utility room." She unlocked the crooked door and yanked it open. "As you can see, we've got enough water for at least a few weeks. Here, take these." She handed out water-purification tablets and testers, the size and width of a key. "These testers scan and filter-clean untreated water; a green light will blink when it's safe to drink."

Osteen cupped an assortment of pill food and pointed at a sealed opaque bag. "What's that?"

"Medications, first aid, toilet needs. I'm afraid all we have is a makeshift outhouse behind us in the alley. So I got us sanitizers."

"We didn't expect the Hilton, Connie. You done good," Osteen said.

"It's going to be tight when we bring in other recruits," Malone added, "but for now . . ."

Malone looked down at Major Troy, who'd been quiet. Troy sat on the floor and gazed at the wall in front of her. Malone brushed off some lint and went to sit by Troy. Osteen noticed the change in atmosphere and put her hands in her back pockets as she peeked outside through a shattered window.

Osteen sat down across from Troy and Malone and watched them look at her. Osteen said, "You're waiting for me to ask 'What's up?'"

Malone pointed to Troy. "Go ahead, MaryAnn."

Troy pulled up her legs closer and wrapped her arms around them. "May I ask, General, what happened to Officer Ginger Pompadoux?"

"Why do you ask?"

Troy looked to Malone for support.

"General, a woman's body was discovered yesterday afternoon," Troy said. "On the beach about a mile from where we last met with Andrica."

"What are you implying?"

Malone took over. "The body hasn't been identified yet, but General Braun knows about the body and asked his aide for satellite communications traffic on a three-mile strip of beach for the night officer Pompadoux was last seen. There is none. Other than a file note of a blackout."

Osteen looked at them, into each of their eyes, from one to the other. She could tell they knew.

"And you think it peculiar that there seems to be no plausible reason for the blackout," Osteen said.

Malone looked at Troy, who said, "We suspect he thinks the blackout was deliberate."

"My, oh my. I wonder if Andrica is the culprit," Osteen said.

# 66

GENERAL ROY BRAUN, DRESSED IN BATTLE CAMOUFLAGE, HIS MODified Laser-Wreak beside him, strapped himself into the Army hover beside his gunner. It was 0200 hours. Hostile emissions had been picked up twenty minutes earlier in "slum-dog" near the beach. Intel indicated Osteen could be in the area; it would take too long to risk ground troops. The hover was ten minutes away. Four black sewn-in stars on his shoulders paraded the General's jacket, while four identical stars were emblazoned across the front of his Army-issue cap. The medal traditionally inked on the breast of his battle fatigues was his Combat Infantryman Badge, which he'd earned in China-India during World War III—the other war which was supposed to end all wars.

"I'll spot for you," he said to his gunner.

"Very good, Sir."

The hover screamed in low and tight, using a hard-to-track southwest approach fronted by ruined buildings and hanging scaffolding. Braun could see what looked like a gang of thugs split off in different directions and disappear behind concrete ruins. Braun tracked through the foot-thick plated window below him, using army-issue night-vision battle glasses. He tapped them and a burst of radiation lured the enemy signal, which he locked to his gunner's. "Right fourteen degrees, two klicks," he ordered the pilot.

"Yes, Sir."

"Fire," he said to his gunner.

It was a perfect shot. The blast tore up the city block which had surrounded the signal. The hover arced skyward, pushing the General hard against his seatback.

"Congratulations, General," the pilot said.

"Thank you." Braun patted the leg of the gunner beside him. "Well done."

"Thank you, Sir."

The following morning at his office, he studied the full report, with accompanying pictures; the General was upset to learn that only Troy and Malone had been eliminated. There was no trace of Osteen. General Braun puzzled and fumed.

Braun called Popov at 0900 hours. "Number two and number three have been eliminated." He could hear her think.

*Where do you think she is?*

"I don't know, Chair Popov."

*I'm meeting with Andrica in half an hour. She had to cancel yesterday. I'll do what I can.*

General Braun closed down his glasses and told his staff not to disturb him. He went through all his notes and re-listened to all the conversations, going as far back as the original vetting, when she'd told him she'd run him up the flag. I should have called her bluff right then and there, he thought.

An hour later, Braun had finished his "emergency think-run," hoping to jog something loose as to Osteen's whereabouts. *She could be anywhere,* he thought. And then he came to understand something, which, for the first time ever, made the general stop running for a moment on his track. *She'd set him up, and had compromised her own one and two to do it.* The General couldn't believe her ballsy plan, but it was clear as day. His team had pulse-searched for hostile emissions, and there had been an enemy signal transmitted right back on the first go. There had been no suppressing fire needed by his gunner, and the "perfect shot" had been available for him to take, just like that. Osteen had prepared it all, and Troy and Malone—her friends as far back as academy—had never had a clue.

.................................

THE GENERAL WOKE UP IN A SWEAT. HE BOLTED UP IN HIS BED AS quick as the snap of a mousetrap and gasped. He couldn't remember what he'd been dreaming about when his wife asked him what the matter was. He questioned himself as to why the dream had occurred the one night he'd allowed himself to sleep at home in over two weeks. But it had come to him in a flash. He knew where Osteen was.

Within an hour, General Braun had managed to wrangle a forty-eight-hour leave of absence from Popov, for personal reasons. "But I can assure you I'll be working," he'd said. She hesitated, but didn't press him, for which he was grateful. In Braun's military mind, he knew he was in the fight of his life against an opponent who was not only lethal but who had no scruples. He would operate alone; and he told no one, not even his closest aide, what he intended to do or where he'd be going to do it.

Braun instructed his wife that she was to leave for several days. When she questioned him, he gave her the don't-ask look and said, "I've made the arrangements; take this," he handed her an envelope, "and follow the instructions exactly."

Braun returned to his study, put on his glasses, and dispatched several memos, the longest one to Popov. He packed a small tactical go-bag, and just after two a.m. he kissed his wife goodbye and walked out of his home. It was unlikely anyone would recognize him, as the usually uniformed general was dressed in civilian clothes, looking like a Hawaiian tourist, topped off in a Panama hat. The post-day heat fanned his face like a hair dryer. He pitched an arm up to the first taxi-hover he saw, feeling renewed confidence as it descended and the ramp lowered. After putting his bag behind him, he strapped himself into the passenger seat and glanced at the pilot.

"Take me to the west side, toward Launch."

A brief time later, General Braun stepped out of the taxi-hover—a mile from the supershuttle *Orion*—and secured a room at a cheap motel. He spent a few moments in the lobby chatting with the night clerk, who wore sunglasses. He, too, no doubt, had a hidden agenda. In his room, Braun changed into battle fatigues not adorned with his name or rank insignia, and exited the motel through a back door. He patted himself one last time to be sure he was packing. He stealth-walked to the North Gate, the main entrance to the launch, all the while looking at the giant vertical ship. When he neared launch Security, he had to crane his neck to see the cone of the enormous shuttle. A full moon was behind it, which backlit the monster. *And this is a toy compared to* Welkin-Alpha, he thought.

Braun retrieved his military ID from his pocket and flashed it at the uniformed guard at the gate. The guard snapped to attention and saluted.

"Sir."

"At ease. Listen carefully. I'm going aboard." Braun pointed to *Orion*. "Do not make any announcement of this to anyone, either before or after. Understood?"

"Yes, Sir." The guard unlocked the gate, and Braun stepped through.

"Is anything being loaded right now?"

"Not that I know of, Sir."

"Who represents most of the onboard workers right now?"

"One moment, Sir." The guard pressed the side of his glasses as he inquired. "Electricians, Sir."

"Have an electrician about my size come to this spot where you and I stand."

Ten minutes later, Master Electrician Lieutenant Bjornson shuffled to the gate. Braun went with Bjornson into the Security building. The guard returned to his post. Fifteen minutes later, Braun emerged from the gatehouse in Bjornson's electrician uniform, complete with tool belt. Bjornson had changed into a guardhouse uniform—Captain Zaweeka.

"It's okay, Bjornson. You act the Captain, and I'll 'Sir' you."

Bjornson took Braun past two more guards before reaching a loading platform next to a shut-down forklift. "You can enter through that door," Bjornson said.

"Okay, Bjornson. Those drawings you gave me"—Braun pulled them out of his inner pocket—"show me where we are again and take me through what I need to know."

When Braun was satisfied, he took Bjornson's walnut-sized control module and glasses, and made adjustments. "Good. Not one word about this to anyone. Clear?"

"Yes, General."

"One last thing. Confidential, as with everything else. Have you seen a woman named or called Osteen on this ship?"

"No, Sir."

"All right. Back up; I don't want to run you over. It's been a while since I've done this." General Braun started up the forklift, picked up a pallet marked Cryogenics, and rolled to the loading ramp. He took up Bjornson's module and uttered a command. The loading door retracted inward, and Braun took the machine into *Orion*.

# 67

ONCE ON THE SHIP, BRAUN VOICE-ACTIVATED THE LOADING DOOR to close, and tucked away the module he'd been given. He knew trying to find Osteen would be like looking for one starling in a swarm in a night sky. She'd be moving, in blended disguise like he was. The General knew she was here because of her knowledge of the ship, which she'd learned on her former assignment: Plan A—Defense. From his examination of her file and astute recall of previous conversations, the General concluded Osteen was distraught about not being selected, and she aimed to correct this egregious error. She'd used and expended officers Troy and Malone, and most likely Pompadoux, to reach this point.

The inside of the super shuttle was enormous and busy—Braun tried to imagine what the moon-based ark, *Welkin-Alpha*, was like—as he swerved to avoid trams and android-operated worker-scooters in the central corridor. At intersections, Braun stretched his neck right and left to locate the ship's sides, which amazed him, as the ship was standing, vertical. In the last seventy-five years, specially developed metals had become one-quarter the weight of former ultra-composites, but were much stronger. He approached an elevator and commanded it to open via the module. Inside, when the door closed, he realized it was a temporary elevator that hoisted up—over, if the ship were horizontal—a thirty-foot-wide conveyor belt. He could see the belt through the elevator window. Braun had been on the shuttle once before, when it was surrounded by scaffolding. He'd had an opportunity to tour the ship several weeks before the change of Plan, but, regrettably, at the last minute had had to cancel.

He consulted one of the drawings and ordered movement to bay thirteen. The hoist rose on a yellow light and stopped on a red light one minute later. The half-doors slid back within inner channels, and Braun emerged into the bay with his forklift.

As he neared Cryogenics, he could see lights, and soon he heard voices. He parked the machine to the side and slid off the seat. He glanced at his drawings a last time and, without a word to anyone, walked through a side door and went left. He walked for a full minute past two more doors and swung open the third, which brought him to the sleeping room for transient workers Bjornson had told him about. General Braun heard a snore, moved to the opposite side, and tapped his glasses. A top bunk was what he wanted. His glasses, with periscopic-reflect, revealed an open one on his right. Braun climbed the ladder up to level three and lay down on the bunk.

Braun considered Osteen's needs. She had to eat, and she worked out as much as he did. If she didn't have a private gym available, she'd find one or make one.

Braun, a spiritual man, though not a religious one, asked his higher power to bless his wife and son and willed himself to sleep.

Several hours later, the General was woken by a ship-wide announcement. "Lieutenant Bjornson, report to ship Security." The announcer's voice sounded like Osteen's. *That's her. Game on.* Braun felt a vibration and pulled out the control module. It glowed intermittently, flashing bright and dim. Braun climbed down the ladder, found the latrine, and flushed the module down a toilet. He pulled out a second drawing Bjornson had given him and studied it, looking for stairs; he needed to change his location. He didn't want to use the public elevator and found the closest stairway, but his survival instinct told him to go to the one a bit farther ahead. He got there and walked up half a flight. He stopped and looked at the carbon-graphite side strips he was grabbing to climb and realized they were actual rails which would allow trolleys to roll just above a conveyor belt. He remembered from the map that sick bay was ahead and exited from the stairway.

General Braun saw the backs of two clinicians and walked to an alcove housing a sofa and two chairs. He sat on the sofa and remembered to tear off the Velcro of "Bjornson" from his chest and stuck it underneath the cushion. He sensed someone coming and lay down on the sofa, pulling his hat over his eyes and crossing his arms over his chest. He snored lightly. He heard the person walk near and stop beside him, then resume the walk and go out a door. He waited for it to become still and crept to a supply closet, where he found medical scrubs. He donned a green top and matching bottoms over the uniform Bjornson had traded with him, and put on a green medic's cap. He slid his own cap into a pocket and went back to a corner in the alcove and pulled a curtain. He sat behind it on the floor to wait out Osteen and see what she would do next.

Three hours later, nothing had happened except for one person passing back from sick bay, the opposite way. Sick bay should be unattended, Braun thought. It was 0600 as Braun scrounged sick bay and found what he'd been looking for. He removed his top shroud and put on a white lab coat with official medical signature and coat of arms. He rolled Bjornson's shirt collar below the lab coat and rolled up the inner shirt's sleeves. It wasn't perfect, but it would have to do for now. He located food pills in a closet and pocketed a few. He used the sick-bay restroom to pop the pills and drink from cupped hands. Braun went back to the alcove and sat behind the curtain, but close enough to peek around it. He would wait one more hour for Osteen to make a move.

..................................

OSTEEN REMAINED IN CONTACT WITH *ORION*'S SHIPBOARD SECURITY office for fifteen minutes after the five minutes it would have taken Lieutenant Bjornson to report to Security. She had initiated a system of checking every two hours into workers' modules with the help of Eva, her final recruit, another major who said she was honored to serve in memory of Troy and Malone, whom she had known since childhood. Lieutenant Bjornson's module hadn't kicked back. Osteen's senses went on high alert.

She tried again to raise Bjornson by having Eva call privately. No answer. After another ten minutes, Osteen had a terrible hunch.

Osteen reached out to engineering and called for the senior engineer in charge, one Damian De Sousa, who had the current shift. She ordered him to report to her in Bunker 2. When Osteen arrived at Bunker 2, he was already there. Osteen drew him inside and airlocked the door.

"Mr. De Sousa, I have no nefarious intent, but you must be honest with me."

"Yes, General. How can I help?"

She saw him eye her breasts as she poured two cups of tea from a thermos she'd taken with her and told him to sit.

"We may be under attack."

De Sousa looked at the stars on her uniform. He glanced at her legs and breasts and looked up to her face.

"I'm sure you know, Mr. De Sousa, that although we, the military, will not be journeying on this shuttle to Moonbase-1, we are responsible for everyone's safety until liftoff."

"I do."

"Here is my question. If we had to destroy this shuttle to prevent it from falling into enemy hands, is there a way to do that?"

"Yes. But it wouldn't be necessary if the enemy didn't know how to fly it."

"Listen. Our enemy has all the plans and is up to flying this shuttle. Which compromises Moonbase-1 and the starship."

De Sousa studied her and stroked his chin.

"Hold on," Osteen said, cupping an ear beneath her glasses. "I see." Osteen pursed her lips and stood, turned a few degrees from De Sousa. She angled her hip and could feel him ogle her. "Raise the Security level to high alert. Inform Chair Popov." Osteen faked taps on glasses not turned on as De Sousa watched.

"We can blow the ship's engines, General," De Sousa said.

Osteen sat down and nodded. She appeared thoughtful and took a sip of tea. "Here is my last question. This is premature: but if it came to that, would you know how to do it, and could you do it remotely?"

De Sousa nodded.

"We must go back to the engine room, to ready those arrangements if they are needed."

"Not necessary, General Osteen: I can override the system and set the blow electronically with two special devices I am required—as senior engineer—to have on my person." He unzipped a pocket on each thigh and removed a hand-sized module from each.

Osteen looked. "How do . . .?"

De Sousa positioned the two modules and pantomimed joining them. "When they join, I command them to lock. Everything is ready. If the order comes to blow, I tap in a code from my glasses."

"Are you the only one who can command 'Lock'?"

"No, General, anyone wearing my glasses can command. I switch these glasses and turn over the modules when other senior engineers relieve me."

"Suppose you forget the code?"

"I don't have a given code, General. I tap in S-O-S in Morse code with these glasses." De Sousa lay the modules down, removed his glasses, and fingered them in his lap. "The system takes over from there."

At that, Osteen drew her stun gun, aimed at the middle of De Sousa's chest, and pulled the trigger.

There was a muffled chuff and no smoke. Osteen restored the stun gun to her inside pocket and swallowed the last sip of tea as she watched De Sousa's chest and then capped her thermos. He lay back in the chair, unmoving, glasses still in his lap, open eyes staring at the wall.

Osteen turned her glasses back on and gave them one quick tap, which signaled Eva in ship Security. "Transmit Damian De Sousa's file to me. Include his Security clearance with matching algorithm. Establish remotes, and link both him and me to the engine room." Osteen secured the modules in her separate pockets and zippered De Sousa's glasses in her other vest pocket.

Osteen dispatched one more memo, to Andrica, while she watched De Sousa. When he stirred and became aware, she drew his arms behind him and broke his fingers one by one except for his thumbs. She took from her pocket a Chinese thumb restraint and placed each end around a thumb. His wails couldn't be heard through the air-locked door as she popped two purple pills into his mouth. To make sure there would be no surprises, she removed his belt and bound his feet to the chair. When he yelped his last and his face fell forward in an induced stupor, Osteen reflected on why she had wanted him to be awake when she broke his fingers: to feel every pain and endure the humiliation. All of it. It would be fun to watch him try to remove his thumbs from the restraint, she thought.

# 68

ANDRICA SAT ACROSS FROM POPOV IN A SITTING ROOM SEPARATE from Popov's office. Popov attempted to be casual and offer the girl some comfort. They both sipped tea with spices. Andrica was trying to control the tapping of her soft leather heels on the floor. The taps were muted, but Andrica accepted that she was nervous, not impatient. Popov noticed Andrica seemed preoccupied and gave her time to settle. They both smiled, and the silence hung.

"You are aware I've asked you here for specific reasons," Popov said. "But before we enter those discussions, bring me up to date with your dolphins, your humans of the seas."

Andrica made the effort to smile again. She'd had a difficult day at academy. She'd prepared the wrong assignment for a mathegenics class, and before the class Charles had intercepted her and given her flowers. After the wasted class, she reread his note accompanying the flowers and became even more in a muddle. Her eyes bothered her again, and she'd cursed Charles.

"Thank you. I haven't made any advances, but I've noted my dolphins appear to understand more about pitch, tones, and, in general, music, than any type of oral word."

"Is there a reason?"

"I don't know. This has been noted before over the years by others, but I was hoping my efforts would have made them more susceptible to human singing."

"By chance," Popov leaned forward, "have you transmitted discordants to them?"

"Yes. But all they do is swim faster and leap more."

"Could the discordants be an aphrodisiac?"

"No. I tested for that."

Popov nodded.

"Charles gave me a new idea, but he doesn't know it. He happened to mention that some old languages were whistled. Turns out, lots of old-time village people whistled parts of their languages so they could be heard hillside to hillside."

"And?"

"I've just started with this, but I see more swim-speed variations, and I'm receiving responses on new frequencies."

"Keep testing. You have cornered something."

Popov let out a sigh, looked out a window screen, and back at Andrica.

"Do you have any idea where General Osteen is?" Popov asked.

Andrica shrugged.

"I've veered off course with you," Popov said. "I can't bring myself to ask what I should ask you."

"Am I in some kind of trouble?"

"You shouldn't insult us, Andrica; we know Osteen has recruited you and others."

"Others who have been blown to smithereens," responded Andrica, not looking at Popov.

"Would you believe me," Popov said, "if I told you I'm having as much of a struggle being here with you as you are being here with me?"

"Yes."

"Why does it have to be this way?"

"Just go ahead, Chair Popov, ask your intended questions."

"You, me, and Osteen, and the rest of her cohorts, aren't the only females who have been taken advantage of."

"My life has been decent," Andrica said.

"Then how could General Osteen have twisted you around so?"

"I can't have a baby."

"This may surprise you, but I'm glad you told me this, and here's why."

POPOV HAD DONE THE BEST SHE COULD WITH ANDRICA AND HAD TO refocus. She and one of her aides were on the way with the newest M-L-M to Iceland, a neutral zone, to meet the heads of state and commanders in the Greenland-Denmark war. That the Chair of WCM chose to conduct this meeting and go to them, without Braun, would emphasize the moment. Ever since resources of natural gas and meteorite iron had been discovered beneath Greenland's ice eight years ago, Denmark had fought to regain control of the nation. In particular, meteorite iron was used in the super-lightweight metals for space launches.

In spite of the importance of the trip, Popov had her mind on other issues: the preparation of *Orion*—smooth boarding of the first load of trekkers, Cryopreservation on *Welkin-Alpha*, the conspiracy of Osteen, the M-L-M inoculation and scientometrics of society staying behind, the translation of alien signals, and this damned, mad, futile war. She'd forced droogs to the back of her mind, and she couldn't explain why, other than their beastly savagery had no place on this Earth.

WITHOUT CONDESCENSION, POPOV EXPLAINED THE MATHEMATICS behind M-L-M, as well as what she could of the music, to the commanders and their aides in Iceland. She spoke of unique mathematics connecting the music and how music was continuing to develop in M-L-M. "Mathe-Lingua-Musica," she said, "is getting stronger by the day. We hope to reach the point in this language where false statements become inexpressible." Popov posed the entire meeting as a huge and vital experiment in which these two warring nations could make history right here, right now. Indeed, after her remarks, the leaders seemed proud to be the "chosen."

After the overture of music, a revised *Invictus*, calibrated to entrain harmony against adversity, before the meeting even reconvened in M-L-M, Popov sensed history being made. The setup music had been extraordinary; intimations of Danish and Icelandic-Greenland folk music segueing to a mental enlargement that moved one to understanding, satisfaction, unification—all in unique rhythms. It was as if they'd all taken a journey—con amore—to a reunification of the spirit. No one was able to speak for several minutes after the music played.

At the end of the meeting, the world's longest and most savage war of present-age, a war that had claimed eighty million lives and left over nine hundred million wounded, was downgraded to a Conflict. What's more, all parties agreed to reconvene at the same time, same place, in two weeks.

Popov hugged everyone present and, without speaking further words which would interfere with the moment, she left.

.....................................

AN HOUR LATER, AFTER HER AIDE HAD INFORMED DE COSTA, THE latter contacted Popov. "Are you sitting down?" Before she could answer, De Costa said, "The chance of surviving as a species has improved to 71 percent."

She cried as she hugged her aide.

However, a few minutes later, General Braun called with the worst news Popov could have imagined.

"The shuttle is under siege," he said.

# 69

WAITING BEHIND THE CURTAIN, BRAUN LISTENED TO THE SHIP. HE heard drilling, thuds, and pneumatic hammers from all directions. He heard muffled shouts, and several times he heard whistles, which he imagined were used to emphasize shouts. Everything seemed rushed to Braun, including his heartbeats. All of his life had been rushed, he thought. From his earliest memory, he had been taught discipline, posture, demeanor. He couldn't understand why at the time and rebelled, and been punished for recalcitrance. Thinking about it here, he realized he'd been rushed into a life of tradition, dedication, and overwork. He allowed himself a moment of emotion as he remembered being rushed into team sports, pushed into mathematics, forced into gyms, but never had a chance to play with friends, never mind by himself. He was about to tear up, but caught himself. *What the fuck is happening to me? I've got a job to do here. Not one second to waste.*

It was time, Braun concluded. He'd expected it to be like this. She wouldn't seek him; he would have to come to her. From what he could tell, ship preparations never stopped. He listened again to thumps, hums of trams, cargo doors opening and closing. He figured Osteen's guess would be that he would sneak around in the middle of the night, not in broad daylight. Braun calculated she would stay keen at night and get what rest she could during the day. He thought of getting Popov's approval to collect his crack troops and storm the ship. But this would be too obvious for Osteen, and she had to have thought of it. *No, don't give her a reason to think of a larger plan.*

General Braun left sick bay and held an ear to the nearest door in the hall. The door was locked. He went to the next door to trace his way back to the forklift; it was quiet behind the door, and he opened it. No one was there, but a jacket covered the back of a chair facing medical monitors. The general removed the name tag, Symmons, from the jacket and applied it to his own empty Velcro. He was glad to see his forklift where he'd left it, still loaded with the same pallet. With no one nearby, he removed his medical garb and looked like electrician Symmons under a hard hat he found under the seat. He folded the other clothes and placed them under a canvas behind the seat, along with Bjornson's cap. Before stepping into the machine, something made him reach again under the canvas: more drawings, some micas, and another toolbelt. He pocketed the new drawings and re-drew the tarp. *Let's go exploring.*

General Braun reconnoitered two further levels without seeing anything out of the ordinary. Near workmen, he dropped off the pallet he'd been carrying, enabling him to move faster and make quick turns. The next bay, number sixteen, was foodservice, and he chose to bypass it and come back later from the opposite direction. Osteen would acknowledge the need of foodservice and would figure an enemy would approach it from the direction he'd been.

Braun had requested the guard back at launch Security to one-way him from ship Security—ship Security could not track him, so neither could Osteen nor anyone else on the shuttle. The price he paid for this was not being able to track her either. But if she gave another command aboard the ship—it had sounded like her the last time—there might be a way he could lock her in. Meanwhile, he had apprised Popov on her private feed. He'd told Popov he was 99 percent certain Osteen was on the shuttle and not to contact him lest Popov reveal that feed to Osteen. Popov said she expected he was going to hunt for Osteen when he'd asked for special leave.

"I'm searching as best I can. I'm sure I heard Osteen give an intraship call earlier."

*Move carefully, General. I can't afford to lose you.*

"Have you talked to the girl?"

*Yes. I made progress. But I could not press and get details to help you.*

"I need to know if Osteen has other renegades on board."

*Understood. The situation is delicate with Andrica. I'm sorry I don't have more information.*

"I'll do everything I can, Chair Popov."

.................................

GENERAL OSTEEN WISHED SHE HADN'T ABUSED DE SOUSA. HE didn't try to remove his thumbs, and his stare back at her was resolute. She'd seen this look before on others; they would no longer cooperate, and in this way he was like her. No matter, she was still linked with him to the engine room. Patting her pockets, she confirmed she had what she needed if it came to a last resort. *Keep De Sousa alive,* she thought. *A hostage is an asset.* With this thought in mind, she offered him tea and he nodded. But when he sipped a mouthful, he exploded it out into her face. She dropped the teacup and backhanded him.

"Do not fuck with me, Mr. De Sousa."

He spat blood on the floor and let his head hang in front of him.

She left him for a cot next to the bunker wall. She needed sleep.

Twenty minutes later, after falling asleep, she was awakened by ship Security. An errant forklift had rammed a kitchen hotline, and two people had been electrocuted. What's more, both the kitchen and cafeteria were in darkness.

"So, fire up the goddammed generator."

"It hasn't been delivered yet. We expect it to arrive here tomorrow for install on Thursday."

"Find that generator and get it up there now. I'm not going to wait two days for lights."

She was a General used to giving orders. Eva, one of her recruited cohorts, had been instrumental in helping her establish command of "prelaunch," in the eyes of the preparing crew. Rubbing worn eyes, Osteen readied to give an intra-ship command. She tapped her special glasses. "Senior electricians, report to foodservice. Senior electricians, report to foodservice."

She didn't suspect a ruse; Braun wouldn't give up innocent people. *But who else could it be?*

She shut down the light and locked Bunker 2 as she left. If Braun was involved, she knew where he was. She'd been glad to give the intra-ship command; *let Braun think he's luring me into a trap.*

..................................

THAT'S WHAT BRAUN HAD BEEN WAITING FOR, HER NEXT INTRA-SHIP command. A desperate situation demanded desperate measures. In the dark he grabbed an elbow.

"Please tell me where the command originated from," Braun whispered. "I'm with Security and I need to substantiate it; this could be sabotage."

A light from the woman's glasses moved over the General's face and uniform. "You don't look like Security," she said.

"Smart of you to question." He waited, about to give up and move to another.

"It's from level 19; that's all I can tell you."

Braun nodded thanks and walked away. Alone again, he turned on his glasses, and went to his drawings. He realized he lacked intimate details of the bays. He remembered ship plans he'd taken from the forklift and shifted to them. He found more details for level 19 and refocused. The usual storage: wait—these were bunkers, one through three. Of course, a perfect hideout. But which one was it? He restored the plans to his inside pocket and patted his toolbelt. At the last moment, before he'd deliberately jammed the machine's accelerator at highest-speed and aimed it for the electrical panel where he saw electricians at work, he'd managed to jump off with the toolbelt. He'd raced through a door while all eyes focused on the charging forklift.

Surmising Osteen was on her way to foodservice, General Braun's plan was to reach her bunker and intercept her when she returned. He stepped through a door he recognized and into the elevator-conveyor corridor. *Stealth*, the General told himself. He went through a final narrow door, grabbed both carbonite rails, and climbed.

# 70

OSTEEN WAS IN HER ORIGINALLY ASSIGNED DEFENSE QUARTERS OF *Orion*. She'd confirmed the quarters would be the last to be retrofitted for Plan B. She would change location in two days, sooner if the situation demanded it. Eva, whom Troy and Malone had recruited and Osteen vetted, kept her hidden, off limits, and updated her continually.

Osteen tried one last time to contact Andrica. After the takeout of Troy and Malone, two remaining recruits had bailed, but Osteen knew they would keep the secret because they would be implicated and their careers dashed.

Osteen admitted her situation looked bleak for merging into *Orion* and experiencing liftoff to Moonbase and to a new world. Someone was after her. If she neutralized that someone, another would come, and another. The more her frustration built, the more miserable she felt. She'd fucked up. She'd thought World Army's zap of the ghetto hideout, which she'd induced, would fool Braun into thinking he'd wiped her out. But she still had her personal Plan B. And Andrica was her best hope for escape. It was time to contact her.

"Andrica, I'm glad to have reached you." Osteen said.

*I met with Chair Popov today, and I'm not thinking straight; I'll have to call you back.*

"I met your father last week. He asked about you."

*He did?*

"He did. He's been back a few weeks from a six-month asteroid-mining mission."

Andrica covered her eyes. At one time, mining asteroids had been a plum job. These days, it was for the deplorables, who were directed by cobots. *I . . . can't talk right now. I promise to call back.*

Osteen shut down and thought. She felt a bit bad for Andrica, the sorry little shit, although Osteen realized she'd moved too fast and laid it on a bit too thick with the bit about the father, whom she had never actually seen. She wasn't on top of her game and was making errors—*too little sleep*—she thought to herself, as she rubbed her eyes. She felt as if the walls and world were closing in. In her desperation, she began to second-guess herself and even wondered if she could contact a key droog. Osteen could offer to teach and train them if they could find a way to rescue her from the shuttle. *Christ! Snap out of it. Sleep deprivation is screwing up my head.* She uncapped her pocket thermos and took a swallow to chase a pill she'd popped, and a few minutes later began to feel some relief and experience some clearness of thought.

As she sat contemplating her next move, she figured Braun would try to outsmart her by coming back down to foodservice from level eighteen. So she decided that she would take the elevator down to level seventeen and wait. But before taking the elevator, she reconnected to De Sousa. Any transmission, in or out, even I-Translation of his native Portuguese, Osteen would receive.

.................................

WHENEVER ANDRICA FELT LIKE THIS, SHE WENT TO HER DOLPHINS. On her way to them, she one-armed the male macaw, who cuddled by her cheek. This too had in some fragile way disrupted Andrica's psyche.

When Andrica had told her mom that an acquaintance had recently been in contact with her father, her mom's response was "God help us if he shows himself here. Keep him up there with the damn asteroids."

"Was he that bad?"

"Worse. And I guess it's time I told you the full story."

Later the same Sunday afternoon, Andrica called Charles. All she could squeak out was "I'm with my dolphins, if you want to come by."

Twenty minutes later, Charles arrived with a potted plant. "I've been wanting to give you this. It's called a Luv plant."

Andrica took it and held it up to the sun. "Is this the new species they found in Brazil last year?" She touched and smelled the tulip-like buds.

"Yes. The reds and blues grow together but they don't mate."

"Yet in several months, new purple buds grow between them," Andrica said.

"Yep."

"Thanks for all the flowers."

Charles admired the dolphin lavaliere hanging from her neck and watched her ply the chain with a thumb and forefinger.

They talked about academy, about the alien signals. "Those signals have no effect on my dolphins," she'd said. They talked about M-L-M. Charles avoided any mention of *Welkin-Alpha*. Andrica hadn't been preselected, and Charles had.

"So, are you looking forward to your big adventure, Charles?"

The macaw fluttered to her foot and hopped to the ground.

"Yes and no. I wish you were coming with me."

Andrica looked at her plant and picked it up and placed it in her lap. They were sitting outside on a bench by the dolphin pool as the dolphins clicked to each other and lapped round and round.

"You didn't damage me, Charles. I can't conceive, but it doesn't have anything to do with you."

Charles teared up, and for a moment held his tongue.

"Did you just find this out?"

"The reason why, yes."

Charles moved closer to her, and she turned her head and kissed him.

"I apologize for being such a shit," she said.

"You had every right to be." He held her cheek and kissed it.

He put his arm around her, and they watched the dolphins, oblivious humans of the sea, lapping the pool amid their squeaks and clicks.

"Are you still seeing that general, Andrica?"

"No."

..................................

THAT NIGHT, HOME ALONE IN HER BEDROOM, ANDRICA, WHO'D been thinking about it all day, called Osteen.

*I've been hoping you'd call.*

"I have a couple of questions."

*Go.*

"What did my father say about me?"

*He was sorry for what he had done to you.*

"Does he still have the tattoo . . . cupid . . . on his right wrist? It refers to me you know."

*I thought I saw that, the angel, on his left wrist. Maybe it was the right.*

"So, what do you want me to do?"

*Come to Shuttle Launch, South Gate, tomorrow morning at 0610. My Security, a woman named Eva, will take you to me.*

"Are the others with you?"

*Yes. Except for Connie and MaryAnn, everyone is here. We didn't want to leave you, Andrica.*

"Okay. I'll be there, and I'm coming alone."

*Why would I think any different?*

"Are they trying to dislodge you?"

*No. We'll discuss the plan when you get here with the rest of us.*

They tapped off. Andrica had wanted more details for Popov. Andrica's father didn't have any tattoo; Andrica had confirmed the fact with her mother an hour ago.

..................................

FOR THE MOMENT, OSTEEN DIDN'T KNOW WHAT TO THINK ABOUT THE conversation. Andrica had emphasized a little too much the word "right" referring to the wrist of her father's tattoo. So, Osteen mentioned his left wrist. Osteen's quick thinking seemed to settle the issue. But Andrica emphasized she'd be coming alone—when there was no need to mention that. Osteen made a decision. She went back to the bunker, grabbing a dolly she'd seen a few minutes ago. She gagged De Sousa and rolled him from Bunker 2 to Bunker 1, on the side of the bay. *The fallback*, Osteen thought, *is Andrica becomes my hostage*. She tapped her glasses to contact Andrica again.

*Forgot to mention: when you see Eva at south gate, she will quiz you. Show her your ID and tell her to take you to Bunker 2. Gotta go. See you in the a.m.*

Osteen ungagged De Sousa, pulled his head back, and tossed nutrition pills and lozenges into his throat.

..................................

GENERAL BRAUN HAD PLACED HIS PHONE ON DO NOT DISTURB, AUthorizing only one contact to ring through. So, when his phone rang, he took the call from Popov.

*Andrica has contacted us, General. I have information.*

"Good. Let's have it."

*She was told by General Osteen, who is aboard the shuttle, to meet Eva, a Security guard, at South Gate at 0610 tomorrow.*

"What else?"

*Andrica will be taken to Osteen in Bunker 2.*

"Okay, then." The General thought. "Let's hope the girl is on the money." Braun thought again. "Let Andrica pass through. Don't initiate any hostile action."

..................................

WHEN BRAUN REACHED THE ENTRANCE TO THE BUNKER BAY, HE stilled in the silence for over two minutes. Not hearing anything different, he ventured closer to the Bunker shown as 2 in his drawing. Everything was dark. His night-vision glasses and heat sensor revealed nothing. Convinced that Osteen was waiting for him at foodservice, he crept to the door of the bunker. A minute later, he pulled the door open. Not having been ambushed, the General walked in and pulled the door ajar. He was still standing in darkness when he heard the door close, and the tumblers lock behind him. Then the lights came on.

# 71

"WELCOME TO BUNKER 2, GENERAL. I'VE BEEN EXPECTING YOU."

Braun's face reddened. Where was she? The voice came from the walls.

"No need to blush, General; or is that anger I see in your sickly face?"

God damn her. "Go fuck yourself, Osteen."

"You will pay for that remark, General."

"You thick snot." Braun realized he'd lost his cool, his professionalism, but he couldn't help himself. "In my military, we don't put up with insubordination."

*My*, he says. *We*, he says. So, I'm excluded from *his* military. Osteen's hatred built as she concluded that the General's "we" implied all the men he served with, but didn't include her.

"A foolish mistake you just made, Roy. Your personal journal reveals you want your son to journey on *Welkin-Alpha*. Something about extending your lineage. I found a way for him to make the journey and was going to use that in my negotiations. Not anymore. Your son will burn to ashes here on Earth, just like you."

Several minutes later, Braun sat on a crate in the bunker, his head in his hands. The bunker remained quiet. He didn't think Osteen would cut him out of negotiation. It wasn't like her to not push her leverage, her angle. The General wasn't thinking right, and he didn't review the exact words he'd spoken to her. He was shut down and didn't understand why. And his electronics had been scrambled; he couldn't get through to Popov.

"Here's how it works, General. I can see you; I can hear you. And I override all controls in your bunker. I may or may not have you make contact on the outside, but if and when I do, make one false move and I will blow the engines on this shuttle and neutralize Plan B. Understood?"

"And how will you do that?"

"Glad you asked. Sitting next to me is senior engineer Damian De Sousa, indisposed at the moment. He's educated me on how, and I'm wired into him and the engine bay."

"'Indisposed,' you say. Maybe you've got nobody there."

"Listen." There was a snap and "EEEEYYYYYAAAA." Osteen continued: "The snap before the yell was De Sousa's left thumb, which is now broken."

Braun turned purple. He yearned to say *Your problem, Osteen, is that you've never been properly fucked*, but he stifled himself just in time.

..................................

POPOV FIDGETED. IT WAS 12:30 A.M., AND GENERAL BRAUN HAD not given her his update, due at midnight. The General was prompt in all matters. She would have to wait. She had WCM Commo-Scramble, but his mission was critical and she couldn't risk interception—Commo-Scramble would be a last resort. A short while later, Popov teleconferenced her six WCM colleagues of the emergency.

"We should storm the ship," Gunderson said.

"But she could have General Braun hostage," Tuan said. "If so, we should hear her demands first."

"Losing Braun would be unfortunate," Gunderson said. "But we'd get her off the shuttle—she's the leader of the mutiny, right?"

"If we storm the ship," Anand said, "she could sabotage it."

"How?" Boucher asked.

It went back and forth. The main decision to be made was whether or not to let Andrica deliver herself at 0610, as instructed. Through all of the discussion, Wang Chen De Costa said nothing. He was aware of his son's love for Andrica.

Gunderson's use of the word *mutiny* scraped against Popov's insides. Could Liftees mount a mutiny? she asked herself. Would a Liftee try to steal a place on the ship?

"Here's my decision," Popov said. "General Amin Farzad, internal Security, will assume complete military command on my orders. I will instruct him to surround ship-launch, outside the gates, with ground troops. The combat troops will hold there, but will be ready to break down the gates and storm the ship if it becomes necessary for me to give that order. And Andrica will go as planned to the south gate to be taken to Osteen."

General Farzad was proud Chair Popov had selected him to take over World Army in General Braun's absence. He'd already spoken with General Blackston and had received his full support. Farzad made a few calls, and within two hours the launch site was encircled with five hundred troops and twelve creeper tanks. He and his troops were positioned and ready to roll when Chair Popov gave the order.

..................................

WHEN OSTEEN HEARD WHAT WAS HAPPENING FROM EVA, OSTEEN had already suspected the vibrations she felt were from a defensive maneuver, otherwise commandos would have stormed by now. But as long as she held the fate of Supershuttle *Orion* in her hands and was in a bomb-proof bunker, the Army would do nothing. Soon Popov herself would learn the true situation and negotiate.

..................................

"IT'S ME, GENERAL. DE SOUSA AND I ARE IN BOMB-PROOF BUNKER 3," she lied. "I'm going to enable you to speak to WCM Chair Popov. Assuming she's smart enough to accept your own feed and repel any other locking feed, apprise her of the situation and my demands. Remember what I told you: this shuttle means nothing to me. Miscalculate, and I promise you I will blow these engines."

..................................

POPOV TAPPED HER GLASSES AND TOOK THE GENERAL'S CALL. "THERE you are. What's happened? I was about to try to get you on Commo-Scramble."

*We are on a form of it now. Osteen has enabled us to communicate, but she can't hear us.*

"Why? Why doesn't she call me directly?"

*Aside from making this a personal vendetta, she fears being tracked.*

"Continue."

*I've been locked in Bunker 2 on* Orion. *Osteen claims she and her chief engineer, Damian De Sousa, are in Bunker 3.*

"At 0610, Andrica is to be taken to Bunker 2."

*Understood. Here's what you need to know. Osteen had De Sousa set the engines to blow. Osteen can initiate the destruction, and if we make any aggressive move, she will blow these engines. What's more, she will survive the blast. The Bunkers are bomb-proof.*

"What should we do?"

*She has demands. But first, she wants to hear that I've explained the situation to you.*

"Tell her you have. I'll wait."

Several minutes later, the General returned to the negotiation. *She wants ten million dollars plus five thousand in world coin, unmarked and untraceable, delivered to her in an Army hover, said hover to be Untracked-Pristine and left for her personal use.*

"What does Untracked-Pristine mean?"

*When she flies off, no one can track the hover; no one will be able to find her. Remember, she's wired to De Sousa, who will accompany her to the hover. No false moves. As it stands, we can't make any move on her.*

"We have no choice, do we? Even if she's bluffing."

*I don't think so; I'll stall her as much as I can, but get the money and tell General Blackston to arrange the Untracked-Pristine.*

"Anything else?"

*Tell Blackston she'll know if the hover is not as ordered. She can still hover off and blow the ship on remote. Osteen told me the shuttle means nothing to her.*

"General Farzad, on my orders, has amassed ground troops and creepers around the perimeter. Get back to me in one hour, General. And make sure Osteen knows I will not speak with anyone on public-tran."

Popov had no sooner closed off the conversation when Magnuson burst through her doorway.

"Lobashevsky! He's gone nuts."

# 72

"MISTER MAGNUSON, EXPLAIN YOURSELF."

"He's gone off his rocker. He's catatonic. He might have had a seizure."

"God help us." Popov shouted to her aide, "Get me Salk."

She turned to Magnuson. "If we lose Lobashevsky, there will be more than tsunamis and meteor strikes. Bring him to Time Travel Control at once; you can retrieve his work later. Salk and I will meet you at TTC."

Magnuson cradled his head in his hands. "We are so close."

"Magnuson! Bring—him—now."

.................................

WHEN LOBASHEVSKY WAS CARRIED OFF THE ELEVATOR IN A stretcher by Petitjean and Magnuson, Popov was dismayed to see that his eyes had rolled up into his head. "Can you fix him? Can you bring him back, Doctor?"

Salk placed the plasma-steth over Lobashevsky's chest and listened. He took out a tiny vial with a built-in plunger and pricked it into a fold of skin in the middle of the chest. He propped up the patient with a cushion and opened his mouth—"Let's try this." He placed an almond-colored pill deep into Lobashevsky's throat with medical tweezers and asked for a warm, wet sponge.

By the time Lobashevsky had opened his eyes, his heartbeat and temps had returned to normal, and Popov had scheduled Lobashevsky's Return to the exact spot from where he'd been Lifted. She thought back to her agonizing decision to Lift Salk. Thank God she had.

"How do you feel, Veced?" Magnuson asked.

Lobashevsky's eyes glared, and he looked frightened. "Do not go near that other extragalactic transmission," he rasped.

"Why?" Magnuson said. "What happened?"

"They found the end of Pi. Pi ends." He tried to sit up.

"Don't disturb him," Popov said. "Veced, we thank you for all you have done for us. I want to tell you: the next time you awaken, you will be back in the same outdoor field you left, and this will be merely a dream."

"You must not try to decode the extragalactic," Lobashevsky said frantically, his eyes glaring.

"Did you leave us your notes and most recent decodes on the other signals?" Magnuson said.

"Yes. Under my chair. And in the bedroom, under the mattress, is the most up-to-date alphabet."

Magnuson smiled and leaned down to kiss Lobashevsky on the cheek.

Lobashevsky said, "I'm being released?"

"Master," Petitjean said, "you were never incarcerated here."

"The gulag has changed, I'll admit." Lobashevsky eyed everyone. "But, as they say, the more things change, the more they remain the same. You do not fool me."

Three minutes later, Popov excused herself. "Thank you, Dr. Salk. Mr. Magnuson, you and Petitjean collect all of Lobashevsky's most recent notes, and his adapted alphabet. Bring the originals to me; make copies and distribute them to WCM, Liftees, and First Tier."

Popov returned to her office, shutting the door behind her. She then instructed world-bank to express ten million dollars and the coin at once, and placed a call to General Blackston.

.................................

BRAUN, COOPED UP IN THE BUNKER, YEARNED FOR HIS TRACK. HE was a stallion, chained in a holding pen, who clawed and hoofed for the open lea.

Braun hollered again from his bunker. "I'm to report to Chair Popov in five minutes. If I don't report to her—"

"Don't get yourself all worked up, Roy. You will make your report when I allow it. Make sure my demands have been met. You are to inform Chair Popov that I expect Andrica to be on time. You may report to her now."

*Yes*, Popov said. *The money and coin have been stored on the hover. The hover will be delivered when you tell me to release it.*

"She expects the girl, Andrica, to arrive on time."

*My Security has her safe and secure behind commandos. She will walk alone to South Gate at 0610 hours.*

"I'll pass on the information. Tell me when to call you back."

*Stall one hour if possible. If you can't, one half hour.*

.................................

THE NEXT MORNING, ANDRICA APPROACHED THE SOUTH GATE. She'd been briefed, but she had her own agenda after hearing from Popov how Osteen had set up Troy and Malone, whom she'd liked. As she walked toward the gate, Andrica thought of all the conversations she'd had with Osteen. Andrica concluded that she trusted Popov a lot more than Osteen, who had taken this too far.

Andrica showed her ID to Eva and was admitted at South Gate. However, before she could take a step inside, Andrica was instructed to turn over her electronics and was patted down. Convinced she wasn't hiding anything on her person, Eva took her to a door next to the loading bay and contacted Osteen.

"I have her with me by the loading dock," Eva reported.

When Eva moved to twist the door closed behind her, Andrica yanked the mini-taser hanging from Eva's belt and shoved it into her abdomen. *Chuff!* The guard folded and Andrica sat her on a chair inside. Andrica looked around to see if anyone had seen or heard what had just happened, and saw two people walking in the opposite direction fifty yards from her; beyond them, a tram went across her field of view. Andrica pulled over a table in front of the chair and positioned Eva's head on the table as if she were taking a breather.

# 73

AFTER LOBASHEVSKY WAS RETURNED—HE WOULD HAVE SAID "REpatriated"—Magnuson rushed to the unit and tipped over the chair in Lobashevsky's sitting room. Magnuson pulled out all of Lobashevsky's papers and notes, including the ones up underneath near the chair springs. He unpinned all the polar maps, grid maps, and other papers from the paranoid man's walls. Magnuson saved the bedroom for last; and when he turned over the mattress, he found Lobashevsky's pièce de résistance: his newest alphabet.

The next morning, Magnuson, Pemberton, and Petitjean sat with everything, including the Russian's original notebook which had started this odyssey. They were to employ the Russian's newest mathematics, and Chair Popov asked to be the first to see results. Popov assigned the new Samoan musicologist, Teuila Malala, Aasen, Krebs, and Bromsky the task of pressing on with music, reverse-coding into dissonances, using Lobashevsky's newest mathematical developments and alphabet. Popov agreed to let Toni Praeger and Liu Hui continue their collaboration on possible rhythms in the collection points between primes. No one, herself included, had the faintest idea of how to penetrate these collection points, if that's what they were; but Praeger and Liu Hui were optimistic. "Godspeed," Popov told them.

Salk was busy, working out the most efficient way to inoculate all those who would remain on Earth. For the selected—the *Welkin-Alpha* travelers—he was able to prove by DNA-RNA simulation that a fetus could be fed M-L-M during the long sleep aboard the ark. He kept thinking that if in M-L-M there is no reference to war, violence, rage, et cetera, the homunculus would grow without any reference to the concept; therefore, would humans ever need to rediscover and develop the contaminated concept? Salk wasn't the only one who itched with the wild notion of peace obviating any virus of evil.

.................................

PEMBERTON, PETITJEAN, AND MAGNUSON CONCENTRATED ON THE first dozen Mersenne primes, the first four of which were 3, 7, 31, and 127. Popov had distinguished herself by discovering sequential Mersennes seventy-two to eighty-six, but the next individual Mersennes approached billions of digits, and the numbers representing further Mersennes were infinitely larger and couldn't be handled. Lobashevsky's alphabet contained ninety-six separate characters, and the first four characters in the order and system he'd written them corresponded to the first four Mersennes. These, he said, were the most frequent characters in thirty out of the thirty-one separate alien transmissions. These four most common characters were aligned with the four most common utterances in M-L-M. In this fashion, Magnuson, Pemberton, and Petitjean assigned further alien-signal patterns to further utterances in M-L-M and to larger Mersennes. They were certain they were on the right track, but ran into trouble the deeper they went into Mersenne. Trying to imagine the length of these prime numbers was like trying to imagine the scale of our galaxy.

They played back the thirty separate intragalactic transmissions which were, decoded into digits, built on Mersennes. It was a ton of math for present-day computers to handle, and they were awed that so much had been encoded by those civilizations. The experiment brought them to where Lobashevsky had deciphered *Welcome-like, Peace-like,* and *music,* and they felt positive in confirming Lobashevsky's work thus far.

"The way to reach farther into Mersenne is to find atonal algorithms," Pemberton said. "Perhaps when we skip a segment, we come *true* again." He looked to his iguana, this time stretched on the floor. "Am I right, Galileo?"

"We may have to enlist Popov," Magnuson said. "It's her specialty; she found later Mersennes."

"That's a great idea, but we can't distract her from her main charge," Petitjean said; "and from what I've heard, she is still working mathematics on her own time. What about Thaddeus? Didn't he do something similar, using Benford's Law?"

...................................

THADDEUS SMITH SPENT THE EVENING LOOKING OVER THE WORK done by Magnuson, Petitjean, and, in particular, Pemberton. Through the night he studied Lobashevsky's most recent notes, graphics, and calculations. He was astounded at the peasant's genius and wondered how many others in the world had similar gifts yet went unnoticed or were abandoned.

In a move to concentrate his efforts, Thaddeus asked Popov to release him from the WCM Board so he could devote his time to working with Pemberton and Petitjean on advanced Mersennes-M-L-M.

"It's a unique challenge, and I see a quicker way to transmission translations."

"Regulations stipulate that I maintain a full WCM complement," Popov said.

"I understand. But I've asked Magnuson, and he's agreed to temporarily take my place."

"He has?"

"Yes. He hesitated, but then he said working close to you would be an honor."

In the end, Popov approved. Thaddeus realized Magnuson felt left out. He was the most responsible for Lobashevsky's breakthrough and knew we were on the cusp. But Thaddeus also knew Magnuson's considerable mathematical skills lay in other areas. Thaddeus had no time to bring one up to speed, no matter how keen the mind. He needed Petitjean's specialties and the unique Pemberton who was, without question, a raw genius.

# 74

ANDRICA HAD A TASER, WHICH SHE'D JUST USED FOR THE FIRST time. She put on the guard's glasses and vest as she briefly considered that she was on her own and had no idea where Bunker 2 was. One way or another, she planned to meet Osteen, but on her own terms. And toward that goal, Andrica took the next logical step.

"Excuse me," Andrica said to a woman walking with a gym bag, "where are the bunkers?"

The woman pointed up. "Bay 19."

"Thank you."

Andrica found the elevator and pressed 19. As the elevator began to move, she felt a gentle pressure against the bottom of her feet. She rode the elevator with her right hand in her pocket, holding the taser secreted within. The elevator reached floor 19, and Andrica withdrew the taser as the doors opened. She looked around and saw no one. Then she noted what looked like a bunker to the left and began—

*Where are you? Do you have Andrica?*

Andrica remembered that she wasn't wearing her own glasses and had donned the glasses of the guard she had tased. She recognized Osteen's voice and, instead of answering into the glasses, she stood ramrod-still. While ignoring the call, she saw another bunker on the right and suspected a third lay behind another elevator across from her. She reached out and noted embrasures on a fixed post nearby, which were sticky to her touch, making her wonder whether a sign had been removed. So, which one is Bunker 2?

*I asked you a question. Answer me.*

Andrica said nothing and kneeled between the elevators.

Osteen grimaced. Time to call Braun. I'll cut his balls off if he thinks he—

*General Braun, you have two minutes to rectify the situation.*

"What situation? What are you talking about?"

*Andrica is not here. My Security guard is not in contact.*

"Whoa. I don't know anything about this. Let me call Popov."

*I'll call you back in two, General.*

"Chair Popov, what did you do with Andrica? Osteen says she didn't show, her Security guard is not responding, and we've got two minutes to fix this."

Popov cradled her head. *Hold on. I'm calling Andrica. I can't raise her. Stall. Tell her I don't know what happened. I'll keep trying.*

*Braun. Osteen here. Status.*

"General Osteen, I speak the truth. We don't know what happened. She was last seen entering the shuttle with a Security guard. Popov is trying to raise her. The young lady must be acting on her own."

*Bullshit, General. You don't think I'll blow—*

"General Osteen, all your demands have been met except for this one snafu here. Let me recall Popov."

*Braun, listen to me closely. The final two minutes of your life start right now.*

*I can't reach her, General Braun*, Popov said.

"Pray," Braun said.

Braun was not a poker player. He never liked the odds. Like most mathematicians, he never played the lottery, and he didn't gamble. Braun never made a bold move unless he was sure the odds were in his favor. This time, he gambled.

*This better be good, General Braun.*

"Thank God you called me, Osteen. Andrica is in Bunker 3. Please don't ask me how she got there—I don't know. But Popov has contacted her and she's in Bunker 3."

Osteen was in a fix. She didn't plan on using Bunker 3 and couldn't check it remotely because Bunker 3 was lined for nuclear waste, preventing and obviating the need for "see and hear" inside. Osteen's demands had been met—the hover, the money, everything. She could forget the little shit, wherever the hell she was. Osteen had never known Braun to lie; she had to give him that. Why would he lie now? Unless he was desperate. Osteen had to know; it was her nature to know an enemy. If Andrica wasn't in Bunker 3, she would make Braun squirm and murder him before she took off. If Andrica *was* in Bunker 3, Osteen had a perfect hostage, unlike De Sousa who would resist her to the end.

.................................

ANDRICA SAW THE REFLECTION OF SOMEONE WALKING. THE PERSON faced another elevator whose sheen reflected her. It looked like it could be Osteen, and she was holding something in front of her. Andrica knelt down as much as she could, as soft steps approached. She noticed the sweat on her palms as she held the taser in two hands. This was all happening too quick. She dared not peek, but when the reflection disappeared, and she sensed Osteen reaching her side, she flung up her hands and activated the taser.

*BOOM!*

The crack concussed Andrica, and she thought she was dead as she heard something ricochet off the wall behind her. Her hands shook, and she couldn't open her eyes. She peeked to see Osteen on her back, revolver still in her hand. She scrambled and took Osteen's still-warm gun as she laid down the taser. She quivered a moment as she realized she would be dead if she hadn't been kneeling with her own head close to the floor. Andrica had managed to tase Osteen, but she was alive.

She removed Osteen's glasses, took off the guard's glasses, which she was still wearing, and put on Osteen's. Andrica tapped and got green.

"General Osteen, this is Eva. Are you there? I was tased by the girl. I don't know where she is, but she has my taser."

"You are speaking with the, oh, have it your way, *girl*, who tased you. General Osteen is now, shall we say, under my command. You are to report to World Army at South Gate."

"Yo. Is that you, Andrica? This is General Braun; I report to Chair Popov."

"Yes, it's Andrica. What do I do now? Osteen's moving."

"Shoot." Braun realized Osteen would wear a protected vest. "Aim for her twat."

Andrica, hesitating, gave Osteen time, not enough time to burst like shrapnel from a mat, but enough time to swing a leg across Andrica's and bring her down.

*BOOM!*

*The irony of it*, thought Andrica, as she stood up again, looking at Osteen on her back. *I didn't even* try *to fire her stupid gun. Her kick jolted me into pulling the trigger accidentally. But I got her right in, what did the General say, twat?*

# 75

THE WCM AND ALL THREE TIERS, PLUS THE LIFTEES AND THE MOST gifted of academy attendees, combined their efforts to adopt and implement the findings of Pauperito, Ramanujan, Lobashevsky, and the others. It was like a cluster of tots on an Easter-egg hunt. Here a formula was adapted, there a modulo tweaked, here a fluxion, as each person assembled fittings to a gigantic mathematical jigsaw puzzle. But it was Charles, in a mathgust of illumination, who worked around the restrictions of *bounded error, polynomial* and leaped along the infinite continuum to the far ranges of $\pi$. He was able to do so after toiling with Toni Praeger, referring to prepared analyses left by the Persian master, Muhammad al-Khwarizmi. As if by magic, the dream he'd had of Archimedes explaining the obelisk's gears occurred to Charles. Vivified, the image of the giant pawl stopped him cold, and when the counter-pawl leaped into his view, Charles headed down a new pathway. Everyone realized the solution was near as Charles, bypassing anything connected to Lussier, conquered the next rungs on the ladder. Teuila Sefo Malala recognized the musical implications, and Charles, again, this time reaching back to Euclid's musical magic square, nailed it with her help. She and Charles translated the signals and, with help from Bromsky, showed the way to consolidate Mathe-Lingua-Musica.

Why it had become so difficult now made sense to everyone assembled. In order to *arrive* in intragalactic circles, to participate and communicate with other civilizations, to be admitted, the people of Earth had to be mathematically, linguistically, and musically capable. Previously, Earth had only been the vivarium of these other worlds: faulty and not worthy at best; infused with a virus of evil—*do-not-contact*—at worst. Earth's virus, in word and deed, contaminated its people and inflamed their language. Nobody wanted anything to do with them.

All thirty of the intragalactic signals followed newly discovered quasi-patterns to $\pi$'s never-ending numbers. Charles's algorithms enabled them to reach into the most distant unending ranges of $\pi$ to finish an alphabet corresponding to signal patterns, which were related to Mersenne Primes. The WCM found that the beginning Mersennes, the first thirteen, were the most common, and were associated like vowels or the most common letters in Earth languages. Late Mersennes showed rhythms and silences, which appeared to complete the alien communications. The alien transmissions built on preceding dissonance according to Mersenne prime. It turned out that each atonality was, as suggested by Popov, a collection spot, a holding area. Using data-pattern-recognition built with Bayesian probability, a modified Benford's Law, and the newest theory from Praeger and Liu Hui, the mathematicians were able to dig out the most frequent characters-utterances-musical notes, and thereby decode the messages for every one of the thirty intragalactics. The messages demonstrated a more or less common theme:

GREETING --- WELCOME --- ARE ADMITTED --- WE ACCEPT KNOW ONLY PEACE --- HAVE YOU [MAY YOU HAVE] COMMUNICATED MUSIC ---MATHEMATICS --- TRUTH

This was the translation of the initial bursts of signals only.

Earth's response in M-L-M was:

HELLO FROM EARTH. WE GREET YOU IN PEACE. MUSIC MATHEMATICS. WE OFFER THIS MUSIC TO YOU

The selection Popov used at the last Siberian-Canadian meeting was revised, mathematically coded, and transmitted. After sending this music, we ended with a consubstantial close:

THANK YOU. PEACE. MUSIC. MATHEMATICS.

*MIRABILE DICTU*. THE FIRST RESPONSE TO A SENT M-L-M TRANSmission came twenty-four hours later, as predicted by Lobashevsky, when communication methods mathematically *wrapped*. The patterns, and thus their message to us, became:

RECEIVED --- CONTINUOUS WELCOME --- MUSIC TO YOU --- SEND [WRAP] MORE VIBRATIONS RHYTHMS MUSIC--- GOOD PEACE --- GOOD MUSIC --- GOOD TRUTH --- Pi 3.14159 . . .

Within three days, all the original intragalactic signals had responded to Earth's message. Nothing was received from the previous extragalactic, or from anywhere else outside the Milky Way.

IN A CONTRITE ADMISSION OF PIQUE, REED RETRACTED HIS MOtion to impeach Popov and asked the court to drop proceedings against her. Although he was mournful about the lives lost, he understood Popov had operated with best intentions. It was noteworthy that Reed had sent his message in Mathe-Lingua-Musica, complete with his own attempt at music.

A WEEK LATER, POPOV, FOR THE SECOND AND LAST TIME, SHOWED up unannounced at General Braun's offices. When Braun spotted her, he stood up and, with a smile, came out to greet her before his aide even had time to announce her.

"Delighted to see you," Braun said. "You look relieved."

"Thank you, General. In your business, do you ever get relief?"

General Braun put an arm around his boss and patted Popov on the back. "No. I can't say I've ever felt full relief, in this business."

"I'm sure you want to know why I'm here. I'll tell you, and I'll offer a way you may get some relief."

"First, let me fix you tea while you bring me up to date," the General said.

"Thank you. Because of you, our starship's launch is on schedule; everything's 'GO.' And this segues to my next bit of news for you. Your son."

Braun's mouth dropped open as he delivered Popov's tea and set it before her.

"I've told you about Reed and the problems he had caused me. He feels remorse and would not reconsider my offer to reinstate him on *Welkin-Alpha*." Popov smiled.

Braun's eyes widened as he looked at Popov over his teacup.

"I asked if I could substitute your son in his place. 'Gladly,' he said."

Braun set down his cup and fought back a tear. He recovered and beamed. "Thank you, Chair Popov. And please extend my thanks to Reed. Damn good of him." The General had spoken with command and authority. Popov noted, not for the first time, that when a man speaks like the General just had, it is an attempt to cover sensitivity, which some perceive as weakness. However, M-L-M would account for this, and hopes for humanity warmed through her as she considered the expansiveness of possibilities.

Popov sipped her tea. "Go ahead and contact your wife and son, General." She got up and went to the pictures on his wall. "I'll take a moment to look at your hangings in the lobby—I'll be back in five minutes," she said and stepped out the door.

Five minutes later, on the dot, Popov walked back into General Braun's office. "Now, here is how I might offer you some relief."

"Whoa," Braun said. "You already did. You mean there is more?"

"We are back down to sixty percent, due to—well, you know all about this droog thing. Not the greatest odds for survival if we can't fix all the rest of us remaining behind quicker and flush out those vicious unfortunates who refuse to absorb M-L-M."

"The droogs," boomed the General.

Popov took a sip and sighed. "Deceit, treachery, and killing are rampant in all lands. Even with mass inoculations, it will take time for humanity to absorb the full benefits of M-L-M."

"I keep thinking about that," the General said. "How do I counter these continuing, inevitable Conflicts? Droogs have reduced the stick-

and-run but are, we believe, aiming for another Javina. We'd be lucky to wipe out one droog for every hundred normals, even if we ultra-smart-bombed."

"Which is the main reason I've come to you. My experts tell me we have all but used up our Lift opportunities. Pauperito had warned us about this. 'The mathematics can't hold,' he'd said, 'you have to scale back.' I've Returned a few Liftees, but have retained Salk. Pemberton Returns today, which reminds me, he wants his iguana, Galileo, given back to his aunt."

The General chuckled.

"We've been lucky. General, I can offer you one new Liftee for six months. This opportunity for assistance is yours."

General Braun blinked. He glanced at the picture of his grandfather on the wall next to Popov. "Okay, then." General Braun looked at the photo of the same grandfather on his desk. "Just give me a moment."

Popov had seen his eyes dart to the pictures of his grandfather. "Make it the best possible choice for all of us who will remain here, General."

"Thank you for reminding me. Hmmm. Haven't told you because I haven't found a smoking gun, but I'm seeing irregularities by the Canadians in Siberia. But bigger problems will come from the droogs. What I need is an experienced and skilled tactician . . . the Corsican . . . of course, the Corsican. My grandfather considered him the most skilled tactician in history."

# 76

AFTER HER MEETING WITH GENERAL BRAUN, POPOV HONORED AN appointment she'd made with Andrica. "Can we meet by my dolphins?" Andrica had asked. "Delighted to," Popov had replied.

Andrica looked healthy and confident as she showed Popov around and let her perch the female macaw.

"I think she likes you," Andrica said, looking at the bird puffed up and sitting on Popov's shoulder.

Popov smiled a huge grin. "Nice to know someone does."

"You're too hard on yourself. I think we owe you an awful lot," Andrica said.

"Thank you, and we owe a great deal to you, Andrica." Popov wanted to gush something else to Andrica but took her time.

After a pause, she said, "You were very brave, Andrica."

Andrica said nothing, but reached up to pat the bird. The macaw fluttered to Andrica, and she held it in her lap. She patted the bird.

"I've scheduled you for a minor operation with my gynecologist," Popov said, looking straight ahead at the horizon.

Andrica looked at her.

"And I've made other arrangements for you. You will journey with Charles on *Welkin-Alpha*."

Andrica glanced at Popov's abdomen. "Are you . . .?

"I am; after a procedure, I will not be."

Andrica wiped away a tear, and another, the first tears since . . . It took her a while to speak. In the silence, both women understood much more, and more deeply, than by using combinations of clumsy words.

They watched and admired Andrica's dolphins as they shimmied and wiggled.

"Does Charles know?" Andrica asked.

"No, Charles does not know, and I shall never tell him."

They sat. The dolphins lapped the pool in harmony. The macaw was at peace.

"You will make a great mother," Popov said.

..................................

POPOV HAD ONE LAST MEETING. SHE'D ASKED CHARLES TO BE AT "Skyview," the peak of the obelisk, which she'd reserved ahead of time. Upon meeting, they'd smiled and embraced for over two minutes, and not one word was said. But in the stillness, surrounded by glass, they'd communicated a lifetime.

"Bon voyage," Popov said.

"Thank you," said Charles.

..................................

WHEN CHARLES WENT TO FIND HIS FATHER, HE HEARD HIS FATHER'S voice call out "Up here" as he walked in.

He was sitting on Charles's bed.

"Why no math problem to solve by the aquarium door today?" Charles said.

For the first time that Charles could remember, they both smiled at each other.

"Mighty proud of you," his father said. He walked to Charles and hugged him clumsily. His father tried to say too much for the moment, but Charles remembered what had happened with Popov.

"It's better, maybe . . . can we just hold each other, Dad?"

His father stopped with a chuff, and did.

..................................

GENERAL BRAUN SAT AT HIS DESK WEARING TORN, FIELD-STAINED battle fatigues, reviewing the latest WCM sims, which had fallen another 8 percent. Two days earlier, he and his aide-de-camp had been attacked by an Indonesian droog who had breached Security while Braun was conducting a field review of troops, and his aide had been killed. However, in spite of the attack and loss of life, they were able to Lift the Corsican.

Braun looked away from the reports and noted the keepsake he kept under the glass covering on his desk. Staring at him was the last stanza of a Kipling poem:

*Once there was The People—Terror gave it birth;*
*Once there was The People and it made a Hell of Earth*
*Earth arose and crushed it. Listen, O ye slain!*
*Once there was The People—it shall never be again!*

The General's secretary walked into the office and handed him a note from the Corsican. As General Braun read the note a second time, he had the feeling he was being summoned. *Why, the arrogant little . . .*

Braun stormed into the adjacent office without knocking and saw a man with a heavy face perusing maps he'd pinned to a side wall. The man, bemedaled in full military dress, turned to Braun and looked at him like he was about to spit.

"You will remove your hat," Napoleon said.

# 77

FINAL ARRANGEMENTS FOR BOARDING *WELKIN-ALPHA* WERE COMplete. Yet, as with anything of this magnitude, there were bound to be errors, intentional and unintentional. And a few errors happened by a combination of the two.

In the controlled atmosphere of *Welkin-Alpha*, it was imperative that no virus or sickness attain a foothold. Modern medicine had cured just about everything except the common cold and a couple of rare viruses. Salk was in charge of clinical examinations, and he and his charges ran all possible tests on final travelers of the last shuttle trip. While doing so, two persons, a young woman and a young man, were discovered to be infected with the one remaining virus that quickened dementia. This finding resulted in their being disqualified to make the trip and thus created two open spots. The spots would be filled from a confidential waitlist, administered by First Tier and controlled by Popov.

By fate, the second person on the waitlist had, for whatever reason, taken his own life. Suicide had quadrupled in the last hundred years and was another blemish on humanity. Salk looked at the data of the suicide and was heartened when he saw similarities. The problem was Popov; she would insist that the next person on the waitlist take the open spot.

That evening, Salk, who was admired by Popov for his creative determination, and who'd had his restrictions relaxed, managed to visit the prison and inquire about Ishmael. He no longer was on death row, but his term was set at six years.

"He has six years to serve," the warden said.

Salk explained Ishmael's story. "And I've confirmed these facts."

"There is nothing I can do. I'm sorry."

"May I take a minute to contact WCM?"

The warden nodded and leaned back in his chair.

"Chair Popov, I know—"

*What are you doing at the prison?*

"I'm attempting to get Ishmael released and ready to travel. For the sake of humanity."

*Dr. Salk, we've discussed this before. I won't authorize it.*

"Then I won't let you Return me. I won't go back to my time.

*You are not in a position to defy me. The warden will bring you to me.*

"Do you want another suicide?

*Doctor Salk!*

In the end, the warden, under orders from Popov, released Ishmael. Salk knew she wouldn't take a chance at destabilizing Salk's past to risk punishment in the present. Ishmael was beyond grateful and filled the spot of the suicide without a problem. He was clear of illness and had kept up with meaningful advancements in Mathe-Lingua-Musica.

..................................

LATE THAT SAME EVENING, POPOV PUT DOWN HER HARP AND TAPPED a quick memo into her glasses. The incident with Salk had upset her, but she realized she'd been forewarned and would use this experience as an opportunity. Any Liftee could now threaten to cause trouble, as their services had, for all practical purposes, ended. She needed to send the few remaining Liftees back to their time, including Salk. This seemed harsh, but if one of them got into an accident—*Salk at a prison*—or if Liftees banded together and made threats in order to enter the ship—Popov slapped her head, wondering why she hadn't acted earlier.

The following morning, Popov went to Salk.

"Is Ishmael happy?" she asked.

"Yes. Thank you."

"I know no matter how I tell you this, you will take it personally. But you have done me a great favor."

Salk looked puzzled.

"For reasons you best understand, we need to send the remaining

Liftees back for, as you put it, the sake of humanity. I do trust you, Doctor, and we will be forever indebted for your services. But . . ."

"Oh, I understand completely. I knew it was coming, but I had to free that poor, innocent young man."

"So you did, Doctor."

Salk smiled at her. "Your gifted people can take it from here. My records are up-to-date and precise; you will have no trouble."

By noon, every Liftee had been Returned, including the Corsican. Though General Braun was impressed by Napoleon's clever ideas of causing key droogs to turn against some of the droog cells, he was a handful and difficult for Braun to control. The relief Popov felt was palpable but tiring; she wanted to play her harp, but she couldn't; there was much to do, much to coordinate, much to check, recheck, and overcheck. Instead, she took a few moments to shed real tears.

After a heartfelt cry, Popov reared up and got herself back on track. She tapped her glasses.

"Apprise me, General Braun.

"Then appoint your best person; I need you here.

"Then appoint your next-best person. Don't delay. Meet me here at 0800 tomorrow to go over launch Security and post-launch priorities.

"Very good, General."

..................................

ON BOARD *ORION*, FOR THE FINAL TRIP TO MOONBASE-1, FEELINGS were mixed. Where there was hope, there was anxiety. Where there was anxiety, there was fear. No one would admit to it, but it was visible on their faces and heard in their voices. But, one way or another, the long journey was about to begin.

..................................

NINE DAYS LATER, WHEN EVERYONE HAD COLLECTED AT MOONbase-1 and had boarded Starship *Welkin-Alpha*, the two-hour indoctrination film was re-shown. Everything was explained again in M-L-M by administrators who stopped the film at key points to take questions and ensure understanding. M-L-M was the language used. Everyone on *Welkin-Alpha* had been taught it and implanted with Neuro Responsive Simulators. They had been bio-fed, tested, and cleared in Mathe-Lingua-Musica. After the film, passengers, in preset order by age and pretests, were led to Cryopreservation. They bathed a last time and entered the egg-shaped cocoons. Those who'd been given donated sperm were monitored by implanted nanobots that read vitals and made adjustments as needed. After three weeks, the bots would engage the master nanobot in the embryo. A week after, M-L-M would begin feeding into the embryo. This feed would be slow and sure and finish before the baby's birth. The process was essentially the same for all other pregnancies.

In the midst of it all, Charles caught up with Andrica. "I'm a couple of eggs over," he said, with a laugh.

"Ha," she said, as she glanced at the open exoskeleton that would enclose and seal him. "I hope you're not as nervous as I—"

He kissed her full on the lips. "I am. Maybe more so."

Andrica hugged him and wouldn't let him go. An administrator tapped Andrica's shoulder a second time.

"I'll see you in Kepler-1649c," Charles said.

"You can name the baby if it's a boy," Andrica said.

"What if it's a girl?"

"I shall name her Hypatia, the female mathematician of antiquity."

"If a son, I shall name him Euclid."

.................................

TEN HOURS LATER, THE FUSION ENGINES FIRED. THE ENGINES thrummed a full minute as cobots finalized course, aspect, velocity. After leaving the solar system with required velocity, the interstellar ramjet propulsion system would take over for good.

.................................

THE GREAT SHIP ROSE. FOR THOSE WHO WATCHED FROM MONITORS on Earth, there was in them a hope that grew as the starship coursed in the inner solar system and would too soon dim from monitors. Was this hope a strange feeling? No. But, later, as soon as the first trigger was pulled, as soon as a first cry of anguish was screeched, all hope had been diluted and soon forgotten.

Weeks later, all Earth peoples quieted once more as new sounds stirred. Ram-scooped hydrogen ripped into the starship's main engine. A unique click-like, koan-like hum engulfed them from monitor speakers. Remaining humanity stopped what they were doing and listened as the sounds diminished and the mother ark breached their home solar system, never to be seen or heard from again.

# EPILOGUE

POPOV STILL FELT VESTIGES OF MORNING SICKNESS. SHE STOOD at the window screen by the auditorium and patted her abdomen. *Funny*, she thought, *all the advances in medicine, all the weal and woe, and the mind will twist reality trying to reject a change. Like this wamble inside of me.*

*My fate, my personal legacy remains here on Earth*, she reminisced, *and I've done the best I could. One war has ended. The new Chair, Boucher, will have to put his talents and M-L-M against the droog revolution*. Although Thaddeus requested to continue his work alone, Magnuson has been a solid replacement at WCM. *They will be up to it*, she thought. *Newest simulations confirm humankind has a 51 percent chance of survival, but optimism reigns. And this too will be my legacy, in a far-off different world*, she thought as she laid both hands on her abdomen, no longer feeling any twinge. *A transcendent symbiosis.*

She looked to the heavens from the window and thought music. Popov's reign had ended because she had resigned early, explaining she would devote the rest of her life and skills to the consecration of Mathe-Lingua-Musica.

The buoyant Popov parted the stage curtain to a thunderous standing ovation, with whistles and bravos building on each other. It was the apotheosis of her career. She took position in her lounge on center stage and smiled to the musicians on both sides of her as the lights dimmed to candle. Thus, it was on this day, in that time before the end of time, a time of atonement and unrest, a time of hope and abandonment, a time of advances and setbacks, that the new stewards of Mathe-Lingua-Musica closed their ceremonies with *An Anthem to Humanity.*

# ACKNOWLEDGMENTS

TO THE FOLLOWING WHO READ VARIOUS DRAFTS: ALAN KENNEDY, who read the manuscript three times and who continues to be my best critic and teacher. My sister, Judy, a professional organist who helped me with some of the music scenes. My late friend, Larry Dolinsky, who gave a comprehensive read and provided detailed suggestions to keep me on track. John Lovett, who read an early draft, intimated the right improvements, and gave me a key suggestion. David Gardner, whose suggestions most always prevail. Gus Borgeson, who was relentless until I began to understand. Jennifer Harris, who read and commented on the final galley.

My grateful thanks to my editors, Amanda Chiu Krohn and Ryan Smernoff, whose professional work and counsel pulled me to a higher level. And, of course, my thanks to all the crew at Keylight and Turner Publishing.

A special thanks to Bob Lynch, my mentor. Sunday afternoons at 1:00 p.m., I went to "class" and mentor Bob would guide me through "what's next?"

Others include fellow writers from the original writing group where I began this book, and a host of friends and writers who encouraged me. Forgive me for all those I've forgotten to mention.

Finally, my wife, Nancy, steady as a rock, who kept me in line and counseled me when necessary as I struggled to get this book out there. Thank you, Nancy!

While writing this book, I did think of all future offspring down the road ahead. Will we leave them with a big mess, or will humanity rally and think of future generations?

# ABOUT THE AUTHOR

**RAY ANDERSON** IS A HIKER AND THE AUTHOR OF THE AWOL THRILLER novel series, which includes *The Trail* (2015), *Sierra* (2016), and *The Divide* (2020). Anderson has done a radio column on hiking. He has also written columns for the Appalachian Mountain Club (AMC) newsletter. Anderson lives with his wife, Nancy, near Boston. When not reading or writing, he walks, listens to music, and tries to keep up with grandchildren.

Printed in the USA
CPSIA information can be obtained
at www.ICGtesting.com
JSHW020240060424
60652JS00002B/12